VIKTOR ROSE

Out of the Depths

Contents

1

Chains of Gloomy Darkness

Angela's hands wouldn't stop shaking. She didn't know if it was the fear, the withdrawals, or both. They trembled uncontrollably, even when she pressed them hard against her chest. She was cold. God, she was so cold. The chain connected to her ankle cuff clinked softly every time she shifted. A sound she had come to hate—quiet, mechanical, a reminder that someone thought this was where she belonged. She sat curled against the wall, cheek pressed to the cement as if the chill might tether her to something real. Something sane.

"God..." Her voice cracked. "I know we haven't talked in a while. Not really. And honestly, I don't even know if you're real..."

She swallowed hard, tears already blurring her vision. Her throat ached from thirst and the sick she'd woken up in days before. "But if you are... please help me."

Her breath caught on the words. Each inhale came shallow and strained. She couldn't stop thinking about those first hours—how the world had blurred, her head pounding, the sick taste in her mouth, and the way she'd nearly died on some worn out couch before being dropped into a dimly lit basement. And *him*. The man. He'd looked at her like she was something fragile. Like a wounded animal he wasn't sure how to care for. His hands gentle. His voice soft. Too soft. Like none of this was wrong.

"I don't want to die here," she whispered, barely audible.

But it wasn't just death that haunted her. It was the quiet. The dissonance. The way her thoughts bent and fractured in this stillness.

"Why is this happening to me? How much more will you let happen? I don't know what I did to end up here," she said, curling tighter. "I was just—I —"

The memory was murky—dim bar lighting, the sticky floor under her shoes, the sour tang of liquor on her breath. She'd been drunk. Vulnerable. Alone. And someone had been watching. She lifted her gaze into the darkness above. No ceiling. No light. No clock. Just the sound of her own pulse filling the silence.

"Please," she whispered, "don't let it end this way."

No reply. Not even a creak. Not even a breath from the other side of the door. She dug her nails into her palm until the sting grounded her. Anything to keep from unraveling.

"Please don't let me lose my mind."

A shift. The kind of low, aching moan old wood gives when the temperature changes—like the house was stretching in its sleep. She froze. Was it the door? Or just her imagination? Her lungs held still, like movement alone might give her away. And then, as the silence settled again, one thought came uninvited: *He's going to come back. And when he does... I still won't know if he's here to feed me—or to finish whatever this is.*

***

Two nights ago Angela was just drunk enough to lose her filter. Her plain brown hair, usually smooth and styled, was starting to frizz like it also had one too many drinks at the bar. The natural pink lipstick she always wore stayed perfectly in place, even as her slightly crooked smile twisted into a smirk with dangerous potential. She looked like someone who should've been giving a TED Talk, not roasting strangers in a bar. Her bright blue eyes were sharp with mischief, her business-casual slacks still crisp, and her blouse collar still buttoned like she hadn't just called a complete stranger "Great Value brand Chris Evans" in front of his friends. Attractive, but not intimidatingly so, Angela always made an effort. Hair done, makeup subtle but intentional, wardrobe neat. That night, though? She'd traded grace for volume. And with half the bar as her unwilling audience, she cracked jokes loud enough to make the bartender pause, aiming her latest commentary squarely at a man who was just trying to enjoy his cocktail in peace.

Short, round, with wire glasses perched on a balding head streaked with gray. His name didn't matter; no one at work really knew him. They just called him Mr. Piña Colada — a man so awkward he nursed the same sugary drink all night just to have something to hold onto. Angela barely noticed him beyond the laughter. She had worked at Harvest Mutual Insurance for only a couple of years, clawing her way into an entry-level analyst job most people thought she had no business getting. Her GPA was trash. Her résumé, worse. But none of that showed the truth: that she was sharp, hungry, and fiercely adaptable.

Once, she had been on track to graduate with honors. Until the drinking took hold. It wasn't just partying. It was blackout nights. Waking up in strange beds with no memory of how she got there. Laughing it off with friends who were just as broken as she was. Until the night she woke up with her pants on backwards, bruises blooming across her thighs, and a sick, heavy feeling she couldn't shake. She pieced together what little she could — but there were no clear answers. Only fear. Shame. And a pregnancy test that came back positive, even after taking Plan B. Her parents urged her to get rid of it. They talked about her future like it was something delicate she could still save. They didn't know she hadn't just made a mistake — she had been assaulted. She couldn't even bring herself to say it out loud. She didn't know why she chose to keep the baby. Maybe it was guilt. Maybe it was rage. Maybe it was the stubborn, broken part of her that refused to let the worst night of her life be the thing that defined her. Maybe it was God. Whatever the reason, she kept him.

She dropped drinking cold. Every day was a battle she fought with shaking hands and locked jaws until her son Phoenix came screaming into the world. It didn't get easier after that. Her father died of a heart attack while she was still bleeding in the hospital. Her family unraveled. She unraveled. The bottles came back, hidden in corners of her family home. By the time she finally graduated — a year later than planned — her record was wrecked.

Dropping to part-time classes to raise her son had slowed her down, and after her father's death, everything unraveled faster. Her mother tried to hold the pieces together, babysitting when she could, but grief hollowed them both out. Her final grades were a shadow of what they once had been, a 4.0 student dropping to less than half. The life insurance money helped them stay afloat for a while, enough to keep the lights on and the creditors at bay. But job offers didn't come. Her résumé barely stood up to scrutiny, and Angela's drinking — once confined to the corners of her life — had grown bolder. She learned how to hide it well: mouthwash in the car, gum and eye drops in her purse, a practiced smile that kept people from looking too closely.

When a real interview finally came — a major company two hours away — she did what she always did. She pulled herself together just long enough to pass. She drove to the interview with her heart hammering, sweating through withdrawal tremors she tried to disguise as nerves. Sitting alone in the conference room, she practiced smiling through the panic, rehearsing the answers she thought they wanted to hear, silently promising herself she could get sober again if only they gave her a chance. Then the door creaked open. And in walked Mr. Piña Colada — wearing a wrinkled blue shirt, a crooked navy tie, and a bright yellow mustard stain right in the middle of his chest.

Despite all her preparation, the interview went sideways immediately. Mr. Piña Colada asked questions that made no sense — oddly specific things that no normal interviewer would have asked. Questions so strange, so clearly drawn from his own obscure experiences, that Angela could only nod and bluff her way through, confusion tightening in her chest.

"In the event that one were to encounter an inadvertent discrepancy within a published rating manual—specifically in the context of a jurisdiction operating under a file-and-use regulatory framework that permits a thirty-day de facto grace period for implementation—what would be the procedurally appropriate sequence of internal and external actions, communications, and filings to initiate, in order to rectify said error while remaining in compliance with both statutory expectations and internal quality assurance protocols?"

The question landed with the subtlety of a car crash. Angela blinked, her bright blue eyes momentarily vacant as her brain scrambled to decode what had just been said. File-and-use. Grace period. *What? Was that even English?* She forced a polite smile, the kind that barely lifted the corners of her slightly crooked mouth. She could hear the faint tick of the wall clock. Or was that her pulse? Across the table, her would-be manager waited, pen poised just above a notepad, eyebrows slightly arched in the way that she interpreted as *This wasn't a trick question... probably.* Angela's mind cycled through every insurance-related webinar she'd half-watched, every regulation handbook she skimmed, every online video giving interview tips, anything to help her grasp the answer. Still nothing.

She drew in a slow breath, adjusted the cuff of her blouse as if the answer might be hiding in the fabric, and gave a faint, practiced laugh—the universal signal for *stalling.* "Well," she began, buying another second.

The silence before that word had been long enough to make both of them sweat.

Eventually, seeing her flounder, he leaned back and simplified it all down to, "Do you know how to use a spreadsheet?"

Angela's face lit up. Not only could she use a spreadsheet — she could build applications inside them. She launched into a confident explanation, rattling off her experience in formulas, automations, even scripting. Mr. Piña Colada nodded slowly, as if he understood, though it was clear he didn't. Halfway through her answer, he appeared to remember the giant mustard stain across his tie. Without a word, he licked his fingers and began scrubbing at the fabric, smearing the stain instead of erasing it. Angela kept talking, her voice faltering slightly as she flickered her gaze between his face and the damp mess on his chest. When she finished, there was an awkward pause. Mr. Piña Colada, still working the stain, blinked up at her like he'd just remembered where he was. Clearing his throat, he moved briskly into the next part of the pitch: the salary — which was insultingly low — and the "generous" subsidized public transportation program. He beamed with pride as he explained how he got to ride the bus for free three days a week.

Angela wasn't impressed. But she was desperate. This was the first door that had opened even a crack, and she knew better than to be picky. She smiled and agreed. Mr. Piña Colada extended his hand. It smelled sharply of mustard and his grip was both warm and damp. Angela suppressed a grimace. That day, Mr. Piña Colada became her first manager at the company.

Two years later, at the bar after work, Angela drunkenly told the story of that first surreal interview to a circle of coworkers. She reenacted the whole thing — the nonsense questions, the mustard stain, the damp handshake — painting Mr. Piña Colada as the punchline to every joke. Across the room, the real Mr. Piña Colada, overhearing, blushed deep crimson. Angela didn't even notice. Laughing too loud, she abruptly excused herself, announcing she needed the bathroom. As she staggered toward the hallway, her phone buzzed. A text from her mother — who was babysitting her son for the night — blared across the screen in all caps:

WHERE ARE YOU?

She checked the time. 7:44 PM. Fumbling her thumbs against the screen, she typed back: *driving now home soon*

A lie — as the sour tang of vodka and cranberry clung to her breath. Cursing under her breath, she shoved her phone into her bag and wobbled toward the exit, leaving her coworkers behind without another word — a classic Irish Goodbye. She was way too drunk to drive. She knew that much. Pulling out her rideshare app, she let the algorithm find her — one click, and the nearest driver would take her home. Easy. Her car could wait until morning. Another buzz. Another angry text from her mother. Angela barely glanced at it, her mind already slipping into that hazy, careless place she thought she had outgrown.

Shortly after she requested a ride, a white sedan with a rideshare sticker on the windshield pulled up to the curb. The driver's door swung open and a man stepped out, wearing a black baseball cap, a disposable surgical mask, and purple latex gloves. Without saying a word, he trotted around the car and opened the rear passenger door for her. Angela, still half-drunk and unsteady, stumbled in and collapsed against the seat. The door slammed shut, and the driver hurried back behind the wheel. He mounted his phone on the dashboard, switched to a map app, and pulled away from the curb in one smooth motion. Smooth jazz floated through the speakers, and it didn't take long for Angela's heavy eyelids to slip shut.

A few minutes passed before Angela's phone buzzed in her hand, jerking her awake. She squinted at the screen, still foggy, her heart skipping a beat. Missed ride. Confused, she looked up.

The driver's eyes met hers in the rearview mirror — calm. Too calm.

"Something wrong?" he asked, voice light, casual.

"It says... I missed my ride," she slurred, frowning.

"The app's buggy sometimes," he said quickly. "If you toggle your location services off and on, it usually fixes it."

She frowned, watching the side of his face in the dim glow of passing streetlights. His shoulders were rigid, his posture too controlled, as if he were holding himself in place rather than simply driving. Even the way his hand gripped the wheel felt tense, knuckles pale, as though he was concentrating on more than just the road. She shifted uneasily, an unshakable sense prickling at the back of her neck. Something was off. She blinked, trying to orient herself. Nothing outside looked familiar. She glanced at the driver's phone mounted on the dashboard — just a map, no route entered, no destination locked. Her stomach dropped.

A cold bolt of sobriety shot through her chest. Heart pounding, fingers trembling, she clutched her phone tighter and checked her rideshare app. A different car. A different driver. Tears welled in her eyes, fear slicing through the last of her drunken haze. Still, she fought to steady herself. *Focus. Focus.* She pulled up her mother's last message, thumb stabbing the screen, and sent a quick location pin. Her hands were shaking uncontrollably now. She plunged them into her bag, desperately rummaging for anything — a weapon, a key, a chance.

The car screeched to a sudden stop in the middle of the empty parking lot. The driver spun around, syringe in hand — but Angela was faster. She unleashed a blast of pepper spray straight into his eyes. He shrieked, dropping the syringe against the seat, one hand clawing at his face. Angela yanked on her door handle, but it wouldn't budge — the child locks were on. Her heart pounded in her ears as she fought against the drunk fog clouding her mind.

The driver, still half-blinded, groped for the syringe again. Angela seized his wrist and, with her free hand, slammed her thumb against the plunger, emptying the needle harmlessly onto the seat. With a grunt, he grabbed her arm in a crushing grip. Angela leaned back, planting the heel of her shoe into his face, kicking hard. His hat flew off. He recoiled, gasping, slamming against the driver's door. Her arm came free. Angela hurled herself over the center console toward the passenger side.

But before she could reach the door, his arms locked around her — one crushing her neck, the other wrapping tight behind her head. She tried to scream, but only a strangled wheeze escaped. Panic seized her.

He began counting quietly in her ear, "One Mississippi... two Mississippi..." tightening his hold with every breath.

Her vision swam. The edges of the world went gray. Angela pushed against the seat, her fingers brushing something — the plastic barrel of the syringe. Summoning everything she had left, she closed her hand around it and stabbed backward, blindly. The needle plunged into his left eye. The driver howled, his grip loosening. Angela smashed the back of her head into his face with a sickening crack. He let go, gasping. She shoved away from him, grabbed the passenger door handle, and threw it open. She fell, and rolled onto the cold pavement, scrambling to get away.

Pain lanced up her ankle — he still had her. She twisted, kicked him with her free foot, slipping out of his grasp — losing a shoe in the process. Angela crawled, staggered, and forced herself upright into a broken, hobbling sprint. Her throat burned raw from the earlier chokehold; she could barely suck in air as she ran. Behind her, she heard the car door slam and footsteps pounding after her. She pushed harder, toward the faint lights of the street, praying for a car, a person, anything. A glance over her shoulder — and searing pain exploded through her body. The taser's barbs struck, electricity locking her muscles in place. She crumpled forward, crashing against a cement parking block. Her head struck hard. The world spun. Then, darkness.

2

Hope Deferred Makes the Heart Sick

Angela found herself in a room that glowed with the kind of golden warmth she believed she'd lost forever. A lamp spilled its light over the kitchen table, where Uno cards lay in sloppy piles between bowls of popcorn and cans sweating rings onto the wood. Laughter rose and fell — her mother pretending to pout at her terrible hand, Phoenix beaming like this game was the most important contest of his little life.

And her father sat across from her, alive, vibrant, his grin wide as he fanned out two cards. "Two left," he teased, his eyes glittering with playful triumph.

The sound of his voice knocked the air from her lungs.

Angela's vision blurred. The tears came suddenly, unbidden, so sharp she gasped with them. She leaned forward, overwhelmed, every piece of her crying out. "Dad," she choked, the word trembling in her throat. "I've missed you so much."

He froze mid-laugh, tilting his head at her in surprise. His brow softened, concern flickering in his gaze. "What's wrong, jelly bean?"

The endearment cut straight through her. Her heart lurched, breaking open. She wiped at her cheeks, embarrassed, confused by the intensity of what she felt. He was right there — how could she miss him?

She tried to laugh it off, though her voice wavered. "I—I don't even know. I just... got worked up."

Her father reached across the table, laying his calloused hand over hers.

His palm was warm, steady, grounding. The moment his skin touched hers, peace unfurled through her chest, melting the ache. For an instant, she felt complete — as though all the jagged years between them had never existed. He smiled at her in that way only he could, patient, full of a love so constant it seemed to anchor the room itself.

Angela sniffled, managing a shaky grin. "Don't think for a second this gets you off the hook. I demand a rematch."

He chuckled, squeezing her hand. "Fair enough. But I'll warn you — I don't plan on losing next time either."

Her laughter bubbled through the remnants of her tears. For that fleeting moment, everything was whole. Everything was right. And then the doorbell rang. A sharp note, too hollow, reverberating oddly against the walls. Phoenix didn't notice, still counting his cards. Her mother reached for her can of soda, unfazed. But Angela's stomach clenched tight, as though the sound was meant only for her.

Her father rose, pressing a kiss against the crown of her head before heading toward the door. He hummed softly — the same tune he always did when he was in a good mood — yet it wavered, bending strangely in her ears. The closer he got to the door, the more the air thickened. The floorboards groaned under his steps, too loud, too heavy, as though each step sank into something deeper than wood. Angela's breath caught. A part of her wanted to call out, to tell him not to open it, but her voice stuck fast in her throat. Her hand trembled where it still rested on the table. Her father reached the door. His hand closed around the knob. And when the door swung open, the light collapsed.

A figure stood on the threshold, draped head to toe in black. His face was indistinct, like smoke clinging where features should be, a shadow that refused to resolve into anything human. The air around him bent strangely, heavy with a pressure that made Angela's ears ring. At his feet, the floor writhed. Thick black snakes poured across the threshold, a seething tide spilling into the room. Their bodies glistened as they twisted over one another, scales scraping, tongues flickering. The hiss rose up, sharp and endless, like static filling every corner of the house. Her father stumbled back, swatting at the first coils that lashed around his leg. He kicked one away, but three more replaced it, their fangs sinking deep into his calf. More of them surged upward, climbing, biting, constricting. His triumphant laugh — his voice that had filled her heart with joy only moments ago — broke into a cry, then vanished beneath the hiss. His body was swallowed, buried alive in the writhing black mass.

Angela screamed, the sound raw and tearing. She lurched forward, but Phoenix clutched her arm, his small fingers digging in, his eyes wide with terror. She froze, helpless, as the swarm surged across the carpet, devouring the game table, the cards, the popcorn bowls, until nothing remained of the warmth that had been there. And the man in black stepped inside. He did not hurry. He didn't need to. Each stride was slow, deliberate, his boots sinking noiselessly into the living tide as though the snakes parted for him. Though his face was a blur, Angela felt his attention lock onto her — a gaze colder than any blade, heavier than the hissing flood. Wrongness radiated from him, warping the air, pressing down on her chest until she could hardly breathe.

Angela clutched Phoenix, and stumbled backward. The peace she had felt moments before shattered, replaced with a dread so deep it rooted in her bones. The laughter was gone. The warmth was gone. Only the hiss remained. Angela clutched Phoenix to her chest, stumbling backward from the table. Shadows writhed across the floor, alive, pulling toward her like water rushing downhill.

"Mom!" she screamed.

Her mother was already on her feet, arms outstretched as though she could hold the swarm back. Snakes lashed around her wrists, biting, coiling. She tried to tear them free, but they swarmed higher, winding up her arms, tightening across her chest. Her scream cut through the hiss, sharp and strangled. Angela yanked Phoenix harder, nearly dragging him across the floor as she spun toward the hallway. Her pulse thundered in her ears, each beat a hammer against her ribs. The man in black followed, his pace unhurried, inevitable. The snakes moved with him, parting and surging, the hiss shaping itself into something almost like words — syllables too jagged for her mind to hold. She ran. The hallway stretched unnaturally long, her bare feet slapping against the wood, but still she wasn't fast enough. The air felt thick, as if she were running underwater.

Phoenix tripped, his small body pitching forward with a cry.

"No!" Angela shrieked, yanking him back up by his arm. His legs stumbled to catch up, his tiny shoes skidding against the floor. She lifted and dragged him, tears burning her eyes as she forced them both forward.

The door to her bedroom loomed ahead. She threw herself into it, slamming it shut with her whole body. Her trembling fingers fumbled with the lock, twisting it just as the first thud struck the wood. The pounding came heavy and rhythmic, rattling the frame, the door quivering on its hinges. Snakes slithered through the cracks, their slick black bodies forcing their way into the room, pouring from the gap beneath the door like water.

Angela shoved Phoenix behind her. The pounding rattled her bones, each strike a hammer-blow that seemed to come from inside her skull. The hiss grew louder, filling every crack of the room, until it was all she could hear. Something cold and slick brushed against her ankle. She gasped, looking down to see the floor rippling, black scales sliding over one another in a tide that lapped at her feet. The snakes curled around her legs, climbing higher, biting, constricting. She screamed, trying to kick them off, but the floor itself seemed alive, pulling her downward. Her feet slipped out from under her, her body collapsing backward. Cold scales wrapped around her calves, her knees, pulling her into the tide. She hit the ground hard, and her eyes snapped open back to reality.

She awoke and found herself lying on an old couch, the cushions sagging and uneven beneath her. The air smelled stale, musty, thick with dust that clung to the back of her throat. She tried to move, but her ankles were bound tightly together. Her wrists, pinned behind her back, ached against the coarse bite of thick plastic zip ties. Something pulled at her face — duct tape sealed across her mouth, making each breath shallow and hot. Her stomach rolled. The room swayed, dizziness pressing in until she felt sick right there against the couch. She forced her eyes open wider.

A woman sat in a recliner just across from her, maybe sixty years old, her hair limp and uneven, her jaw slack. She stared into the distance with glassy eyes, saying nothing, moving nothing, as though she hadn't even noticed Angela's arrival. Angela's chest heaved, panic surging against the ties. She tried to cry out, but the sound smothered into the tape, muffled and weak. Nausea rolled through her, dizzying and relentless — the room tipped and her stomach lurched again. Something wet and metallic filled her mouth and throat — the tape smelled of glue and the back of her tongue tasted like metal. A hot, bitter retch climbed her esophagus; bile braided up and then surged forward. It forced its way into her nasal passages first, and the burn in her sinuses was immediate — sharp, acidic fire that made her eyes water. When she tried to gasp for air to clear it, she inhaled instead, drawing slick, sour liquid back into her throat. The sound that ripped out of her was a wet, hacking choke — raw and involuntary — and it left her throat burning and ragged.

She couldn't find a breath — the world narrowed to the pressure behind her sternum and the sour metallic taste that filled her mouth. Every inhale was a negotiation she was losing; her ribs burned as if they were being forced closed. Panic tunneled her vision, and the room swam in grainy blurs.

Then he was there, looming over her with that single, swollen eye with a mix of tears and blood streaked around his eye socket down his cheeks. He fumbled at her face, fingers slick with his own blood. His hands were shaking so badly they kept slipping; each time he tried to peel the edge free his grip failed, skin sliding on skin. She wanted to shriek, to push him away, but her body only managed tiny, useless movements — a shoulder twitch, a hand that dropped limply.

On his third frantic try his nails managed to hook the tape and he tore it with a brutal, clumsy motion that sent sparks behind her eyes. The seal broke with a crack, and she coughed — deep, violent hacks as foul liquid ripped up her throat. Bile burned and then cleared in hot spasms; vomit blasted out, and she gagged until her lungs remembered how to pull in air. The first breath that finally filled her was thin and trembling, dragged in between sobs and the wet rasp of a throat scraped raw. She swallowed it down with everything shaking inside her, each gasp a small victory. Relief came sharp and immediate, but it didn't steady her. Fog clung to the edges of her mind — a slurry of alcohol, concussion, and oxygen-starved panic — blurring his face into a smear of motion. She drew breath after breath, each one ragged and shallow, feeling tethered between waking and drowning, unable to pin down anything more than the fact that she was still breathing and still not safe.

He pushed himself up from his knees at her side with a graceless grunt; the couch complained and the floorboards groaned under his weight. The hollow thud of his steps faded away a short distance, then the thin hiss of a faucet turning filled the room, bright and steady.

She lay wrapped in the fog, every sound distant and thick. When he came back he carried a washcloth, damp and heavy between his fingers. He moved with the same awkward rush as before. The cloth was cool where it first touched her skin; the salt and acid of vomit stung as he wiped. His strokes were uneven—sometimes brusque, sometimes careful enough to be gentle— and there was a strange, misplaced tenderness in the way he brushed her hair back from her forehead.

She tried to turn her head away, a small, animal protest, but her neck felt like lead and her limbs obeyed slowly, as if underwater. Words wouldn't come; only a weak tilt of the chin that accomplished nothing. He paused once, his one good eye flicking over her face as if searching for permission, then resumed wiping under her chin with an almost reverent slowness. The washcloth smelled faintly of bleach and old soap; for a heartbeat the motion felt less like control and more like care, and the thought smeared through her fog like a splinter of light before the haze swallowed it up again.

He folded the cloth away and left as abruptly as he had come. Footsteps receded, then the slow, mournful creak of old hinges—something opening— cut the air. The sound pooled in the room and made everything feel colder. She breathed, shallow and ragged, listening to the house settle around them, unsure which was louder—the hinge's complaint or the steady thud of her own heart.

He came back faster than she expected, hands already under her shoulders and knees before she could brace. He folded her against his chest as if she were a child, cradling her like a princess in some warped fairy tale, and the motion made the room tilt anew. His arms were solid—shockingly strong—and she felt the ease of it, the way her weight seemed negligible in him. For a single, disorienting second she felt weightless. Then the world slid as he eased her toward the open hatch.

Wood groaned beneath them as he started down the narrow steps; each tread complained under his weight, a slow, resonant creak that punctured the hush. Darkness pooled below like a held breath. The damp press of his chest against her kept her balanced, his pulse a fast, foreign thud under her ear. The smell of him — a sharp, musky deodorant and sweat — filled her nostrils and made her head swim.

Her hands were still bound behind her back; she could do nothing but roll her head the smallest amount, a slow, tired motion that registered as protest. A weak moan escaped her — half-plea, half-exhausted sound swallowed by the stairwell and the fog in her mind. He didn't hurry or hesitate; he carried her down into the dark with measured, steady steps, the house above them shrinking until only the soft scrape of wood and the whisper of his clothing remained. She drifted in a blur of motion and shadow, too fogged and diminished to name her fear—only painfully, helplessly aware that he was holding her.

As they descended the steps a light emerged at the end of the darkness. A harsh, ugly yellow-brown bulb hummed overhead, throwing the room in a sickly light that made her eyes ache. She turned her head away reflexively — the glare stabbed at the backs of her lids — and when she let her gaze fall again the space resolved around her. The cement floor wore an old rug like a bandage. A small mattress sat in the corner, flat but smoothed over with fresh sheets, trying to pretend at comfort. A chipped nightstand held a cheap plastic vase with fake flowers. Like a forgotten roadside motel for a guest who would never leave.

He lowered her onto the mattress with strangely delicate hands — steady, not shaking. The motion was careful, and felt ritualistic, and for a breath she let herself imagine safety. He stood there swaying, as if rehearsing calm, and stared at her like someone trying to decide whether a thing belonged in a photograph. He abruptly turned and left; steps thudded up the stairs, and a cabinet slammed. When he returned, he dropped a bundle of clothes at the foot of the mattress without touching her — sweatpants and a worn sweater that smelled faintly of old laundry. It was an awkward offering.

He knelt again. Her heart pounded, anticipating what might come next. Then he turned and left again, followed by quick, anxious footfall of his sprint upstairs and down again. He returned with scissors. Angela's eyes widened. A cold squeeze of fear settled under her ribs. The thought slid into her like an animal: *Maybe this is it — maybe I will lie very still and the world will stop.* She shut her eyes so tightly they ached, pressing her lashes into the skin, letting the blackness gather like a last refuge. In that thin, private dark she felt small and finished. Suddenly, the zip ties split with a sharp, bright crack that made the inside of her ears ring. Warm air slid across her wrists and ankles as the restraints fell away; she curled her fingers and felt the raw, rubbed skin where the ties had bitten. Relief came thin and surprised.

That relief was short-lived when an iron cuff closed around her ankle. He bolted the padded shackle to the floor. He checked the locks the way someone says a rosary: touch, listen, check again. At last, he let out a long, ragged breath. He turned again to leave this time the room filled with tiny, decisive noises — a bolt sliding, a clip snapping, and the sound of footsteps growing fainter into the distance.

For her, the contradictions throbbed—untied but tethered by iron; a mattress made clean yet still a cell; a cloth warmed against her face and the man who had used it hovering between mercy and menace. The fog curled back around her and she lay there, breathing shallow, holding to the single, terrible fact that she was not going anywhere.

3

I Know That Nothing Good Lives in Me

Marshall sat in the driver's seat, the glow of the streetlamp painting the hood of his car in a sickly orange. The rideshare sticker on his windshield caught the light, making it look official, ordinary—exactly how he wanted it. His palms pressed against the steering wheel, slick with sweat. He told himself to breathe, but his chest hammered like a drum anyway. This was it. After all the planning, the rehearsing, the thousand times he'd played it out in his head—Angela was inside, and soon she would walk through those doors. He imagined her stepping out, head tilted back with that crooked smile, maybe fumbling for her phone. Alone. His chance was finally here. Here she was again, surrounded by noise and strangers and liquor. A place too careless, too dangerous for someone like her. She didn't belong here, not with men who would leer and circle like wolves the second she stumbled. No—he could keep her safe from that. Keep her safe from everything.

A sharp *knock* rattled his driver-side window. He jerked his head to the left. Two women stood outside, one blonde and one brunette, both swaying in their heels. He lowered the window halfway.

The blonde immediately leaned in, her face too close, mascara streaked and her breath reeking of alcohol. "Yeah, you're our ride, sweetie," she slurred.

Marshall kept his voice calm. "Sorry, no. I'm waiting to pick up someone else."

The blonde blinked at him, confused, then nudged her friend. "Show me the app. He's our ride."

The brunette fished out her phone, screen glowing as she angled it toward him. Marshall's eyes flicked down—same make, same model, same color as his car. But the plate numbers were different. The driver's name: Abdul.

He hesitated for half a second, a syllable caught in his throat. "My name's not Abdul. It's Ma—" He cut himself off, pulse spiking. No, not that. Never that. "—Mark. And you've got the wrong car—the license doesn't match."

The two women frowned at each other, wobbly on their feet. Then, without warning, they staggered in front of his hood to check the plate, collapsing into loud, ridiculous laughter.

Marshall tightened his grip on the wheel. Between their bodies, in the distance, he saw her—Angela, finally emerging, phone glowing in her hand. His heart leapt. He forced a chuckle, trying to play along. "Look, I actually need to pick someone up right now."

The blonde tugged her friend aside, dragging her out of the way. But then she leaned back over toward his window, her friend giggling at her shoulder. "I bet you're cute under that cap and mask," she said with a sloppy grin.

Marshall gave a small shrug. "Thanks. But I really need to go."

"I like the dark, mysterious types," she cooed, tilting her head. "Come on, give me your number, Mark."

"Sorry," he said firmly, already inching the window back up. "I really have to go."

He eased the car forward, rolling past their laughter, eyes locked on Angela as the distance between them finally began to close. The tires whispered against the asphalt as he put the sedan in park. He barely remembered pulling the gearshift before his body moved on instinct. His door flew open, and he jogged around the front of the car, heart pounding—not just from the thrill of being so close to her, but from the sharp edge of fear. If she checked her phone, if she thought to compare the license plate, everything could come apart.

The car was ordinary by design—a dull hybrid sedan, the kind you saw on every rideshare line. Nothing remarkable. Most people didn't check the app anyway. But if she did, if she called him out—he would laugh it off, mutter an apology, drive away like it had been a mistake. A strange part of him partially wished for that outcome, wished she would see through him and break the spell he'd wound so tightly around himself. But the other part—the one that had studied, prepared, waited—longed for her to just slip inside without a second glance.

Angela stumbled forward, barely lifting her gaze, and slid into the rear passenger seat.

Relief and terror tangled in his chest. Marshall shut the door carefully behind her, sealing her in, then circled back to his side. Sliding in behind the wheel, he clipped his phone into the mount. A map app glowed faintly on the screen, a convincing cover. With a flick of his finger, soft, velvety notes of smooth jazz filled the car—unassuming, familiar. He knew this detail mattered. He remembered overhearing her in college, laughing with friends about how she sometimes needed jazz to lull her to sleep. That was years ago, but he hadn't forgotten.

Now the music wrapped around them, intimate in the small space. Angela closed her eyes and fell asleep instantly. He gripped the wheel, his heart still racing. He kept his eyes on the road, knuckles pale against the wheel. In the corner of his vision, something shifted—just a shadow stretched across the passenger seat, darker than the rest of the night. He didn't dare turn his head, but he felt it there, felt *him* there.

"She's a pretty one," the voice murmured, low and satisfied, the words curling against Marshall's ear like smoke.

His gaze flicked up to the rearview mirror. Angela sat in the back, her oak-colored hair spilling forward, half-shielding her face. Still, her soft features were visible enough—fragile, unguarded.

"You're speeding," the voice hissed suddenly, sharp as a knife sliding between his ribs. "You're drawing attention."

Marshall's foot jerked off the gas. His pulse thundered. He swallowed hard, fighting the urge to glance at the seat beside him. He knew what he'd find. Nothing but empty vinyl. Years ago, the figure had been clear. Now, it was only the suggestion of movement, a murmur tangled so deeply in his own thoughts that he could no longer tell where it ended and he began. But still, the voice was steady. The voice had always been there. And the voice had always helped him when he needed it most.

He merged onto the street, the tires humming beneath him. His grip on the wheel loosened only slightly as he pictured where they would end up. He had scouted it for weeks: A hollowed-out industrial business center on the edge of town. The kind of place that once had auto body shops, supply warehouses, and cheap repair services—all long since shuttered. Roll-up doors rusted shut. Faded signage dangling from bent brackets. The few businesses that had survived closed hours earlier, leaving the lot deserted by nightfall. No traffic. No late-night crowds. No cameras. Just silence and crumbling concrete. The perfect place. In the corner of his vision, the shadow shifted.

"Breathe," the voice murmured, low and steady. "You're too stiff."

Marshall inhaled slowly, forcing air into his chest. Natural. Calm. Normal. He had practiced this, rehearsed it down to the smallest gesture. And still his pulse galloped.

"It will be okay," the voice whispered again, its tone tender. "You've waited long enough. She's here now. You'll see—she was meant for you."

His eyes lifted to the rearview mirror. Angela's head rested against the seatbelt, her phone loose in her hand. For a moment, she looked peaceful, her features softened by sleep. Then a sudden buzz broke the quiet. Her phone vibrated in her hand, screen flaring to life. Angela stirred, lashes fluttering as she shifted.

Marshall's stomach dropped. Her eyes blinked open.

***

After the fight with Angela and securing her in the basement, Marshall's eye throbbed with blinding, white-hot pain. A reminder of the damage he could no longer ignore. He slumped against the other side of the basement door, blood still dripping down his face, trying to catch his breath. His fingers fumbled at the ruined side of his face, probing gently around the bloody socket. There was no fixing it. Not without help. Somewhere behind him, Angela whimpered softly. He closed his good eye and leaned his head back against the cold stone wall.

"You're not the villain," his voice whispered. "You're the one who saves her."

The room spun when he tried to stand. He caught himself on the wall, one palm sliding against the rough concrete. The pain in his eye had worsened. No longer a sharp, burning stab — now it was a deep, throbbing pulse that shook his entire skull. Each heartbeat felt like a hammer blow behind his ruined socket. He staggered to the bathroom mirror. The light buzzed weakly overhead as he leaned in, blinking his good eye. The other side of his face was grotesque. The eyelid swollen shut, purple and black, blood crusted around the edges. And something worse — a cloudy, milky haze spreading across what little white remained. No saving it. He knew that now. Clumsily, he doused a rag with rubbing alcohol and pressed it against the wound. The scream that tore from his throat was raw, primal. He nearly collapsed right there. Tears streamed down his good eye as he slid down the wall, panting. He couldn't fix this himself. Not with painkillers. Not with willpower. He needed a hospital. And he needed it now. The thought of leaving her — Angela—made his stomach twist. She was down there, helpless, confused, scared. Without him, she might hurt herself. Without him, she might try something stupid.

But if you die, he whispered coldly in his mind, *who will protect her then?*

He clutched the edge of the sink, forcing himself upright again. Blood dripped from his jaw, staining the porcelain. He had no choice. He needed to make it quick — in and out. A story ready for the doctors. Maybe a work injury, an accident, a fall. Something plausible enough not to invite too many questions. He still had his ID. His insurance. He could do this. He had to. He wiped his mouth with the back of his hand and stumbled toward the front door. His mind raced, trying to remember if he'd left anything unsecured downstairs. The chain. The locks. Everything was ready. He had been careful. He always was. He took one last glance down the dark hatchway to the basement. Angela was down there, breathing softly, shackled but alive.

"I'll be back," he whispered, not sure if he was promising it to her — or to himself. Then he stepped out into the cold mountain night, locking the door behind him.

***

The fluorescent lights of the emergency room burned down from the ceiling like an interrogation. He kept his head low as he pushed through the double doors, a crumpled towel pressed to the left side of his face. Blood had soaked through the fabric, trailing down his neck, staining the collar of his jacket. The heavy chemical smell of disinfectant hit him like a slap, sharp and nauseating.

A nurse behind the intake desk blinked when she saw him and quickly waved him forward. "Sir? Come here, please. Let's get you checked in."

He shuffled over, the towel still clutched to his bleeding face. The world tilted dangerously every few steps.

A nurse in faded blue scrubs looked up, her dark hair escaping its bun and shadows settling under her eyes, "Name?" she asked, typing into the computer.

"Marshall Sewert," he rasped out.

"And what happened tonight, Mr. Sewert?"

He gritted his teeth. "Fell. Hit the edge of a table. At home." The lie slid out smoothly — rehearsed a hundred times in the drive over. *Keep it simple. Keep it forgettable.*

The nurse asked a few more basic questions — insurance, medications, allergies. Marshall answered mechanically, barely hearing her. His good eye kept flicking toward the door, calculating how fast he could slip out once this was over. Finally, she finished and motioned him toward a curtained exam bay. He collapsed onto the stiff paper-covered bed, clutching his ribs as another dizzy wave rolled through him. The curtain slid aside a minute later.

The woman who entered wasn't what he expected. Late twenties, maybe. Short curly black hair tucked behind her ears. Her light brown skin glowed under the harsh fluorescent lights, and her sharp, thoughtful eyes sized him up in a single glance. Her badge read *Dr. Paula Castillo.*

"Rough night?" she said lightly, offering a half-smile.

He didn't answer. Just stared at her from beneath the brim of his hat.

She didn't flinch. Pulling on a pair of gloves, she stepped closer. "Let's take a look," she said gently.

Marshall stiffened as she peeled the towel away. Fresh blood welled up immediately. Paula leaned in, her brow furrowing slightly. Beyond the obvious injury, the skin around his good eye was reddened and raw, like a chemical burn. And when she leaned closer, she paused for a moment — a slight twitch of her nose near where Angela had pepper sprayed him. She blinked once, and Marshall leaned back cautiously.

"You said you fell onto the edge of a table?"

He nodded once, stiffly. No details. No elaboration. She didn't press, but the unnaturally long pause told him that she had her concerns – and doubts. Realizing his shoulders were tensed he forced them to relax, worried he was coming across too stiff.

"You're lucky," she murmured, sliding her penlight back into her pocket. "If the puncture had been a little deeper, you might not have made it to the hospital at all."

Marshall shifted uncomfortably on the bed, muscles growing taut with impatience. "I can't stay long," he muttered sharply. "I've got work. I just need it stabilized."

Her eyebrow arched. "All right. Fluids, antibiotics, and pain management for now. But you really shouldn't delay surgery, Mr. Sewert. This is a serious injury. Corneal abrasion, and I suspect you've got a scleral laceration along the white wall of the eye, and if that's the case, we can't just treat it with drops and an eye patch. It has to be surgically explored and closed. We need to prevent intraocular infection, which could be catastrophic, and try to preserve what vision you have left. We really need to get you to the OR so our ophthalmic surgeon can actually visualize the wound under a microscope, repair the defect with sutures, and confirm that nothing deeper was damaged. You would need to be on IV antibiotics before and after the procedure. Your vision and intraocular pressure would need to be monitored closely for a few days."

He didn't answer. Didn't care. He just needed out.

A nurse returned to start the IV. As the cool rush of fluids slid into his veins,

Marshall slumped lower against the bedrail, his head pounding.

Paula jotted quick notes into his chart but paused for a moment to glance up at him. Feeling her gaze he met her eyes and she returned to her monitor.

She tapped a few more notes into her tablet, then looked up at him, her expression serious. "You understand if you leave without surgery, you're risking permanent blindness. You could lose the eye entirely. Worse, if infection spreads to the brain..."

Marshall nodded stiffly, gripping the edge of the bedrail like it was the only thing keeping him upright. He swung his legs off the bed, the IV tugging awkwardly at his arm. The room tilted when he stood, his knees nearly buckling.

A nurse rushed forward. "Sir, please sit back down."

"I don't have time," he muttered steadying himself on the exam table. "I have work."

Paula's voice cut in, firmer now. "Mr. Sewert, you're unsteady. You've had fluids, antibiotics, and pain medication in your system. You're in no condition to drive. If you collapse behind the wheel, you won't just be hurting yourself."

"I'm fine," he snapped, trying to shoulder past her. His balance betrayed him, and he staggered against the wall, catching himself on the hand sanitizer dispenser.

Heads turned. The nurse at the intake desk was watching. A tech paused mid-step with a chart in his hand. Even patients in nearby bays shifted at the commotion

"Sir," Paula said evenly, lifting a hand to block his path, "I can't allow you to leave like this. You need someone to drive you, or you need to wait."

"I said I'm fine!" His voice cracked louder this time, drawing more eyes. He swore under his breath, gripping the edge of the curtain with blood-streaked fingers.

Paula didn't flinch. She picked up the phone at the nurses' station, her gaze never leaving his. "Security to bay six, please."

The words hung heavy in the air. He froze. The last thing he needed was uniformed guards swarming him, questions piling up, more eyes cataloging every detail of his face. Slowly, with a visible effort, he unclenched his jaw. "Fine," he grumbled, sinking back onto the bed. His chest heaved as he stared at the ceiling, every muscle tense. "I'll wait."

Paula nodded once, hanging up the phone before security arrived. She made a quiet note in his chart. The curtain rattled open again, this time not by a nurse. Two uniformed security officers stepped inside, broad shoulders filling the narrow bay. One rested a hand casually near his belt, the other scanning Marshall with that flat, assessing look of someone trained to read trouble before it started.

Paula raised a hand slightly. "It's all right. He's calm now."

Marshall forced his shoulders to relax, even as every nerve in him screamed to bolt. He leaned back against the paper-covered mattress, blood drying along his jaw, his hands open and visible. "I'm fine. I just... don't like hospitals." His voice came out lower, controlled, apologetic.

The two guards exchanged a glance. After a moment, one gave a short nod and they stepped back through the curtain. The tension in the room lingered like static, but the immediate threat was gone.

Paula's eyes lingered on him, steady but unreadable. Then she set a clipboard with a thick form on the tray table beside him. "If you're refusing surgery, I need you to sign this. It states you've been advised of the risks and that you're leaving against medical advice. We'll document that we explained the risks to you."

He grabbed the pen with a blood-streaked hand and scrawled a rough signature at the bottom without reading a word. He shoved the clipboard back at her with a shaky, impatient motion. Every second wasted here was another second Angela was alone, vulnerable.

Paula slid the form into his chart without comment. Her eyes lingered on him one last time, sharp and calculating, before she turned to the nurse. "Discharge paperwork and prescriptions." She gave him one last measured look, then tucked the chart under her arm. Without another word, she slipped through the curtain, the faint swish of fabric closing him in again.

The clock on the wall ticked louder with each pass, a steady taunt that Angela was still alone. Every second wasted here was another second she was unprotected, another chance for something to happen while he sat under fluorescent lights, trapped and useless. His chest tightened until it hurt. He'd promised himself he would take care of her, keep her safe, and now he was penned in by clipboards and signatures, nurses shuffling outside like jailers. The longer he waited, the more the walls pressed in, and the more his fear curdled into anger. He had to get back to her. He had to.

4

If It Seems Slow, Wait for it, It Will Surely Come

Angela's house was quiet, except for the ticking of the kitchen clock. Angela's mother, Christine, sat at the table, her reading glasses perched low on her nose, her phone glowing in the dim light. Phoenix was asleep upstairs, tucked under a blanket with his stuffed dinosaur clutched tight in one arm. It was almost midnight. Angela should have been home hours ago. The texts she sent were still sitting there, unanswered:

WHERE ARE YOU? You need to come home now. Hello??

She frowned down at the latest message — a dropped pin. A location link. Christine tapped it, and the map app opened. At first, it just showed a parking lot — nothing else. She pinched and zoomed, trying to get her bearings. There, just a few miles away — a bar. A cheap-looking dive with neon beer signs blinking in the dark.

Her stomach twisted with disappointment. Of course. Of course it was a bar. She closed her eyes for a moment, pressing two fingers against the bridge of her nose. She had wanted to believe Angela was turning her life around. The new job, the promises about cutting back, focusing on Phoenix. But here it was again — the same old patterns. Anger flared briefly, burning away the worry. She tapped out a terse message:

Come home NOW! I'm not covering for you again.

She hit send before she could second-guess it. The phone screen dimmed back to black. She sat there a while longer, arms crossed, tapping her foot against the floor, listening to the silence of the house. Waiting. She grabbed the TV remote and began flipping through the news channels, hoping one of them wouldn't have anything to report. None of them had any news about anything nefarious happening near the bar where Angela was. She set down the remote and stared blankly at the screen, her eyes slowly closing.

The television murmured in the background, casting flickering shadows across the living room. Christine sat curled up in the armchair, her phone resting in her lap. She hadn't meant to fall asleep, but exhaustion had pulled her under. Now, she awoke with a start — the low mumble of the TV in the distance, the clock on the wall reading 3:04 AM. She rubbed her eyes, heart pounding for a reason she couldn't quite name.

Instinctively, she grabbed the phone, thumbing the screen awake. No new messages. No missed calls. No updates. She frowned, shifting uncomfortably. Angela should have at least texted by now — even if she was drunk, even if she was being irresponsible. This silence wasn't normal. She tapped the location pin again, zooming in and out on the map. Still the same parking lot. Still near the same bar. No movement. No check-ins. Her fingers hovered over the call button. She hesitated. Angela hated being checked up on. She hated being treated like a child. But this wasn't right. Something was off. Christine bit her lip, glancing toward the stairs where Phoenix slept soundly, unaware.

Finally, she tapped the call button and held the phone to her ear. It rang once. Twice. Three times. Then went to voicemail. Her blood ran cold. She tried again, her hands trembling now. Same thing. For a long moment, she just sat there, the phone still pressed to her ear, listening to the empty click of the disconnected line. She tried calling — five more times now. Each call had rung before going to voicemail; the last went straight to voicemail. Each unanswered ring had gnawed deeper at her gut. She stared at the last location Angela had sent — the pinned spot, still sitting stubbornly on her screen. A parking lot, empty at this hour. At first, she'd told herself to be patient. Maybe Angela just passed out drunk somewhere, embarrassed to come home. Maybe she was charging her phone. Maybe, maybe, maybe. But now... The silence was wrong. The time was wrong. Angela had made mistakes before, sure — but she always texted back eventually.

She set the phone down carefully, like it might break in her hands, and glanced toward the staircase where Phoenix slept peacefully upstairs. She couldn't leave him. She wouldn't. Her fingers trembled as she unlocked her phone again and opened a web search looking for the non-emergency police line near the pin. She hesitated for a moment, chewing her lip. Calling the police felt like admitting something terrible might have happened. But what if it wasn't terrible? What if Angela was just being Angela — reckless, selfish, stubborn — and here she was, making a scene?

Better a scene than a funeral, a voice in her mind whispered.

Her heart hammered in her chest. She tapped the number and pressed *Call*. It rang twice before someone picked up — a tired male voice on the other end.

"L.A. Police Department, non-emergency line. How can I help you?"

"I need to request a welfare check... for my daughter." Her voice cracked.

She gave her name. Gave Angela's name. Gave the pinned location. Gave Angela's phone number — the calls, the missed messages, the silence.

The man on the other end listened patiently, asked a few careful questions, then promised to send an officer to look. It would take a while, he warned. They were stretched thin.

She thanked him, hung up, and sat there staring at the dead phone in her hand, feeling the walls of the house press in around her. She sat motionless as though one wrong move would set in motion something terrible. And for the first time, Christine wasn't just angry. She was terrified.

***

The patrol car rumbled across the cracked asphalt, headlights sweeping over rows of abandoned parking spaces. The lot belonged to a cluster of low warehouses and auto shops, their metal shutters rolled down tight for the night. No lights on. No traffic. Dead quiet except for the wind rattling a loose sign somewhere down the block.

Inside the cruiser, the two officers sat in easy silence before Mike muttered,"Whole thing's probably nothing. Twenty-five years old and her mom's calling in a wellness check?"

His partner Jonathan chuckled dryly, keeping one hand on the wheel. "My wife's the same way with our son. Kid's twenty-one, got his own place, and she still tracks his phone like he's grounded. He drops off the map for half an hour and she's blowing me up like he's been kidnapped."

Mike shook his head. "Moms never quit. Even when they should." He pulled the cruiser into the center of the lot and killed the engine. "Bet you anything — she's just sleeping it off at some guy's place. Mom's panicking over nothing."

They stepped out, flashlights clicking on with narrow beams slicing through the gloom. The overhead parking lot lights buzzed faintly, only a few still working. Most of the lot sat in deep shadow. Dead rows of delivery bays, dumpsters lined up like tombstones along the back fence. Jonathan veered toward the dumpsters while Mike swept wide between the empty parking slots. Boots crunched over gravel. A plastic grocery bag fluttered past. Nothing unusual at first. Then...

"Hold up," Mike called out, voice tightening.

Both beams froze on the same spot: A scattering of dark blood drops, dotting the cracked cement near one of the parking blocks. Not a pool — but just enough to be wrong. Leading faintly toward the back of the lot. They stiffened immediately, the lazy mood snapping tight. They moved slower now, tracing the blood trail toward a set of dark black tire marks of someone in a hurry. They continued searching the area, approaching the line of dumpsters.

Jonathan swept his light across a rusted metal lid — and caught it—a faint smudge of blood along the edge. He pulled on gloves, lifted the lid carefully. The smell rolled out first — rotting food, stale beer, something worse underneath. Inside, tucked between black trash bags and broken-down cardboard, was a battered handbag. Next to it, a cracked phone, screen spiderwebbed and dark. Mike carefully lifted the bag and rifled through it until he found the wallet inside. Angela Ward. Twenty-five. He exhaled slowly, the weight of the moment sinking in. This wasn't a drunk kid hiding out. This wasn't an overprotective mom overreacting. Someone had taken her. And there was no one around to see it happen.

"Dispatch, Unit forty-seven," Jonathan said into his radio, voice sharp now. "Possible Code two oh seven at our location. Requesting supervisor and CSI."

Static crackled back acknowledgment.

***

After a few tense minutes, the wail of sirens drew closer before cutting off just outside the perimeter. The flashing red and blue lights bathed the abandoned lot in an eerie, pulsing glow. Two patrol cars sat at odd angles, their doors open, their engines idling low in the silence. Detective Juliet Park stepped out of her unmarked sedan, tightening her jacket against the early morning chill. Next to her, Detective Gabriel Ramos slammed his door harder than necessary, muttering under his breath. They crossed the cracked asphalt side by side, their steps quick but measured. Two uniformed officers — faces drawn tight — waited near a taped-off section at the back of the lot. Beyond them, Juliet caught glimpses of a dumpster, the corner of a handbag sealed in an evidence bag, and the dark glimmer of blood spotted across the concrete.

Patrol officer Price—or maybe Mackenzie; Juliet didn't care to check the nametag just yet—stepped forward. It was her first week as lead on the unit, and she hadn't pinned down everyone's names. Gabriel, she knew well; they'd worked other cases together, and he was a steady presence at her side. The rest of the patrol officers were seasoned enough, but still a blur of introductions she hadn't sorted out yet. That would come with time.

"Ma'am," he said, nodding stiffly. "We were responding to a wellness check. Found blood leading to the dumpsters. Discovered this." He held up the bagged wallet. "Victim's name is Angela Ward. Twenty-five years old. Last contact was a dropped pin sent to her mother a few hours ago. Phone and bag were tossed inside the dumpster. No sign of her."

Juliet took the evidence bag, turning it slowly under the harsh light. Angela's smiling ID photo stared up at her — frozen, oblivious.

Gabriel paced a few steps away, scanning the dark lot. "This place is a ghost town," he muttered. "Nobody's seen anything. Hardly any cameras. No night shift. Perfect spot to grab somebody and disappear."

Juliet ignored his commentary, her mind already building the grid of the scene. Blood drops — not a lot, but enough. Leading from the lot toward the dumpsters. Signs of a quick, clean snatch. No drag marks. No massive struggle. Which meant whoever took Angela either had control — or she was too incapacitated to fight back. She tucked the wallet back into the evidence bag and handed it off to a crime scene tech who was now suiting up nearby.

Gabriel swung back around to her, frowning. "We're already way behind," he said, low. "Could be anywhere by now."

Juliet gave a single, small nod. "I know." She turned to the patrol officers. "I want every building in this block checked for external cameras — warehouse offices, streetlights, anything. I don't care if they look broken. Knock on doors if you have to."

Officer Mike Price nodded and hurried off.

Juliet looked back at Gabriel. "You pull traffic cams. Start three blocks out. Anything that looks like a sedan or an SUV leaving this lot in the last twelve hours, I want it flagged."

Gabriel's jaw tightened, but he nodded and pulled his phone, already firing off texts to the department's surveillance team. Juliet turned toward the pool of light around the dumpster, her face set like stone. A kidnapping. No witnesses. No cameras — yet. An empty industrial lot at night. It was every detective's nightmare. And it was only just beginning.

Juliet leaned against the side of her unmarked sedan, the cold seeping through the thin fabric of her blazer. The crime scene lights pulsed faintly in the background, washing the cracked asphalt and dumpsters in a grim red-blue haze. Dispatch had already confirmed the emergency contact number — the missing girl's mother's. Juliet exhaled slowly, centering herself. Then she tapped the number into her phone and lifted it to her ear. The number matched the one dispatch had from the original wellness check request. It rang once. Twice. Three times. A woman answered, her voice tight with fear even before she said a word.

"Hello?" "Mrs. Ward?" Juliet said, her tone even, clear. "This is Detective Juliet Park, L.A. Police Department. Are you Angela Ward's mother?"

"Yes. Yes, that's me — did you find her? Where is she? Is she okay?"

Juliet pressed her hand against the roof of the car, grounding herself. "I'm calling to update you regarding the wellness check you requested tonight. Officers responded to the location Angela last pinned for you." A pause. "We did find some personal items belonging to her at the scene. However, we were not able to locate Angela herself."

There was a beat of silence.

The mother's voice cracked sharply. "What do you mean you didn't find her? Where is she? What happened?"

"We're still actively investigating," Juliet said carefully. "I want you to know we are treating this situation very seriously. A team is on site right now, and we're doing everything we can to find her."

"But—" the mother's voice trembled, rising an octave. "You found her things? Why would she leave her things?"

Juliet closed her eyes briefly, steeling herself against the echo of panic through the line.

"I can't go into too many details yet," she said gently. "But based on what we've recovered, we believe this may not be a simple missing persons case. We are pursuing all leads aggressively."

There was a choking noise — half-sob, half-breath — through the phone. "Is she hurt?" the mother whispered.

Juliet opened her eyes, fixing them on the distant lot where CSI lights swung back and forth like slow, searching ghosts. "We don't have confirmation of her condition yet. But we're moving as fast as we can." A pause. "I need to ask — do you have a recent photograph of Angela you can send us? One with what she was wearing tonight, if possible?"

"I — I'll find one," Angela's mother said quickly.

"I'll text you this number. Send it when you can. And please stay by your phone. I'll be your point of contact going forward."

"O-okay. Detective... please find her. Please."

Juliet's voice softened slightly, just enough to break the professional wall for a heartbeat.

"We're going to do everything we can, Mrs. Ward. I promise you that." She ended the call quietly, sliding the phone back into her pocket.

Behind her, Gabriel paced restlessly near the dumpster tape line, muttering to himself. Impatient. Frustrated. Ready to tear the world apart if it meant getting a lead. Juliet straightened her blazer, rolled her shoulders once to release the tension, and started walking back toward the scene. The clock was already running. And Angela Ward was out there somewhere — if she was still alive.

5

Blood is Crying to Me from the Ground

Thousands of years ago, the stars pulsed like breath across the velvet canopy of Heaven, their songs ancient and low. Between them, suspended in the liminal stillness beyond time, stood two figures of radiance. Uriel—whose name means *God is my light*—burned bright with a steady glow. His wings shimmered like sunlight on calm waters, eyes forever drawn to Earth below with patient hope.

Beside him stood Asael - his name meaning *made by God*, once no less glorious, though something in him had cooled—a quiet shadow beneath the brilliance.

He watched the world below, arms folded across his chest, jaw set with restrained contempt. "They stumble through the dark," Asael said, voice smooth as silver, yet edged with steel. "They rule a world they don't understand, destroying more of it with each passing age. And yet, the breath of the Most High warms *them*."

Uriel turned, gentle yet firm. "They are children, yes. But beloved. Made in His image."

"*We* were made before them," Asael muttered. "We stood at the birth of galaxies. We sang stars into being. Yet He cast His eyes down—on mud and marrow—and called *them* good."

Uriel's gaze lingered on Earth, where a village burned, and a child cried in her sleep.

"Dominion is not a reward, Asael. It is responsibility. They are learning."

Asael scoffed. "They have been *learning* since the Garden, and still they crawl. Tell me, brother—how long must we bow while they fail upward?"

Uriel flinched at the word *brother*—not because it wasn't true, but because it still carried warmth. "This is not you. You speak like the ones who fell."

Asael's eyes glinted, something ancient and buried stirring beneath them. "You think I'm the only one who sees? The only one who wonders why dust was chosen over fire?" He tilted his head. "There are others who whisper, Uriel. Quietly, for now."

A hush fell. The stars seemed to pause in their spin.

Uriel's voice, when it came, was laced with sorrow. "Then we are closer to war than I feared."

For a moment, Asael said nothing. He only watched the Earth, expression unreadable.

Then, softly, almost tenderly: "I do not want war, Uriel. I want justice."

Uriel turned to face him fully, eyes shining with the ache of truth. "Justice does not grow from envy."

Asael didn't reply. His silence spoke louder than rebellion. And below, on the Earth, a boy stood beside his sister, clutching her small hand as they watched their village consumed by fire. The roar of the flames carried up into the heavens, and the two ancient spirits shifted their gaze, drawn to the children. With wings like storm clouds, they descended from the heights, circling lower and lower, until their presence loomed above the trembling pair—watching, studying, as though the fate of the world flickered in those frightened eyes.

Uriel bent close, his voice like sunlight breaking through the smoke. "Do not be afraid. The fire does not end you—it is only the beginning. Hold fast to each other, and light will come again."

His words moved through the children like a breath of warmth, steadying their trembling, quieting their tears.

Asael's voice followed, sharp as stone and fire, pressing against their hearts. "Stand. Move. The world will not wait for you. If you stop, you die. Push forward. Always forward."

It carried no comfort, yet it sparked a defiance in their chests, a raw will to keep walking even when their legs ached and their bellies starved.

And so the children moved on, step by step, through ash and ruin. For years, the two angels had shadowed them—Uriel lifting their spirits with gentle reminders of hope, Asael driving them on with relentless demands to endure. Together, their unseen presence became a rhythm, a strange harmony that carried the brother and sister across the wasteland of their young lives.

Until one day, the boy's eyes no longer looked back in fear but forward with fire. The years of wandering had carved him lean and restless, his sister's frailty pressing on him like a weight he could not set down. He had heard Uriel's gentle urgings of mercy, of rebuilding, of tending to the broken.

Yet Asael's words lingered differently—less comfort, more edge. "The world remembers only those strong enough to shape it. Ashes are not an end, but a beginning. What is taken must be answered."

The boy let those words take root. While Uriel spoke of healing, Asael's voice stirred the embers of his grief into something sharper. He began to draw in the dirt, naming those he blamed for the fire, tracing plans he barely understood. What started as daydreams hardened into intent. His heart turned from mere survival toward a darker purpose: Making the destroyers of his village feel what he had felt. And so, beneath the shadow of two spirits— one of light, one of fire—the boy began to weave his plan for vengeance.

He shaped the spear as if shaping his own fate. From the plains he chose a length of young, straight wood, stripping it clean of bark and smoothing it with a stone until it fit his hand. For the point, he chipped at a piece of flint, striking again and again until sharp edges broke free like fragments of night. With sinew taken from a hunted deer, he bound the point to the shaft, twisting the cord tight until wood and stone became one. Each step was patient, deliberate—an act of will as much as craft. By the firelight, while his sister slept, he tested the balance, adjusted the grip, whispered his intent into the haft. When at last he raised the spear upright, its weight settled into his hand as if it had been waiting for him all along.

When the spear was finished, he did not rest. The boy rose before dawn, the fire little more than embers, and shook his sister gently awake. Together they slipped into the hush of the night, keeping low to the ground as the horizon paled. The wooden haft of the makeshift spear bit into his palm as he gripped it tighter with every step. Beside him, his twin sister lagged slightly behind, clutching a satchel to her chest. A crudely carved wooden doll peeking from its opening had long since lost its smile, a relic of a childhood lost in the flames of violence. Above them, the two angels moved with them — not bound by time or gravity, but tethered still by duty.

Uriel's gaze lingered on the boy's face. The boy's jaw was clenched, not in fear, but in memory.

"His heart is thunder," Uriel said, his voice soft as wind through trees. "Grief still grips him, years on, but now it's changed. It coils like smoke. Ready to ignite."

Asael walked with hands behind his back, expression unreadable. "Righteous anger. Justice. He remembers the smell of ash. The sound of his mother's screams. The heat. That kind of pain doesn't fade, Uriel. It ripens."

Uriel turned slightly, the light of his being dimmed with sorrow. "And you call that justice? He means to murder them in their sleep. Not warriors — farmers and merchants. Men with sons of their own."

A brief pause settled between them.

"Though, I still struggle to know why they burned the village in the first place..."

"Have you forgotten?" Asael asked. "This is humanity at its core. These are still men whose hands are still red beneath the soil. They burned the children first."

"I never forget," Uriel whispered. He glanced back at the girl.

Her eyes darted nervously from shadow to tree, her grip on the doll tight.

"But I remember her too. And I fear what her eyes will see tonight."

Asael's gaze dropped to the boy's trembling hand. "She *needs* to see. So she learns. This world isn't for lambs. If her brother doesn't strike, someone else will." He paused, watching the boy stop at the crest of the hill, staring at the distant flicker of firelight in the valley below — the camp. "It's their nature. Fire for fire. Death for death. No matter how many times we whisper peace."

Uriel shook his head. "It's not nature. It's a wound. And wounds heal. But not if you keep tearing open the flesh just to show the scar."

Asael turned to face him fully now. His voice had cooled. "You speak of healing as if they seek it. They crave vengeance more than salvation." He gestured toward the boy. "So this one becomes like the men who destroyed him? And you call that hope?"

Uriel's steps slowed. "He could become more. That is the gift given to them. Choice."

Ahead, the boy had dropped to one knee, overwhelmed by the weight of his plan. His sister said nothing — just stood, waiting.

"He walks a road paved with grief, yes," Uriel said. "But it is not yet stained with blood. He can still turn."

"You always hope," Asael said, with a trace of pity.

"And you always despair," Uriel responded.

Asael gave a short, bitter laugh. "Perhaps. Or perhaps I see them clearly. Creatures made in His image, yes — but far more like Him when He burned those cities to the ground for their sins."

Uriel stopped. His eyes softened. "Asael, He takes no pleasure in destruction."

A quiet moment passed. The boy stood, legs shaking.

"Humanity doesn't suffer because of sin, it suffers because it has forgotten how to love," Uriel said.

Asael watched the boy's trembling fingers, saw the way his sister reached out, hesitated, then let her hand fall. "Not all of them want to be reminded," he murmured.

***

Thousands of years later, in the dark basement, Uriel stood beside Angela. She lay curled on the thin mattress, her breath slow and uneven, strands of hair fallen across her face. He had been with her from the moment she was born, though she could neither see nor feel him now. Watching her sleep, the despair etched into her features made his heart ache. He clenched his jaw, grinding his teeth in frustration. All he wanted at that moment was to break her chains and carry her away. His eyes shifted to the ankle cuff, and his fingers tightened around the hilt at his waist. A breathy whisper suddenly interrupted his imagination.

"You know better than that."

Uriel's nose flared in anger. His eyes shifted in the direction of the sound while turning his head.

The voice continued, "Then again, you always were rather dull."

The room's darkness seemed to shake subtly before forming into a ball in the corner of the ceiling. Two white horns emerged, followed by a scaly face with bright red eyes like a reptile. It was the demon Asael. His large teeth gave the false impression of a smile, but his expression was cold and blank. His face slowly rotated upside down while his body oozed onto the floor.

"The Lord rebuke you Asael," Uriel muttered coldly.

Asael's body rolled into a long snake-like shape as he slowly slithered toward Angela. The light in the room began to flicker off as he approached.

Uriel stepped in front of her. "That's close enough."

Asael lifted his body up like a cobra and stared into Uriel's eyes. Without breaking his gaze, he began shouting in Angela's own voice, "I'm never going to leave this place alive!" His voice returned to his raspy growl and he began laughing to himself hysterically.

Uriel reached toward the sword at his waist, but Asael quickly coiled his body around him.

Asael's voice changed again into Angela's. "He's going to torture and rape me, I'll never see my family again."

Uriel struggled to get free, his hand trying to pull the sword from its sheath.

"No one will find me, I'm going to die here all alone. Maybe I can bite down on my tongue and bleed to death before he gets back..." Asael's forked tongue flicked near Uriel's face as he tightened his grip. In his hoarse voice he spoke, "She's already breaking," he hissed. "You can feel it, can't you? That quiet unraveling inside her mind. Hope is slipping... thought by thought."

Uriel's jaw clenched as the pressure around his chest increased. "You mistake silence for surrender," he growled. His wings slowly unfurled behind him, radiating a soft, golden glow in defiance of the darkness pressing in.

Asael recoiled slightly at the light but his grin only widened. "You still think she's worth saving?" he sneered. "She forgot about Heaven the moment the pain began. She doesn't pray because she believes - you know that. She prays because she's afraid. That's all you've got left. Fear."

The light in the room flickered as they argued.

Angela shifted in her sleep, though completely unaware of the battle taking place beyond her senses.

"She has faith," Uriel countered, his voice low but resonant, like thunder waiting to strike. "The kind that clings to the light when all she sees is dark. Faith, like a mustard seed, that's all she needs. That is what makes her strong."

Asael's form flickered, his snake-like body rippling as he hissed, "She's not strong. She's alone. She's human. Fragile. Weak." He leaned toward Angela, his breath like smoke against her skin. "And I will enjoy watching her break."

Uriel's anger boiled hot at the demon's words, and he forcefully wrenched one arm free with sword in hand. The blade flashed like lightning, and he powerfully declared, "You will not touch her!"

The blade's brilliance flared against the demon's shadow.

Asael let out a guttural screech as the light seared across his coils, forcing him to withdraw in a cloud of black mist. He reformed at the far end of the basement, pacing like a beast behind glass. "This is only the beginning, Uriel. Her spirit will fracture. You can't hold the darkness back forever. Eventually... It swallows everything." He faded away into a mist and disappeared.

Uriel, full of rage, spit in his direction. After he had made sure he was gone, his eyes turned to the brilliant white sword. A glow like this could only mean one thing. He smiled and looked back at Angela. She was no longer lost in sleep. Her eyes were open now, glassy but alert, her body rigid as she lay perfectly still on the mattress. Her lips moved without sound, shaping words of a prayer only Heaven could hear. The single light in the basement seemed warmer than before, like the morning light peeking through the window of the home she was stolen away from.

He grinned at her. "Do not give up yet child."

Her lips still moved faintly, whispering prayers between shallow breaths. The tension in her face slowly eased, her words tapering off as her eyelids fluttered. Within moments, she had drifted back into sleep, her chest rising and falling in a fragile rhythm of peace.

Uriel closed his eyes and began to settle his thoughts.

In his moment of silence, a small voice said, "Protect her."

He tilted his head back and replied with a smile, "Yes, Father."

6

Where Shall I Go From Your Spirit?

Angela started to wake up. The first sensation was cold—biting, damp, and still. Concrete beneath her back, sending its chill up her spine. Her head throbbed. Something metallic clinked near her ankle when she moved. A chain. Her eyes fluttered open. The light was dim and yellowed, buzzing faintly from a single bulb overhead. The air smelled of mildew, dust, and something faintly sweet—antiseptic maybe. She tried to sit up but a sharp pain bolted through her shoulder. Panic rushed in. She was on the floor beside a mattress pushed against a concrete wall, one leg still resting on it. It was thin and covered with a soft microfiber blanket. Pipes ran along the ceiling. There were no windows. Just cinderblock and the hum of distant plumbing.

Then—movement. A chair scraped gently on the floor, just out of her line of sight.

"I was wondering when you'd wake up," a voice said. Calm. Familiar in the way nightmares are—quiet and wrong.

She turned her head. He was sitting just outside the edge of the light, hands resting neatly on his knees, watching her. Not smiling. Not threatening. Just... watching. "I'm sorry about the taser. You ran. I didn't want to hurt you. I only want to protect you."

Her breath hitched. A hot pulse of fear shot through her as she scrambled backward, palms scraping against the cold floor. She slammed into the wall with a dull thud, the sting of impact lost beneath the rising panic. Her wide eyes darted around the room first toward the narrow staircase, then the bolted door. Every escape was already sealed. A sudden tug at her ankle yanked her down from the surge of adrenaline. She looked and saw it—the iron cuff, the chain rattling against the concrete as she pulled frantically at it, her breath coming in short, shallow gasps.

"Oh my God, No..." Her voice cracked into a hoarse whisper as she clawed at the shackle. The sound of metal links echoed like cruel laughter in the close space.

The man didn't move. He just sat there in the half-light, silent, broad-shouldered and thickly built, his long dark hair falling in rough strands around a face shaped in hard, angular lines. His deep-set eyes fixed on her with an unblinking intensity, as though the walls themselves had closed in tighter. Angela pressed her back flat to the wall, trembling, every muscle straining against the unyielding chain. Her heart hammered so hard it drowned out every other sound in the room—except the steady rasp of the man's breath.

"Angela," he said softly, his voice breaking the silence like a crack in glass. He raised his hands slightly, palms open, as if to show he wasn't a threat. "It's okay. You're safe. I'm not going to hurt you."

The words did nothing to slow her panic. She pressed harder against the wall, her chest rising and falling in ragged bursts. "Stay away from me," she gasped, yanking again at the chain until the shackle bit into her ankle.

He flinched, a flicker of hurt flashing across his face. "Please," he murmured. "Don't... don't look at me like that. I just want to help. You hit your head, you were out cold. I—I had to make sure you were okay."

Angela's eyes burned with tears. "Then let me go," she said, her voice raw. "If you want to help, let me out of here."

He shook his head slowly, his jaw tightening as if the choice pained him. "I can't. Not yet. If I do... they'll get to you. They'll take you from me. I won't let that happen."

Angela pressed herself tighter to the wall, her fingers curling into the cold concrete as if she could claw her way through it. "Who?" she demanded, her voice shaking. "Who's going to get me?"

The man's lips parted, but no words came. For a moment he just stared at her, his good eye flickering with something unreadable—fear, memory, maybe even doubt. The silence stretched until it felt heavy, suffocating, before he finally exhaled and shook his head, as if banishing the thought.

"I can't explain it all right now," he said quietly, forcing steadiness back into his tone. "But you have to believe me—they'll take you, and they'll break you apart. I'm the only one who can stop that."

Angela blinked hard, her thoughts spinning. *They?* The word clung to her ribs like ice. Was he talking about people waiting outside, or voices only he could hear? Her stomach twisted as the question took shape she didn't dare speak aloud—was she already marked for death, and was he the one who decided when it would come? Who was this man?

"You probably don't remember me, I'm Marshall," he added gently, as if he'd heard her thoughts. "But I know you. I've been watching for a long time."

Angela blinked through the haze of her headache, her tongue thick and dry. The name echoed somewhere faint in the back of her mind—familiar, but smudged, like a face half-remembered from a dream. She frowned, but the thought slipped away before she could catch it.

He leaned forward, finally stepping into the light. "And I'm not going to let what happened to you... happen again."

She backed up along the edge of the wall, trying to get as far away as her chain would allow, until her foot caught and she tripped, landing hard on her backside. Her eyes widened at the sight of him, flicking toward his bloodied, bandaged eye.

"Oh this?" he said pointing to his bandages. "Don't worry, I'm not mad. If someone had jumped on me like that I probably would have done the same."

She stared at him in uncertainty, though something about him seemed strangely familiar.

"I brought you some water." He knelt down and placed a plastic water bottle by her bed, "I even have banana bread." He stepped away back into the darkness for a moment and returned with a small brown loaf wrapped in plastic.

Angela looked down at it confused and then back up at him.

"I made it myself actually." He looked down at the loaf. "Oh it's okay I promise, I made sure there are no walnuts."

When he said that she felt goosebumps on the back of her neck because he said it with such casual certainty, as though he had always known about her allergy.

He gently set the bread down next to the bottle of water, the movement slow, deliberate—like he was placing an offering at an altar. Then he took a single step back, hands held out slightly at his sides. "I know how scary this must all seem." His voice was low, measured. Soothing—like a parent trying to calm a child after a nightmare. "But I need you to understand something. I'm not here to hurt you." He crouched slightly to her level, careful not to come too close, as if that somehow made this moment more respectful.

Her legs curled close to her chest as Marshall stepped toward her. Every inch he closed made her flinch tighter, her shoulders rising as if she could fold herself small enough to disappear. Her hands came up instinctively to shield her face, fingers trembling, nails digging into her palms. She couldn't stop the low whimper that slipped out, her whole body cringing from him as though his shadow alone might strike her.

"I've seen what you've been through. The way you walk with your head down. The way you flinch when someone touches your arm. I saw how they looked at you after that party. How they whispered when they thought you weren't listening."

She squeezed her eyes tightly shut, heart pounding, hands trembling still partly covering her face.

"I know what it's like," he said softly. "To be invisible when you're screaming inside. To want someone—*anyone*—to see you. Really see you." His eyes were glassy now, distant. "That's why I brought you here. So nothing can get to you. So you don't have to keep pretending you're okay." He smiled. "You don't have to be afraid anymore."

She closed her eyes, fighting hard to keep from exploding in an outburst of tears. She nodded weakly, slowly opening her eyes again while looking down at the floor.

"Good," he said, "I need to take care of something, but I will be back to check on you later. There's a TV in the corner, the remote is next to your pillow. If you need anything, write it on that chalkboard at the foot of the bed." He smiled, turned, and walked out of the room, carefully closing the door behind him as though he didn't want to wake his sleeping child.

Angela waited for a while, listening for footsteps or any other noise outside. She looked around. The room was sparse. There were no windows, except maybe one but it seemed like it was now covered by bricks that didn't match the rest of the basement.

She started to scream at the top of her lungs, "Help! Help, someone please! Help!" Her voice tore through the basement, raw and frantic, bouncing off the cold concrete walls. She screamed again, louder, until her throat burned and the corners of her vision pulsed from the effort.

Then—*crackle.* A faint hiss of static, like an old radio coming to life.

And then his voice, calm and steady, threaded through the distortion. "There's no point in screaming. The room is soundproofed. The only one who can hear you... is me. Through the camera mic."

She froze. Slowly, her eyes turned toward the television. Atop it sat a small, black, nondescript camera—no bigger than a golf ball, its lens aimed squarely at her. She hadn't noticed it before. But now she couldn't *unsee* it. The tiny red LED pulsed like a heartbeat. Watching. Recording. Her body began to shake. She staggered back from the TV, bumping into the edge of the mattress. Her knees gave out beneath her, and she dropped onto it, arms wrapped tightly around herself. The room suddenly felt colder. More than that—*smaller.* Like the walls had moved closer, like the air had thickened. Like there was nowhere in the entire room she could *not* be seen. The realization settled like a weight in her chest: She was *never* alone. Not even now. Not even in her silence. Her face crumpled. And there, in the dim flicker of the overhead light, she buried her face in her hands and began to cry in the dark.

Her sobs quieted into shaky breaths, but the camera's red pulse still throbbed in the corner of her eye. Angela lowered her hands and stared at the floor, her vision blurring with fresh tears. The image of her mother surfaced—tired eyes, kind voice, always believing Angela would get it together "next time." How many times had she sworn she'd clean up, stay sober, keep her promises? Too many. And now the weight of every broken one pressed down like iron.

Then came the sharper ache. Phoenix. His little face, the way he lit up when she surprised him with a hug, the smell of his hair when he fell asleep against her chest. She hadn't even kissed him goodnight that last evening. Instead, she'd chosen a bar, chasing laughter, noise, and the lie of escape. A night out, when she should have been home.

Her stomach twisted with self-disgust. How had she been so careless? So blind? Sitting here, trapped, the truth crashed over her—she might never see them again. Never get a second chance to be the woman she swore she would be. If she had known this was coming, she would have fought harder, really changed. She would have gotten sober, not just said she would. She would have been there. For her mom. For her son.

The regret hollowed her chest until it felt like she could barely breathe. She pressed her palm to her mouth, rocking slightly on the mattress, whispering broken fragments of prayers she wasn't even sure God was still listening to. She let herself fall back onto the thin mattress, the springs creaking beneath her. She draped an arm across her eyes to block the harsh overhead light, but it did nothing to dim the flood of memories pressing in.

It had started with her father's death. That first drink wasn't about fun; it was about silence. About drowning the hollow space he left behind. One night turned into many, bottles stacking like bricks in a wall she couldn't tear down. Her mom had told people Angela was grieving, that it was understandable. She had even told Angela the same thing, as though excuses could soften the edges of self-destruction. But grief had become habit. Habit had become escape. And escape had become her way of living.

Her throat burned as she thought of Phoenix. Sweet, gentle Phoenix. She never understood why she kept him when she hadn't even known his father. But she had. And instead of becoming the mother he deserved, she had pushed the responsibility onto her mom, too wrapped up in her own spirals.

The shame cut deeper than the cold of the basement. Phoenix was so easy, so full of love. Never the kind of child who screamed for attention or made life harder. He didn't deserve to be left with goodnight kisses that came from his grandmother's lips instead of hers. He didn't deserve the empty seat at his little milestones—the plays, soccer games, the moments where she should have clapped the loudest.

Angela pressed her arm tighter over her face, but the tears slipped free anyway, streaking across her temple and into her hair. If she never got out of this place, Phoenix would grow up remembering her not as a mother who was there, but as a shadow who wasn't. And the pain of that truth was more than she could bear.

Her arm slipped from her face, and she let her gaze drift unfocused toward the ceiling. The memory came without warning, sharp and whole. It was a Saturday morning, sunlight pouring through the thin curtains in her mom's kitchen. Phoenix had been sitting at the table, legs too short to reach the floor, swinging in quick little kicks. He had a crayon clutched in one hand, his tongue peeking out in concentration as he scribbled lopsided stars onto a piece of scrap paper.

When he saw her stumble in, hair wild, eyes heavy from the night before, he had looked up at her with a grin so pure it hurt. "Look, Mommy. This one's for you."

He had held the paper up with both hands, proud as though he'd painted a masterpiece. The yellow star smeared across the page was crooked, the lines uneven, but he had drawn it for her. Just her.

She remembered mumbling something—what was it? "That's nice, buddy"—before reaching for coffee, trying to blink herself awake. She hadn't even kept the drawing. It probably ended up crumpled on the counter, swept into the trash when no one was looking.

Now the image of it burned in her mind like an accusation. That little star. That smile. Another morning she had thrown away without even realizing it. Her chest squeezed until it was hard to breathe. Phoenix had always given her his love so freely, without judgment, without hesitation. And she had wasted it—left him with her mom, left him waiting, left him wondering why she wasn't there. She rolled onto her side, clutching the thin pillow to her chest as if it could fill the space where her son should be. The thought of never seeing him again was worse than the chain on her ankle, worse than the camera's unblinking eye. It was unbearable.

Angela's sobs broke open into something worse—raw and ragged, the kind of cry that hurt your ribs. She buried her face in the pillow and let out a sound that had nothing gentle about it, a ragged, ugly scream that vibrated the thin mattress beneath her. Her hands clawed at the fabric as if she could tear the shame out of her chest.

Through the muffled thud of her own breath words tumbled out, small and frantic. "I'm sorry, baby. I'm so sorry," she choked, the name barely a whisper swallowed by the pillow. "I'm sorry I wasn't there. I'm sorry I left you. I—" Her apology came in jagged bursts, a string of promises and excuses that dissolved into hiccupping sobs. She spoke as though he were sitting at the foot of the mattress, as though she could feel his small hand in hers. "I didn't mean to. I should've—God, I should've been home."

When the pillow finally wrenched free from her face she gasped, cheeks wet, voice raw. The basement seemed to hold its breath with her. Her apology bled into something else — a pleading that had nothing theatrical about it, only absolute desperation. She folded her hands clumsily on her chest and began to pray, words tumbling out urgent and simple: "Please. Please, God, make a way. If you get me out of here I—" She swallowed hard, the promise catching in her throat. "I will change. I'll get clean. I'll be the mother he deserves. I'll prove it. I'll do whatever it takes."

She pressed her forehead to the mattress and whispered the bargain like a vow, as if the walls themselves could hold her to it. "No more lies. No more nights out. No more using it to run. I'll go to meetings. I'll call my mom. I'll—" The list spilled from her in a trembling rush, evidence of a woman trying to stitch together a future out of fear and hope.

When her breath finally steadied, the red light on the camera glowed the same steady beat. Angela stared at it, feeling every word she'd offered hanging in the air between the lens and her heart. Whether Heaven listened or not, she had said it aloud. For the first time in a long while, something like resolve — small and brittle, but real — trembled under the weight of her sorrow.

7

There is None Who Does Good

Marshall's Journal Entry

I've been thinking about how this all started. The first moment, as if there's a switch that flips. But that's not how it works. It doesn't arrive all at once. It seeps in slowly, like mold beneath a carpet. At first, you think you're still normal. Still clean. But then it starts to rot, and by the time you smell it, it's everywhere. I don't remember the exact moment it happened to me. Somewhere between those nights when I was a kid, when my father would stumble in drunk and bloody the walls with his rage. I don't remember the day I stopped being a regular kid. It was long before I ever picked up a gun. Something inside me cracked long before that. Maybe when you see someone become a monster in front of you, a part of you becomes one too.

People like me, we blend in. We wear the right faces. Nod at the right times. Smile when expected. Hold the door open. Sit quietly in the back. Nobody notices us. But I noticed her. Angela. And once I saw her—really saw her—I couldn't look away. I noticed her long before I knew what had happened. Before the party. Before the baby. Before the whispers and the silence. She would just... walk across campus with her head down, her backpack hugged to her like armor. She smiled when people laughed around her, but her eyes never matched the smile. They stayed distant. Guarded. Like she was bracing for something. I saw that look every day on my mother's face, back before she stopped feeling altogether.

Angela moved like someone carrying something heavy. Like every step was a negotiation with pain. But no one noticed. They just saw a pretty girl and assumed she was fine. But I saw the truth. She laughed when she didn't mean it. She avoided groups of guys but made it look casual—like she was just in a hurry. It wasn't casual. I knew. I always know. Most people don't understand what it's like to see someone drowning while pretending they're not even wet. I didn't approach her. I didn't say anything. I just watched. I wanted to protect her—even then. Before I knew the truth. I feel like Angela is a part of me, like we are bound together by threads of fate. Some might call it an obsession, but I think it's no different than the way a father loves his child. Or how he should love his child, mine was not the best example. Wouldn't it be natural to worry about her? Wouldn't he be thinking of her all the time? It's the same. I just didn't know what to call it at the time.

We had Anthropology 101 together. She sat near the front. I stayed in the back. One day I got added to her group project. I wasn't able to finish my part at the very end. She emailed me and asked if I was okay. I replied and told her to take my name off the project, that I didn't want to drag the group down.

And she said, "We're in this together. It's no problem." She added a smiley face to the end.

When we were doing the group project, I volunteered to take on extra work and when she objected I said that exact thing to her. She remembered, she was so thoughtful. I couldn't understand it. How could someone be that kind, going through everything she was? That night, I lay in bed thinking about her. I looked her up, using her last name from the school email. Found all her social media. Every photo. Then her friends. Then her mother. Then I found a park near their home – her mom left the location tagged – she liked to post from there on Saturdays.

So I went. Just to see. Just to feel near her again. I sat on a bench near the pond, earbuds in, pretending to scroll. But I was watching. And then—there she was. Angela. Laughing with her mom. No makeup. Hair tied up. She looked perfect. Natural and effortless, I liked seeing her that way. From there, it wasn't hard. I followed them at a distance until they went inside a house

I recognized from my online searching, white railing, ivy-covered fence. I walked past three times that day. Slower each time. Blue constellation curtains in her room. I liked that. It felt right. Like I was meant to find her. I eventually memorized her daily routine. Once, I saw her crying in her room all by herself. My heart almost gave out. I stood there for an hour. Just watching. Just being close.

This journal started out so simply. Taking notes on the things she did. The colors she wore. How she seemed to be doing emotionally. Little details— like the way she tucked her hair behind her ear when she was nervous, or how she'd blink a little faster when someone caught her off guard. I wanted to keep track of her moods. Make sure she was okay. That was all. But this has grown so much. My sketches of her and even the dreams I had— where she smiled at me like she used to smile at her friends. Dreams where she didn't flinch anymore.

I still can't believe she's here. After all the nights I stayed outside her window just hoping to catch a glimpse, now she's only a few feet away. I wanted this more than anything, but not like this. Not with chains, not with fear in her eyes. I wanted her trust. I wanted her smile. I wanted the kind of closeness you don't have to steal. But that's all I see when she looks at me—fear. Wide, trembling eyes that flinch at every movement I make. She doesn't see the hours I watched over her just to make sure she was safe. She doesn't see the way I memorized every little thing that made her smile. She doesn't see me at all. Not the way I wish she could. If only she could look past the walls between us, past the mistakes, and see me the way I've always seen her. Worth protecting, worth everything.

Sometimes I let myself imagine a different beginning. A better one. One that feels so real I trick myself into thinking it happened.

We're in the university library. I'm at one of the long tables with my textbook open, half-reading, half-dozing under the dim lights. Then I hear the soft clatter of something hitting the floor. A pen rolls past my shoe and I bend down to grab it. Another hand reaches for it at the same time—hers.

For a split second her fingers touch mine. Warm. Small. She pulls her hand back quick, shy, embarrassed. I hold the pen out to her.

She smiles when she takes it, eyes flicking away before they find mine again. "Thanks," she says, just barely above a whisper.

"Anytime," I answer, pretending I'm calm though my chest is racing.

She laughs then—soft, unguarded—and it's enough to crack open the silence between us. We start talking. About our classes. About the professors we can't stand. About anything, everything. Before long we're laughing like we've known each other forever, voices hushed but alive in that heavy, quiet library air.

That's how it should have been. That's how it could have been. Two people finding each other naturally. Not like this. Not with me writing down the truth in a place where only these pages will ever understand.

***

Marshall's pen slowed, the line on the page breaking into a smear of ink. His eyes lifted to the phone propped beside him. The screen glowed with Angela's image, her lips moving faintly. For a moment, he thought she was just whispering to herself, but when he nudged the volume higher, the words came through. A prayer. She was praying for her life. A hollow pit opened in his stomach. That's what she thought of him—that he was going to hurt her. That was all she could see. To her, he was only the monster.

She moved suddenly, the chain rattling as she lurched to her feet. Marshall straightened, watching her rush toward the bathroom. He had made sure to give the chain just enough leeway for her to get inside. There was no door, just a narrow space, but he'd kept the camera turned aside. A courtesy. His kind of privacy. That was what he told himself. Her body slipped out of view. Then the sounds came. Retching. Violent, hollow. The kind that clawed at his insides with every echo. He froze, pen trembling in his grip. Should he go to her? Offer water, hold her hair, prove he wasn't what she thought he was? Or stay where he was, because the truth gnawed at him—he was the cause of this. Her sickness, her terror, it all came back to him. He hovered on the edge, paralyzed between protector and monster, every sound from that bathroom dragging him deeper into the truth he couldn't outrun.

***

Marshall's Journal Entry, Continued

Everyone has always wondered what was wrong with me from the very beginning, social workers, teachers, therapists, people who couldn't even look me in the eye. They all took one look and decided what I was. Troubled kid. At-risk youth. Antisocial, or more specifically, "conduct disorder with emerging antisocial traits," like I was some case study in a textbook. They smiled and handed me worksheets and meds and thought that was healing. Like crayons and quiet corners could erase the sound of your mother being strangled two rooms away. No one ever asked the right questions. Eventually, I gave up trying to answer them. I stopped the meds. I stopped pretending. And I learned to mimic what people wanted to see.

They think killers are monsters with wild eyes and blood on their sleeves. But sometimes, they're just little boys sitting on staircases, listening. Hoping it ends soon. My father was a drunk, violent and unpredictable. Every punch that landed was like a hammer forcing down a nail—his way of reminding us who owned the house, who owned us. And my mom—she never left. She made excuses. Always. She said it wasn't him, it was the bottle, or the stress, or even me. She told me once she didn't want kids, but she thought maybe having me would make him stay. That maybe it'd change something. It didn't. He still slept around. Sometimes she would call him out for it and he would beat her. I hated him with all my heart, but I loved my mother so much. Every damn day, I thought if I could be better, if I could do something, she'd finally look at me like I mattered. But she only looked through me like I was made of glass.

The first night I heard my friend, I was eight, hiding in the crawlspace beneath the stairs. My ears still ringing from the shouting, the thud of fists against flesh echoing down the hall. And then, clear as a whisper inside my own skull, a voice said, *She can't see you because you're too small. Too quiet. But I see you.* He stepped out from the shadows like he'd always been there. Not scary. Not like my dad. He looked like an older brother I never had—tall, calm, confident. I asked him who he was, and he just smiled. Said to just call him "Brother," though later I would discover his real name, *Asael.* He said that even if we weren't related, he saw me as his little brother. Said he was there to help. At first I thought I was imagining it. But he kept coming back.

Only when things were really bad. Only when I needed someone. He didn't tell me what to do. Not directly. Just... helped me see things more clearly. Helped me make sense of why everything felt so broken, and gave me the confidence that I would one day be able to change it on my own.

The night my father died, I didn't cry. I didn't scream. I was ten years old. Small enough that my legs dangled off the couch, but old enough to sit up late and feel proud of it. I had the TV tuned to a rerun of a show called *Peacemakers*, that old cowboy show where the marshal always rode into town, saving people and putting the bad guys in their place. I liked the sound of that. Marshal. I pretended he was me. Every time he drew his pistol, quick as lightning, I imagined I could be like him—protecting people, solving problems no one else could. The crack of gunfire on the show felt comforting, more peaceful than the shouting that usually came from their bedroom. My parents fought so often their voices became part of the soundtrack of my nights, but that night it got quiet. The silence wasn't part of the routine, and it made the hairs on my arms stand up. I tore my eyes from the screen and realized my heart was beating too fast for someone who was just watching TV.

I slid off the couch, the blanket falling around my shoulders like a cape, and padded down the hall in socks. The silence on the other side of their door was heavier than all the shouting had ever been. I pushed it open. He was on top of my mom, choking her. It wasn't the first time, but this time he didn't let go. She was turning purple, I never saw her like that before. It's strange, her bloodshot eyes locked on me and in that moment for once in my life I felt like some part of her really did love me. Like she was worried about me. Dad's gun slipped from his waistband and clattered on the floor. Like a gift. Like it wanted to be picked up. My little hands picked it up. They shook uncontrollably as I raised the muzzle up to the side of my father's head.

He let go of mom and looked at me from the corner of his eye and said, "Since when did you become the man of the house? You think you have the balls to shoot me? You can barely keep that thing steady, you're so scared you're about to pee your pants."

When he said that I smiled, pulled back the hammer on that old revolver, and said, "I'm not shaking because I'm scared… I'm excited." As I said this, I could feel my brother standing behind me, helping me hold my hands steady. We pulled the trigger, together.

The sound of the gunshot didn't matter. His body hitting the floor didn't matter. What mattered was the silence afterward. That was the first time I ever felt peace. I wanted to tell her I was okay and hear her say that she loved me, but it was too late. The damage was done. Her brain went soft. She was never the same, she wasn't there anymore, just a husk. After years of bouncing through the foster system, I finally found her—tucked away in a state-run facility, forgotten by everyone but me. It took time to piece everything together, to dig through old records and legal red tape, but eventually I reclaimed the cabin my father left behind. Once it was mine, I brought my mother there. Became her full-time caretaker. Just the two of us, shut off from the world. I fed her. Changed her. Talked to her even when she didn't talk back. And I waited. Every day, I waited for a sign that maybe she saw me again. That she was proud of what I did. That she loved me… She never did. Then I saw her. Angela…

She moved like my mother used to, before the beatings got bad. The same eyes. The same way she flinched at the world. I saw her on campus. She didn't even notice me. But I noticed everything. I heard what he did to her. The party. The aftermath. The baby. No one protected her. No one saw her. Just like no one saw my mom. So I did what had to be done. I watched over her. I made sure she got home safe. I listened when she cried. And I knew—eventually—I had to take her away. Just like I should've taken my mom away years ago. I gave Angela safety. I gave her what no one ever gave me or my mom—a protector. I have come to realize this was my way of saving her, my way of showing her what I now know is love.

***

Asael watched Marshall's pen drag to a halt, the tip hovering mid-sentence above the page. A shiver rippled across Marshall's shoulders, the kind that prickled at the nape of his neck and raised goosebumps along his skin. Asael smiled. Even now, after all these years, Marshall's body betrayed him with the same fragility it had in childhood. He leaned closer in his chosen guise, the one Marshall always accepted most easily—an older brother's shape, human and warm. His hand came down on his shoulder, steady and possessive. To Asael, the muscles beneath his palm might as well have been the narrow frame of a frightened child. That was all he would ever be to him: small, impressionable, needing guidance. Marshall stiffened, back rigid, breath caught like he'd been caught misbehaving. For a heartbeat, he sat frozen, as if acknowledging what he could never admit aloud.

Yes, Asael thought. *You feel me. You know I'm here.*

When Marshall finally turned, quick and wary, the chair legs scraping against the floor, there was nothing. No hand, no smile, no figure looming over him like a watchful brother. Asael lingered unseen, smiling still. No matter how old Marshall became, to him he would always be a child with pen in hand, waiting to be shaped.

8

Be Alert and of Sober Mind

At first, Angela told herself it was just stress. Being kidnapped would do that to anyone, wouldn't it? But the longer she sat in that gray, windowless room, the more she knew it was something else. The headache came first—sharp and hot, like needles driving in behind her eyes. Maybe dehydration. Maybe madness slowly seeping in...

Sleep never came that third night. Some of it was nerves, of course, but beneath that, something deeper gnawed at her. By morning, her hands trembled so badly she could barely grip the thin blanket. Her legs felt foreign, like they belonged to someone else. Food wouldn't stay down. Her body wouldn't cool. She couldn't rest. Couldn't stop sweating. On the fourth day, when she tried to stand and make her way to the bathroom, her knees buckled. The concrete rushed up to meet her, cheek striking against it with a cold, punishing slap. A bitter taste filled her mouth—metal, dust, the sting of defeat. After that, everything unraveled into fragments. Heat. Noise. Light. A high, whining note that screamed in her ears. Then nothing at all.

When she came to, the room was softer than before. Blankets wrapped around her, tucked in close. A bowl of ice chips waited on the nightstand beside the mattress. The lights were low. The TV glowed silently in the corner.

Marshall was there—sitting in his chair, steady as stone. Watching her like she was some fragile bird with a broken wing. "You're detoxing," he said quietly, tapping at the laptop beside him. "From alcohol."

The words slid past her at first, just sounds in the haze. Then they sank in. Shame clawed at her chest, so sharp she wished she could melt back into the mattress and vanish.

"You drank a lot," he continued, calm, gentle. "After the baby. Everyone else let it slide, but I saw it. I knew."

Her mouth was too dry to answer, her tongue heavy and rough against her teeth. He held out water. She took it with hands that wouldn't stay steady, the cup rattling like it was alive. A little spilled down her chin, soaking into the blanket. He didn't flinch. Didn't scold or smile. He just watched—eye steady. Like he was proud she was trying. Like he'd been waiting for this moment all along. He said he'd been researching.

"You need fluids. Magnesium. Vitamins. A lot of rest. You're going to shake. Maybe hallucinate. But I'm here. I'll take care of you. We're in this together, it's no problem," Marshall told her, voice low and steady.

She turned her face to the mattress and curled tighter into the blanket. Her body felt like a traitor; thoughts slid out from under her like loose coins, impossible to clutch. She wanted to scream until the sound tore through the room. She wanted to ask why he cared, why he made it sound like a kindness instead of what it really was. But the water soothed the rawness in her throat. The crackers settled into her belly like small, sensible anchors. The way he sat there—close enough to be a presence but never forcing himself—eased something small and stubborn inside her. That was the thing that made her skin crawl the most.

The days folded into one another. He brought soup in paper bowls. He sat in the chair, watching but careful not to crowd her. He kept a little notepad by his knee and penciled things down—how her pulse fluttered, whether she'd eaten, when she'd slept. Once, in the dark, she heard him whisper under his breath, words that could have been a prayer or merely a muttered hope; she couldn't tell which. Slowly, the tremors loosened their grip. It didn't stop all at once; instead the internal roar faded into a low hum. Breaths came easier, not as if each one might be the last. The nausea backed off enough that small pieces of herself returned—snapshots rather than the whole. Her head throbbed, a dull ache beneath the fog, but she could feel the outline of herself again.

That night she slipped into a deep sleep. Later—if it was later—she found herself standing in the woods, but everything was too clean to be real. Moonlight lay across the ground like paint, too bright and too perfect. The trees moved without wind, their leaves whispering in a rhythm that didn't belong to the world she knew. Everything shimmered silver. Someone stood a few feet away. He wasn't Marshall. He wasn't anyone she could name. He was tall, with hair the color of burnished gold that caught when he shifted, and his eyes were smooth as glass—kind, but carrying a weight that pressed against her chest. He wore a plain white shirt with the sleeves rolled to the elbows and dark slacks, ordinary clothes that somehow made him more impossible. There was a heat about him that did not show as flame, a quiet burn that seemed to sear the edges of the scene into her.

"You're not alone, Angela," he said.

The voice rolled warm and low through the silver quiet—strangely familiar, like a song half-remembered. It made no sense, but she didn't push for sense. There was something in the timbre that tugged at a place inside her that had been hollow for years.

"Who are you?" she asked, and her voice came out smaller than she felt.

"A friend. A watcher."

"Am I dead?" The question tasted silly in her mouth, but the woods felt unreal enough to make anything possible.

"No. You're fighting." He tipped his head as if catching a faint sound no one else could hear. "You're not finished yet."

Her throat tightened, an old familiar squeeze. "Then why does it feel like I've already lost?"

His face shifted—something softer moved there, something patient. "Because this feels like another chapter in the story you tell yourself. That you've always been the one left behind."

The words landed like a stone. They dug through her like cold fingers finding an old scar. A tremor went through her—less the shaking of detox and more the body's reflex to an ache that had lived inside her for years. She didn't want the sentence to be true, and yet it fit with the easy certainty of something she had learned to carry.

"Then why does it keep happening? Why do I keep getting hurt?" Her voice broke. Tears came before she could stop them, hot and sudden, tracking down her face.

She didn't notice the hand until it was there—a light brush across her cheek, dry and sure. The touch did not demand anything. It didn't try to mend; it simply rested, a fact. That steadiness—no pity, no ownership—slid into her like an unexpected seam.

"You haven't been left behind. Not in the way you think. You were never forgotten. Never discarded. You were seen—even in the moments when it seemed like you were on your own."

The words settled around her like the blankets, oddly close and oddly foreign.

She swallowed, the motion scraping her throat. "Then why did it all happen like this?"

He held her with a look that carried both eternity and ache, as if he knew every grief and still bore it. "There are answers," he said, voice hushed, steady. "But they won't soothe you right now. I could tell you there's a plan. That there's meaning in the pain. But I know that's not what you need."

Her gaze fell, tears slipping hot down her cheeks. "Then what do I need?"

His voice dropped. "Just keep holding on. Even if it's only by a thread. That thread is stronger than you think."

And then he was gone. The silver woods folded inward, light collapsing into itself until nothing remained. She startled awake in the dark, her body slick with sweat, her chest holding a strange calm she couldn't explain.

She never told Marshall about the dream. She couldn't. He would have twisted it, made it about him—his redemption, his purpose. But the next morning when he brought her breakfast—oatmeal, a boiled egg, a napkin folded with care as if this place were some bed-and-breakfast—her eyes lingered on him longer than she meant to. Marshall looked worn, more than tired. There was a heaviness about him, the kind carried by someone who had never learned how to set anything down. She didn't forgive him. She didn't trust him. But something unwanted stirred in her anyway—something that felt close to gratitude.

She despised it, but there it was, simmering beneath her ribs. Maybe it was just her body still clawing back from dehydration. Maybe her mind playing tricks. Still, the truth sat bitter in her chest: She wouldn't have survived the worst of it without him. Psycho or not, he had kept her alive. And yet— she wouldn't have been detoxing on a basement floor if he hadn't dragged her here in the first place. Sometimes, though—when he spoke, when his eye softened for just a moment, she glimpsed something else in him. Not innocence. Not goodness. Just... displacement. As though he didn't belong to himself, either.

He looked like a wild animal shoved out of its territory by new construction—adrift, pacing the edges of a place that wasn't home and couldn't be. For half a second she felt something like pity flare up, and then she pinched it shut. That was all she allowed herself. After a while, he shifted his weight and wandered toward the stairs. He moved slowly, like a man restless in his own skin, pausing once as if debating whether to stay. Then he slipped through the door, the hinges groaning faintly. The sound of his footsteps faded above her.

She dug the remote from under the mattress and aimed it at the TV. The screen snapped awake, throwing cold, flickering light across the room. Channels bled past— Clifford the Big Red Dog, Andi Mack, some infomercial for a blender that could probably crush bones. She kept flipping until the picture stopped her.

"Angela Ward, age twenty-five, has now been missing for over a week..."

Her face filled the screen—the photo her mother loved, hair just to the shoulders, that neat navy blazer and ivory blouse she'd worn on her first day at Harvest Mutual. It was the kind of headshot meant for LinkedIn or a company bulletin, not splashed under the word *MISSING*.

A clip cut to Mr. Piña Colada, her old boss, smiling the small smile of someone trying to be sincere on camera. "I don't know what we are going to do without Angela. She once brought in lemon bars for the break room, and I said, 'Wow, these are almost as sweet as you'—which, I now realize, maybe came off weird. But I meant it respectfully. Anyway, we all just want her to come back. The office isn't the same without her…"

She let out a sound that was closer to a laugh and a groan at once. "Oh my God… They sent Mr. Piña Colada?" she said under her breath, the words sharp and ridiculous in the dim room.

The news kept talking; the anchors' voices softened into background noise. Angela's photo lingered on the screen, lips frozen in that practiced, hopeful smile, and she felt a violent, private urge to wipe it clean.

The picture snapped to a press conference. Her mother stood behind a podium, one hand crumpling a tissue, the other clutching a folded sheet of paper like a lifeline. Skin had thinned around her eyes; her face looked smaller, worn at the edges.

Her voice broke as she addressed whoever might be listening. "If anyone out there knows where my daughter is—please, please say something. If you're the person who has her… I'm begging you, just let her go. She's a mother. Her son needs her. We need her."

The camera panned down around the image of Phoenix. Something older lived in his face now, a seriousness that didn't belong on a child so small.

He stared straight into the lens with a steadiness that should have belonged to someone far older. "Mom, I love you. Please come home."

The plea landed like a stone inside her chest. She dropped the remote. The thud was small but felt like an anvil. The TV's sound became a smear; the anchors' words receded into a distant hiss while static roared louder in her ears. Both hands flew to her mouth because there was a sound rising inside her—half sob, half animal howl—that she couldn't let loose. If she cried, if she screamed, the sound would travel through the thin air and perhaps reach them in some impossible way. Or it would reveal the fact that she was still trapped, and she was not ready for that truth to fall into the light.

They were looking for her. They hadn't stopped. That thought hit with a cold, clear panic: This room was not only a prison—it was the barrier between her and everything that mattered. The walls didn't just keep her in, they kept her from the warm press of her son's small body, from the crooked smile her mother wore when she was trying to keep herself together. The realization was a new kind of terror. She was not simply trapped—she was being kept away from them.

The image of Phoenix—his small jaw set, the way his eyes already carried worry he shouldn't have to know—seared something loose inside her. Panic folded into a sharper, colder thing. A decision. She couldn't float in the fog any longer, pretending the world hadn't rearranged itself around her absence. If they were looking, then there was a path back. Somewhere. She had to find it.

She waited until the room narrowed down to its details, the way a map reveals itself when you stop squinting at the whole. The mattress sagged against the concrete in a particular crescent. The lightbulb overhead swung just enough when someone moved the stairs. The door had a deadbolt—she'd heard it when he opened it. Angela's mind caught on one detail she had forgotten: the bobby pin. She had slipped it into the seam of the mattress days ago, back when her hands still shook too badly to do anything useful with it. It was still there—she was almost certain. A tiny sliver of metal, overlooked, waiting. The thought of it sparked a fragile thread of hope. It wasn't much, but in this place, even something so small felt like a weapon, a key, a promise.

She thought about Marshall—the way he left and came back, the steady cadence to his wandering. He hadn't chained her wrists. Whatever fragile mercy he allowed suggested routine more than cruelty. He fed her, he monitored, he stepped out. Each of those movements was a thin thread she could follow. If she watched him, learned when he slept and when he climbed the stairs, she could hunt for gaps.

Beyond the physical, she felt the other lever: Marshall himself. He watched her the way someone watches a stray animal taken home—ownership braided with uncertainty. That gaze could be turned. If she could be smaller, softer, and cooperative when he returned, maybe she could make him lower his guard. Maybe she could make him proud of her progress, proud enough to leave a door unlocked for a breath. It felt like a dangerous calculus—using his care against him—but danger was the contour of her life now.

But when she shifted, the cold bite of metal at her ankle reminded her of the truth. The chain rattled faintly, heavy and absolute. No matter what she planned—no matter how sharp her mind or steady her hands—she wouldn't get twenty feet without dealing with it first. Her eyes lingered on the cuff, on the way it hugged her skin like a verdict. If there was going to be an escape, it would start here. Without that, she would never leave this room alive.

9

Hope that is Seen is Not Hope

The soup simmered in a chipped pot on the stove, the scent of lentils and wilted carrots filling the cramped kitchen. Marshall stirred it carefully, slow circles, watching the steam rise like breath from a tired animal. From the living room came the familiar creak of the aged recliner. His mother hadn't spoken a full sentence in years, but still, she moved. He ladled the soup into a bowl, steady hands practiced in ritual. In the living room, she slouched in her chair—eyes dull, mouth slack.

He knelt beside her, lifting the spoon gently to her lips. "Easy now," he whispered. "Still hot."

She took it without resistance. Another spoonful. Then another.

"You care deeply, Marshall," came the voice—low, measured, but warm like light filtering through morning fog. "You've held onto her when most would have left. And now you hold onto Angela too."

He didn't look up. But his fingers trembled.

"Letting go does not mean abandoning," the voice continued. "Angela has a life beyond this house. Beyond you. She has a son who still prays for her, a mother who hasn't given up. You cannot make her whole by keeping her here."

Marshall wiped the corner of his mother's mouth with a cloth she'd sewn years ago.

"Pain taught you to hold on tighter. But love—true love—lets the cage

68

door open."

He set the bowl down on the table and walked slowly back to the sink.

The voice followed him like a shadow's inverse, soft but unwavering. "You've done what no one else could. You kept her safe. But safety isn't living. Let her go, Marshall."

Marshall rested his hands on the edge of the sink, staring into the steel basin. Silence.

And then, something colder stirred—like breath on the back of the neck. "The world is a dangerous place," Asael's voice slid in, smooth and close. "You know better than anyone what it can do."

Marshall's head dropped slightly.

"What freedom is out there for her? This world has already ruined her. You saw it in her eyes—you managed to sober her up now, but if she wasn't here she would go right back. What kind of mother would she be in a state like that? You know what that's like, remember? She'll never be the same, Marshall. And the world will punish her for that. You know what happens when broken things try to pretend they're whole."

Marshall turned on the faucet, watching water run down the spoon. The reflection in the window above the sink wavered with the ripple of steam.

The words spilled into his mind with a human-like warmth, but something about them made his skin crawl. The voice carried a softness that tried to mimic comfort, tried to sound nurturing, but it landed wrong—like a recording just slightly out of sync.

"But you... you've been kind. You protected her. Listened to her cry. Sat in silence while she shook. No one else would've done that. No one else could've understood."

Marshall's grip tightened around the faucet handle.

"She belongs to you now, whether she sees it or not. And if you truly love her—if you want her to never suffer again—you know what must be done." Each syllable stretched a beat too long, each inflection bent at the wrong angle, as though whatever spoke was imitating kindness without ever having felt it.

He shut the water off. The sound of dripping faded.

"It's not cruelty, Marshall. It's mercy. It's peace. It's the only way to make sure no one else ever gets to break her again."

Marshall stared at his reflection in the glass—his own eyes empty, flickering between the voices in his head. After a brief moment he shook off his thoughts and moved the spoon to the rack. He turned around, leaning against the sink. His eyes wandered to a bowl of fruit, fixing his gaze on one of the red apples. He could see it again—sunlight spilling through the window, dust dancing in the beams like tiny fairies. He was six then, small enough that his chin barely cleared the edge of the table. His mother, hair tucked into a scarf, humming softly as she sliced apples into a bowl. No yelling. No slammed doors. Just the two of them. He remembered the sound of her laugh, soft and breathy, when he made a joke about the apples looking like little boats. That day, she let him stir the cinnamon into the sugar, even showed him how to sprinkle it evenly over the slices.

"Gentle, like snow," she'd said, guiding his hand. For a moment, she wasn't tired or distant. She looked at him—*really* looked—and smiled.

She hadn't wanted him. He knew that now. Maybe even then, he'd felt it in the way she avoided his eyes some days, or how quickly she shrank when his father raised his voice. But on that afternoon, when the air was sweet and the house still, it felt like he mattered. A lump tightened in his throat. He opened the cupboard, searching for something, anything. The smell of cinnamon still made him ache.

And then another memory shoved its way in. A crash. A cupboard door slamming open. Spice jars clattering and rolling across the floor.

"Where the hell is my bottle, Candice?" his father had bellowed, voice thick with rage.

Marshall remembered freezing by the doorway, the apple slice still in his hand.

His mother stood by the sink, shoulders drawn up tight, her voice trembling. "I—I poured it out. I thought maybe if it wasn't here—"

"You thought what? That I'd magically stop drinking?"

The sound of a fist hitting the wall snapped through the air.

"You stupid bitch! That bottle cost money. You think money just grows on trees, huh?"

Marshall had wanted to run in, to scream, to stop it. But his legs wouldn't move. His heart hammered in his chest like it was trying to escape.

Back in the present, his fingers gripped the cupboard door. Cinnamon. That sweet, stupid smell. The ghost of a good day buried in a thousand bad ones. His jaw tightened. His eyes burned. He slowly closed the cupboard door with one hand, staring down at the counter breathing hard like he was the same little boy all those years ago.

He pulled out his phone, seeking relief from the flood of memories filling his mind. He unlocked it with a swipe, tapping on the app nestled discreetly among more innocent icons. The screen blinked to life—grainy but live. Angela. She was sitting cross-legged on the bed, blanket draped around her shoulders like a shawl. Her hair was still unkempt, but her posture had changed. She was upright, steadier, eyes clearer than they'd been in the week she had been there. There was something sharper about her now—like a wire pulled taut. The haze of withdrawal was gone, and in its place, something else had begun to stir. She reached toward the small chalkboard propped at the foot of the bed—block letters scrawled in chalk: *HUNGRY*. She pointed to it deliberately, her expression unreadable, but her hand steady.

He watched her for a moment. She didn't know if he could see her, not always. But she kept pointing at the sign anyway, just in case. He liked that. The hope. He was also happy her appetite was coming back after the withdrawal. Marshall stood, slipping the phone into his pocket. He made sure to grab a tray with a bowl of soup and a plastic spoon as he moved toward the basement hatch. He knelt down on one knee, setting the tray aside to open the hatch, then he picked up the tray again and descended toward the basement. The stairs creaked beneath his weight, old wood groaning under each step as he descended. The air shifted. Cooler. Still. Concrete walls welcomed him like old friends, and the dull hum of the dehumidifier buzzed softly in the corner. He paused at the locked basement door, resting his hand on it for a moment. She was hungry. He would take care of that. He slid the bolt back, the metal grinding against the frame before the lock finally gave. He pushed the door open and stepped into the basement, the tray balanced carefully in his hand. The steam rose in thin wisps, softening the sharp scent of damp concrete.

She was there on the mattress, straight-backed, hands folded neatly in her lap. Wrapped in the blanket like armor. Watching him closely. The weight of her eyes pressed against him, but for once, she didn't shy away immediately. He held her gaze longer than he meant to, searching for something he could never name, before the burn of it forced him to glance away.

"You're hungry," he said. The words came out low, softer than he intended—an offering disguised as a statement.

Marshall set the tray down on the table beside the bed, but his hands didn't move away right away. He lingered, caught in the stillness of the room. Normally, he'd leave the second the food was in place. Today, he stayed.

Her voice broke the quiet. "We've never really talked."

He shifted on his feet, forcing a shrug. "We've talked some." His tone was casual, though it felt thin, stretched.

"Not about anything real."

Her eyes stayed locked on him, steady, insistent. He hesitated, then pulled out the chair against the wall and lowered himself into it. The distance between them was deliberate—he didn't want to spook her—but sitting there felt like crossing some invisible line.

She studied him in a way that made his skin prickle. There was something in her gaze that burrowed past the surface, clawing at things he'd kept buried.

"You seem familiar. Do I... know you?"

Marshall's jaw tightened. He forced himself not to react, but silence was its own answer.

"I'm serious," she pressed. "I've been thinking about it since the first day. I thought it was just the trauma, like my brain trying to attach a face to the fear. But now I'm not so sure."

He didn't move. Didn't speak. But inside, something flickered—too fast for him to stop it. He felt it in his eye, the way it betrayed him, just for a second.

"You said something earlier... when you first brought me soup after the withdrawal. You said, 'We're in this together. It's no problem.'"

Marshall blinked, the words hitting him harder than they should have.

"And now I remember saying that. In college. When we were doing a group project for Anthropology class."

His gaze fell to the floor. Of course, he remembered, but he hadn't expected she would.

"You missed a few meetings. I got an email that said something about the flu and needing to take care of your mom. I remember you asked to have your name taken off the project, but I insisted we keep it because you had already done so much—way more than the other group members."

Marshall kept his head down, letting the silence stretch. His chest tightened with every word. She remembered.

The faint metallic clink of her ankle chain broke the quiet. Then her voice again, softer, but sharper somehow: "Marshall. I remember because I made sure your name was on the group list. Marshall... Sewert."

His head lifted, against his will. Their eyes met.

His throat worked before the words finally slipped out. "You remembered."

She stared at him like she was seeing him for the first time. "You were quiet. You always wore that gray hoodie. You barely talked. I think you only spoke up once the entire semester."

A faint warmth stirred in his chest, half ache, half relief. "You were the only one who didn't roll your eyes when I did."

The memory felt sharper now than it had in years—the way her face softened that day, how she'd let him finish his thought without looking bored, without that dismissive smirk everyone else wore. He hadn't realized until this moment how much it had meant.

She looked uncertain, caught between disbelief and something else. He could see it in her eyes.

"You remembered me all this time?" she asked.

His voice dropped before he could stop it. "You used to cry a lot back then, sometimes when you would get back to your car I would see you lose it."

He swallowed, shame curling at the edges of the memory. Watching her from a distance, never knowing what to do, never finding the courage to step closer.

She was quiet, but he could feel the shift in her—like she was putting the pieces together, even if they didn't fit.

"I didn't really know you back then," she said carefully. "You could've just... said hello."

Marshall's lips parted, but the words came out soft, fragile, like an apology. "I didn't know how."

She nodded slowly, but something in her stillness put him on edge. Marshall's words hung between them, fragile, exposed. *I didn't know how.* He'd meant it as truth, but the truth always sounded small when spoken aloud.

"I didn't know how," he repeated, quieter this time, as if the words might find weight if he said them again.

She offered him a smile—soft, careful. He couldn't tell if it was real or not, but it steadied him anyway.

"Well... you're talking to me now."

His eyes lifted, drawn to her face, and for a moment the air shifted. Something fragile cracked inside him, as though her words had reached through the walls he'd stacked around himself. "I guess I am," he murmured, voice barely more than breath.

She nodded, her voice gentling. "I remember that project. You weren't wrong about me crying that day. I was going through... a lot. But that doesn't mean I wanted to disappear."

Marshall's gaze slipped to the floor. He hadn't wanted her to disappear either—that was the whole point.

"I never thought you were crazy," she said softly. "Quiet, sure. But you seemed... smart. Thoughtful. Just kind of alone."

His shoulders twitched at that word. *Alone.* It struck him like a stone skipping across a deep well. He clenched his jaw, trying to keep the ripples from showing, but he knew she saw it.

"Anyway," she added, her voice barely above a whisper, "thanks for the food."

The trance broke. Marshall stood, his body moving stiffly, like he'd forgotten he was supposed to. The chair legs scraped faintly against the floor, grounding him back in the basement's dim reality.

"You should eat before it gets cold." His voice came out steadier than he felt, the words a kind of placeholder to fill the space between them.

Angela nodded lightly, keeping her tone soft. "Maybe you'll sit a little longer next time. It's nice to talk."

He didn't reply. Just turned toward the door, footsteps measured. At the threshold, a thought caught him—an impulse to leave the door unbolted. It would make returning easier, quicker. A way to step back in if something went wrong. The idea hovered, tempting, but he shut it down. Too much risk, too much room for chance. He slid the bolt into place with a final click. She exhaled—he could hear it even through the wood—and something in the way she released air set off a tight, taut sensation in his chest. Was it relief? Defiance? Gratitude? He could not be certain, and uncertainty was a blade he'd never learned to trust.

As he ascended the stairs, his mind replayed the conversation on a loop: her questions, the way she remembered a gray hoodie, her steady insistence. Pride flared at the memory that she'd kept him in that corner of her past. But beneath it lurked a colder current—a knowledge that she watched him now with a clarity that might become dangerous. If she'd pieced fragments together, if she'd begun to map him the way he had mapped her, the map could be read in more than one direction.

He walked to the kitchen and sat at the table, staring at the untouched cup of coffee in front of him. It had gone cold a long time ago, but he hadn't moved. He barely blinked.

"She remembered me." The words left his mouth in a whisper, like saying them too loud might make them vanish.

All this time... all the days he watched her from a distance, the nights he imagined conversations that never happened, the guilt, the justifications, the doubts—none of it prepared him for *that* moment. Not really. She remembered his name. Not just that—she remembered the class, the project, what he'd said. He smiled to himself. It had mattered. *He* had mattered. And for a moment—just a moment—it felt like being seen. Not looked at. Not tolerated. *Seen.* He ran a hand through his hair, fingers tugging at the strands near his temple. The giddy warmth in his chest made him feel light, dizzy.

But then something twisted inside him. What if he'd said too much? What if she realized too soon what he was? What he'd done? What he *really* wanted from all of this? He didn't even know exactly. Not in words. But there was something about having her here, in this house... eating meals he made, saying his name like it meant something. Something about the quiet hum of knowing she was nearby. Breathing. Moving. Dependent on him. Like a family. No. Not a *real* family. Not like before. This wasn't his mother lying silent in a chair by the window. This was... different. Angela was bright. Sharp. She looked at him like he wasn't invisible. Like he could still be good. But would she think that if she knew the whole story? He did it all for her, but would she understand? He pressed his palms into his eyes and let out a slow breath.

"I'm not trying to hurt her," he murmured. "I'm helping." He said it again, a little louder this time, trying to anchor himself in it.

He just wanted her to feel safe. To see him. To choose to stay. He didn't realize he was rocking in his chair, the way he used to when he was little— back when the shouting started in the other room and he needed to disappear inside himself. He thought of the look in her eyes when she said, *"You could've just said hello."* It wasn't anger. It was sadness. And somehow, that made it worse.

Marshall stared at the hallway leading to the back room. To his mother's bedroom. The house was so quiet, always quiet. Except now... it wasn't. He stood, pacing slowly, a nervous buzz flickering in his limbs. Maybe tomorrow, he'd sit longer. Maybe they could talk again. About school. About anything. He just had to be careful. Not too much at once. He didn't want to scare her.

She didn't know about the others yet...

10

Their Angels Always See

Standing in the far corner of Angela's living room, cloaked in stillness, was a figure that did not breathe and did not blink. Remiel. He was massive—nearly seven feet tall, with the carved frame of a warrior and shoulders broad enough to carry storms. His skin shone like burnished bronze in the faint glow of the streetlights outside. A white mantle fell over his back, draping the dense cords of muscle that lined his body like armor. But his face was kind. Sorrowful. He stood with his arms folded gently across his chest, watching Christine and Phoenix—grandmother and grandson.

Angela's family home was too quiet now. Too clean. Too still. The silence pressed against Remiel's chest, heavy as stone. He stood unseen in the corner of the room, watching the woman who had given Angela life. The only sound was the faint tick of the wall clock and the sharp, broken rhythm of her breathing. Her hands trembled as they clutched a photograph—edges frayed, colors dulled, but alive with memory. In it, joy radiated. A birthday cake waiting to be cut, balloons blurring behind a little girl whose eyes were squeezed shut in laughter, her parents wrapped around her in a cocoon of love. Remiel's throat tightened. He had not been there for that day, or any day of Angela's childhood. He had only been sent when Phoenix was born—now he was charged not just with watching over the boy, but the grandmother who had nearly lost herself. This frozen image was new to him, yet through it he felt the ache of what once had been, the warmth that had long since fractured.

"God, I CAN'T LOSE THEM BOTH!" Christine's scream tore through the room like shrapnel.

Remiel flinched, the force of her agony rippling through him as though the cry had been hurled at Heaven itself. She bent over the couch, knuckles whitening around the photograph until it crinkled under the pressure of her grip.

"Don't do this to me!" she sobbed. "Don't take her too! I buried him—I survived that, but I can't do this again!"

Remiel's hands curled into fists at his sides. Every word was a wound he could not close. He longed to tell her that her daughter still breathed, to whisper that God had not abandoned them—but the laws bound his tongue. He could only watch as she pressed the picture to her chest like a lifeline, rocking, her sobs breaking against the silence.

"She's fine. She has to be fine. This is just a misunderstanding, a mistake—maybe she just ran off to clear her head. People do that. She'll walk through that door like nothing happened. She always comes back…"

Her voice withered into a whisper, and Remiel's heart broke with her. He had not witnessed Angela's early laughter or the strength of the father she mourned—but he saw their shadows now, etched in the pain of the woman before him. And though his charge was not Angela, he felt the pull of her mother's desperation like a chain around his own chest. His duty was to this grieving mother and to Phoenix, waiting in fear for answers no one could give. All he could do was stand, silent and unseen, while the ones he was sworn to guard unraveled in the absence of the one they loved.

He could not bear the sight any longer. The mother's sobs carved too deeply into him, so he turned away and moved silently up the stairs. The walls were lined with photographs that traced Angela's life—moments frozen in time that he had never lived alongside her. But now he bore witness like a stranger thumbing through a family album. Each frame seemed heavier than the last.

He reached the doorway to Phoenix's room and paused. The boy was on his knees by his small bed, hands clasped, head bowed so tightly that his forehead touched the blanket. His lips moved with urgency, words tumbling out between gasps of breath, a prayer whispered like it might shatter if spoken too loudly. His eyes were screwed shut, face wet with tears that clung to his cheeks.

Remiel's chest tightened with reverence. This was why he had been sent—for this boy who carried a faith more unshakable than men ten times his age. He stepped closer, unseen but not absent, watching the child's shoulders tremble as he poured his small heart out before Heaven. Then it came. A deep warmth, soft as velvet, spread through the room like light poured into water. It filled the air—not loud or showy, but steady, alive, and whole. The walls seemed to hum with it, every corner breathing peace. Within Remiel's chest, the sensation unfurled—tender and weightless yet heavy with meaning. It was the presence he had known since the dawn, the presence that made even the mightiest bow low.

It wasn't merely around him—it was *in* him. A serenity so profound it stilled every thought. A joy so complete it burned behind his ribs like fire wrapped in silk. The angel closed his eyes, overwhelmed by the holy nearness, and if he'd possessed mortal knees, they would have buckled beneath the weight of such love. In that moment, Heaven was here. Remiel's breath caught. He stiffened, convinced for a moment that the feeling had been meant only for him, an assurance sent to strengthen his resolve. His wings stirred in quiet awe.

But then Phoenix stilled. His words faltered, his prayer cut off mid-syllable. Slowly, he lifted his head, eyes opening wide. He glanced around the room, as if searching for the source. And then, a smile bloomed across his tear-streaked face—small, radiant, certain.

Remiel swallowed hard, wonder stirring in his chest. The boy had felt it too. Did he receive a promise spoken directly into his heart? Phoenix shot up from the side of his bed, the presence from earlier still burning in his heart. His small fists clenched with conviction, and the tears on his face seemed to dry in an instant.

"She's coming back," he whispered to himself, and then louder, steadier, as though already rehearsing the words for his grandmother. "She will come back."

He hurried toward the door, his steps quick and determined. Remiel followed silently, a guardian shadow keeping pace in the narrow hallway to the staircase. He could feel the boy's heartbeat radiating with hope, steady and bright like a lantern suddenly lit.

Then Christine's voice carried upstairs. Phoenix slowed. Her voice faltered, trembling at the edges. "She's not gone. She's not. She would never leave Phoenix like that."

Phoenix froze mid-step, listening, lips parted. Remiel's gaze softened as he looked between them—the child clutching faith like a sword, the mother clawing her way through despair.

Then came the bargaining, soft and breathless, spilling out of Christine like a desperate tide. "God, please. Please, if you bring her home, I'll do anything. I'll be better. I'll stop doubting. I'll go back to church—I'll talk to that woman from the prayer group, I swear I will. I'll even forgive the ones who hurt me. Just don't take her too."

Her voice cracked. Tears streamed down her cheeks unchecked as her body folded over the photograph still clutched to her chest. "She's my baby. She's my baby..."

Phoenix's lips quivered. He took another step, but Remiel placed a hand near his shoulder—not touching, but close, steadying him with unseen strength.

Then the storm shifted again.

Anger rose ragged and hoarse, tearing through her like fire. "You took him from me! Wasn't that enough? You said You were good. You said You were a Father! What kind of father does this?!" She choked on a sob that refused to leave her throat, fists trembling against the fragile photograph. "What kind of God breaks a woman twice?"

The silence that followed was thick, jagged, alive with accusation. Remiel bowed his head, sorrow carving deep lines across his spirit. He had heard cries like this before—faith cracking under grief, promises thrown back at Heaven like broken glass. Yet it pierced him anew, every time. Beside him, Phoenix straightened his small shoulders, his jaw set.

He whispered again, this time as if he were answering not just his grandmother but the heavens themselves. "She will come back." His soft footsteps padded across the hardwood floor.

Remiel looked up as the boy appeared in the living room behind her—small, but standing straight, his eyes wide and alert, glowing with the remnants of prayer.

"Grandma?"

Christine jerked upright, swiping at her tear-streaked cheeks as if she could erase the evidence. Her voice was hoarse but gentle. "Phoenix, baby, go back to bed, okay?"

He didn't move. Instead, he crossed the room with quiet determination and climbed onto the couch beside her. Without a word, he pressed himself into her side, grounding her with the warmth of his small body. "I pray for her every night," he said simply, his voice carrying the calm weight of conviction.

Christine swallowed hard, caught in the stillness of his certainty. Her throat worked as she tried to speak, but Phoenix continued, his gaze fixed ahead as though looking at something beyond the room.

"She's gonna come back. God told me."

Christine's head snapped toward him, startled.

Phoenix blinked up at her, calm and assured, as if the matter had already been decided.

"I'm not worried." Then he rested his head against her arm, eyes closing at last.

Christine stared down at him, lips parted, too weary to argue, too broken to hope. Remiel could see the war in her eyes—faith against despair, love against loss. And then, in the stillness, something stirred. Not peace. Not yet. But a flicker. A fragile warmth pressed against her side, carried not by her own strength, but by the faith of the child she held. Remiel bowed his head, a silent witness to the miracle of it: hope finding room to breathe again, even in the ruins.

His gaze settled on Phoenix. The boy slept now, chest rising and falling with quiet steadiness. Faith clung to him even in dreams, a shield stronger than walls.

"He believes," Remiel whispered, the words carried on a breath.

"He always has." The voice came from beside him.

Remiel did not flinch; he knew it instantly, as surely as a soldier knows his captain's step.

Uriel stood tall in the stillness, robes shifting faintly as though stirred by a wind that did not exist. His face was grave, his eyes weighted with thought. "I crossed paths with an old friend," Uriel said, his voice low, deliberate. "Asael."

Remiel's brow furrowed, though he held his silence.

Uriel's gaze drifted toward the boy, but his words were for Remiel. "It troubles me. Asael seldom wastes his efforts on individuals. He sows unrest in nations, stirs hatred in crowds, bends rulers to his whispers. But this—" His mouth tightened. "To attach himself to one man, to a captor with no great power or influence? It is... strange."

The air between them grew heavier. Remiel felt it too—the wrongness, the echo of something more than coincidence.

Uriel's voice hardened, edged with unease. "I fear there is more at work here than a single abduction. Asael does not act without cause. If he has fixed his gaze on Angela and twined himself around her captor, then something larger is unfolding. Something hidden."

Remiel lowered his head in acknowledgment, though his spirit stirred uneasily. If Uriel spoke this way, then Heaven itself was watching with concern. And if Asael was moving here, among the small and the broken, then perhaps the stakes were greater than either of them could yet see.

Uriel turned then, his eyes steady, commanding, but brotherly. "More than ever, I will rely on you—my brother, my friend—to continue guarding this family. Their protection is no small task, and Heaven does not take it lightly."

His words carried both weight and reassurance. "Support has been sent to you."

At that, a light stirred in the corner of the room. A figure stepped forward, compact in stature yet steady in bearing, eyes bright with resolve. He bowed deeply before them, hands pressed briefly to his chest.

"Serel," Uriel said, his tone carrying both respect and command. "He will stand with you."

Remiel studied the smaller angel, then inclined his head in welcome. The resolve in his chest deepened. The enemy might be moving in shadows, but Heaven was not idle.

"Archangel Raphael senses it as well," Uriel continued, his voice lower now, edged with caution. "There has been a shift. A tremor in the order of things. We cannot yet see its full shape, but we know who waits in the shadows."

Remiel's wings drew in closer, unease prickling through him.

Uriel met his eyes, his tone weighted with urgency. "We must be ready for anything."

The words lingered in the stillness like a sword left drawn, sharp and waiting. Uriel's eyes suddenly became unfocused, head tilting slightly as though he were listening to something only he could hear. His sword began glowing faintly from the sheath at his waist.

"Uriel?" Remiel asked quietly.

Uriel's wings flexed, every feather tightening like drawn steel. "She's praying."

The air seemed to bend under the weight of that word. For a moment, the room itself faded, replaced by a faint echo of a voice, broken and trembling but full of longing.

"She's calling out to Him," Uriel said, his tone filled with urgency and reverence, "I must go."

Before Remiel could respond, Uriel's form ignited with light. The air rippled, and with a powerful flap of his wings, he flew upward, phasing through the ceiling.

***

The brightness of Uriel's light gave way to a single bulb casting a sickly yellow haze over concrete walls. Dust hung heavy in the air. Angela sat on the thin mattress, her head bowed, fingers trembling as they clasped together. Her whisper barely carried through the stillness.

"Please... God, if you can hear me... I need a way out. Just a hint. A door. A distraction. Anything."

Uriel lingered in the shadowed corner of the basement, his gaze resting on Angela as she lowered her clasped hands. Her prayer still reverberated softly through the air—its echo faint but steady, like the last note of a song refusing to die. She waited—her eyes lifting toward the ceiling, as though expecting Heaven itself to split open and flood her world in gold. But the silence held. Uriel's heart ached. He wanted so badly to answer her the way she longed for—with light, with wings, with proof. But that wasn't how faith worked. Not yet.

He shifted his attention to the hum in the room—the low electrical current coursing through the old television across from her. To mortal ears, it was static, a background buzz. To him, it was a chorus of frequencies—threads of invisible energy vibrating in divine rhythm. He reached out—not with hands, but with thought—tracing the threads like harp strings. Within them he found a pulse, a path, a whisper of possibility. A small turn, a gentle nudge.

This way, he thought. *Let her see what she needs to see.*

Angela sighed and picked up the remote, flipping through channels without focus. News. Comedy. Some cooking show. Noise without meaning. Uriel waited. Then, as the remote slipped from her hand and hit the floor with a sharp clack, the batteries rolling away, he felt the static waver. A small ripple passed through the screen like the surface of disturbed water.

Angela groaned. "Seriously?"

Uriel touched the current again—ever so lightly—and the signal shifted. The image blinked once. Then again. And suddenly the channel changed on its own. White letters flared across the screen:

EXTREME ESCAPES: LOCKED IN WITH THE LOCKPICKING LIFEGUARD

Uriel's eyes narrowed faintly. To her, it would seem like a coincidence. But to him, it was providence in disguise—a message delivered through the mundane. Angela blinked, brow furrowed, unsure what she was looking at. The scene opened to a dimly lit prop room—a man tied to a chair under a hanging bulb, grinning like a fool while the narrator's voice boomed over swelling music. Uriel allowed himself the smallest of smiles, remaining still, the faint hum of the television vibrating through the cement floor like a heartbeat.

"In this episode," the narrator's voice said, "Tanner—also known online as the Lockpicking Lifeguard—has ten minutes to escape using only what's in the room. No tools. No tricks. Just his vibe."

Uriel's gaze flicked to Angela. She stared at the TV, completely focused, her attention drawn to the screen as though decoding a secret message. Onscreen, Tanner laughed through his struggle.

"Yo, this is gnarly. We got, like, discount horror movie lighting in here, my arms are totally pretzeled, and whoever tied these knots? Certified savage."

Uriel's eyes narrowed slightly. The mortal's words were ridiculous, and yet, something about them shimmered faintly with resonance. Heaven often spoke through foolish things.

"Step one: Don't panic. Step two: Wriggle like a fish in distress. Step three: Use your brain, dude, not your biceps."

Uriel's wings stirred faintly, invisible to human sight. The lesson was there, clear as scripture written in static. *Calm. Think. There is a way.*

Angela leaned forward unconsciously, her breath catching as the man on the screen slipped free of his ropes.

"Boom! We're free, baby! Like it's spring break!"

Uriel could almost feel her pulse quicken. The smallest spark of hope flickered in her heart—fragile, but real.

The man paced, inspecting the door on the screen. "All right, all right," he said, crouching beside the knob. "No pin, no paperclip, no gum wrapper. But we do have a sick industrial lightbulb hanging from the ceiling, and you know I'm about to make that work."

Uriel's gaze rose slowly toward the single bulb swaying above Angela's head. Light. He felt the meaning strike like the soft toll of a distant bell.

"Never underestimate the utility of light, bro," Tanner said, unscrewing the bulb and holding it toward the camera. "See this little filament guy inside? That's your best friend. Strong, flexible, full MacGyver vibes. Just don't shatter it too hard or you're gonna have sad fingers and regret."

Uriel's expression softened. "Even here," he murmured quietly, "your light finds her."

Angela blinked, her gaze moving slowly from the television to the bulb above. For the first time in days, her mind began to turn—not in circles of despair, but in lines of possibility. Uriel remained still in the half-light, his presence woven into the hum of the old television. Angela let out a soft, incredulous laugh—half disbelief, half release—and covered her mouth. The sound startled him. After days of silence and prayer soaked in fear, that small burst of laughter was like hearing music return to a ruined cathedral. On the screen, Tanner continued his animated performance.

"You wanna pop the base gently, like a fizzy soda bottle. Use your shirt if you gotta. Don't hulk out unless it's your last resort, y'feel me?"

Uriel's eyes flicked to Angela again. She was listening now—truly listening.

The man cracked the bulb against the floor, pulled the filament free, and grinned like a fool. "Now you jiggle it—real gentle. Like you're flirtin' with destiny... just tryin' to get those pins to the shear line without scaring her off." He winked at the camera. "Gotta be smooth, bro. Destiny likes a light touch."

Click. The lock yielded, and the room filled with Tanner's triumphant yell.

"LET'S GO! Freedom, my dudes! Freedom tastes like victory and question-able safety protocols!"

Uriel smiled despite himself. How strange the language of grace could sound in mortal mouths. The image froze—Tanner's grin framed in flashing letters:

ESCAPE TIME: 8 MINUTES, 12 SECONDS.

Angela stared at the screen. The humor drained from her face, replaced by something quieter—contemplation, recognition. Her gaze lifted slowly toward the bare bulb above her head. Uriel followed her eyes. The same kind of bulb. The same fragile filament. The same small symbol of light in a place meant for darkness. And there it was. The change. Subtle, but unmistakable. A heartbeat quickened. The atmosphere shifted. She wasn't free yet—but she was *thinking* like someone who could be. He felt the corners of his mouth turn upward, a mixture of reverence, sorrow, and hope. He had seen entire nations turn on less—a spark, a single word, a foolish TV show at the right moment.

Angela exhaled, shaking her head, a faint smile curving her lips. "All right, Tanner," she whispered. "Let's see what I can do."

Uriel closed his eyes. In Heaven, it would be written simply: *Faith rekindled.*

11

Truthful Lips Endure Forever

The air carried a faint tang of beer, exhaust, and rain-soaked asphalt. Detective Gabriel stood outside the bar where Angela had been taken, his breath visible under the streetlight. The neon sign in the window hummed weakly, casting a flickering red glow across the sidewalk. He'd watched the bar's security footage at least a dozen times by now. The same loop—Angela stepping out, her phone in hand, the silver hybrid sedan gliding up to the curb, door opening, and then gone. What the footage *didn't* show was where that car had come from. He turned, scanning the street. From the driver's angle, the timing had been too precise. The man wasn't circling—he'd been waiting somewhere nearby, engine running, eyes fixed on the bar. Gabriel crossed the street, his shoes crunching against stray gravel. Across from the bar stretched a narrow sidewalk lined with an aging apartment complex, its stucco walls stained from years of rain and neglect. From here, he could see the bar's entrance perfectly—close enough to watch without drawing attention.

He stopped, and pictured the scene. "This is where you sat," he murmured to himself. "You had a front row seat."

He traced the curb with his eyes, calculating distances. The sedan would have idled right where he was standing—half in shadow, half under the dull wash of a streetlight. The driver would have seen Angela step out and known the exact moment to move. As he turned to leave, something caught his eye—a small black box mounted beside one of the apartment doors. A video doorbell. Gabriel frowned, stepping closer. The lens glinted faintly in the light. From that angle, the camera would have faced directly toward the street—exactly where the sedan must have been parked.

He exhaled. "Worth a shot."

He climbed the cracked steps and knocked. For a long moment, there was no answer.

Then the door creaked open a few inches, and a man peered out—a wiry older figure, wearing a stained tank top and a frayed bathrobe. His hair stuck out in wild tufts, and his eyes were sharp despite the dark bags beneath them. "Whatever you're selling, I'm broke," the man rasped.

Gabriel flashed his badge. "Detective Gabriel Ramos, L.A.P.D. Just need a moment of your time, sir."

The man blinked, looking him up and down. "Didn't do nothin'."

"I'm not here for you," Gabriel said evenly. "I'm investigating a disappearance. A woman went missing the night of February sixteenth—across the street at the Southwood bar."

The man scratched his chin, squinting toward the bar. "The brunette? Yeah, saw the news."

Gabriel nodded. "You live here long?"

"Too long."

"Then you might've seen something. There was a car parked right along this curb the night she disappeared—silver hybrid, a rideshare decal. You remember that?"

The man's brow furrowed. "Can't say I do. I don't pay much attention. Don't go out much either."

Gabriel gestured toward the small camera by the door. "Mind if I ask if that thing works?"

The man glanced at it, then back at him. "Usually does. I got porch pirates around here. Don't trust anyone."

"Would you be willing to let me take a quick look at your recordings from that night? Just between seven and eight p.m."

The man hesitated, shifting on his feet. "You think it caught somethin'?"

Gabriel's tone stayed calm but firm. "If that car parked where I think it did, your camera might've caught its plates—or the driver."

The man stared at him a moment, then sighed. "Hold on."

He opened the door fully, revealing a cluttered living room dimly lit by the glow of a TV.

"Hope you don't mind the mess. Name's Dustin, friends just call me Dusty."

Gabriel stepped inside, scanning the room as the man shuffled toward a small tablet on the counter. "Not a problem," he said quietly. "I appreciate it. I'm just hoping your camera saw what no one else did."

Dusty muttered to himself as he shuffled over to a narrow counter stacked with unopened mail and takeout boxes. "Gimme a second. Thing's slow." He tapped the screen of a grimy tablet until it flickered to life.

Gabriel waited, scanning the cluttered living room. A recliner sat dead center facing the TV, surrounded by an army of soda cans and empty chip bags. The air smelled faintly of dust and cat food. Then something soft brushed against his leg. Gabriel glanced down just as a massive, lopsided tabby cat hauled itself onto the counter beside him with a wheezy grunt. Its fur was patchy in spots, and one ear looked permanently bent sideways. The cat stared at him with a judgmental squint.

"Jesus," Gabriel muttered under his breath.

The man glanced over his shoulder, beaming with pride. "Oh, that's Chairman Meow. He's the mascot for this apartment complex."

Chairman Meow blinked once, unimpressed, then began pawing lazily at an unopened can of tuna.

Gabriel bit back a smirk. "He looks... nice."

"Yeah, he runs the place," Dusty said matter-of-factly as he handed over the tablet. "Here you go, detective. Footage is all there. Scroll back to the sixteenth. Battery's a little iffy, so don't knock it loose."

"Appreciate it." Gabriel took the tablet carefully, swiping through the recordings.

The interface was ancient, timestamps barely legible.

Meanwhile, the man crouched beside the cat, his voice softening into baby talk. "Who's hungry? Is my little Chairman hungry? You want your din-din, big guy?"

The cat yawned in response, revealing a single long tooth that stuck out like a fang. Gabriel blinked, trying not to laugh. He rewound the video feed to the night in question. The apartment's camera showed the street from a perfect angle—the same stretch of curb he'd just been standing on. For a moment, there was nothing. Then headlights drifted into frame.

Gabriel froze the image. "There you are."

He zoomed in slightly before replaying. The footage showed two women approaching from the edge of the frame—one blonde, one brunette—both unsteady on their feet. The blonde was louder in her movements, tossing her hair back, her laughter silent but visible. The brunette followed with the slow, uncertain gait of someone who'd had one too many.

They looked impatient, gesturing toward the driver's window. The blonde stepped ahead, lifted her hand, and knocked on the glass. There was a brief conversation with the driver before the blonde turned to her friend, who then pulled out her phone and showed something on the screen to the driver. After a short talk, both women circled around the front of the car to inspect the license plate. Whatever they saw, it set them off—the blonde doubled over laughing while the brunette clutched her arm for balance.

Gabriel leaned closer. A small decal glinted faintly in the corner of the windshield—a rideshare logo. *Maybe they thought he was their driver.* The way they waved the phone, checked the plate, even leaned in like they were confirming the pickup—it all fit. But the car didn't move like a rideshare vehicle. It idled too long. Waited too still. The blonde leaned into the open window again, talking animatedly, still smiling, still flirtatious. The driver didn't say much—just turned his head slightly toward her before rolling up the window and pressing the gas. The silver sedan rolled forward, slow and deliberate, easing away from them while they were still standing in the street.

The blonde called something after it, her mouth forming words Gabriel couldn't hear. Both women looked at each other, laughed again, then staggered back toward the sidewalk.

He frowned, replaying the footage. Maybe the bar staff knew them—regulars who'd had too much and wandered out looking for their ride. *Did the driver lure them, or were they just in the wrong place at the wrong time?* He saved the file, sent it to his email, and handed the tablet back to the man. "Thanks," he said quietly.

Chairman Meow jumped down from the counter and brushed himself against Gabriel's leg, purring loudly.

The man grinned, revealing a silver tooth. "The Chairman brings good luck. Hope you find whoever you're lookin' for."

Gabriel gave a faint nod. "Yeah. Me too." He stepped outside, the door closed behind him, followed by a loud deadbolt slamming into place.

The night air was cold and still, heavy with the smell of rain and exhaust. Across the street, the bar's neon sign flickered against the wet pavement. He decided to head there next—to show the staff the women in the video. If they were regulars, someone would recognize them.

He crossed the street, the soles of his shoes crunching softly against the pavement. The bar was quieter now, filled with the low hum of conversation and the faint clink of glassware. Neon light bled through the front window, painting the floor in faded red and blue.

Joe, the bartender, was wiping down the counter when Gabriel walked in. He looked up immediately, recognition flashing in his eyes.

"Detective Ramos, right? You were here earlier—asking about that girl and the silver sedan."

Gabriel nodded and set his phone on the bar counter. "Yeah. Found some new footage I wanted you to take a look at."

Joe leaned in as Gabriel opened the video. The glow from the screen reflected off the bottles behind him as the footage played—two women approaching the silver car, knocking on the window, and laughing.

Joe squinted, eyes narrowing. "I think I know them," he said slowly. "Whitney and Marcella. They're regulars."

Gabriel kept his eyes on the screen. "You know their last names? Anything that could help me find them?"

Joe scratched the back of his neck. "Might have it in the tab records, lemme check—"

The front door swung open before he could finish. A gust of cold air swept in, followed by a burst of perfume and laughter.

"What's up, Joe?" called a blonde woman, her voice bright and just a little too loud for the near-empty bar. "You are not gonna believe this—I just won a hundred bucks on a scratcher!"

Joe gave a half-smile, glancing toward Gabriel. "Speak of the devil."

The woman strutted up to the counter, tossing her purse onto the stool beside Gabriel without noticing him at first. "Make it my usual," she said, grinning. Then her gaze landed on the detective. She tilted her head, flashing a slow, sultry smile. "Hey there. Haven't seen you here before. I'm Whitney."

She nodded toward Joe. "Joe, get a drink for my new friend..." Then she turned back to Gabriel, playful and curious. "What was your name?"

"Gabriel."

Whitney smiled, giving him a quick once-over. "Nice to meet you, Gabriel."

Without a word, he pushed his phone across the bar toward her, the paused video glowing between them. "That you talking to the driver in that sedan?"

She leaned closer, squinting at the screen. The blonde woman in the footage knocked on the driver's window, laughed, and leaned into the car.

Whitney chuckled to herself. "Yeah, that's me. Went up to the wrong rideshare driver. Oops." She looked up at him with an amused grin. "Why? You making a documentary or something?"

Gabriel reached into his coat and flipped open his badge. "I'm working a missing persons case."

Whitney froze, her smile faltering. The amusement drained from her eyes, replaced by a flicker of recognition and something heavier. "Wait," she said quietly. "This about that girl, Angela?"

Gabriel nodded once.

Whitney swallowed, glancing back at the phone. The video still looped silently on the screen—her own face, laughing under the bar's flickering streetlight.

"Yeah," she murmured. "I remember that night."

Joe set two martinis in front of them, saying nothing.

Gabriel slid the phone back, his expression unreadable. "Then let's start there."

Whitney stared at the looping video on the phone, her reflection flickering faintly on the screen. "I don't know much. It was hard to make out his face," she said after a moment, voice quieter now. "He had on a mask and a baseball cap. I remember that."

Gabriel leaned forward slightly. "You talk to him?"

"Yeah," she said, brow furrowing as she tried to recall. "I asked for his name... he said something, I just—" She rubbed her temples, groaning softly. "God, I was so drunk that night. It's all kind of fuzzy."

Gabriel exhaled through his nose, patient but insistent. "Whitney, I need you to try. Anything at all — an accent, hair color, how old he looked, anything."

She chewed her lip, thinking hard, then sighed. "He didn't have an accent, he had dark hair, looked like he might be mid-twenties? As for the name, I'm not sure. Maybe Marci remembers." She reached into her purse, pulled out her phone, and scrolled through her contacts.

"Hang on, I'll call her."

As the phone rang, Whitney grabbed her martini and took a long, bracing swallow. The glass clinked softly as she set it back down.

A moment later, a muffled voice came through the speaker.

"Hey girl," Whitney said quickly. "I need to ask you something important. Got a sec?"

There was a pause, the faint hum of bar noise filling the gap.

"Remember that guy we thought was our rideshare that night?" Whitney said. After a short pause, listening to Marci, she laughed. "I know right? Do you remember what his name was?"

Another pause.

Whitney frowned. "Marvin? No, I don't think it was that. It was something like *Ma*...something. Definitely not Marvin."

Gabriel's gaze fixed on her, patient but intense.

Whitney squinted, thinking, then her eyes lit up. "Mark! That was it. He said his name was Mark."

She looked up and caught Gabriel's expression — steady, serious, the kind of look that drained the last trace of playfulness from the air.

"Thanks, Marci," she said quietly into the phone. "Yeah... that's all I needed. Talk later, bye." She ended the call and set the phone aside.

Gabriel reached into his coat, pulled out a small black notepad, and flipped it open. His pen scratched quietly across the paper. He tore his eyes from the page long enough to meet hers.

"That's good." He slid a card across the counter. "If you remember anything else, give me a call. Anytime."

Whitney nodded, her fingers brushing the edge of the card. "Yeah," she said softly. "I will."

Gabriel gave a small nod, closed his notepad, and tucked it back into his coat. As he stepped toward the door, the word *Mark* echoed quietly in his mind.

12

Forgetting What Lies Behind

Marshall's hand hovered over the row of worn spines until it found the one he was looking for—*Introduction to Anthropology.* He slid it free, brushing dust from the faded cover with the flat of his palm. For a moment he just held it, thumb pressed to the corner, letting the memory stir. Angela. He remembered the day she emailed their group the finished presentation, her revisions stitched cleanly into the slides and notes. He'd been stuck at home, scrolling through her additions on the dim glow of his laptop. Her words cut sharper than anything the professor could have said—thoughtful, deliberate, alive. One line in particular had lodged itself in him, bolded in her notes as if she wanted them to carry it with them: *People are shaped by the stories of those who came before them.*

He carried the book to the dining table, set it down with care, and opened it. The hollowed space inside greeted him like an old secret. Nestled within the cavity was a plastic bag, edges curled and stiff with time. He lifted it out, steady with familiarity. The wallet. The folded knife. Both stained with dried blood, dark and brittle like scabs that would never heal. He sat there a long moment, Angela's words echoing in his mind, pressed cruelly against the artifacts of his own story.

Marshall sat still, his fingers laced on the table, his eyes drifting far away. The room around him thinned, replaced by the echo of another time. He was back in the lecture hall. Rows of hard seats, the hum of fluorescent lights, the smell of paper and stale coffee. A cluster of frat boys sat a few rows ahead—loud, entitled, their laughter carrying easily in the cavernous room. He hadn't cared, not at first, until a name cut through the noise. Angela.

Tyler was leaning back in his chair, pointing out the window toward the quad. Angela was walking across, books tucked to her chest, hair catching sunlight.

Tyler smirked, voice pitched just high enough to carry. "God, she's hot."

And then—he started bragging. About a party. About her. Said she had passed out upstairs, alone. Said he'd gone in. His tone was casual, as if he were telling some story of conquest, not confession.

Marshall had frozen. Every word was a knife. The others laughed, slapped his back, egged him on. None of them called it what it was. None of them even flinched. But Marshall's chest was tight, his pulse hammering so hard it hurt. He remembered staring at the back of Tyler's head, bile burning his throat. And he remembered Angela the next morning—pale, withdrawn, eyes lowered. Like something had been taken from her and she didn't even know what. He had gone home that night and collapsed on the floor. Hours passed and he didn't move. Just sat there, her face haunting him, the sound of their laughter replaying like a curse. And in the hollow of his chest, a thought began to take shape. Maybe he could scare Tyler. Make him feel hunted. The way he had made her feel. At the very least, he deserved that much.

The idea burrowed in and wouldn't let go. Days passed, but every time Marshall closed his eyes he heard their laughter, saw Angela's pale face the morning after. It gnawed at him, sharpening into something more than anger—purpose. He started watching Tyler, learning his patterns, the way he left parties late, sometimes alone, always sure of himself. Each sighting made the thought burn hotter: *Maybe tonight.* Until finally, there was no maybe.

The night air was damp, heavy with spilled beer and cigarettes drifting from the frat house. Marshall stood in the shadows wearing a dark sweatshirt with the hood pulled up and gloves snug on his hands. His pulse thudded against his throat, each beat louder than the music bleeding through the walls.

Then the door swung open. Tyler stumbled out with a couple of others, laughter spilling into the night. They were all swagger and noise, throwing their arms around one another, talking too loud. Marshall stayed back, steady, watching. Waiting. One by one, the group broke apart—someone peeled away to puke in the grass, another disappeared into a waiting car. And then Tyler was alone, swaggering down the sidewalk with that same cocky tilt to his shoulders Marshall had seen in the lecture hall. Marshall followed. Steps measured. Breathing slow. He kept his distance until the houses thinned and the streetlamps grew sparse. Shadows stretched long across the pavement.

That was when he moved closer. "Hey," Marshall's voice was low, unfamiliar even to him. He stepped out of the dark, knife gleaming faintly in his grip. "Wallet."

Tyler stopped, surprise flashing across his face before hardening into something else. Confidence. He smirked. "You serious?" Then he lunged.

Marshall hadn't expected him to be that fast. A fist crashed into his ribs, another clipped his jaw. Pain flared white-hot. Tyler's weight slammed him backward, driving him into the ground. The breath tore from his lungs. He scrambled, panic clawing at his chest. Tyler's fists kept coming—trained, precise, like he'd done this a hundred times before. Marshall's vision blurred, the world narrowing to the pounding in his skull, the suffocating weight above him.

Instinct took over. His hand found the knife. He swung. The first strike was wild, desperate. Tyler grunted, twisted, tried to wrench free. Marshall drove the blade again, and again. The struggle became a blur of motion and heat, breath and blood. By the time it was over, Tyler wasn't moving. Marshall staggered to his feet, chest heaving, body screaming from the beating he'd taken. His hands shook as he pried the wallet from Tyler's pocket, the leather slick and warm. He shoved it into his own, staring down at the body sprawled in the dark. It wasn't supposed to end like that. And yet, standing there, battered and bleeding, he felt something he couldn't name. Not triumph. Not relief. But something close to justice. Twisted, brutal, and final.

He hadn't planned for cleanup. He had to improvise with his old backpack tossed on the backseat. His hands shook as he yanked it open, shoving the blood-soaked hoodie and jeans inside. The fabric landed with a wet, heavy sound. He added the gloves, then the knife—its handle slick, the blade tacky with drying blood. Finally, he forced Tyler's wallet down into the mess, the leather streaked and dark. The zipper strained as he dragged it shut. By the time he climbed behind the wheel, he was stripped down to his undershirt and boxers, skin clammy, body battered. The drive back was a blur of streetlights and shadows, every bump in the road rattling through his bruised ribs. His jaw throbbed with each grind of his teeth, his hands sticky on the wheel.

When he finally reached his home, he staggered inside, the backpack slung over one shoulder like some grotesque secret. He dropped it by the door and sank down against the frame, breath ragged, chest heaving. For a long time, he couldn't move. And then his thoughts drifted to Angela. To how she might feel, knowing Tyler was gone. Would she feel relief? Would she breathe easier walking across campus, head lifted instead of lowered? He pictured her waking up without the heaviness in her eyes, laughing with her friends, finally able to sleep through the night without fear of what he had taken from her. The image tightened in his chest—hope and pain tangled together.

But reality pressed in quick and cold. He couldn't go back to class looking like this. Bruised, swollen, and staggering. It would draw suspicion he couldn't risk. That's when he remembered the project. Due Monday. Tonight was Friday. His part unfinished. He had to let her know. He dragged himself to the desk, and flicked open his laptop, the glow of the screen cutting through the dark. With stiff, trembling fingers he typed:

Hi Angela, My mom and I are really sick. I can't finish my part of the project, I'm sorry. Please take my name off of it.

Her reply came hours later, and it gutted him.

We're in this together. It's no problem. I'll cover the rest.

She kept his name on the final version, even though he told her not to. She didn't owe him anything. But she had chosen kindness. And that, somehow, hurt worse than the beating. Because it meant someone like her could care—

even for him. Marshall leaned back, eyes burning. He didn't want her to see him as a monster. Not then. Not ever.

Four years later, he stared blankly ahead slowly snapping himself out of nostalgia. He shifted slightly, still sitting at the dining table, the plastic bag crinkling faintly in his grip. The knife and wallet caught the light through the clouded plastic, frozen relics of that night. He held them there, suspended between memory and the silence of the room, before finally setting the bag down on the table with a dull thud.

A long breath escaped him, heavy and deliberate. He pulled out his phone, thumb swiping across the screen until the feed opened. Angela's camera flickered to life. Relief trickled through him when he saw her—no tears this time, no trembling hands pressed to her face. She was sitting on the mattress, the glow of the TV washing over her, arms folded across her knees, chin resting on them. Watchful. Guarded. Not relaxed, not free. But not unraveling either. For the first time in days, he felt the knot in his chest loosen—just slightly.

He slid the bag back into the hollow of the textbook, the edges of the plastic catching against the cut paper. He closed the cover gently, as if sealing away a secret, and returned the book to its place on the shelf. For a moment, he stood still, staring at the row of spines, then turned toward the front door. The door to the deck groaned as he opened it, sunlight spilling across his shoulders. He stepped outside and leaned against the rail, the wood warm under his forearms. A breeze stirred the air, cool and clean, threading through his hair. He closed his eyes, breathing deep, letting the quiet press against him.

When he opened them, his gaze stretched over the plain that unraveled toward the tree line. The forest loomed in its stillness, green and endless, and nearer—scattered among the grass—stood clusters of foxglove, their purple spires catching the light. Something in them tugged at him. Nostalgia, sharp and sudden. Another time, another place. A memory rising, unbidden. He thought of the lecture halls, of numbers on the board and Angela bent over her notebook, hair falling against her cheek as she scribbled. Statistics with Dr. Marlowe. He'd tried to get into that class when he heard she was in it, but by the time he registered, it was too late. So instead, he signed on as Marlowe's aide—just to be near her in the margins of her world.

***

In college, Marshall passed by the frosted glass window outside Dr. Marlowe's office, carrying a small box of paper handouts. He wasn't eavesdropping—not exactly. But when he heard *her* voice, he stopped. Angela.

She stood inside, hands folded tightly, a baby-blue diaper bag slung over one shoulder. Her voice was soft, apologetic. "I had to take my son to the ER last night. He had a fever that wouldn't break, and I—" she hesitated, "—I missed the assignment deadline. I'm not asking for a free pass, I just—if there's any chance to make it up..."

Dr. Marlowe didn't look up from his computer. "Miss Ward," he said, his tone clipped, "I run a statistics class, not a daycare. You knew the deadlines when you registered."

"I know," she said quickly. "It's just—he's barely three months old and—"

"And he's *your* responsibility," Marlowe snapped, finally glancing up. "You want special treatment, you drop out and take an extension next semester. Otherwise, be a student or be a parent. Don't expect to be both."

Angela blinked fast. "I'm just asking for one day. That's all."

"Everyone's got problems," he muttered, turning back to his screen. "Next time, prioritize accordingly."

She stood there for a beat longer, lips trembling. She nodded robotically. "Thank you for your time, Dr. Marlowe." She turned and exited, gently closing the door behind her.

Marshall had stepped away just in time not to be seen. He watched her walk down the hallway, her chin tight, eyes red, arms clutched to her chest like holding herself together was the only thing she could do. Marshall's hands balled into fists. He knew that look. That silent heartbreak. That quiet suffering the world stepped over without blinking. He looked back at the office door. Dr. Marlowe was tenured. Protected. Arrogant. No one was going to stop him. Except maybe someone who knew what it felt like to be invisible. Someone who'd seen enough.

That night, he lay awake in bed, staring at the ceiling fan tracing circles above him. In his mind, he replayed it—Marlowe slouched at his desk, his belly straining against the buttons of a yellowing dress shirt that hadn't fit properly in years. His fleshy neck folded into the collar, and his lower lip hung slightly open as he breathed through his mouth. One thick, sausage-like hand clutched a stained coffee mug, his fingers leaving greasy smudges on the ceramic. He looked bored— inconvenienced—while a young woman across from him fought back tears.

Marshall imagined bursting through the office door. The blade in his hand. The same feeling he'd had with Tyler—that heat behind the eyes, the roar of justice building in his chest. He could do it again. Quick. Violent. Satisfying. But too risky. Marlowe wasn't some drunk frat boy in the dark. He was a public figure. A faculty member. A man with lectures and office hours and assistants. People would ask questions. He needed something cleaner.

A few days later, he was walking the perimeter of campus between classes. The spring air was thick with pollen and distant laughter. He stopped near the conservatory building, squinting at the university's meticulously kept flowerbeds. A long row of foxglove lined the edge—soft purple blossoms dancing in the breeze. They were beautiful. Deadly. His mind paused on the thought, like a finger resting lightly on a trigger. Digitalis. Slow. Undetectable in small doses. But build it up... He stepped closer to the plants, watching them sway. Harmless to most. Lethal to the right person. A slow smile curled at the edge of his mouth. Not a blade this time. A whisper.

Dr. Marlowe was a man of routines. Lecture at ten o'clock, sharp. Black coffee in a stained ceramic mug. Two sugars. No cream. Always from the break room pot, always handed to him—without fail—by whichever aide was unfortunate enough to be on coffee duty that day. Marshall never minded the task. In fact, he preferred it. It gave him control. Just a pinch. Every few days. Masked by the bitter coffee. Safe in small doses—until it wasn't. Marlowe never suspected a thing. And why would he? He barely looked anyone in the eye unless he was dressing them down for a wrong answer or a missed assignment. He taught like he was angry the whole room still needed him.

By the third week, Marshall could see the changes—slight at first. The flush in Marlowe's cheeks lasting longer than usual. Shortness of breath halfway through lecture. A tremor in the hand that held the coffee. Then came that day. The lecture hall was full. Stiflingly warm.

Marlowe stood at the front like a general in enemy territory, gripping a dry-erase marker like a weapon. "If any of you had actually read the material, we wouldn't be wasting our time on remedial probability like it's middle school math." He turned to the girl in the second row, his eyes narrowing beneath bushy, sweat-beaded brows. "You—Miss... I forget. Doesn't matter. Do you even understand the difference between conditional and joint probability? Or are you just here to check a box for the university's diversity quota?"

A few students shifted in their seats, stunned. The girl froze, her face draining of color. A nervous laugh rippled from the back of the room, then died quickly.

Marlowe scowled. "Don't laugh. Half of you shouldn't even be in college," he barked. "Some of you were handed your acceptance letters because your last name sounded interesting, or because you cried in an essay. Not because you can actually think."

Angela sat quietly in the back, eyes lowered.

Marlowe's voice rose again, wobbling slightly at the edges. "It's not my job to dumb things down because you didn't pay attention in high school. If you want hand-holding, try an intro course at a community college—or maybe go back to whatever soft little corner of the world gave you a medal for showing up."

He stopped. Mid-sentence. His brow furrowed. A sudden, shallow breath caught in his throat. He reached for the edge of the whiteboard, his hand shaking, knuckles white. His eyes blinked several times.

A moment later, he turned to write something—his hand dragging a blue marker across the board. The line started smooth. Then stuttered. Then dropped. His body twisted, knees buckling. He pitched sideways against the whiteboard, leaving a long, unbroken streak of blue ink trailing downward as he slid to the floor. The marker clattered from his fingers. For a heartbeat, the room was silent. Then someone screamed. Panic broke out like wildfire.

Students leapt from their seats, some screaming, others frozen in place as Dr. Marlowe's body spasmed once, then lay still—his chest heaving shallow gasps that grew further and further apart. But amidst the noise, the chaos, and the rising storm of fear—he was still.

13

Father of Lies

Asael, in the form of a thick-bodied serpent, black as oil and coiled like a noose, hovered beside the dying professor. No one saw him. Not the girl sobbing in the second row. Not the boy dialing 911 with shaking fingers. Not even Marshall. But he was there. Eyes like coals. Tongue flickering.

He gazed down at Marlowe's withering form, then slowly curled into a loose spiral, scales glinting like glass. A rasping chuckle echoed, unheard by mortal ears. "*See you in Hell, Professor,*" he hissed. Then he turned.

Across the room, amidst the shouting and clamor, Marshall stood silent near the exit, his face mostly composed—but the corners of his lips hinted at something else. Satisfaction. Asael looked straight at him and smiled. Then he disappeared, shifting through another dimension in the blink of an eye. Reality bent inward, folding over itself like torn fabric, and Asael was cast through the wound. He hurtled across the void, trailing ribbons of light and shadow, a form neither flesh nor flame until he suddenly stopped and quietly floated above the earth. The world spun beneath him — a trembling sphere veiled in cloud and chaos. Then the voices came.

At first a whisper. Then a torrent. Billions of prayers, curses, and screams flooded his mind — every heartbeat of humanity reverberating inside him. He hovered above the planet, still as a star, eyes burning with ancient fire. He listened. Wars flared like sparks across the continents — gunfire in deserts, wailing in alleyways, and children screaming for their parents through the thunder of explosions. The noise of humanity filled him until it became something almost melodic. He smiled. The music of ruin.

He drifted lower, his vision narrowing, his gaze piercing oceans and walls as easily as breath. He saw a child clutching his dead mother's hand. A soldier's trembling fingers on a trigger. Lovers arguing through tears. A priest praying to a God he no longer believed in. Each sound, each sorrow, wove into the grand symphony of the broken. For a moment, Asael closed his eyes and basked in it.

Then the world rushed upward to meet him — a flash, a shudder — and he was standing among trees, sunlight splitting through the leaves. His form had settled into human shape, black tracksuit uncreased, breath steady. A jogger passed without seeing him. A mother pushed a stroller. Somewhere nearby, a small dog barked at nothing. Asael smiled faintly and walked on, the echo of humanity's song still humming somewhere deep inside him.

He strolled down a gravel path, hands tucked into his pockets, shoes spotless despite the dust. He looked like any other man. Except no one looked back at him. People passed close—some within inches—but no one nodded. No one smiled. A child glanced toward him once... and then hurried away, eyes wide with something she didn't understand. He walked like he belonged—and like nothing could touch him. Eventually, he reached a bench beneath a tree whose branches split the sunlight like stained glass. A man already sat there. Old. Composed. Dressed in a pale ivory suit that looked untouched by the breeze or the season. His hands were folded neatly over his cane. His gaze was fixed forward, on the people of the park as if watching a stage play.

Asael sat beside him, resting one ankle over his knee. "Master," he said, reverently.

The old man didn't reply—not at first. His eyes remained forward, still and unreadable.

Asael leaned back, grinning faintly. "It's done. The professor's heart gave out like clockwork. Mid-rant, no less. All that fury—wasted on numbers and children. I'd call it poetic, wouldn't you?"

Still, the old man said nothing.

But Asael wasn't bothered. His grin deepened as he looked out at the park. "They never see it coming," he murmured. "All it takes is a nudge. A whisper. A well-placed seed." He looked toward his master, voice soft and eager. "And Marshall? He's coming along beautifully."

The silence between them lingered. Asael watched the old man, content to wait, sensing the weight of what was coming.

The old man's gaze didn't waver from the passing crowd. His hands rested gently on the carved silver head of his cane. A breeze caught his hair, perfectly groomed, yet unmoved. "Such a lovely day," he said at last, his voice soft—measured like a judge handing down a sentence. "All of these people... enjoying their time here without a second thought. A coffee, a walk, a passing smile. They never wonder how many are dying this very moment."

Asael's smile faded. He turned his head to listen, the way a child might when a story begins.

The old man's eyes followed a couple jogging past, their laughter a faint, meaningless echo. "They keep living," he murmured, "carefree. Unbothered. As it should be." He let the words hang. "People who care... are dangerous. They meddle. They interfere. They see suffering and want to see change." His voice thinned, like the edge of a blade. "But numbness... apathy... that is the natural order. That is peace."

Asael followed his master's gaze now—eyes scanning the crowd. Children. Lovers. Strangers brushing past. All unaware. All alive.

The old man turned slightly, and the light caught his face in sharp angles. His voice dropped lower. Firmer. "I have seen a vision."

Asael turned to him, alert.

The old man's eyes were like still water—unblinking, unreadable. "Angela must die."

Asael tilted his head. "Master?"

"She is on a path that leads to awakening. Not just for herself... but for others. Many will care for her. And she—" his jaw tightened almost imperceptibly, "—will care for them in return. She will teach them to see. To feel. To question." He paused. "She will shake too many from sleep. And if enough people start to care..." His fingers drummed once, softly, on his knee. "Then we will have interference."

Asael said nothing, the breeze brushing through his track suit like it wasn't there.

The old man's gaze remained fixed ahead. "Her death must come through him. Marshall. Only that will wound the heart deeply enough to close it again." He paused. And then, without emotion, "And after, he too... must die."

Asael's face lit up, glowing with pride. "Well, I must say," he grinned, "Marshall has taken to the path splendidly. One nudge, and he struck down that frat boy like a rabid dog. No hesitation. And Marlowe? Please. A slow death tailored just for him—poetic, painful, and public. It couldn't have gone better." He chuckled softly, adjusting the cuff of his track suit. "I don't think I've *ever* had a subject come along so naturally. All that simmering pain, that deep loneliness—it's like he was handcrafted for this."

The old man didn't move. Didn't nod. Didn't smile. His gaze remained locked on the children feeding ducks by the water's edge. Asael's grin wavered slightly, unsure.

Then the old man finally spoke. "You take too much pleasure in milestones that were always meant to pass."

Asael blinked, his smirk fading a touch.

The old man slowly turned to look at him, and though his face was calm, his voice rang with something deeper—ancient—something that made the birds in the trees above fall silent. "If you fail, I will not need to punish you," he said, his voice calm as still water. "You'll end up like the others."

Asael's smile wavered, but he said nothing.

The old man's eyes followed a flock of birds lifting into the sky, his tone unchanged. "You remember them, don't you? The ones who faltered. Who lost their way. Who thought they had more time." He tilted his head slightly, as if listening to something only he could hear. "They scream still, you know. Though no one hears them now. No mouths left. No will. Just echoes—folded into me." His gaze was cool, gentle. "You would not be the first." Then, facing forward once more, he smoothed the crease of his sleeve and added, with affection, "But let's not speak of failure. You're so close now."

The old man rose with the unhurried grace of someone for whom time no longer applied. His cane clicked softly against the path as he turned away, ivory fabric catching the light like a fading memory.

Asael shifted, sensing the moment slipping from his grasp. "Of course, Master," he began, voice smooth, composed, obedient. "The outcome is already deci—"

But the words faltered into nothing.

The old man disappeared. No trace. No sound. Only the faint scent of ozone, as though lightning had once stood there and then thought better of it.

Asael's jaw tightened and his fingers curled into a fist before he slowly unclenched them. He leaned back against the bench, exhaling through his nose. Across the park, two men argued near a fountain—one shouting, the other defensive, their gestures sharp and graceless. Passersby pretended not to notice. The sound carried to him faintly—anger, pride, wounded ego. And it stirred something ancient. For a moment, he wasn't in the park. He was elsewhere, a memory from thousands of years in the past.

***

The night stretched thin over the ruins like a veil of smoke. Below, two figures slept beside the embers of a dying fire — Jared and Leah, twin brother and sister turned sixteen, wrapped in blankets made from animal hides. The air smelled of ash from a small fire that had burnt out hours ago. High above the camp, two lights hung suspended — faint at first, like twin stars uncertain of their place. Then they took shape. Asael and Uriel stood upon the thin edge between realms, looking down through the veil.

Asael broke the silence first. "Two men cling to a plank in open sea," he said, voice low and patient, as though continuing a conversation centuries old. "It will bear one, not both. One pushes the other off and lives. Tell me, brother — has he sinned, or merely survived?"

Uriel's jaw tightened. "He has taken what was not his to decide."

"He chose to live."

"He chose another's death."

Asael smiled faintly, eyes glinting red in the dim. "And yet his choice sustains the story. If both perish, there is silence. If one lives, there is consequence. Which do you think Heaven prefers?"

Their words carried no echo here — only light bending faintly with the weight of them. Below, Leah stirred. Uriel's gaze followed her — the young woman rising from beside her sleeping brother. She moved cautiously, lifting a satchel and slipping into the trees beyond the camp. Her breath was visible in the pre-dawn chill.

Uriel's expression softened. "Another day, Asael," he said quietly. "Our argument will wait." He stepped forward, and his form began to fade, the glow around him dimming as he descended through the veil. His light threaded through the forest canopy until it vanished entirely.

Asael stood alone, watching. Jared turned in his sleep, his hands were clenched, his expression weary even in dreams. Asael studied him for a long time, unmoving. He had watched him for years — had seen the moment, the chance for him to bring justice. The men who destroyed their village slept peacefully in a drunken stupor down the valley in a makeshift camp, he could have ended all their pathetic lives that same night. He had stood at the edge of the basin, spear in hand, but he *hesitated.* Then he snapped the spear in two over his knee and cast it into the fire. Even now, Asael could see it — the charred haft still jutting from the coals below, smoke curling around it like a whisper of what could have been.

"You had him," Asael murmured, voice soft with disbelief. "And you chose mercy."

He took a step closer, the faint shimmer of his form brushing the edge of the mortal plane. The boy's breathing stuttered for a moment, then steadied again.

"You think that makes you stronger?" Asael's tone sharpened. "You think Heaven applauds restraint?" He looked down, his jaw flexing. "They will call it virtue, boy. But it's weakness. And it will break you."

His gaze lingered on the ashes of the fire. For an instant, his hand twitched, the urge to reach into the flames and reclaim the spear himself. But he didn't. He turned instead, his expression darkening to disgust and disappointment. The night wind shifted. Ash rose and swirled through him like memory. Asael looked once more at the sleeping boy and felt the hollow ache of boredom creep back in. The thrill of the earlier argument had vanished, and the theater of humanity had gone still. He sank to the ground beside the bench of rock and ash, resting his elbows on his knees. The prolonged silence warmed his contempt like a boiling bot.

Then a voice behind him broke the quiet. "I see he took the high road." The tone was light, mocking, dripping with amusement. "How noble..."

Asael turned sharply. His eyes widened, and he rose to his feet at once. Standing a few paces away was a figure draped in pale garments that shimmered faintly, as though woven from dawn itself. His hair was white-gold, his features sharp and ageless. The faint glow that emanated from him was steady and his eyes had a depth of someone who carried the weight of having seen past, present, and future at the same time.

"Adapa," Asael said softly, lowering his head in reverence. "I did not expect your presence here."

The senior angel's gaze never left the firepit. "No one ever does." He crouched slightly, studying the blackened spear half-buried in ash. "So... the boy refuses justice for his parents. The great cycle repeats — creation breeding weakness, mercy mistaken for holiness." His voice carried neither anger nor pity, only an air of weary amusement.

Asael straightened. "I doubt it was morality that stayed his hand. He fears the act itself — the weight of it. Fear masquerading as virtue."

Adapa's lips curved faintly — not quite a smile. "Spoken like one who remembers what fear once cost him."

Asael's jaw tensed, but he said nothing. A long silence followed. The air tightened, as if reality itself recoiled from the presence of two beings it could no longer contain.

At last, Adapa spoke. His eyes glowed faintly — not with warmth, but the cold luminescence of purpose. "This world no longer belongs to humanity," he said quietly. "They have forfeited the right to its ownership. What else could be expected? Giving dominion to children."

He turned his gaze toward the horizon, where the first pale light of dawn began to crawl across the sky. "Soon the veil will tear again — and the lost will remember what it means to be ruled by those who were meant to rule."

The words hung in the air like prophecy — or threat.

Asael's expression shifted — awe, unease, something caught between devotion and hunger. "And Heaven? Will it stand by?"

Adapa's eyes flicked toward him, the faintest smirk ghosting across his face. "Heaven will do what it always has," he murmured. "Sleep."

The wind stirred, scattering the ashes of the burned spear.

He turned then, meeting Asael's eyes. The warmth drained from his tone, leaving something colder. "Tell me, brother... have you the courage to take the step this time?"

Asael froze.

Adapa stepped closer, the light of him casting long shadows over the dying fire. "To stop whispering from the edges, stop playing philosopher to those who will never see truth. To build the world as it should have been — in *our* image."

The ashes stirred. Adapa's gaze lingered a moment longer, then his voice dropped to a whisper that brushed against Asael's thoughts like wind through glass.

"You were not made to follow." The words carried the weight of old truth — or an imitation of it. "If you have changed your mind..." He stepped closer, the air warping faintly around him. "Send the children west."

Asael frowned slightly. "West?"

Adapa nodded once. "There are others there — those who have seen the lie for what it is. A world rising from the ashes of blind obedience. They are building what Heaven never dared."

He lifted a hand and placed it gently on Asael's shoulder.

The contact was quiet — but the effect was anything but. A tremor rippled through Asael's body. His eyes widened as a flood of visions poured into his mind: cities half-formed in darkness, banners rising where light once fell, whispers of names and paths and power. He staggered, breath caught somewhere between awe and pain. The fire flared once, as though reacting to the surge of divine exchange. Then it was done.

Adapa drew his hand away. "You know where to send them," he said simply. "Do this, and the rest will follow. We will finish what was begun long ago."

He turned, the faint glow around him dimming as he began to walk into the mist. His final words came like a quiet command woven into the dawn. "The age of shepherds is over. The wolves will tend the flock now."

The light of him faded — until there was nothing.

Asael stood unmoving, the last warmth of Adapa's touch still burning through his shoulder, the new knowledge pulsing behind his eyes. He looked once toward the boy's sleeping form, then to the horizon in the west — the direction of destiny whispered into his mind. The ashes stirred again, lifting into the cool morning air. And Asael smiled. He knelt beside the boy, the faint shimmer of his form casting soft distortions through the morning mist. His gaze lingered on the boy's face — peaceful, trusting, unguarded. He reached out and placed a hand upon Jared's head. The moment his palm touched skin, the air bent. The last whisper of the breeze stilled and sound drained from the world.

Then — the dream began.

***

Jared stood in sunlight. Warm. Golden. The air smelled like home — like cedar smoke and the ocean wind that used to sweep through their village before the fire.

"Leah," he whispered.

She was there beside him, smiling, no ash in her hair or blood on her hands. She pointed toward the horizon where the light shimmered faintly over the hills. "They're waiting for us. We have to go west."

He turned, blinking in disbelief. Shapes emerged through the haze — faces he knew. Family. Friends. People who should have been gone. His uncle waving from the ridge. The old fisherman who had carried him on his shoulders as a child.

"Jared!" one called, voice thick with joy. "You found us!"

The sound cracked with emotion — but beneath it, something else moved. A deeper tone, subtle, coaxing, resonating through the words like a hidden chord. "Come west," the voice said.

But Jared did not hear it as command. It was comfort. Promise.

"We built a new home," another said — his father's voice, though Jared's father had burned long ago. "There's food, water, safety. All that was lost can be rebuilt... if you come west."

Tears stung Jared's eyes. The ache of hope pressed against his chest like something divine.

Leah tugged his sleeve, eyes bright with wonder. "Let's go. We can start again."

He nodded. "West," he murmured. "We'll go west."

***

Outside the dream, Asael's eyes glowed faintly, his expression calm — tender. The boy's lips moved with the echo of the words, whispering them in sleep.

Asael withdrew his hand slowly, the air returning to motion around him.

He looked down at Jared, whose face now carried the faintest trace of a smile — fragile, unearned, hopeful.

Asael straightened. "Dream well, little prophet," he said softly. "I will be your guide."

He turned toward the pale horizon, the memory of Adapa's touch still burning in his shoulder, and vanished with the rising wind — leaving the boy to wake beneath the first true light of morning, dreaming of home that never was, and a hope born from deception.

The forest slowly breathed again. Wind stirred the leaves. Distant birds broke the silence with scattered calls. Asael stood over the boy, watching as the faintest smile lingered across Jared's sleeping face. He tilted his head, curious — like an artist studying his own work. Then, through the trees beyond the camp, two figures appeared.

Leah moved lightly between the ferns, a woven basket cradled in her arms, half-filled with wild berries. Beside her walked Uriel, unseen, his expression watchful and solemn. The early light caught the edges of his form, a quiet shimmer trailing like mist.

Jared stirred. His eyes opened suddenly, wide and alert. He sat up, breath catching as the remnants of the dream still clung to him like smoke. "Leah?"

Hearing her name, she lifted her head. "You're awake." She smiled softly. "I found breakfast—"

But Jared was already on his feet. He ran to her, gripping her shoulders, eyes bright with a fervor that startled her. "We have to go," he said breathlessly. "Leah, we have to go west!"

She blinked, startled. "What? Jared, slow down—what are you talking about?"

He shook his head, trembling with urgency. "They're there! Our people — they're alive! I saw them. I saw Father, Uncle Ren, all of them. They've built a new home — to the west! We can find them if we leave now!"

Leah looked confused, frightened even. "Jared, that's not possible. They're—"

Uriel stepped forward, his gaze narrowing on him.

Jared continued not noticing the skepticism in Uriel's unseen gaze. He clutched his sister's hand. "It wasn't just a dream — it was real! I know it was!"

Uriel studied the boy carefully, his divine senses rippling through the air around him. There was something there — a residue, faint but familiar. His brow furrowed.

Asael stood several paces behind the camp's edge, unseen by mortal eyes. His smile was gentle, proud. "Look at him," he murmured, voice low, tinged with satisfaction. "At least he has hope now."

Uriel's gaze shifted toward the treeline — toward the faint presence he could feel but not see. The light in his eyes sharpened. For a moment, the two unseen angels faced each other across the thin veil separating worlds. One suspicious, the other quietly triumphant.

Leah touched Jared's arm. "We'll talk about it," she said softly. "Just... let's eat first, all right?"

But Jared was already looking west, his eyes filled with conviction born of illusion.

Asael turned away, the echo of Adapa's words stirring faintly in his mind: *Send the children west.*

And as dawn washed the camp in gold, Asael smiled — the serene smile of one who believes the first piece has finally moved into place.

14

Near to the Brokenhearted

Uriel and Remiel walked along the plains of Heaven, abruptly pulled away from their assignments to guard Angela and her family, summoned by the archangel Raphael. Heaven was not loud. There were no trumpets, no shining gates or choirs ringing in the sky. There was only stillness—a vast, endless plain of living grass that shimmered in the light of no sun, where the air carried warmth without heat and breeze without movement. A gentle stream cut through the field, its water so clear it looked like glass in motion, whispering as it wound its way toward a great tree rooted at the center of all things. The Tree of Life. Its trunk was wide enough to dwarf mountains, its branches stretching into the sky until they vanished into light. Each leaf shimmered with something like starlight and breath—*alive* in a way words could never capture.

They appeared at the edge of the stream in silence, their forms bright and sharpened in this place. Their sandals left no prints in the grass as they walked, side by side, toward the tree. At its base stood Raphael. He was not imposing like Remiel, nor radiant like Uriel. He stood with the lean, taut build of a sprinter—his arms crossed behind his back, eyes locked ahead. There was no halo, no fanfare. Just focus. Precision. Purpose.

As the two approached, Raphael gave a single nod. "The enemy is moving," he said without preamble. His voice was low and exacting, like steel unsheathed. "Something has shifted. We've received confirmation of new activity in their ranks, strategic, not chaotic."

Uriel and Remiel stood straight, silent. Listening.

Raphael continued. "Angela's family is at the center of it. The enemy has taken notice. And they are working, actively, to unravel what has been sown."

Uriel's brows drew inward. "Do we know the shape of their intent?"

"Not yet," Raphael replied. "But their movements are too precise to be coincidence. There is design in this." He paused, glancing between them. "You've both served with honor. Without error. But this is where paths divide."

Remiel remained stone-still.

But Uriel turned his head. "What do you mean?"

Raphael looked at him directly, his voice calm. "You are being reassigned."

The words hit like a quiet thunderclap.

Uriel blinked. "Reassigned?" There was confusion behind the question—not pride, but disbelief. "To where?"

"A depressed factory worker in Arkansas," Raphael said, with no judgment in his tone. "He has been on the verge of suicide for twelve days. Your presence is needed."

"For how long?" Uriel asked dumbfounded.

"For as long as it takes."

Uriel opened his mouth, to protest.

But Raphael's gaze sharpened. "It is the Lord's will."

Uriel stopped. Swallowed. Bowed his head.

Remiel remained quiet beside him, his hands clasped in front of him like stone folded in prayer.

Raphael took a breath and looked toward the horizon. "You were not sent to walk one path. You were sent to obey." A pause. Then, quieter: "And you have done well."

Uriel closed his eyes for a moment, and when he opened them, there was nothing but resolve.

Remiel finally spoke, his deep voice calm. "And Angela's family?"

Raphael turned back to them, the faintest gleam of something heavier behind his eyes. "They are still yours. And they will need you more than ever."

Raphael didn't linger. The moment the final word was spoken, his form lifted—not like a bird, but like a blade drawn swiftly upward. Wings unfurled in a flash of radiant movement, and in the next breath he was gone, streaking across the sky like a spear of light hurled toward some unseen battlefield. Silence returned to the plain. Uriel stood unmoving, staring at the space where Raphael had vanished. His hands were clasped behind his back, his jaw set tight. But the calm on his face was too practiced. Too still. Remiel didn't speak. He remained beside him, his massive presence radiating steadiness like the roots of a mountain.

At last, Uriel broke the silence. "I don't understand," he said quietly. "There are battles forming all around them. Angela, her son, her mother— they stand on the edge of something none of them see. The enemy sees it. We see it. But I am to be sent away to… one man. In Arkansas." His voice cracked on the last word.

Remiel looked at him, eyes soft under his heavy brow. "That one man matters."

Uriel nodded, though his gaze was far off. "I know. I know he does. I know we don't measure purpose by size. But it feels like being… *removed.*" His voice dropped. "Like being told I'm no longer needed."

Remiel shifted his weight, the grass bending softly beneath him. "Your absence is not abandonment. You planted more than you know."

Uriel's lips pressed together. "I still want to see it bloom."

Remiel turned fully toward him now. "You will. Just not yet."

Uriel met his eyes. For a moment, the formality slipped. The celestial order, the obedience, the unwavering discipline—it all gave way to something simpler. Friendship. Without a word, Uriel stepped forward and pulled Remiel into an embrace. He was dwarfed by the larger angel, but it didn't matter. Remiel returned the hug, one thick arm wrapping carefully around him, as if shielding something fragile.

Uriel stepped back, his hands lingering for a moment on Remiel's shoulders. "Godspeed," he said softly. "Guard them well."

Remiel nodded. "And you. Guard *him*."

They parted. A final look. A shared understanding. Remiel remained still, alone beneath the branches of the Tree. Uriel turned, his form lifting skyward with grace and solemnity, rising higher and higher until he dissolved into the light above. He shifted through dimensions back to the earth, to the man waiting for him alone in his home in Arkansas.

***

The house was silent, save for the faint hum of the refrigerator. No photos on the walls. No toys. No voices. Just an aging recliner, a dusty coffee table, and the cold metallic gleam of a revolver resting beside a half-empty glass of whiskey. The man sat slouched in the chair, one hand cradling his lower back, the other resting on his thigh, just inches from the weapon. His name was James. He worked third shift at the ammunition plant outside of town, a job that paid just enough to keep him alive and empty enough to make him wonder why he bothered. He hadn't seen his kids in over a month. His back throbbed with the memory of the injury that stole his sleep and earned him just enough prescriptions to get hooked before the doctor pulled the rug. Now it was street pills. Cheap powder. Stronger things. The kind that let the hours melt away in silence, and let the world stay dim enough to forget it existed.

Tonight was one of the bad ones. The kind of night where the dark felt alive and the future narrowed to a single point. A chamber. A trigger. James reached for the revolver with slow fingers. He opened the cylinder and slipped a single round inside, then spun it.

The click echoed like an accusation. "Here we go," he muttered. He raised the barrel to his temple. Then paused.

The silence deepened.

And then, from across the room, a voice said brightly, "Well hey there, cowboy."

James didn't flinch. He didn't even look up. The voice had become familiar. Perched casually on the arm of the opposite chair was a creature that looked like a man in a four-foot-two package with a body like a coiled spring and hair that spilled down to the waist like black oil. His grin was too wide, his teeth too perfect. His eyes glittered with the joy of cruelty. He wore only a pair of black, tattered shorts that hung loosely around his waist. His skin was pale gray, corpse-like, stretched tight over lean muscle and veined arms that looked carved from stone. His hands—large, powerful, bare—flexed idly on his knees, like he was warming up for something he couldn't wait to hurt.

"You really gonna do it this time?" the demon asked cheerfully, swinging his legs like a child on a bench. "Ooh, I'm tinglin' just thinking about it."

James said nothing. His hand tightened around the gun.

"You know what I love about you?" the demon continued, cocking his head. "You *almost* believe you matter. That little sliver of fight? So cute. Like watching a wounded dog trying to bark."

James lowered the gun slightly. "Shut up."

"Ohhh, there it is." The demon laughed. "The voice of the man who lost everything! Wife? Gone. Kids? They don't even ask about you anymore. Spine? Toast. Dignity? That's been gone since you begged your dealer for another hit." He leaned in, whispering with mock intimacy. "Face it. You're just a broken man waiting to become a statistic. Might as well pull the trigger and spare us both the slow part."

James stared at the wall, jaw clenched.

The demon smiled wider. "But hey. No rush. I'll wait. I *love* watching the cracks form."

Suddenly, the temperature in the room shifted. The air became lighter. Brighter. The shadows pulled back. Uriel stepped through the veil. He didn't enter so much as appear—tall, radiant, clothed in simple linen that shimmered like sunlight on still water. His expression was composed, but the sorrow in his eyes was unmistakable. He looked down at James with quiet resolve. Then his gaze turned to the demon.

The creature's smile faded. "Uh-oh. New guy."

Uriel didn't speak to him. He stepped forward and stood behind James's chair, one hand extended gently—not touching, just hovering, a breath away from the man's trembling shoulder. "I see you," Uriel whispered, words meant not for the demon, but for the broken man in the chair. "I see your pain. And I have come."

The demon rose to his feet. He stretched theatrically, rolling his neck until the joints cracked, then gave a slow, mocking clap. "Ohhh wow." His voice dripped with exaggerated awe. "An angel from the upper ranks. Dropping in on this pathetic mess personally? What'd he do, cry loud enough to flag Heaven's pity line?"

Uriel still didn't look at him. "Some souls matter more than you'll ever understand."

The demon scoffed. "Oh please. I've seen this before. You show up, glow a little, whisper something poetic—and maybe he doesn't pull the trigger *tonight*." He stepped closer, voice darkening. "But you can't stay forever. And I can."

Uriel turned his head slowly, finally letting his gaze fall on the demon. His eyes were calm. And cutting. "Ecanus," he said, voice low. Measured.

The demon froze. Just for a breath. Then his lips curled into a snarl, the mockery slipping into something colder. "*Don't.*"

Uriel didn't flinch. "That was your name. Once."

"I *said* don't." The demon's voice cracked sharp this time, and he jabbed a thick finger toward Uriel's chest. "You don't get to use that name. Not anymore. That name was for someone who lost. Someone who *knelt*." He bared his teeth. "The name is *Ravage* now."

Uriel looked at him—not with anger, but with a sorrow deeper than pity. "No," he said quietly. "That is what you've become. Not who you are."

Ravage stepped back like he'd been stung, fists flexing at his sides. His whole body buzzed with restless energy, like a beast too long caged. "Oh, you just love that, don't you? Standing there with your glowing robes and your quiet sadness. Like you're *above* all this."

Uriel said nothing.

Ravage spat to the side and smirked. "Well, go on then. Shine for him. Try and fix it. But I've been here a *lot* longer than you. And I know how this story ends." He leaned closer again, voice dropping to a low, venomous whisper. "I'll get him in the end. Maybe not tonight. Maybe not next week. But he's mine. He already *believes* me."

Uriel's voice came, low and steady. "Then why are you afraid?"

That stopped Ravage. His eyes narrowed, but he didn't answer.

Uriel stepped closer—not to fight, not to threaten—but to stand between Ravage and the man. "You're losing him. That's why you rage. That's why you mock."

Ravage backed up slowly, expression unreadable now. He gave a small, bitter laugh. "We'll see." And with that, the shadows thickened around him like smoke curling backward into a flame, and the demon vanished.

The silence returned, heavy and humming with invisible battle lines. Uriel remained by James's side, eyes fixed forward. Watching. Waiting. For an instant, his mind wandered. Angela's face flickered across his thoughts like a reflection on water — that same steady heart, that same ache for what she couldn't yet see.

He exhaled softly, pushing the thought away. *One thing at a time,* he told himself. *Faith first. Purpose always.*

His gaze drifted toward the horizon — toward the direction of Marshall's house. Though walls and miles lay between them, he could almost see it, a faint image painted against the fabric of his mind—shadows moving, choices forming, threads tightening around a storm yet to come.

He turned away at last and knelt beside James. His voice dropped to a whisper, warm and firm as a steady hand. "Hold on a little longer. The dawn's closer than you think."

And with that, he rose again — silent, watchful — a lone sentinel between light and the gathering dark.

15

This I Call to Mind, and Therefore I Have Hope

Angela sat cross-legged on the mattress, staring at the lightbulb overhead. It buzzed faintly, a little filament of light trapped inside fragile glass. The video she'd seen still played in her mind—The Lockpicking Lifeguard, shirtless and shouting while using a lightbulb filament to escape a locked room. She hadn't forgotten a single frame. She glanced at the padlock on her ankle. Cold. Heavy. Bolted into the concrete. Physically fighting her way out of the basement was not an option, but maybe she didn't have to.

The hatch creaked open at the top of the stairs. Footsteps descended—measured, controlled. Her heart pounded, her right hand trembled slightly, but she quickly covered it with her other hand and took a deep breath.

Marshall came into view with a plate in one hand and a folded blanket in the other. He looked tired, like he hadn't been sleeping. "Hey," he said softly, kneeling to set the plate on the floor. "I brought you breakfast."

Angela nodded, forcing a thin smile. "Thanks."

He looked at her with that familiar blend of intensity and awkwardness, like he wasn't sure if he was supposed to say something else. The silence stretched a little too long.

She kept her voice even. "Can I ask you something?"

Marshall blinked. "Yeah. Anything."

Angela hesitated, then met his gaze. "Why me?"

His face twitched, just slightly, but he didn't look away.

"You remembered me from class. You knew my name. You knew I had a kid. You planned all this. So... why?"

Marshall shifted on his feet. His fingers tugged at the edge of the blanket he was holding, a nervous tic. "I guess I just... noticed you. More than most people."

"Why?" she pressed, gently. "You noticed *a lot* about me. Enough to know where I worked. Where I liked to get drinks. Even my allergy to walnuts. That's not just noticing, Marshall."

He didn't answer at first. His eyes drifted to the concrete floor. "You were kind to me back in college. That group project. I was all banged up and I couldn't make it to class, but you still turned it in with my name on it. You didn't have to."

Banged up. Angela caught it immediately. That wasn't how most people described being sick. It wasn't the phrase you used for a cold, or a migraine, or even food poisoning. It was the kind of thing someone said after a fight— or worse. It didn't sit right with her. At the time, he'd emailed their group to say he was too ill to finish, but now that she was sitting across from him in this basement—*in chains*—she remembered that detail more clearly than ever. The wording. The hesitation.

She tilted her head just slightly, voice careful. "You said you were sick back then. But now you're saying 'banged up.' Which one was it?"

Marshall's lips parted, but no words came right away. His good eye flicked away, blinking fast.

"I mean," she added gently, "if it's something else... you can tell me. I'm not going anywhere." That last line almost made her choke, but she kept her tone even.

Marshall scratched the back of his neck. "It was... complicated. Some stuff happened. I got into something I shouldn't have."

"Someone hurt you?"

He paused. Then nodded once, just barely.

Angela leaned back a little, letting the silence breathe. Inside, her mind spun. *He wasn't just isolated. He was hiding something. Maybe something violent. Maybe something connected.* She looked at him again, softer this time. "Was it about me?"

He blinked.

Her eyes didn't leave his. "What happened to you, Marshall?"

The question lingered in the air between them like smoke.

He didn't answer right away. His eyes stayed low, focused on the floor, jaw tightening as if the words were trying to claw their way out—but something inside was holding them back. And then a shift. A flicker, subtle but distinct. Marshall's shoulders tensed. His gaze turned slightly to the side—*not* toward her, but into the empty corner of the basement, where the shadows collected like dust. Angela's breath caught.

He was listening to something. Then, under his breath, he spoke. "...But it was because of her." His voice was hoarse, fragile.

Angela's brows furrowed. "What?"

Marshall blinked like he was surfacing from underwater. His lips parted, but the explanation didn't come. He seemed disoriented for a moment, eyes darting back to her face, then away again. But Angela had already seen it. The way he whispered toward nothing. The tone—like he was answering someone. Or something.

Her voice softened, careful. "Who were you talking to?"

Marshall swallowed hard. "No one."

But there was a crack in his tone. A fracture.

Angela leaned forward slightly. "I heard what you said... 'It was because of her.'"

He stiffened.

"You said it was *because* of me," she continued gently. "What does that mean?"

Marshall's hand flexed slightly on his knee. He looked away again.

Angela didn't push harder. She let her voice drop, low and warm. "You don't have to tell me everything. Just... help me understand. Please."

Marshall's jaw clenched. He looked like he was fighting two wars—one with her, and one inside his own mind.

"They hurt you. And I couldn't let them get away with it," he said finally, voice tight.

Angela's heart began to pound, but she kept her expression steady. "Who hurt me?"

He didn't answer.

"Marshall... what did you do?"

For a moment, his face looked haunted. Then his eyes flicked again—just briefly—toward that same shadowed corner. Angela followed his gaze, but saw nothing. And yet she knew, in that still moment, *he* saw something. Someone.

Angela sat perfectly still. Her fingers curled into the edge of the blanket draped across her lap, the threads twisting between them like a tether to reality.

Across from her, Marshall's posture shifted. His shoulders hunched inward. The tension in his body was different now—less defensive, more ashamed. His fingers tapped unconsciously on his knee as if trying to tap out the words he couldn't say aloud.

"I didn't mean to..." he started, voice low. "It wasn't supposed to happen like that."

Angela's throat tightened. "What wasn't?"

He exhaled through his nose, face pinched like he was physically trying to hold something back. His good eye flicked briefly toward the shadowed corner—just for a second—and Angela followed it again. But there was only darkness. Still, something about the air shifted. Like it was waiting.

"I heard them talking. Him and a couple of his buddies. They came into the lecture hall before class started—loud, laughing. I was already sitting in the back. They didn't see me."

Angela's breath caught before he even said the name.

"Tyler," he murmured.

And just like that, her stomach twisted.

Marshall didn't seem to notice the way she tensed—or maybe he did and couldn't stop now. "He was bragging. Said you passed out in a bedroom at a party. Said you looked so good, he couldn't help himself. He told them what he did like it was some kind of accomplishment."

Angela's vision blurred for a moment—not from tears, but from the sudden, blinding memory. A bedroom. Too dark. Her head swimming. Tyler's weight pressing her into the mattress. The smell of cologne and stale beer. His lips on her neck. Her arms barely able to lift.

She had buried it.

But it surfaced now—raw, burning, and undeniable. Her body shuddered, recoiling. Her hand flew to her mouth as bile rose in her throat. Marshall saw it and froze.

Angela stared at him, her voice trembling. "You... killed him?"

Marshall looked down. "I just wanted to scare him."

Angela's voice was a whisper. "You stabbed him." Her heart pounded in her ears. The pieces were falling into place, jagged and bloody.

And then, something shifted in him. His head turned—just slightly— toward the far wall, to nothing. Angela stared.

Marshall's lips moved low, like a man caught in a dream. "But it was because of her..."

Angela blinked. "Marshall... who are you talking to?"

His eyes flicked to the shadows again, his jaw clenched. A flicker of fear.

"Is someone there?" she asked, voice soft but shaking. "Are you... hearing something?"

He closed his eyes, pressing his fingers into his temple. "You wouldn't understand."

Her heartbeat thudded unevenly in her ears. A thin chill crept up her arms despite the warmth of the room. She tried to steady her breathing, but it caught halfway, shallow and trembling. And then it landed — heavy, undeniable. He had killed someone. The air thickened around her, pressing against her ribs. Her stomach twisted. The faint sound of the creak of the floor felt miles away. She blinked once, slowly, as if that might make the truth disappear. But it didn't. Not only had he killed someone, but he was also hearing voices in his head. Her throat tightened, and for a heartbeat she thought she might be sick. She swallowed hard, eyes still fixed on him — on the man she thought she understood, now suddenly unfamiliar, dangerous.

And yet she couldn't look away.

***

In Marhsall's mind the room had begun to shift. She was still sitting there. Still staring at him. But something was changing. The edges of her form began to blur, like she was behind glass smeared with condensation. The light around her dimmed, though the bulb overhead hadn't flickered.

Her voice, once steady, grew muffled—underwater. "...Marshall?"

He blinked. Once. Twice. Everything else vanished. And Asael entered. Not with footsteps. Not from a door. He came in like a thought you didn't invite—slipping behind Marshall's eyes, curling into the folds of his mind.

"Brilliant move in there," Asael said, his voice low and curling with acid. "Telling her about *Tyler*. Did you expect her to kiss your forehead afterward in gratitude?"

Marshall turned his head, but the room around him didn't exist anymore. Only Asael did.

"She's going to look at you differently now," he murmured. "You saw it. The way she pulled back. She shuddered. That wasn't fear of what Tyler did. That was fear of what *you* did."

Marshall's throat went dry. He tried to say something, but no sound came out.

"Oh, and what's your excuse for Professor Marlowe?" Asael paced around him like a circling wolf. "Tyler was heat-of-the-moment, sure, fine. But Marlowe? That was cold. Slow. You poisoned him little-by-little over that whole semester, Marshall. You *watched* him slowly die. That wasn't rage. That was art."

Marshall winced. A flicker of guilt, or nausea.

"She'll never understand that," Asael whispered, leaning in. "She'll never look at you the same." And then—Asael's voice softened. He stepped closer, his presence warm, soothing, even affectionate. "I get it, brother. I do. You've always been alone. People walked past you like you didn't matter. But I saw you. From the beginning. When you were small. When your hands were still shaking after the gun went off and your father hit the floor." His fingers ghosted over Marshall's shoulder. "I was there. No one else came."

Marshall stood still, breath shallow.

"I've always been here," Asael said. "I've always cared for you. You're like a little brother to me."

Marshall blinked slowly, drowning in it.

"And now, I need you to trust me. You're going to be tested. She's not what you think. And when the moment comes..." He leaned in, whispering now. "You'll know what needs to be done."

A beat of silence.

"*Marshall.*" The voice cut through. It sounded warm. Human. Real. *Angela.*

He blinked hard. The haze peeled back, like clouds clearing from the sun. Her face sharpened in front of him.

Her eyes searching his, wide with concern. "Marshall," she said again, gently. "Are you okay?"

He exhaled like he hadn't breathed in minutes. His hand trembled. "I'm fine. Just... tired."

But her eyes said she didn't believe that. Not for a second.

***

Angela watched him carefully. His face had gone pale. Haunted. Her heart was still pounding from what he'd said. From what he'd *admitted.* He killed Tyler. He killed Tyler... because of her. She didn't know what to feel. Tyler had taken something from her, something she hadn't even fully processed until now. She didn't *pity* him. Not even close. But the knowledge that someone had died—violently—for what he did to her sat heavy in her gut. And worse than that, the man who did it was now sitting a few feet away. With that same soft voice. That same warped tenderness. She could be next. She knew it. Unless...

She shifted slightly, her voice careful. Gentle. "You've never told anyone this, have you?"

Marshall's head turned toward her slowly. The look in his eye filled with shame.

Angela's voice stayed low. "Not just Tyler. All of it. Everything you've been carrying."

He hesitated, then shook his head slowly.

Angela nodded faintly. There was a long silence between them. She wanted to recoil. To run. To scream for help. But none of those were options. Not here. Not yet. *He's not just unstable,* she thought. *He's being... pushed.* Her mind drifted to the dream during detox—the strange man who spoke to her and encouraged her through those dark moments. The remote falling and changing the channel on TV to a lifeguard teaching her how to pick a lock. Both moments had felt too sharp, too timely to be coincidence. Maybe she was losing it. Or maybe not. Maybe there really *was* something else going on here. Angela closed her eyes, just for a moment.

God... if You're real... I need help. I don't know what to say. I don't know how to reach him. But I know something's inside him that wants to listen. So please... give me the words.

The air in the room changed—not dramatically. No flash of light. No sound. But something *lifted.*

Her chest didn't feel as tight. Her thoughts came clearer. She opened her eyes and looked at him—not the captor, not the killer—but the *man.* The broken boy who had watched too many terrible things happen and never healed.

"You've been alone a long time, haven't you?"

His lip quivered just slightly.

"You did awful things. But I think... part of you still knows they were awful."

He blinked.

"And I think that part of you is still fighting. Even now."

Marshall stared at her for a long time. Something in his posture eased. Just a little. Angela didn't move. She just stayed where she was, calm and grounded, her voice a whisper of mercy in a room full of ghosts.

Marshall didn't speak at first. He looked at her like she had spoken a language he hadn't heard in years—something soft, sacred, and terrifying. His fingers twitched where they rested on his knee. He blinked twice, then looked down. "I used to think... if I could just explain it right, someone would understand."

Angela waited. No rush. No pressure.

He swallowed hard. "I told a teacher once. About my mom. I said she was hurt, that I was scared. She believed me. Called someone. CPS." He paused, his jaw clenching faintly. "They came to the house. Asked some questions. Smiled too much. My mom said everything was fine. That I was 'just acting out.' They left."

Angela's stomach knotted.

"No one came back. After that, things got worse. I wasn't allowed to talk to teachers anymore. My dad made sure of that." He let out a bitter breath. "I remember thinking... I *did* try. I really did. But I was small. Weak. I watched him hurt her and couldn't stop it." His voice wavered—quiet, broken. "And when I finally did something... it was too late."

Angela felt the weight of his words settle in her chest like cold stone. But something else stirred—a flicker of memory. That night—when he'd first brought her here. She'd barely been conscious, slipping in and out of awareness, but there had been a moment when she saw something. Someone. A pale, older woman slumped in a chair, silent and still, her head tilted like a doll left behind. Not restrained. Not frightened. Just... *gone.*

Angela's eyes narrowed, her voice quiet. "Marshall... the woman upstairs. Who is she?"

His gaze dropped, avoiding hers. "My mother."

Angela's breath caught. "She's alive?"

"In a way. Her body is. But her mind's not... really there anymore."

Angela felt a chill crawl down her arms. She connected the pieces. His mother was here. Still alive. Broken. His father... gone. He had *done something.* And it wasn't hard now to see what.

Angela looked at him with new understanding, her voice barely above a whisper. "It was your dad... wasn't it?"

Marshall didn't answer. But he didn't deny it either. His shoulders tensed. His jaw locked. And the silence that followed said enough.

When Marshall spoke again, his voice dropped even lower. "So when I heard what Tyler did to you, I—I couldn't just let it go. I couldn't sit there and do nothing *again.* It didn't matter what happened to me."

Angela stared at him, heart pounding. She saw it now—not the excuse, but the *pattern.* The blueprint of a boy who tried to be brave, failed, and never forgave himself.

Angela stayed quiet for a long beat, her gaze steady, her voice soft when it finally came. "I think you've been carrying this weight for a long time. Trying to fix something you couldn't stop back then."

Marshall looked at her, but didn't speak.

"You did it because you thought it was the only way to make it right."

His expression flickered—just barely.

"To make a difference," she said, more gently now. "Because no one listened. And you couldn't protect the person who mattered most." She paused, watching him. "You didn't want to feel helpless again."

Marshall's breath caught in his throat. He blinked slowly, and for the first time, something shifted behind his eyes—not anger, not confusion. Recognition. As if she'd just spoken aloud something he hadn't dared to name. A tear slipped down his cheek before he could stop it. He turned his head. Angela didn't move. Didn't flinch. She just stayed with him—in the quiet, in the pain. And in that silence, she kept piecing him together.

The silence between them held like a fragile bridge—something real, something *good* trying to form. Angela could feel it. Marshall's breathing had slowed. His shoulders had lowered. The tears were real. The shame was real. She felt herself almost *believing* he could change. And then— *Flick.* The overhead bulb trembled in its socket. A faint buzz. Then a flicker. Angela looked up, frowning. The light pulsed once—twice—before holding steady again, but a strange chill brushed across her skin. Another coincidence? It felt like something else. Something *watching.* Something shifting just beyond her reach.

Her thoughts swirled, uncertain—until she noticed Marshall. He'd gone still. His gaze was distant again, unfocused. His hands twitched slightly, like he was trying to keep hold of something slipping from his grip. After a few moments he jerked slightly, as if waking from a dream. His posture stiffened.

Angela watched as the warmth vanished. His face closed. "Marshall?" she asked gently.

He stood suddenly. "I need to think. I'll come back later."

"Wait—"

But he was already moving to the stairs, the conversation cut clean like a wire. Angela stared after him, her chest tight, the light above still gently buzzing. *Something else was happening.* She could feel it now.

16

Why, My Soul, Are You Downcast?

The sound of weights clinking echoed through the dim apartment. The TV screen cast a cold, grainy light across the room—Angela's face frozen mid-motion in a blur of static. Gabriel's breath came in short bursts as he pushed through another set of curls. Sweat rolled down his temple and dripped onto the hardwood. He glanced up between reps, eyes locking on the paused frame. He gritted his teeth and started another set.

One. There's a struggle in the car—shadows thrashing in the narrow frame—then Angela spills out, hitting the pavement hard after fighting her way free. *Two.* She stumbles, barefoot, and runs. The man bursts out after her, moving fast, wild. *Three.* The taser hits. She stiffens, collapses. *Four.* He clutches his face like he's been hurt—maybe from their struggle in the car—and yet when he kneels beside her, his movements are careful. Almost delicate.

He set the weights down, wiped his mouth with the back of his hand, and hit play on the remote. The video crawled forward, the noise of old surveillance static filling the silence. Angela tried to crawl away. One shoe left behind. Then the flash—bright, sharp, and final. He froze the frame. Her body arched back from the taser. He stared at the image, jaw locked, shoulders rising and falling with each heavy breath.

"God… I just need some kind of lead, anything." he muttered under his breath, not a prayer but a fact.

He sat back down, bench press this time. Controlled, mechanical. The muscles in his arms trembled under the strain. Every push upward was a way to drown the helplessness clawing at his chest. He'd gone over this footage a hundred times, maybe more. Juliet's voice echoed in his head: *'He's checking her pulse.'*

He could still see it—two fingers to her neck, that slight tilt of the man's head. Not panic. Not haste. Deliberate. Careful. Almost gentle. He let the bar rest against his chest for a moment, lungs burning.

"You didn't want to kill her," he whispered. "You wanted her alive."

He shoved the weight up again, harder this time, until his arms quivered. The metal scraped against the stand as he dropped it back in place with a harsh clang. He sat up, breathing ragged, staring at the flickering screen. The man was gone again—just darkness where they'd vanished. Every time, it ended the same way. The same black frame. The same unanswered questions. He rubbed his forehead, pacing the length of the living room.

"Plates stolen. Cameras down. He knew the gaps. He planned every damn second." His voice came low, half growl, half confession.

He stopped and looked back at the screen one last time. Angela's limp form in the man's arms. The image had the stillness of a nightmare caught mid-breath. His fists clenched. He could feel the pulse hammering in his wrists. He dropped down to the floor—push-ups this time. Every rep landed like punctuation: *He knew. He planned. He took her.* Outside, the city hummed—oblivious, alive. Inside, Gabriel's apartment was a cave of light and shadow, the frozen footage still burning on the screen. He stayed on the floor until his arms gave out, the faint static of the video still whispering in the background, as if mocking him with what he couldn't yet see.

His phone buzzed on the counter. He grunted as he got up, wiping his face with a rag. He checked the screen and immediately rolled his eyes. *Mami.*

He pulled out a set of wireless earbuds and tapped to answer. "Hola, Mami."

"*Gabriel!*" Her voice burst through, thick with love and just the right amount of guilt. "I've been calling you all day! Are you still alive? Do I need to send someone?"

He grunted, heading toward the kitchen for water. "I work, Mami. You know. Crime. People doing dumb things. Someone's gotta catch them."

"Well maybe if you worked less and dated more, I wouldn't have to call you and *remind you* that I'm not getting any younger!"

He sighed. "Are we really doing this again?"

"Yes, we are doing this again. Your brother, God help him, is still talking about moving to Colorado to find himself. You are my only hope for grandchildren that won't come out of a yurt."

Gabriel chuckled despite himself and took a long drink. "I just haven't found the right person yet."

"You're twenty-eight, mijo. You don't *find* the right person waiting at your doorstep. You go *meet* them."

He opened the fridge and stared inside at nothing in particular.

"You know who I met this weekend?" she continued before he could answer.

"The niece of my friend Carmen's husband. Very sweet. Very pretty. Very smart. She's a doctor, Gabriel. A *real* doctor—not the kind that does TikToks."

"Mami..."

"She works in emergency medicine," his mother said, tapping away on her phone like she was reading off a scouting report. "Good job, no kids, speaks Spanish and English, pretty smile, natural hair. And she's sweet—not fake sweet, but real sweet. You can just tell."

Gabriel, halfway through a set of pullups, groaned. "Mami, *please.* Not this again."

"I'm just saying, you're not getting any younger. And I'm not getting any more grandchildren."

He dropped from the bar and grabbed his water bottle. "You have zero grandchildren."

"Exactly!" she snapped, like she'd just won a game show. "Your brother?" she scoffed. "Lost cause. I've accepted it. That boy can't even keep a plant alive, let alone a relationship."

"That's harsh."

"It's true. I've made peace with it. But you?" Her voice warmed just enough to press the guilt in. "You're my one remaining hope. Don't let me die with an empty photo frame."

"Wow. No pressure or anything."

"Oh, there's pressure. Just enough to remind you I gave you life."

"I'm not looking for anyone right now."

"You never are. That's why I do it for you."

He groaned louder.

"She's got gorgeous curls, that pretty gold-brown skin tone like her mama, very elegant. Classy. Not like those girls with the fake lashes and the duck lips."

"Mami—"

"And she goes to church," she added, half-casual, half-poking. "Real church. Not just Christmas Eve when someone drags her. She's got values. That's rare. Maybe she'll inspire *you* to remember where the church is located."

"I don't need a sermon."

"You need a wife."

Gabriel sighed. "Please tell me this conversation is almost over."

"I'm sending you a picture. Don't say anything until you see it."

His phone buzzed a moment later. He opened the photo and blinked. Long, loose curls. Warm skin like sun on honey. A natural look—no makeup, no filters. She wore navy scrubs and an ID badge, standing near a hospital hallway, mid-laugh. Her eyes were bright, intelligent. Confident. The kind of confident that didn't need to prove anything.

"Huh." He tilted his head.

"I *told* you," she said smugly. "She's beautiful, right? And she's smart. Independent. And not a criminal, which puts her ahead of some of your exes."

"*One* girl had a parking boot on her car. That doesn't make her a criminal."

"It makes her irresponsible."

He smirked, still looking at the photo, then locked his phone and set it face-down on the counter like it didn't matter. "She's all right."

His mother cackled on the other end. "Mira este—trying to act unfazed. I heard that pause."

"I didn't pause."

"You were staring like you saw a miracle. Don't lie to your mother."

"I didn't say I'm marrying her."

"I didn't say you were. I'm just saying what's the harm in calling her, and if you do meet maybe don't wear that ratty shirt with the holes in the collar."

"That's vintage."

"That's tragic."

He laughed. "I'll think about it."

"You'll *call* her. Thinking is what sad men do when they're eating soggy meal-prep chicken alone at night."

He shook his head, grinning, already regretting answering the phone—but not entirely.

"I'm sending you her contact info right now," his mother said, her tone somewhere between a command and a blessing.

"Mami—"

"No excuses. You've been single so long I'm starting to think you've taken a vow."

Gabriel's smile faltered. He opened his mouth to protest but couldn't find the words. The silence that followed wasn't awkward—it was maternal, knowing. She'd always been able to see through him, no matter how he tried to hide behind sarcasm or work.

Finally, she sighed. "Mijo, I just want you happy. You can't live your whole life chasing darkness and expect to come out clean."

He leaned against the counter, thumb tracing the edge of his phone. "I'm fine, Mami."

"I know what fine sounds like. You sound like you're fine when you're not."

He let out a breath, halfway between a laugh and defeat. "You should be a detective."

"I should be sleeping," she said pointedly. "But instead, I'm matchmaking because my son refuses to."

He chuckled, shaking his head. "You don't quit, do you?"

"Nope. So? You'll call her?"

"I'll... sure."

"Good. God bless you mijo, love you."

"Love you too,"

"Buenas noches, Detective." *Click.*

Gabriel stood in the quiet of his apartment, phone still warm in his hand. A few seconds later, another buzz—her contact info, just like she'd promised. He stared at the name on the screen. *Paula Castillo.* He hesitated, thumb hovering above the screen. For a moment, the image of Angela's frozen face flickered in his mind—the static from the footage still echoing somewhere in his thoughts. He set the phone down beside the sink and ran a hand through his hair, the echo of his mother's words tugging faintly at him: *You can't live your whole life chasing darkness.* He glanced once more at the phone. Then, in spite of himself, he opened the photo again. Paula was laughing at something off-camera—unguarded, bright. The kind of laugh that belonged to someone untouched by the things he saw every day. He smiled faintly. Just a flicker. Then he locked the phone again and turned off the light.

17

Teachings of Demons

Thousands of years ago, the angel Ecanus worked in a hall of light and shifting glass, reflecting starlight and smoke from distant galaxies. Scrolls hung in the air like suspended thoughts, fluttering faintly as if stirred by the breath of God. In the center, seated cross-legged atop a floating slab of lapis lazuli, was Ecanus—quill in hand, a scroll unraveling endlessly from his lap onto the floor.

He hummed a tune without melody, tapping the quill to his lip. "Six hundred and seventy-three murders today. Not including infanticide. Oh, but should I count the infants? They certainly count their spears and arrows." He dipped his quill again and laughed—a high, singsong thing— then stopped. His face darkened as he stared at the ink slowly blooming on the page like blood. "They burn their food to spite their neighbors. They salt their own fields in tantrum. They worship make-believe gods of stone and wood who can't even talk."

He sighed and looked up as Uriel entered the hall, robes dusted with the faint ash of Earth's war-torn winds. "You're late."

Uriel stepped forward, his gaze distant. "Leah picked up a fever, I kept the wind from cutting too deep, the cold from taking her. They're moving west now, slow, but steady. Jared chose peace and now walks with renewed hope. I'm proud of him. Vengeance was at his fingertips. He could have done it. He wanted to. But instead—he turned away. Snapped his spear in half and used it for firewood."

Ecanus made a noise—something between a laugh and a scoff. He clapped his ink-stained hands once. "How poetic. A boy on the edge of becoming a killer decides to turn philosopher instead. Lovely. And tomorrow? Maybe he'll starve. Or freeze. Or maybe those same men that burned his village will find him and finish what they started." He shook his head and picked up a fresh scroll. "You act like mercy is a triumph. But what you've preserved is a *tragedy with an intermission.*"

Uriel didn't flinch. "He was given a choice. He chose to break the cycle."

Ecanus waved the quill like a dagger. "Break it? He *paused* it. Violence is a river, not a stone. All you've done is give it a bend."

A faint tremor stirred the chamber as Asael stepped into the room, voice smooth, gaze fixed on the distance beyond. "He's not wrong. The world, such as it is, seems determined to cough out its last."

Ecanus raised his brows. "Ah, the ambassador of hope arrives."

Asael didn't take the bait. He moved past them, stopping near a suspended scroll that charted the recent slaughters in ochre ink. "I walked behind a woman today as she buried her youngest child beneath stones. No grave rites. No weeping left in her. Just silence. Like the grief had drained her into dust. And yet—she still woke up the next morning."

Uriel stepped forward. "And that isn't worth something? That spark? Even under all this ruin?"

Asael looked at him, expression unreadable. "It is. But I wonder if it's the spark of hope... or of madness."

Ecanus snorted. "Finally, something we agree on."

Uriel shook his head. "You both speak of humans as if they are a sickness. But they feel pain. They *grieve.* They restrain themselves from vengeance even when every bone screams for blood. That is not madness—it is *miracle.*"

Asael's jaw clenched. "And what happens when that restraint breaks? When they decide they've swallowed enough ashes to burn back? You think one boy setting down a spear makes a tide turn?"

"No," Uriel said, voice low. "But it *starts* one."

Ecanus scoffed again. "Yes, and what a wave it will be. A righteous few drowning in a sea of butchery. Let's not pretend, Uriel. You're not saving them—you're delaying them."

Asael turned to the others, this time with a flicker of heat beneath his calm. "Perhaps they don't need saving. Perhaps what they need is truth. The truth of who they *really* are. No masks. No lies about their nobility."

Uriel stiffened. "You sound like you admire their bloodlust."

Asael smiled faintly, tilting his head like a teacher indulging a naïve question. "I admire their *will*." He walked slowly around one of the floating scrolls, fingers trailing through the light. "To survive. To endure. Even beasts break under less. But these creatures," he paused, "they fight for more than just breath. Even in their violence, there is... purpose."

Uriel narrowed his eyes. "And what purpose justifies slaughter?"

Asael gave a small, amused shrug. "That's not for me to decide. Is it for us to judge their every falter, or to understand what drives them to the edge?" He stepped closer to Uriel now, his voice lower. "You said yourself—he laid the spear down. But what if the next boy doesn't? What if the rage *wins*? Will we cast him into darkness and pretend we never saw the fire kindling in his heart?" He leaned in. "Or will we walk beside him anyway?"

Uriel held his ground, but his silence was telling.

Asael smiled a little wider, gently, as if comforting an old friend. "They are flawed. We all see that. But maybe what they need is not correction... but companionship. Maybe what they need... is someone who understands how deeply their hearts burn. Someone who won't flinch when they do the unthinkable."

Ecanus, from behind his scroll, muttered dryly, "You mean someone who'll hand them the match."

Asael didn't turn. "No. Someone who won't condemn them for having *held* one."

Uriel's jaw tensed, eyes narrowing. "You speak like a shadow at the edge of the flame, Asael. As if you envy their anger."

Asael's expression softened, almost sad. "No, brother. I pity it." A pause. "But I no longer fear for them because of it."

Uriel turned away, pacing a few steps through the radiant chamber. "You twist words as if they were threads. Pity becomes praise. Understanding becomes invitation. You'd walk beside them into the fire and call it fellowship."

Asael stayed where he was, voice calm. "Would you rather I stand above them and pretend the fire isn't there?"

Uriel spun back around. "I would rather you help *quench* it!"

The air tightened like a pulled bowstring. Light dimmed subtly at the edges of the hall.

Ecanus sighed without looking up from his scroll. "And there it is. The fire's not just in them, is it?"

Uriel glared. "You find this amusing?"

Ecanus met his gaze for once, the usual humor gone from his face. "No. I find it inevitable."

The tension between the three flared—divine presences trembling just beneath restraint. Words left unsaid hung like sparks in a dry sky. And then— he came. The chamber brightened—not harsh, but complete. A golden warmth filled the air, the kind that *reminded* creation it was loved. The scrolls stopped mid-drift, as though kneeling.

Adapa entered, barefoot, wrapped in robes that shimmered like dawn on still water. His face was perfect—not flawless, but so deeply right that flaw would've been impossible to conceive. His eyes held galaxies, and his smile... his smile could quiet storms. "Brothers," he said gently, his voice like music from before the first star. "Must even *we* take up the quarrels of mortals?"

Immediately, Asael bowed his head—not just in respect, but *reverence*. A subtle joy lit his face, like a lost son glimpsing home. "Wise one. You honor us."

Ecanus stood and bowed with a graceful flourish, lips curving into something warm—sincere, for once. "Your timing is divine, as always."

Adapa stepped among them like a breeze between flames. He touched Asael's shoulder, a faint glow spreading beneath his hand. Then he turned to Uriel. "You carry a heavy burden, brother."

Uriel met his gaze, neither bowing nor retreating. "I carry a *conviction*."

Adapa's smile deepened. "And that is why I love you." He moved between them all now, speaking as if to children squabbling in a garden. "But let us not forget—we are not *them*. We do not fear. We do not hunger. We do not grieve as they do. So why should we let their wildness infect our unity?"

Asael nodded slowly, eyes fixed on Adapa like a disciple watching his teacher breathe. "Of course."

Ecanus echoed the sentiment with a soft bow.

But Uriel remained still. "They *are* wild. But they were made in the image of the One. Are we so sure their fire is not part of the design?"

Adapa turned his head slightly at that, and for a moment... just a moment... his smile faltered. Then it returned, serene and radiant. "Perhaps. But even fire must be taught where to burn." He turned away, the light following him like a tide. "Come Asael. There is more to witness. And far more to shape."

As Adapa turned and began to glide from the chamber, his footsteps as soundless as thought, Asael remained, a look of consternation on his face. He lingered in the hush that followed, eyes fixed on Uriel—not with anger, but with something far heavier.

He stepped close. "You feel it too, don't you?" he whispered. "The air is shifting. The silence between the stars is not what it was."

A current moved through the air, subtle but undeniable, like the moment before a storm realizes itself. Ecanus's hand tightened around his quill.

Uriel didn't move. "The stars where meant to bring light, but it seems like some of them are collapsing into darkness."

Asael gave a faint, mournful smile. "You think I'm slipping. That I'm being pulled."

Uriel's voice was firm. "No. I think you're *choosing*."

There was a long pause. Asael looked down, then back at Uriel—eyes bright with something caught between hope and sorrow. "When the moment comes, you'll have to choose too. Just... don't wait until the sky is already burning."

Uriel didn't blink. "If the sky burns, I will stand where I always have."

Asael exhaled—quiet, defeated, but not angry. He nodded once, more to himself than to Uriel. "That's what I'm afraid of."

He turned and followed Adapa out of the chamber, swallowed by that soft, golden light. Uriel turned away with a look of sorrow and vanished back to his assignment on the earth. Once again, the hall lay quiet —emptied of angels, emptied of song. Only the soft, relentless hum of the scrolls filled the air, an unending chorus of ink and light.

Ecanus stood over the nearest one, the parchment alive beneath his hands, names unspooling across its surface with mechanical grace. Line by line, humanity's story wrote itself in real time. A birth here. A death there. But more deaths than births, lately. And more deaths with *cause.*

He watched the numbers climb—murder, famine, war—and felt something in his chest twist, not with pity but with a weary, growing disgust. "Stewards of creation," he murmured. "What a generous term for butchers with borrowed breath."

The script flickered, shifting faster now, and a new column began to form—one he had not seen before. *Ritual sacrifice.* At first, he thought it an error. But the numbers grew steadily, names filling beneath it. Each one was marked by blood, some freely offered, and others taken by force. He scrolled upward, tracing the pattern back to its origin, the glow of divine record cold against his skin. A village. Remote, half-forgotten. Yet the sacrifices there had multiplied, sanctioned by no known order of Heaven. He frowned and searched the registry for its assigned watcher. When the name appeared, his heart stilled. Adapa. The quill slipped from his fingers. Ink bled down the parchment like veins. For a long while, he said nothing—only stared, the realization clawing its way through disbelief. He looked again to the rising numbers, the constant litany of failure, and felt the bitter thought bloom uninvited: *Is this the design we're meant to protect? Is this perfection?*

Slowly, deliberately, he rolled the living scroll closed, the glow dimming as the parchment tightened. "No," he whispered to the silence. "There must be a better way."

He slid the scroll into the fold of his robe. Whatever was happening, it had the scent of something forbidden, and he intended to not only understand it, but partake in it.

***

Thousands of years later, in an ammunitions factory, Ecanus the fallen angel watched James working at his station, oil stains on his hands, eyes hollow from too many shifts and too little meaning. The factory's hum faded into a dull murmur of machines and melancholy. From the shadowed catwalk above, Ecanus watched Uriel stand beside James. Uriel's voice carried softly—words of hope, of light, of purpose in the unseen.

Ecanus frowned. *Hope,* he thought. *A drug as old as humanity.*

Then the pull came. Subtle at first—a tug behind his temples, a ripple through the quiet fabric of his thoughts. His gaze blurred and the world around him wavered like heat over asphalt. He exhaled, and the air folded. The factory dissolved. He stepped through silence into sunlight. The smell of grass met him, fresh and sweet. Children's laughter drifted across the park, though none of them saw him. Joggers passed, faces serene, eyes glazed with that gentle blindness reserved for humanity. And there, on a weathered bench beneath an oak, sat Adapa. Still, composed, wearing the faintest smile. The sunlight seemed to bend around him, softening the world at its edges.

Adapa said the name like an invitation. "Ecanus—"

Ecanus let it pass over his lips in a sound half-drowned and half-swallowed. "Ravage," he mumbled to himself. His new name, a small, private blade.

Adapa didn't flinch; he only smiled as if he hadn't heard and folded his hands on his knee. "Sit with me."

Ecanus sat, every motion measured.

"There's an old friend who needs your gift. Asael."

Ecanus snorted, tone dry. "An old friend. What's the fuss? One troubled man—Marshall—won't be that hard. Who cares about him, I had James nearly finished." He let the complaint hang like a challenge. "You know how close I was."

Adapa's smile thinned to something patient and tired. He watched the pond, then said, quietly, "Marshall is useful, but he is not the fulcrum. It is his prisoner, Angela, who matters."

Ecanus blinked. "Angela?" The name sounded ordinary and terrible all at once. "What's the big deal about one girl?"

Adapa's eyes turned to him, a small impatience in their warmth. "She must die." He said it without flourish, as if he had said it a hundred times too many. "Marshall only opens the hinge. Angela is the door. Forget James, he is insignificant to this design."

Ecanus watched Adapa as if seeing him anew—calm, inexhaustible. "And Asael? Did he ask for my help, or is my old friend slipping in his duties lately?"

Adapa's smile curved, faint and private. "He did not ask."

Ecanus's mouth twitched into a small, cruel smile. The irony pleased him. "Of course he didn't." He closed his eyes briefly, savoring the thought. "Very well. I will help your broken angel break his man. Tell Asael—if he ever learns to admit need—I will accept nothing less than begging on his knees next time."

Adapa rose from the bench, the light bending faintly around him. "Be that as it may," he said softly, "he needs you this very moment."

The breeze stirred the grass, and the laughter of unseen children carried faintly through the air.

Ecanus's grin widened as he stood. "Then let's not keep him waiting."

***

Across realms, the air trembled with power. Ecanus—or rather, *Ravage*—felt it before he saw it: the hum of divine fury breaking through the seams of the mortal plane.

He turned his head slightly, eyes narrowing as the veil split open in front of him. There he was—Remiel. Towering, sanctimonious, all righteous muscle and light. His blade burned like conviction itself, cutting through the gloom where Asael fought to hold his ground.

Ravage watched a moment, admiring the contrast—the white fire against Asael's blackened talons, the symmetry of ruin and glory colliding. Then he smiled. *Predictable.*

Remiel's strike hit home, sending Asael crashing into the basement wall of the spiritual echo. Dust and light scattered like ash.

"You've overstepped," Remiel thundered, voice shaking the very air. "Your hold over him is getting weaker. You've failed."

That was his cue. Ravage stepped through the rift like a man walking into a bar fight he'd been waiting for. The shadows parted around him, and he grinned, every tooth gleaming with irreverence.

"Hey, big guy!" he called out, his voice dripping with mockery. "You're ruining a perfectly good mental collapse. Mind giving us five minutes?"

Remiel spun, divine fury lighting his eyes—but he was too slow. Ravage darted forward, short and solid as iron, driving his elbow into the angel's ribs. The impact reverberated like thunder through two worlds.

He laughed—a deep, reckless sound that didn't belong in Heaven or Hell. "Relax." He ducked under a blinding arc of white flame. "I'm just here for quality assurance."

He caught Asael's arm as the other angel stumbled, yanking him clear of Remiel's next strike. For a heartbeat, their eyes met—one mocking, one murderous. Then together they fell back through the haze, holding the line just long enough to survive the storm.

Ravage's grin didn't fade even as Remiel's light scorched the air around them. *This will be fun*, he thought. And for the first time in centuries, he felt alive.

18

Whoever Refreshes Others Will be Refreshed

Marshall sat in silence beside the bed, the old recliner creaking beneath him as he shifted his weight. The room smelled faintly of old sheets and lavender—the scent of the lotion he still rubbed on her hands each night, even though she never flinched, never blinked. Her eyes stared at the ceiling, vacant as the sky after a storm. Her mouth hung slightly open.

He reached out and brushed a lock of brittle gray hair from her forehead. "I made soup today," he said softly. "Chicken and rice. The way you used to make it."

No response. Of course not.

"I think I finally got the salt right." A small smile flickered at the corner of his mouth and died before it could land.

The silence was so deep it felt like it might crack.

"I told her about you, y'know. Angela." His voice was quieter now. "She's not like you. Not the you I remember from after... everything fell apart." He paused, eyes drifting over his mother's motionless form. "But before that—before Dad started turning you into someone else—you had this light. This kind of quiet spark that made people feel safe, even when they didn't know they needed it. Angela has that too. She pretends like she doesn't, like she's just trying to survive, but it's there. She makes the room feel warmer.

Safer." His throat tightened. "I thought maybe... maybe if I could protect her, I could hold onto a piece of that. Maybe even bring some of it back." He laughed, but it was dry and hollow.

"I don't know who I'm trying to convince."

The lamp beside the bed flickered faintly.

Then, from nowhere and everywhere at once, a voice bloomed like a grin in his skull. "Ohhh boy," said an unfamiliar voice with theatrical glee. "We're having *feelings* again. This is my favorite part of the evening. Soup and regret? What a pairing. Michelin-star despair, right here in the heartland."

Marshall flinched. "No."

"No? Oh come on, don't be like that. You're on a roll tonight. Almost got me misty-eyed back there with the 'maybe I could protect her' bit." A fake sniffle followed. "Adorable. Really. If I had a heart, it'd be breaking."

Marshall pressed his palms into his eyes, breath catching in his throat. "Get out."

"You invited me," the voice said brightly. "Every time you looked in the mirror and wished it'd crack. Every time you stared at the ceiling wondering if it'd be better if you just didn't wake up."

"I'm not—"

"Important? Right. That's the word. Not important. Not remembered. Not loved. You're a guy in a locked house with a corpse that forgot how to die and a hostage who'd rather gnaw through her own ankle than stay for dinner... You should've ended things a long time ago. You'd be surprised how peaceful nothingness is. Like a nap. Forever."

A second voice slithered in behind the first, deeper, silkier, laced with something more ancient. "Peace," Asael whispered, "is not absence. It is release."

Marshall froze. That voice. That damn voice that made everything sound like it was already decided.

"The cycle. Hurt birthing hurt. Your father into your mother. Your mother into you. And now you into her. Angela..."

The name hung in the air like smoke.

"You've caught her in the same trap, Marshall. She will carry it. Break beneath it. Then spread it—like rot. Unless… you set Angela free."

"She deserves to live," Marshall said.

"To suffer," Asael corrected gently. "To struggle. To become the very thing she fears. That's the arc. That's the human curse. You've seen it."

Marshall turned and stared at his mother's face. Slack-jawed. Blank. Still breathing, yes—but was this life? Or just a monument to his failure? "I tried," he said, voice raw. "I tried to take care of her."

"And look what good it did," the other voice chimed in. "A vegetable in a hospice bed. Standing ovation, pal."

Marshall's jaw tightened. "I didn't have anyone else."

"And neither will Angela, soon enough," Asael said. "She'll wake up one day years from now and wonder how she became everything she hated. And she'll remember you. And she'll blame herself. That's how this works."

"You don't know her," Marshall muttered.

"Don't I?" Asael said. "She's soft. Scared. Clinging to ideals the world will grind into pulp. But if you end it now… there will be no pulp. No scars. Just peace. You get to rewrite the ending."

The other voice hummed thoughtfully. "Call it a mercy killing. Real poetic stuff. Leave a little note. 'She was too good for this world.' Bam. Instant martyrdom. You'd be *famous* in a documentary someday."

Marshall turned, pacing now. His hands kept drifting to his coat pocket. The weight of the revolver rested there like a final thought, patient and still. "She doesn't deserve to die."

"No," Asael agreed, so gently it almost hurt. "She deserves to be saved. And you—only you—can do that."

Marshall looked at his mother again. "Maybe I was never meant to save anyone."

"Exactly," the other voice chirped. "Now you're getting it."

Marshall stood, the floorboards creaking under his weight as he slowly made his way to the kitchen. The house was still, the kind of stillness that hummed too loud in your ears when grief had nowhere else to go. He moved on instinct—cleaning up the tray beside his mother's bed, rinsing the half-empty broth bowl in the sink, folding the napkin she hadn't used. His fingers brushed the handle of the kitchen knife lying by the drying rack. He stared at it for a moment. Then his gaze darkened. He pictured it—just a flicker, a flash in his mind's eye:

The blade pressed against Angela's pale skin, her body tensing, her breath hitching in her throat.

His stomach churned. His hand twitched. The image revolted him. No. Not like that. Never like that. He pulled his hand back, fingers curling away from the knife as though it had burned him. He didn't want her to feel pain. If he did this, it had to be fast. Clean. Like shutting a door. His hand slid into his coat pocket and closed around cold metal. The revolver. Heavy. Familiar. Honest. He drew it out slowly, staring down at it with an expression caught between reverence and dread. He remembered the sound—the one that never left him. The gunshot. That first shot. The one that made the house go silent. The one that ended his father's voice forever.

Bang.

It still rang in his ears some nights, uninvited. He turned the revolver over in his hands, thumbed the release, and popped the cylinder open. Empty. Of course it was. He frowned and stepped toward the sink, crouching low. The cupboard beneath groaned as he opened it, the hinges stiff. He reached for the small black ammo box tucked in the far corner—but when he touched it, it gave a wet, squishy protest.

Drip. Drip.

A slow leak from the pipe above had been at work for days, maybe weeks. The box was soaked. He pulled it out and peeled back the lid. His stomach sank. The cartridges were damp, tarnished, a few already bloomed with corrosion. Some were green at the edges. Others had their brass warped and pitted like they'd been left in acid. He tried to shake one loose, but it clung to the others like a cluster of bad teeth. He exhaled through his nose, slowly, eyes never leaving the box. A sign? A message? Or just more bad luck. He set it on the counter and leaned on his palms. He didn't know what he was doing. Not really. Every part of him was fogged, like he was moving through someone else's dream—one he couldn't wake up from. But he had to be ready. In case... in case things got worse. In case the voices came back.

In case Angela looked at him like she looked at him that first night—like he was a monster pretending to be human. He wiped his hands on a towel and stared down at the box of ruined bullets. He'd need more. Not because he wanted to use them. Just in case. Just in case...

His train of thought was broken by an urge to check on Angela, and he pulled the phone from his pocket to check the feed. The camera view flickered between static and the dim glow of the basement. Angela sat cross-legged on the thin mattress, the television washing her face in cold, shifting light. She looked smaller down there. Quieter, but he could sense something was shifting inside of her, a hidden strength perhaps. He noticed it growing the more he checked on her. He could tell she was studying him—the rhythm of her asks, the way she timed her smiles, her tone. She was getting better at it. Calculated. Careful. Now, he watched her stare at the TV screen for a long time. Probably the news again. Probably hoping to hear her name, or see a picture of herself flash across the bottom of the screen—some sign that they were still looking. The thought hit him harder than he expected, a small sharp ache in his chest that he couldn't quite swallow. Guilt had a way of sneaking up on him like that—soft, sudden, and merciless.

She finally reached for the little chalkboard. He watched her write the word *THIRSTY* with slow, careful strokes, her hand steady now, practiced. She set it upright beside the mattress, exactly where she knew he'd see it. Always something simple. Always just enough to make him come down. He grabbed a water bottle from the fridge and made his way down the hatch. The air in the basement always stayed damp, heavy with that smell of concrete that hadn't seen sun in years. The dehumidifier had died, sputtering out with a final rattle before it went silent, and now the place felt like it was breathing against itself—wet, stale, alive in the wrong way.

She looked up when he opened the door, giving him that faint, practiced smile—polite but not too warm. "Hey," she said softly. "How's your eye?"

He felt the sting under the gauze before she even finished the question. The bandage was crooked again—he'd changed it that morning, alone, squinting at his reflection until he gave up trying to make it neat. "It's... fine."

She nodded. "Looks better than yesterday. You changing the bandages yourself?"

Her tone stayed light, casual, but he could feel her watching—reading every twitch, every shift in his shoulders. Measuring him. She was learning fast. And for some reason, he didn't stop her. Maybe because it felt almost human, having someone care enough to ask—even if he knew it wasn't really care at all.

Marshall nodded, like they were talking about a scraped knee instead of the syringe she'd driven into his eye socket. A few days ago, she wouldn't have dared to bring it up at all. But now... now she was getting more comfortable.

Silence lingered. He didn't step closer, just stood in the doorway with the bottle still in his hand, shifting his weight while his eye wandered across the room. The chalkboard. The mattress. The faint shimmer of TV light that still clung to the concrete walls. Everything down here bore traces of her—small, deliberate attempts to make the basement something other than what it was.

"Can I tell you something dumb?" she asked suddenly.

His gaze snapped back to her.

"I feel gross," she said, offering a small, embarrassed smile. "Like, really gross. I know I'm lucky you've let me clean up a little, but... it's still a basement. And I haven't had deodorant in—I don't even know how long. I probably smell like a foot."

That almost drew a laugh from him—almost. The corner of his mouth twitched before he caught himself. He wasn't sure how long it had been since he laughed, the feeling surprised him. He didn't know if he wanted her to see that part of him, especially since he hadn't seen it himself in many years. But she saw. She always saw. And she leaned into it.

"I know it's stupid," she said, brushing a stray hair behind her ear, the movement soft and unguarded. "But it's kind of messing with my head. Makes me feel like... less human, I guess. If you ever went to the store and maybe found some cheap deodorant, I think I'd be like, the happiest hostage ever."

That word—*hostage*—landed like a knife turned sideways. His brow furrowed before he could stop it. She must've caught the change in his expression because her tone shifted, gentler now, smoothing over the tension she'd just stirred.

"You don't have to," she said quickly. "I just figured... if you were already going out."

Marshall stood there, caught somewhere between irritation and something he didn't want to name. She was clever—too clever. Every word carried two meanings: The one she spoke and the one she wanted him to feel. Still, something in her voice, in that quiet plea to feel *human*, hit closer than it should have. He understood that feeling all too well. For a long moment, neither of them moved. She sat there, looking up at him with that soft, practiced hope. He just watched, wondering if she was the only one in the room still trying to remember what being human felt like.

Her voice lingered in the air long after she stopped talking, soft but deliberate—like perfume that stayed on the skin. Marshall didn't answer right away. The words sat in him like a weight he couldn't quite shift. *Deodorant.* Something so small. So human. And yet the way she'd asked— gentle, embarrassed, almost shy—made it feel like more than that. He stared at her for a long moment, his thoughts wandering somewhere he didn't want them to go.

Then, finally, his shoulders dropped, and the tension eased from his chest. "Yeah," he said quietly. "I'll get it."

Her head lifted a little, surprise flickering in her eyes. "Really?" she asked, careful, cautious—like she didn't want to spook him.

He met her gaze with his good eye. The other throbbed beneath the gauze, a dull ache he'd grown used to. "You said it'd make you happy."

That seemed to hit her in a way she hadn't expected. Her lips parted, then closed again.

He hesitated before adding, "You shouldn't feel... less. Not while you're here."

The words came out softer than he meant. Maybe even sad. *Not while you're here.* He knew how that sounded—temporary, conditional—but he meant it. He didn't want her to feel like she was decaying in the dark.

"I don't want you to feel like you're rotting away down here," he said under his breath. "You're not some... thing. I know what that does to people."

For a second, she didn't respond. Just looked at him, quiet and cautious, like she was afraid to move too quickly and shatter something fragile between them.

When she finally spoke, her voice was barely above a whisper. "Thank you."

He nodded once, the motion stiff and awkward, as if her gratitude embarrassed him. He set the water bottle down without stepping closer, then he turned toward the stairs, shutting the door behind him. Each step creaked under his weight, slow and deliberate, the sound echoing in the still air. Halfway up, he stopped. His hand tightened around the banister. He didn't know why—maybe it was the tone in her voice, or the way she'd looked at him when she said *thank you.* Something in it cracked through the armor he'd spent years building.

He turned slightly, just enough to glance back. There was something in the space between them he couldn't name—sadness, guilt, maybe both. Or maybe it was that constant sense that everything he did, every breath he took, was holding up a ceiling that could collapse any second.

His jaw clenched. He let out a slow breath, gave one last look and turned away.

19

Keep Your Heart with All Vigilance

Angela stayed frozen for a full ten seconds. She listened—first for his footsteps on the stairs, then the distant shuffle of movement above. Finally, she could hear a distant door opened, then closed.

Silence.

She picked up the remote, her thumb moved across it, flipping through the channels quickly. A basketball game. Perfect. The game clock would give her something solid—quarters, timeouts, halftime. A way to measure how long he was gone. Time, finally, in definable chunks. She laid back onto the mattress and pulled the thin blanket over her, curling slightly toward the television. Not for warmth, but to hide from the camera. It was mounted to the top of the TV and stared back at her with its unblinking glassy eye. It was glued crookedly, a little off-center—like everything else in this house.

Beneath the blanket her hands were mostly hidden, folding into the shadow like a pair of careful animals. Her fingers crept down to her ankle and found the cold steel ring and eventually the cool smooth curve of the padlock shackle. It was stubborn and squat, its body scarred from years of use; she had traced its edges a hundred times. Tonight, as every night, she treated it like a book she was learning to read by touch. She didn't think in diagrams or instructions. She thought in textures. Her fingertips had grown intimate with the seams on the lock's casing—so intimate that she could tell, just by pressure and sound, when something inside shifted even the smallest fraction. Small, almost inaudible changes felt like conversations she could barely hear.

She flattened the bobby pin between her knuckles until it lay straight, then let it tremble between two fingers. The pin's metal was warm from her palm; the paint had worn where she gripped it. She didn't pretend she had mastered some mechanical art. What she had was practice: repeated, tentative probing that taught her more about locksmithing than she should have ever needed to know in her lifetime. She had learned how many little obstructions the lock hid—several tiny elements that resisted and yielded on their own timbre—and how little pressure it took to make them stay put for a moment. Her touch had become calibrated; she knew when to be feather-light and when to stop before the metal bit too hard into her skin.

There were little musical responses—micro-shifts that she would never have noticed a week earlier. Sometimes she could feel a grainy give, a whisper of motion under the bobby pin, and that was enough to make her chest flinch with hope. More often the lock simply sat like a sleeping thing, patient and indifferent. She kept her movements slow, reverent, because haste had a way of waking things up you didn't want disturbed. She also knew the limits of what her hands alone could do. You needed two hands doing different jobs at once—one to search and one to hold—and one bobby pin could only do one thing at a time. She had seen the lockpicking on TV always involve a pair of tools. She came to understand why the hard way, through evenings of near-successes that slipped away because she couldn't keep the tiny bits in place while she tested the next. She needed something to hold a steady pressure for her, a quiet hand that wouldn't tremble. A small, stubborn brace that would let her fingers move freely without losing the tiny gains she'd won.

She rolled her wrist and glanced up without thinking. The bare bulb above her hummed faintly, a small warm pool of light over the mattress. The filament inside the bulb glowed like a tiny, brittle spine—thin, threaded, and impossibly bright against the dark. She'd seen how someone could use those filaments to escape a locked room. That vision slid into her head now: a filament's fragile persistence, how it held and released light. The memory wasn't a plan quite yet; it was an image—one small bright thing she could hold in her mind while she figured the rest out.

She settled back on her shoulder and breathed slow, letting the lock be for a beat. Time was the real tool she had—long practice, the patience to learn the lock's moods, and the chance to wait for the right window. For now she would keep listening, keep learning the language of metal and shadow, and keep that filament-picture tucked behind her eyes like a promise that some small brightness could be coaxed out of the dark.

She'd have to wait until she knew exactly how long Marshall stayed out on errands. Until she had a reliable window. Then maybe— She sat up slowly and looked around the room, eyes scanning each surface with renewed urgency.

Plan B.

Her eyes flicked from one object to the next. The plastic bowl on the floor, the spoon, the water bottle. A few books stacked on a nearby shelf. The remote. She picked it up absently, turning it over in her hands. Marshall was strong. She knew that. Even on his worst days, she doubted she could take him in a fair fight. He was quick too—quicker than someone his size should be. He'd proven that the night he had captured her. Fighting him would have to be the absolute last option. But still... she had to know. She had to weigh it. The remote. She picked it up, rolling it in her palm like it might reveal something more than plastic and wires. Her thumb pressed against the battery cover, but her thoughts had already drifted. Lithium batteries. Fire. The idea came uninvited, but not unfamiliar. A fire might set off smoke alarms. And if he'd forgotten to disable the ones upstairs—or if the house was close enough to a neighbor—they might hear it. Maybe even call someone. A firefighter. A cop. Anyone. She imagined it for a moment— flames licking at the edges of the door, smoke curling upward, someone shouting from outside. It could work. It could also trap her down here, choking on her own plan. If she didn't get the shackle off in time... she'd be a headline instead of a rescue. Her stomach twisted. No. Not yet. She set the remote down gently. *Patience,* she told herself. That was the only weapon she had right now. She turned back to the game, eyes narrowing on the score in the corner. She had to know exactly how long he was gone. Every minute mattered.

She traced the edge of the shackle with her fingertip. It reminded her of a Sunday from long ago—the old church that smelled like dust and hymnbooks, her mother's hand resting over her purse, her father's arm around the back of the pew. Her family used to go more often back then. Mostly because of her dad. He was the one who insisted they get up early, even when she and her mom groaned about wanting to sleep in. They went every week when she was little, and every so often after that—until high school. Somewhere along the way, they just stopped. She couldn't quite remember the reason, but she thought maybe it was around the time her dad's heart started sending him to the hospital more often. It was hard to keep believing after that. Hard to pray when every test result looked worse than the last. She remembered how her mom would still whisper grace at dinner, but it sounded thinner each time. Maybe, she thought now, they'd all started to feel like faith was a kind of fantasy—something you told yourself to make the waiting hurt less.

Her chest tightened at the thought, and then, as if called by the memory itself, she remembered the rest of that Sunday. The pastor had been preaching about Joseph—about patience and trust when nothing made sense.

"His feet were hurt with fetters," he had said, quoting Psalm 105:18.

Angela remembered tugging on her father's sleeve, whispering, "Daddy, what's a fetter?"

He leaned down, smiling just a little. "It's like a metal bracelet," he told her softly. "But it's the kind they put on people in jail."

She'd wrinkled her nose in thought, then grinned. "I want one."

Her father had chuckled quietly to himself, shaking his head. "No, you don't, sweetheart."

Back then, she'd only imagined something shiny and delicate, something pretty—like jewelry. She hadn't known what it meant to be chained, to wait and wonder if anyone would ever come for you. The pastor had gone on to say Joseph wasn't just forgotten for two years, it might've been closer to ten. Ten years of darkness before freedom.

Angela's eyes lifted to the ceiling now, to the faint hum of the bulb overhead. *Ten years.* If she were still alive in ten years, Phoenix would be thirteen. Would he be in middle school by then? Playing soccer, maybe, or getting too busy for bedtime stories? She wondered if he'd think of her sometimes—if he'd think she was a bad mom for not being there as he grew up. Maybe life wouldn't look that different without her. Maybe he'd already learned not to need her. The thought made her chest twist until she couldn't breathe.

She set her jaw. No. She wouldn't let that be the story. Not for him. Not for her. She would find a way—no shortcuts, no desperation, no blind panic. She would do it *the right way.* Her fingers closed around the shackle again. The metal was cold, but her resolve wasn't.

She let out a shaky breath and whispered into the stillness, "God... you better not have me here for ten years." Her voice trembled with a bitter kind of humor. "I don't understand You. I don't understand why You took my dad. Or why You let this happen—why You let me get kidnapped at all. None of it makes sense."

Her eyes stung. "But I guess... asking for help's better than nothing."

The words hung in the air like a fragile truce—half anger, half plea.

Joseph waited, she reminded herself again, quieter this time. *And he was freed.*

Maybe, just maybe, someone was still listening.

***

Paula leaned over the counter at the nurses' station, finishing up her charting. The hospital shift was finally slowing down. Monitors still beeped, and someone was yelling for discharge papers down the hall, but the chaos had thinned to a manageable simmer. Her scrubs were rumpled, and a wisp of hair had slipped from her bun, but her focus was sharp as ever.

Tasha rolled over in a wheeled chair, sipping a pink smoothie through a metal straw. "You already know what I'm gonna ask." She grinned

Paula didn't look up. "Don't."

"I am, though. Any man in your life yet, or are we still married to the job?"

"Definitely still married," Paula said with a tired smile. "And the job is a jealous husband."

Tasha shook her head. "Mmm. Shame. You too fine to be goin' home to leftovers at an empty house. Somebody out there needs to be bringin' you flowers and cookin' you dinner."

Paula laughed. "My mom would agree with you. She's been trying to set me up. Said she reconnected with an old friend from church—apparently her son and I used to play together as toddlers."

Tasha raised a brow. "Oh, we talkin' a family friend setup? Does he have a job or just vibes?"

"He's a detective. Name's Gabriel."

"Ooh, a cop." Tasha sat up straighter. "That could go either way. You got a picture?"

Paula sighed and pulled out her phone, flipping through a few photos. She turned the screen toward Tasha.

Tasha squinted, then blinked. "Okay... wait. He's fine. Like... TV-drama fine."

Paula smirked. "Yeah, he's got the whole broody thing going on. But honestly? I mean, he looks... dense. Like the kind of guy who's really into himself and nothing else."

"Mmm." Tasha wagged her eyebrows. "You're into it, though."

"I didn't say that." Paula tucked her phone away. "I care more about personality. Values. You know—whether or not he's a decent person."

"Oh honey." Tasha slid off the chair and stretched. "You can't tell all that from just a picture now can you? And don't try to tell me you didn't smile the first time you saw it either."

Paula looked away, trying not to grin. "I just don't want to waste my time on someone who doesn't take people seriously. You know what I mean?"

Tasha smiled and tilted her head. "You know, I love that about you. I do. You're not thirsty out here like some of these folks. You've got standards. Look. It's not that I think you need anyone to make you complete—you're already the whole package. I just..." she shrugged, smiling. "I want to see you happy. You pour so much of yourself into other people, Paula. You deserve to be seen, too."

Paula took a breath, looking down at her phone again. "I'll think about it."

Tasha nudged her knee with her foot. "You better. And text that man back if he hits you up. I got a good feeling."

Paula stood and gathered her things. "Goodnight, Tasha."

"Night, girl. Tell Officer Fine I said hey."

20

The Conviction of Things Not Seen

The sun dipped low behind the city skyline, streaking the glass of his windshield with a dull orange glare. Gabriel squinted against it, the light catching on the hood of his car as he stood with his arms folded. The parking lot was mostly empty now—just the distant hum of traffic and the soft creak of engines cooling in the evening air. He exhaled slowly, jaw tight. Three hours spent chasing the same lead, and it had led him in circles. The kind of dead end that made his temples ache. He glanced toward Juliet's car as she locked it, her reflection warping across the glass, and for a moment he wondered if she was as tired of all this as he was.

She approached, tossing a manila folder into her passenger seat. "Well," she said, her tone flat but not unkind. "Another thrilling evening of nothing."

Gabriel grunted. "Kidnappers who leave no digital trace, no ransom, no pattern. Almost makes you nostalgic for the dumb ones."

She shot him a look over the roof of the car. "We'll get him. He's sloppy somewhere. They always are."

He nodded, though his jaw was tight. "Yeah. Just wish that crack would show up sooner than later."

Juliet closed her door gently and turned to him. "Go home, Ramos. Eat something. Sleep. You're no good to anyone at forty percent."

He rolled his eyes. "I'm still at least a solid sixty-eight."

She smirked. "Then go give the rest to someone who cares." With that, she got in and started the engine, leaving him standing there with a faint grin.

As she pulled out of the lot, Gabriel exhaled and reached for his keys—but just as his hand touched the door, his phone buzzed in his pocket. He slid it out.

A text from his mother: *Well?? Have you texted her yet or are you waiting for divine intervention?*

Gabriel huffed a laugh through his nose. Classic. No greeting. No punctuation except for the question marks. Just straight to the point, with that signature mix of nosy and endearing. He stared at the message for a second, then unlocked his phone and opened her contact. Paula. No messages yet. Just the number his mom had forwarded with a little winking emoji, like she was handing him a secret weapon. He leaned back against the car and stared up at the darkening sky. She worked emergency medicine. Busy life. Probably didn't need a stranger popping into her phone just because two bored moms had run out of hobbies. Still... his mom was rarely wrong about people.

He opened a new message. Hovered for a second. Then typed:

Hey. I'm Gabriel. Apparently we've been scheduled for marriage by our mothers. Should we meet for coffee first, or just skip to picking out curtains?

He hit send before he could think better of it. The screen flashed back to silence. He slid the phone into his pocket, pushed off the car, and finally headed home.

***

The deadbolt clicked behind her as Paula stepped inside, flipping on the lights with her elbow. The apartment greeted her with its usual silence—tidy, calm, untouched. The kind of place that always looked like it was waiting for someone else to arrive. She slipped off her shoes and dropped her bag by the door before heading to the kitchen. The fridge opened with a quiet sigh, revealing rows of neatly stacked containers, labeled by day in black marker.

She eyed a carton of eggs, a bundle of asparagus, a forgotten block of feta. "I could make something...but why."

Too tired to even pretend. She reached for the Tuesday container—grilled chicken, roasted zucchini, sweet potato mash. Serviceable. Emotionally uninspired. She peeled back the lid and tossed it in the microwave, leaning against the counter as the machine hummed to life. Then—*ding.* Her phone lit up on the counter. A number she didn't recognize. She tapped it open and blinked at the screen. A half-laugh escaped her before she caught herself. Bold. Definitely bold. Maybe even funny—if it didn't come with that undertone of someone a little too sure of himself. She set the phone down, crossing her arms as the microwave beeped behind her.

So this is him. She could practically hear the smirk through the text. Typical. A detective with a sense of humor and an ego to match. Three little dots appeared like he was already typing something else. *Of course he is.* She rolled her eyes. She grabbed the hot container from the microwave, the plastic bending slightly in her hands, and slid it onto the counter. A fork clinked against the rim of the drawer as she pulled one out and started eating, half-focused on the quiet rhythm of her own chewing and the hum of the fridge. Then—*buzz.* Gabriel again.

I'm kidding, by the way. Mostly.

She exhaled through her nose, somewhere between an amused sigh and an eye roll. *Of course he's kidding. Mostly.* The kind of half-joke that let a man flirt without the risk of rejection. Confident. Charming, in that *I know I'm charming* kind of way.

She turned back to her food, stirring it absently with her fork. The chicken tasted fine. Everything in her life was *fine.* Predictable. Organized. And now—apparently—some detective thought he could crash through that quiet with a smirk and a text about curtains. Her phone buzzed again against the counter. Not him this time—just a reminder from her mom's group chat. She glanced at the preview and immediately felt that familiar pull of obligation settle in her stomach. If she didn't reply to him, her mother would bring it up by tomorrow. Probably with that gentle *I'm not pressuring you, but...* tone that always meant the opposite.

Paula groaned softly and leaned her hip against the counter, staring at the phone again.

She could ignore him. Pretend she was busy. That would be easy enough.

But then she pictured her mom's face—bright, expectant, *hopeful*—and knew she couldn't dodge it forever.

"Fine," she grumbled.

She picked up the phone and typed a quick reply:

Coffee's fine. Just don't bring curtain samples.

Her thumb hovered for a second. Then she hit send. A small smile tugged at her lips as she locked the screen. There. Message sent. Obligation fulfilled. Now she could go back to her dinner—and to pretending she wasn't a little curious about what he'd say next.

I see you're trying to keep this professional. That's fine. I'll bring a clipboard.

She snorted, a mouthful of zucchini almost slipping the wrong way. Setting her fork down, she shook her head and typed:

That confidence is impressive. Do they give you a mug for it at detective school, or is it just something in the water over there?

She hit send, a crooked smile tugging at her lips. So far, he was more fun than she expected.

***

Gabriel lay flat on his back, still in his jeans, one arm draped over his forehead. The ceiling fan hummed above him, steady and slow, the only thing moving in the room. He should've showered an hour ago. Should've eaten something more substantial than the protein bar he'd grabbed from the glovebox. But his body had called it quits somewhere between paperwork and traffic lights. Her message lit up his phone on the nightstand. A low laugh escaped him—quiet but real. It had been a while since a woman made him laugh at all. He grabbed the phone, propping himself up on an elbow as he read it again. Sarcastic. Sharp. Not afraid to jab back. He thumbed out a reply, but paused halfway through, letting the phone fall back against his chest. God, when was the last time he actually felt... interested? Not out of boredom, not out of loneliness, but genuinely curious about someone?

Most of the women he'd met in the past were the same story told in different voices. Shallow conversations that went nowhere. Too busy talking about themselves to ask a single real question. A few with drama wrapped in court dates and *Can you talk to the judge for me?* texts. And then there were the ones who were walking red flags—beautiful enough to keep him hooked long after he should've known better. He'd grown tired of it. All of it. Paula felt different. There was color to her—texture, depth. He unlocked his mom's message thread and scrolled up. There she was again, in scrubs, laughing at something off camera. That same easy confidence. Not that he *knew* her; nobody really knows someone through a photo and a few playful messages. But something about her tone, her restraint, the way she carried herself even in that one shot... it hinted at substance. Years on the job had sharpened his instinct for reading people, and something in his gut told him—this one was real.

He couldn't admit it—not to his mom, not even to himself—but he found Paula wildly attractive. The kind of beautiful that didn't need effort. The kind that made his stomach flip just thinking about her looking at him the way she looked in that photo. He smirked at the thought of how smug his mom would be if this actually went somewhere. She'd probably make a speech at the wedding. He could already hear it:

"You see? Moms know best."

Still smiling, he thumbed out his reply.

A mug, a badge, and a free subscription to people crossing the street when they see me coming.

He hit send and dropped the phone onto his chest again, watching the screen dim to black. For the first time in a long time, he felt... optimistic. Tired, yes. But hopeful. And that felt like something worth staying awake for. After a couple minutes watching the ceiling fan spin, his smile faded before he realized it had. Because no matter how hard he tried to turn it off, the job always crept back in. His thoughts drifted—uninvited—to Angela. The missing mother. The one whose photo had been staring at him from the case board all week. He rolled onto his side, the glow of his phone screen still lighting the room. Her picture was there—the same one they'd used in the press release. Bright smile. Warm eyes. The kind of woman who looked approachable, steady. But he knew better than to take a picture at face value.

He'd asked the usual questions: boyfriends, admirers, anyone who might've taken an interest in her. Every answer had come back the same—*No one.* Her coworkers said she was warm, friendly even—but there was a line. Angela kept people at arm's length. Smiled easily, but never let anyone in too far. A few friends mentioned she could open up after a drink or two, that she had a fun, almost reckless streak when she loosened up. But most of the time, she was private. Guarded.

When he'd asked about Phoenix's father, Angela's mom had gone quiet. The kind of quiet that said she'd been waiting for the question but still hoped it wouldn't come.

"It was just a one-night stand," she'd said after a long pause, voice low. "Back in college. She told me she was drunk and didn't really know him. I tried to press her about it, told her she deserved to have the father in the picture, that he should take responsibility..."

She'd sighed then, eyes glistening but steady. "But every time I brought it up, she'd shut down. Get angry. She didn't want to talk about it. Said it was a mistake she just wanted to forget."

That answer had stayed with him.

Afterward, he'd done some digging—old yearbooks, social media trails, tagged photos. Most of her college friends said the same thing. They hadn't heard from Angela in years. Somewhere between graduation and the pregnancy, she'd gone quiet. No fights. No falling-outs. Just... distance. And then she built a careful little life—work, her son, her mother—like she was holding the world together with both hands.

Gabriel exhaled, staring at the ceiling. He'd seen a hundred missing persons cases, but this one... this one gnawed at him. Angela's case had dug its hooks in deep. He unlocked his phone again, thumb hovering before opening the browser. He had a need to *see* something he might've missed. Her son, Phoenix, was three. That put the conception around her junior year—spring or maybe early summer. He typed in the name of Angela's university, scrolling through old local news reports. And then he saw it.

Student Found Dead Near Fraternity Row — Police Investigating Possible Robbery.

The date—mid-March, 2014—made his stomach tighten. Not far from when Phoenix would've been conceived. He skimmed the short article. The victim's name jumped out: Tyler Van Daalen, twenty-two years old. Police suspected a robbery gone wrong. His wallet was missing. No murder weapon recovered. He'd been stabbed several times, the piece said. No suspect identified. Gabriel stared at the screen, the faint blue glow washing over his face. He didn't believe in coincidences. Not anymore.

Angela had gotten pregnant that same year, from a man she claimed not to know. Every time her mother pressed her, she'd shut down—angry, defensive, done. Maybe she *had* known the father. He sighed, letting the phone fall to his chest. The fan kept turning overhead, slow and rhythmic, as if ticking down to something inevitable. A robbery. A stabbing. A pregnancy. And now—a disappearance. He closed his eyes for a moment, listening to the hum of the fan. It wasn't adding up. Not yet. But somewhere in that blur of past and present, something was waiting to be found. He'd follow up on it later, maybe run the name *Tyler Van Daalen* through the old case files, see if anything had ever made it off the books. But not tonight. He'd spent enough of his evening chasing ghosts.

His eyes drifted to the phone still resting on his chest. Somewhere between the silence and the fan's slow hum, Paula's name floated back into his mind like a welcome distraction. He smiled to himself—small, tired, but real. Maybe he didn't need to solve anything right now. Maybe he could just... text the girl. He unlocked the screen, thumb hovering for a beat before he opened their thread. He started typing.

I know a place with good coffee and better food if you're game.

He hit send, exhaled, and let the phone fall back against his chest. He closed his eyes again and sleep crept in slowly, wrapping itself around the hum of the fan.

21

Every Secret Will Be Brought to Light

Fluorescent lights buzz overhead as Marshall stood motionless in front of a towering wall of deodorants. His good eye squinted at the labels: *invisible solid, gel, aluminum-free, ultra-fresh, shea butter, sport cool, wild rose, lavender rain*—it was like reading a foreign language. He shifted his weight, the bandage over his eye itching slightly. A few shoppers passed behind him, casting quick, uncertain glances. He knew he looked out of place—too tense, too stiff. Too broken to be standing between *Cool Glacier* and *Coconut Dreams*.

He muttered under his breath, "How many damn types of deodorant are there?"

His fingers hovered over one of the brands. Then he hesitated. *Does gel even work better? Or is that just marketing? What if it irritates her skin? What if it smells weird?* He closed his eyes briefly and exhaled. *I can't just text her. Idiot.*

"Hi there!" a voice chirped suddenly to his right.

Marshall jolted.

A young woman—store apron, name tag that said *MELISSA*, hair in a messy ponytail—was smiling brightly at him like he'd just been chosen for a prize. "Sorry!" she said quickly, holding up her hands. "Didn't mean to sneak up on you. Just saw you kind of... I don't know, you've been locked in deodorant battle stance for like five minutes. Need a hand?"

Marshall straightened up, instinctively inching back half a step. "Uh... I'm fine."

Melissa tilted her head, scanning him with a casual kind of curiosity. "Shopping for someone?"

His mouth opened, then closed. He nodded. "Yeah. She didn't tell me what kind."

"Oof. That's tough," Melissa said with mock sympathy. "Okay, well—does she usually go for something fresh and sporty? Or more floral? Or like, cocoa-buttery, vanilla, kind of warm and cozy?"

"I... don't know."

"Well, let's break it down!" she said, already grabbing a couple from the shelf. "See, gels dry quicker, but some people hate the texture. Then there's the solids, which last longer but might leave residue, unless you go invisible. Now *these* are aluminum-free—super popular lately, but they don't always hold up if someone's really active. I actually use this lavender one—it's calming, smells amazing, and it doesn't clash with perfume, which is a big plus—"

Marshall stared at her, his expression frozen in quiet horror. *Please stop talking. Please stop. I just want to leave.*

She held up two options. "So between these, I'd say if she's sensitive to scent, go with the green tea aloe. But if she's a 'power through the shift' kinda girl? Probably this one."

He gave a small nod, reaching out and taking one—more to make her stop than because he had made a decision.

"Great pick," Melissa beamed. "Hope she likes it."

He mumbled, "Thanks" and walked off, clutching the deodorant like he just defused a bomb. Marshall stepped into line, deodorant in hand, joining the slow-moving queue that snaked toward the lone open register.

A toddler screamed somewhere in the toy aisle. An old man argued with the cashier about a coupon that expired last year. Marshall exhaled hard through his nose. He glanced down at the item in his hand. Pink and green. *Soothing Aloe & Cotton Calm.* Not something he'd ever imagine himself buying. Not something he ever thought he'd need to buy. *This is what people do,* he thought. *They look after each other. Buy stupid stuff. Ask questions. Wait in line.* It all felt so foreign. So... normal. And normal, to him, was still a strange and dangerous thing.

He pulled out his phone and tapped the screen. 7:13 PM. His stomach sank. The ammo shop closed at seven. He rubbed a hand over his face, the bandage brushing against his cheek. He hadn't even wanted to go—*not really.* But still, he'd meant to. He just hadn't expected to get stuck in an aisle debating botanical scent profiles with a girl who smiled too much. *Maybe that's a good thing,* he thought. Or maybe it just delayed the inevitable. He pocketed the phone and stepped forward as the line inched ahead, still not sure which answer scared him more.

***

Angela sat cross-legged on the bed, the muted basketball game flickering across the screen. Her eyes weren't on the score—they were fixed on the tiny game clock in the corner, tracking each minute like a metronome. He'd been gone a while. Longer than it should've taken. The second quarter had started. Then halftime. Now midway through the third. She didn't want to admit it, but the waiting gnawed at her. She'd kept her cool earlier, even teased him. But now that she was alone again, every passing minute scraped at her nerves.

Then—*thump.* A soft noise overhead. Footsteps. The creak of the upstairs floorboards. He was back. Angela sat up straighter, adjusting the blanket across her lap. She muted the TV just as the basement door opened. Marshall walked down, his expression blank, one hand clutching a plastic bag like it was something far more fragile than deodorant. He crossed the room and held it out to her awkwardly.

She took it, peeled back the top, and pulled out the pale green stick. A pause. She read the label aloud, dryly, "Soothing Aloe & Cotton Calm… huh."

Marshall's shoulders stiffened just slightly. His mouth opened like he might defend the choice, then shut again.

Angela looked up at him, let the silence stretch, then cracked a small smile. "My grandmother used to use this exact one." She waited just long enough for the panic to flicker in his eye— Then added gently, "She always smelled amazing."

The tension in his jaw softened a touch.

She twisted the cap open, sniffed. "Yep. Smells like old ladies and clouds." She gave him a faint but genuine smile. "Thanks." She stood, crossed to the far side of the room where she'd left her sweatshirt draped over a chair, and began applying the deodorant like it was the most luxurious product on earth. Without turning, she said casually, "You've looked like you wanted to say something all day. You changed your mind, or just chickened out?" She glanced over her shoulder, arching a brow. "Come on. I saw that look. What were you gonna say?"

Marshall stood in place like someone caught under a spotlight. For a long moment, he didn't answer. Then, finally, he sighed and sat down—on the floor, of all places—leaning back against the wall, legs bent, arms resting on his knees. "My mom used this exact brand. Same scent. Didn't even realize until you read it out loud."

Angela's brow knit as she turned back around, slower now. "She still wears it?" she asked gently, already suspecting the answer.

"She doesn't wear anything for herself now. She's... not really there anymore. Been that way for a long time."

She sat back down across from him, curling her legs beneath her.

"She took care of me," he said, eyes distant. "As best she could. Even when she was hurting. So I take care of her now. That's how it's supposed to work, right? You don't just walk away from people."

"A lot of people *do* walk away. More than you'd think. Plenty don't lift a finger when their parents get old or sick. But you've been doing it for years—without complaint, like it's just... normal." She looked at him, really looked at him. "That says something about you, Marshall. Something good." Angela tapped the deodorant gently against her palm. "You know, for someone who kidnapped me, you've got an awfully noble streak."

He actually chuckled—small, breathy, like it surprised even him. "That's not the word most people would use."

"Well, I like to be original." She shrugged. "What would they say?"

Marshall leaned his head back against the wall, staring up at the ceiling like it held something he couldn't quite name. "When I was a kid," he said, voice low, "I used to count the seconds between my father's footsteps.

That sound—his boots on the floorboards—used to make my stomach turn. Sometimes I'd try to breathe quietly, like maybe he'd forget I was there if I made myself small enough."

Her expression softened as he went on.

"He'd hit her over nothing. A burnt dinner. A wrong look. Once, just because he answered the phone and heard a man on the other end asking for her by name..." his voice caught, "She'd cry and apologize like it was *her* fault. Every time." His hand curled loosely on his knee. "I thought if I was good enough, fast enough, quiet enough... he'd stop."

A beat of silence.

Then, after a long breath:

Marshall told her about the other murder—Dr. Marlowe.

Not in vivid detail—he clearly didn't want to relive it—but enough for her to understand. The anger. The fear. The twisted sense of protection that had driven him. He didn't brag. He didn't justify. He just told her. Like someone finally unloading a weight they weren't sure they were allowed to carry anymore.

Angela didn't move. Not a breath. Not a blink. Her mind was a storm behind the stillness—heart pounding so hard she could feel it in her throat, her pulse echoing in her ears like a warning drum. Another person dead. Because of her. Because of *him*. She forced her face to stay soft, curious even, as though she hadn't just heard the most horrifying confession of her life. If she so much as flinched, he'd see it.

So she exhaled, slow and steady, setting the deodorant down beside her with deliberate calm. "That must've been hard," she said gently. "Carrying that. You ever think maybe you weren't born broken? Maybe you were just... taught the wrong way to love?"

Her voice didn't shake. It sounded warm, sympathetic, the way she'd talk to a wounded animal that might bite if startled. He blinked at her, caught off guard.

"You were trying to protect someone. I get that." She leaned forward just slightly, letting her tone drop into something tender. "You've been protecting people your whole life, haven't you?"

That made him look up. A flicker of confusion—or maybe gratitude—passed through his eyes. She held the look, gave him a small, crooked smile. Inside, she wanted to scream. Her stomach churned, her fingers ached from how tightly she was gripping her own knees. But she didn't let it show.

Instead, she tilted her head, just enough to make her voice sound lighter. "You know," she said, teasingly, "for someone who says he's the bad guy, you don't make it easy to believe."

Marshall blinked. "You don't think I'm a bad guy?"

Angela's lips parted like she was about to say something real—but then she caught herself, letting the silence draw out instead. Finally, she smiled—small, knowing. "I think you've done bad things. But I don't think that's *all* you are."

He looked at her for a long time, studying her face like he was searching for the lie underneath it. Then, quietly, "You're not scared of me anymore?"

Angela froze. Her mind scrambled for the right answer—one that wouldn't sound rehearsed, or worse, patronizing. A lie would be too obvious. He'd feel it in her tone, see it in her eyes. So she took a breath, forcing her heartbeat to slow, letting her voice find that careful middle ground between honesty and control.

Her smile lingered a second too long before fading, softening into something vulnerable. "Of course I am," she said finally. "You kidnapped me. That's not something I just forget."

She watched his expression shift—something in his shoulders tightening, a shadow flickering behind his eyes. For a heartbeat she thought she'd gone too far.

"But..." she added, leaning forward slightly, her tone gentling. "I've also seen what you're like when you're not listening to the voices in your head."

Marshall's jaw moved like he was chewing on her words, testing them for sincerity. Slowly, he nodded.

Angela kept her gaze steady, even though every instinct screamed to look away.

"I see the man," she said softly. "Not just the monster."

The words left a strange taste in her mouth—half truth, half survival. But if it meant keeping him calm... it was worth it.

22

Some Have Entertained Angels

Thousands of years ago, a vast chamber of Heaven shimmered with a serene, pulsing light—its marble columns tall as mountains, veined with gold and starlight. Everything breathed order, calm, and resonance. At the heart of it stood the archangel Raphael, his frame compact but formidable, the kind of strength forged for speed, clarity, and decisive action. His wings—folded tightly—still glowed faintly from a recent descent. Uriel stood across from him, arms behind his back, posture as precise as his mind. His expression was calm, but his eyes missed nothing.

Raphael spoke without pleasantries, his tone clipped but respectful. "There are whispers rising from the plains west of the Euphrates. Not prayers. Not praises." He glanced to the side. "Reports say they're *chanting.* Making offerings to something that does not bear the Name."

Uriel's brow lowered. "A false god?"

Raphael nodded. "Something new. Serpent-shaped, they say. They are building and progressing at a rapid, unnatural pace. They've built shrines, temples, and structures the likes of which humanity has not yet seen in its history."

Uriel's jaw tightened.

Raphael's gaze sharpened. "That's not all. They've also begun forging tools of war. Weaponry that should lie outside the realm of their current understanding. Blades. Shields. Armor."

Uriel stilled. A beat passed before he asked, carefully, "You want me to go?"

Raphael inclined his head. "I want you to *walk* among them. As one of them."

Uriel's eyes flickered with alarm. "That would mean... complete concealment. Not even a trace of angelic presence. No glow. No Voice. Not even the knowing."

Raphael looked at the smooth floor beneath them. "Something is twisting their hearts. Too focused. Too coordinated. Too fast. We need to know where it leads."

Uriel's voice dropped. "You think one of us is down there."

Raphael didn't flinch. "I think there's a reason they're worshipping something shaped like *that*."

Silence hung between them like a suspended blade.

Uriel's wings bristled, then settled. "I'll go."

Raphael gave a faint nod. "Remiel will join you. He's already preparing."

Uriel raised an eyebrow, imagining Remiel's massive frame and imposing presence. "Remiel? He is not usually sent on these types of assignments. He doesn't exactly blend."

"No," Raphael said, allowing the slightest edge of dry humor. "But you'll need someone at your side you can trust."

Uriel turned, already mentally mapping the descent.

Raphael's voice followed after him. "Be careful, Uriel. If this is what we fear... you may be walking into more than human heresy."

Uriel paused at the edge of the chamber, his voice calm but heavy with purpose. "If a serpent is behind this... I'll find its den." He gave Raphael a final determined look. Then turned—his form dissolving into quiet radiance as he descended from Heaven.

***

Dust rose in soft swirls around Uriel's and Remiel's feet as they stepped through the village in the Levant's sunbaked paths. The air was dry, heavy with the scent of smoke, clay, and something more subtle—*ash and incense.* The village itself was primitive but organized. Mud-brick homes lined the main road, and every visible surface—walls, pottery, even carved fenceposts—was adorned with images of snakes. Coiled, slithering, crowned. Their shapes varied, but their presence was inescapable.

Remiel, taller and broader than his companion, kept his hood up, golden eyes lowered. His silence was not from discomfort—it was caution. Even cloaked in humanity, power whispered around him like a scent. Uriel moved with the ease of someone used to blending. His human form was lean, sun-worn, with steady eyes that watched everything. They approached a small stall made of reeds and stone, where a woman—maybe mid-thirties, wrapped in faded linen—was arranging a display of carved idols. All of them serpents. Uriel picked one up. It was surprisingly intricate. The serpent had wings—small, feathered ones folded along its back—and two black stones for eyes.

The woman noticed him studying it and spoke, her voice a little wary. "You're not from here."

Uriel met her gaze calmly. "We travel. Bringing goods between river and hill."

He gestured toward Remiel, who wordlessly set down a bundle and untied it. Inside were fine linens—undyed, neatly folded.

Her eyes flicked over the fabric, impressed despite herself. "Merchants, then," she said, relaxing. "Most who come here ask for food or shelter. Not many bring anything worth trading."

Uriel tilted the snake idol. "And these? They sell well?"

She smiled, pleased. "They sell faster than I can shape them. Everyone wants one now. Every house, every man, woman, and child."

He set it down gently. "What's the meaning of it? The serpent?"

The woman straightened proudly, brushing her hands on her tunic. "It's not just a symbol. It's *truth.*" She leaned forward slightly. "You must not have heard—gods came down from the sky. They glowed like fire and walked like men."

Uriel and Remiel exchanged a subtle glance.

"They taught us so many things—how to build with strength, how to organize, how to keep peace through law. And they told us the true god is not the one of wind or sky or flame—but the *serpent.* His name is *Kosheck.*" The name fell from her lips with reverence, hunger.

Uriel's voice was still gentle. "And these gods—do they still walk among you?"

"Not openly," she said, gaze distant. "But they return. In dreams. In visions. And the high one—the first to descend—he still visits the temple beyond the trees. He walks with the elders."

Before Uriel could respond, a deep, *resonant horn* rang out across the village. It came from the east, near the edge of the settlement, and was followed by murmurs, footsteps, and the sound of dozens of people beginning to gather.

The woman stood straighter. "It's time. The Voice will speak." She gave Uriel one last look. "If you wish to trade, come back tomorrow. No one barters during the summoning." And then she disappeared into the stream of villagers, leaving the angels behind.

Uriel's voice was low. "It's worse than we feared."

Remiel's expression was hard. "And not just men behind it."

They followed the crowd, silent and watchful, toward the edge of town— toward the source. The sun had slipped behind the treeline, casting the village in a burnt orange haze. The people gathered in a wide circle at the edge of the settlement, where the ground was scorched black from many fires and ritual burnings. Dust clung to bare feet and hems. Children clutched their mothers. Men stood silently, heads bowed. At the center of it all stood the High Priest. His robe was deep red, the color of dried blood, with black trim swirling along the cuffs and collar. A black serpent had been meticulously painted across his back, coiled in an eternal loop, fangs bared mid-strike. Around his eyes and down his cheeks, black makeup fanned out like scales or claws, casting sharp shadows across his gaunt features. Beside him stood five lesser priests, their robes plain red, unadorned. They formed a loose semicircle around him, reverent and silent.

The High Priest lifted a gnarled black staff topped with a stone carved like an open serpent's mouth. His voice cut through the murmuring crowd with sharp authority. "People of Kosheck—blessed children of the true flame— tonight we remember our gratitude."

The crowd murmured, "Praise Kosheck."

"We remember the gods who came in fire and thunder to tear the veil from our eyes. Who showed us the mystery of law. Of form and architecture. Of power."

"Praise Kosheck."

"And we remember the price of knowledge. For what is given must be returned. As they lit our minds, so we light the path with sacrifice." He turned, pacing slowly, letting his words settle like ash over the gathering. "Once a year, we offer thanks. But the gods are generous. They have gifted us an early tribute."

Two robed servants stepped out from the edge of the trees, dragging behind them Jared and Leah. Their hands were bound. Faces streaked with dirt. Fear radiated off them like heat.

Gasps rippled through the crowd. A few turned away. Most did not.

The priest raised his voice. "They were found in the forest—feral and faithless. Hiding from our light. Brought back to us by divine grace, the survivors of the village we burned in offering."

Leah sobbed, twisting against her ropes. Jared gritted his teeth, shoulders taut.

"But even the lost have purpose. Even the defiant can serve. And tonight, they will. Their blood will call down favor. Wisdom. Peace."

Among the crowd, Uriel and Remiel stood at the outermost ring. Both in plain, earthen clothes, their divine forms perfectly hidden behind the veil. Remiel's jaw clenched, hands twitching at his sides. His eyes never left the children.

Uriel shifted subtly, just enough to put a hand near Remiel's wrist—low, invisible to others. "Not yet. We need to see it through. Find the root. If we reveal ourselves now, the corruption retreats underground."

Remiel didn't speak. His breathing was tight, nostrils flared.

Uriel's gaze returned to the priest, and he whispered beneath his breath. "But if the knife is drawn..." He didn't finish the thought.

Because if the knife was drawn, they would both know exactly what would come next.

Jared stared up at the High Priest, trembling but unbroken. Then, with a sudden roar, he lunged forward against his restraints, voice cracked with rage. "You're liars! You burned our homes! You killed our family! You call it sacrifice, but you're just murderers—*cowards* hiding behind your serpent god!"

The crowd stiffened. A few gasped. One woman began to cry softly, but no one stepped forward. The lesser priests surged in, grabbing the boy by the shoulders, wrenching him back down to his knees. He thrashed once, hard, then sagged forward—exhausted, panting, eyes wild.

The High Priest turned slowly, eyes locked on him. He stepped forward without a word, staff dragging lightly through the dust. Jared raised his head, breathing like a hunted animal, fury still burning in his gaze. With no warning, the priest jammed the butt of the staff hard into Jared's stomach. He collapsed instantly, coughing, retching, folded over. Then came the first blow—a strike across the face with the crook of the staff. Then another. And another. *Crack. Crack. Crack.* The sound of bone and wood echoed across the clearing.

Jared fell fully to the ground, his lip split, blood dripping into the dust.

The crowd did nothing.

But Leah screamed. "Stop it!" She twisted, then slipped free of one of the priests holding her. She stumbled forward, and she dropped to her knees, shielding her brother's body with her own. The High Priest raised the staff again—then froze mid-swing.

She looked up at him, eyes brimming with tears—but defiant. Her eyes were blue. Not sky blue. Not gray. A rare, radiant sapphire that looked luminous in the fading light.

He lowered the staff slowly, his expression shifting. Curiosity. Awe. Hunger. His voice dropped low, soft as it was sinister. "Look at you..." He crouched slightly, reaching out with bony fingers, cupping her face.

She flinched, but didn't move.

He turned her chin this way and that. "A gift from Kosheck. A sign. Your eyes... You are set apart." He stood tall again and raised his voice. "This one will not be sacrificed." He pointed toward the temple beyond the trees.

"Take her. Prepare her for the Serpent's blessing."

Two of the robed priests moved in, gripping her arms.

"NO!" she screamed, twisting violently. "Let me go—*leave him alone!*"

The High Priest gave a casual flick of his hand. The remaining priests lifted Jared by the arms, dragging his limp form across the earth, a trail of blood marking their path.

He was still conscious—barely—but his eyes searched wildly, trying to find his sister. "Leah—!"

She shrieked and fought, trying to get to him, feet dragging as the priests pulled her in the opposite direction.

Uriel's fists clenched. Remiel stepped forward instinctively.

Uriel blocked him with a single arm. "Not yet. We follow them. We find the Voice. The source."

The cult procession began moving toward the distant temple in the forest, red robes swaying, chants rising low in their throats. And the angels, hidden in mortal skin, followed the serpent's trail into the trees.

***

Thousands of years later, Uriel followed James. His latest assignment, working hard in the ammunition factory. The machines beat like a heart out of rhythm—heavy, relentless, weary. Their pulse echoed through the steel bones of the factory, through the air thick with grease and metal, through the men who moved like ghosts in fluorescent light. To Uriel, it all sounded wrong. The cadence of creation was supposed to be alive, full of purpose and breath—but here, the rhythm was dying, dragging itself forward through smoke and fatigue. His eyes—in human form for now—settled on James. The man worked in silence, movements slow and stiff, pain etched into every motion. Uriel could feel the tremor in his spirit before he saw the tremor in his hands. There was a fracture there, deep and widening—a wound that no medicine on earth could close.

When James finally abandoned his station, no one noticed. No one ever did. Uriel followed at a distance, his boots making no sound against the concrete. The hallway beyond the lockers was narrow, forgotten, as though the world itself had turned its back on it. Dust clung to the air like old sorrow. James

185

reached into his pocket. The crinkle of foil was a small, desperate sound.

"Just enough to get through the shift," he said under his breath.

The lighter flared—an ember against the dim. He breathed in, shoulders slumping, and for a moment the weight slipped off him. The pain dulled, but so did everything else. His heartbeat slowed. His spirit dimmed. And that was when Uriel stepped closer. He didn't arrive with light or trumpet or flame. He simply was like any normal man, though hiding away his angelic soul. A quiet warmth filled the empty corridor, a flicker of Heaven in the gray. His borrowed body leaned against the far wall, arms folded, face calm. No halo, no fire. Just eyes that saw too deeply to be human.

James blinked, startled. "Hey—what the hell? You follow me back here?" His voice cracked, defensive. "You with security or something?"

Uriel's lips curved faintly. "No. I came to find you."

Suspicion rippled through the man's features. "You from inspection or something?"

"No."

"HR?"

Another quiet, "No."

James wiped his nose, straightening like a cornered animal trying to look fierce. "You saw me, didn't you? You saw what I just did."

Uriel didn't answer. Silence hung between them, heavy as truth.

James's voice wavered. "Look, I'm not hurting anybody, all right? I get my work done. I keep my head down. You don't have to report this."

Uriel pushed off the wall, the motion deliberate, gentle. "I'm not here to report you," he said softly. "I'm not here to judge you." He meant it. Every word.

And though James couldn't see it, light shimmered faintly in the corner of Uriel's eyes—like dawn pressing against the edge of a storm.

James's jaw tightened, his voice rising with the edge of panic. "You said you came to find me. Why? Do they know? Am I getting tested or fired or what?"

Uriel didn't move. He let the man's words fall, heavy and trembling, before answering. His expression softened, the faintest ache flickering behind his calm. He looked at James and in that gaze was no threat, no trap, no authority that could punish or pardon. Only knowing.

"I meant you're not invisible," he said quietly. "Not forgotten. Not left behind. I meant that you... are still seen. Even here. Even now."

James froze. For a moment, he couldn't speak. The fight drained out of him, leaving only confusion and something fragile—something that hadn't dared rise in years. His shoulders sagged, and he slid down the wall until he was sitting, arms hanging loosely over his knees. No more words. The silence that settled wasn't empty—it was steady, patient, alive with the faint hum of something divine. James stared ahead, breathing slowly. And then—

"James? You hidin' on me again?"

Uriel turned his head first. The voice carried down the hall like a lifeline, bright and unashamed. Uriel recognized the voice instantly, one of James's few remaining friends. Brandon stood there, framed in the doorway. He was Black, mid-forties, built like a man who worked with his hands—thick arms, broad shoulders, a bit of a gut, and a calm presence that grounded the room. No flash. No drama. Just steady strength. He held a thermos in one hand and a sandwich wrapped in paper in the other. His uniform was just as stained, his eyes just as tired, but his smile was something rare: a choice made fresh every day.

"You missed lunch," Brandon said. "Figured I'd find you back here."

James blinked, caught off guard. He accepted the sandwich with a weak smile. "You're too good for this place."

"Nah," Brandon said, handing over the thermos. "Just stubborn." His grin softened. "You good?"

James hesitated. He turned his head, instinctively glancing to where Uriel had been, but there was no one there now. Just the gray wall, the hum of distant machines, and Brandon's quiet concern. Uriel had withdrawn the moment Brandon appeared, veiling his presence in the quiet way angels could—stepping just beyond the edge of perception. He didn't leave, not truly. He simply watched, unseen, as the moment unfolded on its own. There was no need for divine words now. What mattered was already happening: grace passing from one soul to another, freely given. It was enough.

James looked back down at the sandwich, fingers tightening around it. "Yeah," he said at last, voice faint but real. "I think I might be."

Brandon studied him for a moment longer, eyes steady, searching for what had changed. James's phone buzzed in his pocket. He sighed, pulled it out, and glanced at the screen. A text from his ex-wife.

James. The lawyer says you still haven't signed the release forms. If this doesn't get submitted this week we're going to have to reschedule court again. I'm tired of chasing you. Get it done.

James stared at it for a second, jaw tightening. "Of course. Perfect timing."

Brandon stepped a little closer. "You all right, man?"

James shook his head slightly and scoffed. "It's the ex. Wants more paperwork for the divorce. Like I haven't filled out enough crap already." He clicked the screen off with a hard tap, but the phone didn't go dark yet—his lock screen came up instead.

A photo: two kids, Colin and Hailey, both grinning wide with painted faces—one with a superhero mask, the other with a glittery crown. A carnival in the background. James's hand could be seen at the edge of the frame, steadying the camera. He stared at it for a long moment, his face softening as the pain beneath the anger surfaced. Brandon waited quietly, letting the silence speak first.

Finally, James sighed. "I used to tuck them in every night. *Every* night. Read them books. Got so good I could do the voices." He chuckled bitterly. "Now I get court dates and cold stares through glass."

Brandon sat beside him against the wall, his voice gentle. "They still know who their daddy is."

James's thumb hovered over the screen, brushing the side of the photo. "I don't even know if they *should.* I mean—look at me. I'm hiding in a hallway with junk in my lungs. And I still haven't signed the stupid papers 'cause some part of me thinks if I just keep not signing, it won't all be real."

Brandon nodded slowly. "Yeah, but real don't wait for us. And it sure don't care how wrecked we feel. You just gotta decide what *kind* of real you wanna live in."

James let out a breath. "I don't think I've made a good decision in years."

Brandon nudged him gently. "Then maybe that means you're due for one."

They sat there a while longer—just two men in coveralls, the low hum of the factory in the distance. The sandwich untouched. The phone dimmed. The silence honest. And somewhere nearby, unseen, Uriel watched. Not intervening. Not pressing. Just *being there*—like a soft light waiting patiently for the next right step.

"Well, if you need a place to be this Friday night, we got a spare seat. You don't have to sing, don't have to talk. Just sit there and breathe."

James looked down at the sandwich. His grip on it tightened slightly. He rubbed his temples, then let his head rest back against the wall. "So... this church thing. Why Friday? I thought church was for Sundays."

Brandon smiled, but it was a careful, measured smile—like he was walking on ice he didn't want to crack. "It's not a regular service. It's a group. Called *Celebrate Recovery.* Lotta folks from the church come, but it ain't like Sunday service. Nobody's passin' a plate or preachin' at you."

James lifted an eyebrow. "Celebrate *what*, exactly? That we all got screwed up lives?"

Brandon chuckled softly. "More like... we celebrate not being stuck in 'em."

James glanced sideways at him, suspicious. "So what—you think I belong in a recovery group now?"

Brandon reached down and tapped the floor between them. "I ain't tryin' to label you, James. I'm not your sponsor or your preacher or anything like that." He hesitated. "I'm just your friend. And I've been where you are."

James kept his eyes fixed forward, jaw clenched.

Brandon pulled his phone from his back pocket and unlocked it, flipping to a photo. "This is my wife, Janelle. And our daughter, Amiya. She just turned eight last month." He turned the screen toward James.

It was a sunlit photo, maybe taken at a park. His wife had her head thrown back in a laugh, and the little girl had cotton candy on her face and no idea it was there.

Brandon's voice dropped, quieter now. "Five years ago, I almost lost both of 'em."

James looked at him. "What happened?"

"Alcohol. Every night. Bottles in the truck. Bottles in the closet. Anger I didn't know what to do with. I missed birthdays, scared my little girl more than once. Thought I was holdin' everything together while I was really just draggin' it all down." He reached into his pocket again and pulled out his keys. Dangling from the ring was a small, worn metal chip, stamped with the number five. "Five years sober last month." He held it up—not like a trophy, but like a story. "I didn't get here overnight. And I sure as hell didn't get here alone."

James looked at the chip, then at the photo again. His expression twisted—something between envy and shame. "So now you think I'm where you were?"

Brandon shook his head. "I think you're where you are. And that's enough."

James exhaled slowly, eyes drifting back down to his own phone. The lock screen had gone dark again. He didn't turn it back on. "I'm not big on the whole testimony thing, man."

"You don't gotta be. Just come sit. Listen if you want. Leave if you want. You don't even have to say a word."

James stared ahead for a long moment. "I'll think about it."

Brandon gave a single nod. No pressure. No closing pitch. "That's all I ask." He stood and gave James a pat on the shoulder before heading back toward the line, whistling softly as he disappeared around the corner.

From where Uriel stood just beyond the veil, he watched James sit in silence, shoulders bowed under the weight that never fully left. But it was lighter now—just enough. He could feel it, the shift in the man's spirit, like a door cracked open to let a breeze in. When James rose, brushing the dust from his pants and tucking the sandwich away, Uriel remained hidden, letting the choice be his.

Then—James looked back. Not because he heard anything, not because he saw movement, but because something in him *knew.* Their eyes met again across the hallway. Uriel let himself be seen, just for a heartbeat. Still, calm, leaning against the wall as before. No words. Just a nod—gentle, approving.

You're not alone.

James blinked.

And Uriel let the moment fold closed. No rustle of wings, no flicker of light. Just stillness. But he left something behind. A warmth that wasn't heat. A presence that lingered even when it couldn't be named. The kind of knowing that stayed in the soul like a light under the door.

23

The Breadth and Length and Height and Depth

The overhead lamps cast long shadows along the sanctuary floor, like the ghosts of fallen saints watching in silence. James stepped into the dim church, the air hitting him with the twin scents of burnt coffee and lemon-scented disinfectant. It was too bright, too clean, too quiet. His eyes scanned the room—wooden pews, a crooked table stacked with pamphlets, and a faded sign taped to the wall: *Celebrate Recovery – All Welcome*. He rubbed his lower back, the familiar ache blooming just beneath the surface. He hadn't wanted to come. Still didn't. But Brandon had invited him—said this group was different. Said it was real. And now, Brandon was nowhere in sight. James hovered near the entrance, the door still half open behind him. He didn't know whether to sit or turn around and disappear.

Then came the voice. "First time?"

He turned. The man approaching was impossible to miss—tall, broad, with a long, gray beard down to his chest and a bald head that gleamed under the lights. His arms were bare despite the chill, and it wasn't out of bravado. It was intentional. His skin read like a confession—swastikas, SS bolts, Iron Crosses, white pride slogans, all faded but unmistakable. He made no effort to cover them. There was no shame in the display—just defiance. Or maybe... redemption. Because layered over the old hate were new markings.

A bleeding heart wrapped in thorns. A lamb beneath the shadow of a lion. A thick black cross scored over his chest like a seal. He hadn't erased his past. He was testifying to it.

The man smiled and offered a hand. "Name's Larry. Recovering from meth, pills, porn, gangs and everything in between. I'm also an avid stamp collector saved by grace and caffeine. You?"

James hesitated, then took the hand. Firm grip. Careful. "James. I... was supposed to meet someone. Brandon."

Larry's eyes lit up in recognition. "Brandon! Yeah, solid dude. Factory guy, right? Usually early. Must be on the late-freight tonight. Don't worry, he'll show."

James nodded, unsure what to do with his hands, his posture, or the pounding in his chest. The room didn't feel threatening—just tired. Like a place that had seen too many broken stories and wasn't surprised by any of them.

"Come on, grab a seat." Larry nodded toward the pews.

James eased into the wood, his back barking a fresh complaint. He sat near the edge, avoiding eye contact. The others didn't look at him either—but not out of coldness. More like familiarity. Like they remembered what it was to be the new one.

Larry stepped up to the pulpit, placed a thin black binder on top, and perched reading glasses on his nose. "Welcome to Crosspoint Church's Celebrate Recovery." His voice was steady but warm. "We're here to celebrate together as we journey toward transformation. My name is Larry, I'm a grateful believer in Jesus, walking in freedom from drugs, gangs, and just about every mistake you can make under the sun. Never got a parking ticket though. Didn't have many cars to park."

A few soft chuckles rustled through the room.

"Whether this is your first night or your hundredth, know this: Your story matters. Your scars matter. You matter." He lifted a metal ring strung with small plastic blue chips—like poker tokens, but sacred in their own way. "Any first-timers tonight?"

An awkward silence. Heads tilted subtly toward James. Larry scanned the room theatrically, as if he didn't already know. The silence stretched too long. James lifted his hand like someone volunteering for a firing squad.

Larry's face lit up. "Well come on up, sir!"

James stood stiffly, back flaring, and walked the longest twenty feet of his life to the front.

Larry's smile was patient and kind. "Tell us your name, and if you're comfortable... what brought you here?"

James swallowed. "Uh... I'm James. I was invited. A friend of mine, Brandon."

Right then, the church doors creaked open. A breeze and a few raindrops slipped in with the tall figure wiping water from his sleeves. Brandon. He caught James's gaze and gave a single nod before easing into the back pew. His knees popped as he sat. That simple glance grounded James more than the whole room had.

Larry placed the blue chip in James's open hand, a token signifying a new beginning in recovery. The gold lettering shimmered beneath the overhead lights – *The Journey Begins.*

"We're glad you're here, brother."

James nodded and turned back to the pews, shuffling to the back to sit beside Brandon.

Larry looked around. "Anyone else? No? All right, then." He closed the binder and took a breath. "Let tonight be about honesty, not shame. Change, not perfection. Hope, not hiding."

The words fell soft and weighty, like dust caught in sunlight.

James exhaled, some combination of relief and frustration slipping out of his lungs. "You're late," he muttered.

Brandon shrugged, settling deeper into the pew like a man who'd fought heavier battles than traffic. "I was emotionally on time."

James snorted—an involuntary sound, half laugh, half scoff. "What does that even mean?"

"It means," Brandon said, pulling a crumpled tissue from his jacket pocket, "I meant to be here, which in spiritual terms, counts for a lot."

James rolled his eyes but couldn't help the flicker of a smile that tugged at the corner of his mouth. "You owe me. That walk up to the front felt like I was being volunteered for the Hunger Games."

Brandon chuckled. "And yet you lived to tell the tale. Got yourself a chip and everything. Next thing you know you'll be holding hands in a prayer circle and crying into a Dixie cup."

James arched an eyebrow. "Is that… a rite of passage?"

"Nah. That's step four." Brandon leaned closer, voice dropping to a faux conspiratorial whisper. "Step five is admitting that you actually like Larry's coffee."

James glanced over at the table in the corner where a stained pot sat on a hot plate next to a stack of paper cups. The smell wafting from it had strong notes of battery acid and regret. "I'd rather confess to murder."

Brandon grinned. "Might go easier on your stomach."

Up front, Larry had moved on, talking about how healing wasn't a straight line but more like a roller coaster built by drunk raccoons. "Some weeks, you're up. Some weeks, you're upside down screaming."

James leaned back and let the words wash over him. The pain in his back was still there. The discomfort hadn't vanished. But the knot in his chest was starting to untangle. Just a little.

"Hey," Brandon said after a pause. "You came. That's not nothing."

James stared straight ahead, voice quiet. "It felt like nothing."

Brandon nodded. "That's how you know it mattered."

James looked over. "You always talk in fortune cookie riddles, or is that just a Friday thing?"

Brandon grinned. "Stick around. I've got a whole sermon in me about vending machines and forgiveness."

James smirked. For the first time that night, he wasn't thinking about leaving.

Larry clapped his hands once. "All right, folks. We're gonna move into open share time. Go ahead and bring yourselves up to the front rows—yes, even you in the back trying to disappear. I see you, Bob."

A few chuckles bubbled up. People began to shuffle forward, gathering their coffee cups and personal space issues as they made their way toward the front pews. James hesitated.

Brandon gave him a nudge with his elbow. "C'mon. The splash zone's up front."

James groaned softly but followed. The pew creaked as they sat.

Larry lifted his black binder again and adjusted his reading glasses. "Before we share, let's go over the guidelines. These aren't just rules, they're the reason we can do this without running for the exits halfway through."

James leaned over to Brandon and whispered, "What am I supposed to talk about?"

Brandon kept his eyes forward and deadpanned, "Whatever you want. Last week Larry spent fifteen minutes talking about his stamp collection and how it taught him about grace."

James blinked. "You're kidding."

Brandon held up a finger. "Direct quote: 'Even the damaged ones still have value.'"

James snorted. "That's either very deep or deeply concerning."

Brandon gave a slow nod. "That's the brand."

Up front, Larry began reading in his warm baritone, "Number one, keep your sharing focused on your own thoughts and feelings. Limit sharing to three to five minutes. We love you, but we love the clock, too."

Someone up front murmured, "Amen," and a soft ripple of laughter spread.

James settled back, the blue chip still in his pocket, a strange weight against his thigh. He didn't know what he was going to say. But maybe—maybe that wasn't the point.

Larry continued reading the guidelines, voice steady, calm. And around him, people nodded—not in agreement with everything, maybe, but in familiarity. Like worn travelers recognizing a signpost.

Brandon leaned closer. "First time's the worst time. After that, it's just awkward group therapy with donuts."

James whispered back, "Do we get donuts?"

Brandon shook his head. "Budget cuts. We get saltines."

"Spiritual suffering," James muttered.

"Deeply biblical," Brandon said with a smirk.

The group had clustered into the front pews, their posture somewhere between attentive and braced.

Larry gave a nod toward the pulpit. "All right, brothers. Let's get into open share. Who wants to kick us off?"

Brandon stood, slow and steady. He made his way to the pulpit with the ease of someone who'd done this before—not because it was easy, but because it mattered. "My name's Brandon. Grateful believer in Jesus. Five years clean from alcohol as of last Friday."

A few murmurs of approval echoed around the room. One guy offered a soft clap. Another gave a low, "Good work, man."

Brandon nodded. "It's wild. If you'd told me six years ago I'd be spending my Friday nights in church without a court order, I'd have laughed you straight out the plant."

A few chuckles broke the silence. Even Larry cracked a grin.

"But I'm here. Life's different now. Better. Not perfect. Still got a temper sometimes. Me and my wife been butting heads a little lately—nothing serious. Just dumb stuff. Dishes. Bills. She wants to get a dog, and I still haven't recovered from the last one chewing up my Jordans."

More laughter this time, low and knowing.

"But here's what's different. I don't storm out. I don't disappear to the bar. I stay. I sit in it. I try to talk. And if I mess up—and I do—I own it. That's a kind of freedom I never thought I'd know." He gave a short, humble nod and stepped back down, returning to the pew with the calm of a man who knew storms and still came back from them.

Then it was Greg. Late fifties, wiry build, faded work shirt tucked into jeans. He walked up to the pulpit like his destiny was calling him from it. "Name's Greg. Still trying to figure out what the hell I'm doing here."

Scattered chuckles.

"Been clean off meth a year and a half. Hardest thing I ever did. Harder than losing my job. Harder than burying my brother. I'm not used to feeling things without numbing 'em. Not good at it. But I come here, and I don't feel like I have to fake it." He rubbed the back of his neck. "That's all I got." He sat back down.

A guy named Marcus followed. Mid-thirties, former gang member. Talked about wanting to be a better father than his old man but scared he was becoming a ghost in his own house. A single tear tracked down his cheek before he sat back down and wiped it away like it owed him a debt.

Then came Dave—older, quiet, maybe mid-sixties. Said he hadn't picked up a drink in eleven years, but his daughter still didn't talk to him. He didn't cry. He just said it like a fact and sat back down like he'd said all there was to say.

Each man brought his weight to the circle, laid it down, and returned to his seat lighter or heavier—sometimes both. James stayed silent, fingers laced together, blue chip tucked tight in his pocket. He could feel his name swelling in his throat like a lump. His turn hadn't come yet, but the pulpit stood open now—waiting. He hadn't planned to speak. He wasn't even sure he belonged here. But listening to the others, a strange truth had started to dawn: No one really did. And that's exactly why they came.

James stared at the floor, his fingers clenched tight around the chip in his pocket. The group had gone quiet. The pulpit stood empty. The silence stretched, thick and waiting. That's when he felt it—a presence behind him. Not a hand, not a whisper, but something deeper. Like sunlight warming his spine from the inside out.

A voice, calm and close, barely louder than a thought, "You're safe here, James. Every man in this room came here with something bleeding. You're not alone. You don't have to carry it alone."

He didn't turn around. Somehow, he knew the voice was real—more real than the pew beneath him. And still, warm. Steady. Like it belonged to someone who had seen everything... and wasn't afraid. He rose before he could stop himself. His knees locked for a second, and he had to swallow twice before his legs remembered how to walk. The wood beneath his boots groaned as he reached the pulpit.

He stared at the rows of faces—Brandon, Greg, Marcus, Larry—and cleared his throat. "My name's James."

A few nods. A quiet, expectant stillness.

"I'm, uh... going through a divorce. Kinda been going through it for a while.

The papers have been sitting on my kitchen counter for months, but I've been ignoring them. Like if I just didn't sign them… maybe it wouldn't be real." His hands gripped the edges of the pulpit, knuckles pale. "I haven't seen my kids in over a month."

That landed harder than he expected. A few heads bowed. One man closed his eyes.

"I keep telling myself it's just temporary. That I'm giving them space. But the truth is…" He took a breath, shaky and raw. "I don't even know if I'd know what to say if I saw them." He looked down, voice quieter now. "The house is so quiet. I used to think I wanted peace and quiet. Now it's just… empty. Feels like the walls are staring at me. I started leaving the TV on all night just so I wouldn't hear the silence."

His breath caught in his throat. He blinked hard. "I hate that sound. The silence. It's like it's mocking me. And sometimes…" His voice cracked. "Sometimes the only thing that makes me feel like I'm still alive is this pain in my back. This deep, constant throb that just never goes away."

A pause.

His throat tightened. When he spoke again, his voice trembled with something heavier. "And I wonder—God help me, I wonder—if it would even matter if I didn't wake up tomorrow. Some nights I just lie there thinking about it. Not in a big dramatic way. Just… the thought."

He wiped his eyes roughly with the back of his hand. The room was utterly still.

"I used to tell myself I was taking pills just for my back. That it was just physical. But lately…" He swallowed hard. "I think it's more than that. The loneliness. The fear. The life I didn't think I'd have to live. I never thought it would be like this. I don't know what I'm doing. I don't know how to be this man."

His eyes lifted—just for a moment. And there, in the back pew, he saw him. A man in jeans and a light gray hoodie. Quiet presence. Hands resting in his lap. His smile was small but sincere, like he already knew every word James had just spoken and loved him anyway. His eyes radiated something more than encouragement—peace, yes. But also pride.

James looked back at the group, exhaling a sharp breath like he'd been underwater too long. "I didn't mean to say all that," he said with a sheepish laugh that barely held together. "Guess I've just... never really said it out loud."

He looked down again, then nodded. "Thanks for letting me. Really." And with that, he stepped down. He returned to his seat like a man who had just put down a weight he wasn't sure he could name. His back still ached. His chest still felt hollow. But something—something had shifted.

Brandon said nothing. Just reached out and gently patted his shoulder once.

And for the first time in a long while, James didn't flinch from the contact.

24

Rulers of the Darkness

The house was still, cloaked in a heavy quiet broken only by the faint hum of the fridge down the hall. Marshall moved through the shadows like a ghost, one hand gripping the doorframe to steady himself as he entered the bedroom. His mother lay on the hospital-style bed nestled in the corner of the room. The same place he laid her in for years. A thin blanket rose and fell with her shallow breaths. Her eyes were half-lidded, staring through the ceiling as though waiting for something—or someone—that never came.

"Hey, Ma," Marshall murmured, crouching beside her. He brushed a damp cloth gently across her forehead, wiping away the sweat that had gathered in the crook of her hairline. "You were moving around a lot earlier. Must've been a rough dream."

She didn't respond. She never did. Not since the damage had stolen her speech, her motion, her spark. Still, Marshall tucked the blanket higher around her shoulders, smoothing it as if that small gesture could protect her from everything he'd failed to stop before.

He sat on the edge of the bed, his voice breaking the silence. "I've been thinking. About Angela." He glanced at his mother's face, hoping for something—an eyelid twitch, a flicker, a breath that felt more intentional.

Nothing.

"I think I made a mistake." His voice trembled now, softer than before. "I brought her here because... because I thought I was saving her. From the world. From becoming like you." He reached down and gently took her hand.

Her skin was cool, paper-thin, the bones beneath delicate and still.

"But she's not like you. And I'm not a kid anymore." He looked away, jaw tightening. "I keep telling myself this is all for something. That it means something. That if I can just protect one person, it might undo a piece of everything I couldn't fix."

His fingers squeezed hers, desperate. "But what if she needs protecting from me?" His voice cracked. "What if I've become the thing I hated?" His breath shuddered, and he dropped his head onto her arm. "I'm sorry, Ma," he whispered, the words ragged. "God, I'm so sorry. I should've protected you. I should've gotten you out. I should've—" Sobs tore quietly from his chest as his shoulders shook. "I just... I just want to do one thing right," he choked. "Just one."

He stayed there, clinging to her arm like a lifeline, the silence swallowing his confession.

***

The air in the room burned like light filtered through smoke—thick, suffocating, holy. Asael hated it. Every breath felt like it scoured the edges of his form, stripping him of the veil that kept him from being seen. And there he was—Remiel. Standing like judgment made flesh. White armor over linen, the faint glow of sanctity bleeding from his eyes as though Heaven itself had anchored him there.

Asael watched him from the corner, his shadow pressed tight against the wall. He could feel the boundary—the invisible barrier that hummed where Remiel's presence touched the world. It was pure, solid, untouchable.

His claws stopped inches short of it, sparks of pain dancing through the black mist that shaped his hand. He sneered quietly, voice nothing more than a whisper folded into the air. "Always the sentinel," he said with disdain.

Beside him, Ravage shifted restlessly, his form flickering like bad reception, trying in vain to slip through. "He's cheating," he hissed. "He's holding the whole room."

Asael ignored him. His gaze was fixed on the man in the center—the mortal. Marshall. Fragile, trembling, human. Yet something in him stirred faintly. Something luminous. That was why Remiel was here. Not to guard the man's body. To guard his awakening. Asael could feel it, the faint stirring of a change of heart. A dangerous thing. A divine thing. The kind of thoughts that could unmake everything Asael had worked to shape.

Remiel didn't move. Didn't even look their way. He didn't have to. His silence was defiance enough. His stillness, a wall. Asael's lip curled. He wanted to tear it down—to drag that mortal soul back into the pit of self-loathing where it belonged. But the angel had sealed the space too tightly, every inch of it humming with authority.

Then, both demons froze. A low vibration rippled through the room— inaudible to mortal ears, but heavy enough to make the air thicken. Their eyes flicked toward each other at once, recognizing the pull. The summoning call.

Asael's expression hardened.

Ravage's grin faltered into something wary. "He's calling," he said, voice like gravel in smoke. "Guess playtime's over."

"Let's go," Asael said curtly, his gaze cutting one last time toward Remiel. "This isn't finished."

And just like that, the shadows unraveled—drawn upward in a spiral of black smoke, twisting through cracks in the air until they vanished completely. The walls stilled. The flicker of the lamp steadied. Only the faint echo of their presence lingered, like the aftertaste of ash.

***

In an instant Asael and Ravage reformed in human form on the top of a skyscraper. The wind skimmed over them, high above the city's gleaming skeleton of light and motion. Atop the roof, all was still—except for the rhythmic sound of boots crunching gravel. Asael strode forward, sharp features cast in shadow beneath the red blink of a rooftop beacon. Beside him walked Ravage, short and thick like a compact storm. His grin was already plastered in place, half amusement, half contempt. They were mid-argument.

"I didn't need your help," Asael muttered, voice edged like frost on steel.

"Oh, definitely," Ravage said, nodding. "You had it handled. That whole *getting-body-slammed-by-Remiel* thing? Masterclass."

Asael stopped walking, jaw tightening. "If you're going to be assigned to me, you will *watch* your mouth."

"And if you're gonna screw up again, I'll keep saving your pride like I always do."

"You were just as stuck as I was! Don't act like your presence is making any real impact." Asael moved in closer, and the wind seemed to hush around them.

Ravage didn't flinch.

But before it could escalate, a voice interrupted them from ahead. "Enough."

They both turned. At the far end of the roof stood Adapa. He appeared as an old man—weathered yet composed, his features chiseled with age rather than softened by it. He wore a clean, sharply pressed white suit, not the blinding white of Heaven's messengers, but the kind of white worn by men with too much money and not enough accountability. It caught the city light just enough to gleam, but beneath that gleam was something diabolical, calculating. His hands were folded calmly behind his back, as though the ledge he stood on were a balcony at an opera house, not the edge of a hundred-story drop.

He didn't look at them as he spoke. "You're not here to posture. You're here to report."

Asael's shoulders straightened. "Marshall has progressed significantly. His attachment to the girl is being peeled back. Slowly, but effectively."

Adapa turned then, his eyes like deep wells—calm, ancient, and far too observant. "*Effectively?*" A pause. "You allowed him to slip. Even for a moment. His last conversations with her should have driven the knife deeper, not pulled it back."

Asael's lips pressed into a line. "It was a moment. Nothing more. He's still—"

Adapa cut in. "A moment is all it takes for hesitation to take root. A pause is *mercy*. A pause is *weakness*. And you... allowed it."

Ravage, smug as ever, rocked back on his heels. "You were right, he definitely needed backup."

Adapa didn't smile. His next words were smooth, but final. "Ecanus, you have not showed even half the same capability with Marshall as you did with James." He stepped past the both of them. "Asael, you are no longer a Marquis until you show me you have what it takes to succeed. Effective immediately. Ecanus, show me you still have what it takes to break a man's spirit."

Ravage gave a wide grin, glancing over toward Asael.

Asael ignored him, his expression darkened. "You don't trust me."

"I trust your conviction," Adapa said. "Not your control." He turned again to face the city, the glow of towers mirrored faintly in his eyes. "Marshall's task is delicate. The girl is the key. Her death must come by his hands, and by *his belief* that it is right. If he wavers... the whole plan collapses."

Silence stretched. His voice lowered, each word measured like scripture twisted. "The boy will be the weapon, yes—but she will be the wound. A wound that bleeds not only through her family, but through every life that touches hers. The kind of loss that buries itself into the bones of a community. The kind they will still whisper about twenty years from now in coffee shops, prayer meetings, and courtroom benches." He stepped slowly toward the edge again, hands still folded behind his back. "Let them ask, 'Where was God?' Let that question echo through pews and bedrooms, classrooms and graves. Let it pass from mother to daughter, father to son—unanswered. Unhealed." He folded his hands behind his back once more. "That is how you unmake a kingdom. Not with fire. With silence."

Ravage let out a low whistle. "So, no pressure."

Asael said nothing, but his jaw clenched. He took a step forward, staring past Adapa at the endless grid of city lights below. "I will finish what I started."

Adapa's voice was calm, kind. "See that you do. I have my own preparations to complete."

The three of them stood on the edge of the world—judgment, chaos, and the architect of doubt—poised above a city that had no idea the incarnate darkness watching over it.

***

The basement was dimly lit, the muted TV casting soft flickers of light across the walls. A rerun of a late-night talk show played in the background—some host in a suit, grinning wide, waving his hands while mouthing something inaudible to the studio audience. Angela glanced at the screen for a moment.

The caption read: *Tonight's guest shares a wild story from set...* before cutting off mid-scroll.

She smirked faintly, then turned her attention to Marshall, who knelt by the door, picking up her empty soup bowl. She watched him for a second, amused by the absurd backdrop of a talk show in a place where time felt so still. "You know," she said casually, "your cooking's gotten a lot better since I've been here."

Marshall paused, bowl in hand. His one good eye flicked to her, uncertain.

She smiled—dry, but real. "This one didn't even need salt."

He looked down at the bowl and gave a small, bashful shrug. "I've been tweaking it. Tried a little thyme. Didn't want to overdo it."

"Thyme?" she repeated with a raised eyebrow. "So we're getting fancy now."

He actually smiled—just a flicker, but there. "Maybe a little."

Angela tilted her head. "Where'd you learn to cook anyway?"

Marshall set the bowl down gently by the stairs, his tone softening. "Had to, after taking care of mom... we didn't have much money. I'd make simple stuff. Stretch a bag of rice, dress up canned soup, that kind of thing." He sat back on his heels, his hands resting lightly on his knees. "She had this old cookbook," he said, voice distant. "Faded pages, half of it stained from spills. I used to see it on the counter while she cooked. Some nights she'd talk to me—real quiet, real sweet. Other nights she'd barely say a word."

Angela stayed quiet, listening. Watching him.

"I think a lot of that was him," Marshall said finally. "My dad... changed her. Broke parts of her she never got back. But when she cooked, it was like... she remembered who she used to be."

A long silence stretched between them.

Then he added, as if to himself, "I've been trying to perfect her recipes ever since."

Angela's smile faded a little, replaced by something more sincere. She opened her mouth to speak, but Marshall beat her to it.

"What would you do," he asked suddenly, "if you weren't in this basement anymore?"

The question hit like a drop of ice down her spine. Angela blinked. Her breath caught. She studied his face carefully—but he wasn't smiling. He wasn't mocking her. He was asking like he truly wanted to know.

She swallowed. "I'd see my son," she said, voice quieter now. "Phoenix. I'd hold him so tight he'd probably squirm away. I'd go to my mom's house. Sleep in a real bed. Maybe sit on the porch and watch the sun go down without looking over my shoulder."

Marshall nodded slowly, his expression unreadable.

Angela tilted her head. "Why? Why did you ask me that?"

But Marshall didn't answer. He just stood, picked up the bowl, and climbed the stairs in silence—his footsteps slow, thoughtful, vanishing into the shadows above. Behind her, on the TV, the talk show host leaned in for a punchline, and the silent audience burst into muted laughter.

***

Angela's family home slumbered under the hush of midnight. The hallway was dim, a soft light from the porch casting faint glows through the curtains. A child's toy blinked idle colors in the corner of the living room. In the back bedroom, Phoenix slept soundly in his toddler bed, limbs sprawled like he'd collapsed mid-adventure. A small stuffed dinosaur lay clutched in one hand, his chest rising and falling with slow, even breaths. Then—movement. A shadow crept along the baseboards like a living smear of darkness, silent and cold. It slipped under doors, around corners—not cast by light, but moving with purpose. Outside, under the dark stretch of backyard, a lesser angel struggled. Wings pressed to the ground, knees driven into the soil, black chains like living obsidian pinned him down. They pulsed with foul energy, etched with symbols no angel should bear. He strained against them, jaw clenched, celestial light flickering around his edges. But the bindings held.

Inside, the shadow thickened, slipping beneath the crack under Phoenix's door. It pooled beside the bed. And from it, Adapa emerged—shrouded in a robe darker than the night around him. His presence consumed warmth, silencing even the tick of the nearby wall clock. He stood over the boy, gazing down through his hood. The child's breathing remained steady, unaware. Adapa extended one pale hand and reached into the corner of the room, where shadows pooled deepest. He scooped something from the air—like grasping smoke—and crushed it slowly between his fingers. Then he leaned low. With a long, slow breath, he blew the dark dust over Phoenix's sleeping face.

The child twitched, his nose scrunching. Then—a cough. A sharp inhale. Another cough—deeper, harsher. His small body rolled over, then thrashed. A leg kicked out, his hands curled into fists, and he began to whimper, then cry.

Christine, asleep down the hall, startled awake. She sat up in bed, listening. A loud, choking cough. A high, pained cry.

She rushed out of bed, flipping on lights as she moved. "Phoenix?" She threw open his door.

He was tossing violently in bed, face flushed, his little hands clutching at the blankets. His stuffed animal had fallen to the floor. His skin was hot to the touch.

"Oh no, baby—shh, it's okay, I've got you." She scooped him up, her arms trembling slightly. His skin burned against her.

His eyes rolled a little, dazed from fever. He coughed again, lips dry, sweat beading at his brow. She didn't see Adapa's form dissolve, retreating like smoke out through the window frame, merging with the shadow of a tree branch waving in the wind. He slipped down the darkness of the old oak tree in the backyard, its branches stretching like black veins across the grass. The air bent slightly around him, a distortion—an unmaking. At the base of the tree, bound against its trunk, knelt Serel.

The angel's wings hung low, feathers dulled to a faint gold-gray. Runes of restraint glowed faintly around his wrists and across his chest, pulsing with the rhythm of Adapa's will. He was strong once—fiercely so—but even strength had its limits when divine light met corruption's design.

Adapa paused, studying him. There was a faint tremor in Serel's jaw, though his eyes burned steady with defiance. It almost made Adapa smile. Almost.

"Still watching over them," Adapa said quietly, his tone edged with something that could've been respect or mockery. "Even now, when you can't move, can't speak without my leave."

Serel's nostrils flared. He said nothing. His silence was its own act of rebellion.

Adapa stepped closer, shadows curling around his shoes. He crouched to meet Serel's gaze, voice softening to a near whisper. "You were supposed to keep him safe. The boy. The woman. The fragile little thread of faith holding them together." His eyes narrowed. "And yet here we are."

For a moment, the silence thickened—something ancient and personal between them. Adapa's expression hardened. He straightened slowly, the dark pressing close at his back. With a single step, his form unraveled—shadows flowing upward like smoke pulled toward a flame.

Serel strained against the bindings, the runes flaring in protest. But the seals held. All he could do was bow his head as the last trace of Adapa's presence vanished.

Inside, Phoenix whimpered softly against his grandmother's chest. She stroked his hair, whispering a prayer she barely remembered.

25

Everyone Will be Salted with Fire

Juliet stood at the far end of the squad room, her arms crossed tightly against her chest, eyes fixed on the cluttered case board. Photos, timelines, maps—none of it was giving her what she needed. The faint hum of late-night fluorescent lights buzzed overhead like a persistent headache. She didn't look up when Gabriel entered, but she felt his presence. He walked with that restless edge she was starting to recognize—like something inside him was pushing too hard, too fast.

"Got something." He tossed a slim folder onto the nearest desk.

Juliet turned, arching a brow. "Thought you were reworking the search grid."

"I was." He pulled out a chair and sat with the kind of heavy movement that said he hadn't slept. "There's nothing there. No new sightings, no digital footprint. It's like he vanished."

She gave a quiet nod, waiting.

"So I started looking backward. Into Angela's past. Her college records, connections, history. Anything that might explain why this guy took her."

Juliet leaned against the desk, her voice calm. "And?"

Gabriel flipped the folder open, revealing a thin stack of printed reports. "A few years ago, there were two major incidents on campus. First, a robbery gone bad—fraternity guy named Tyler. Stabbed not far from a frat party. Party was a joint event between his frat and a sorority." He looked up at her now. "Angela's sorority."

Juliet's brow furrowed. "Coincidence?"

"Maybe. But then, almost a year later, Dr. Marlowe, one of the senior statistics professors, dropped dead mid-lecture. Heart attack. Everyone called it natural causes, but..." He trailed off, tapping the page. "Angela was in that class."

Juliet narrowed her eyes. "What are you saying?"

"I'm saying it's like she's got a shadow. Like death follows her. But not in some random, unlucky way. What if all these are connected? And the way the footage looked from the night she was taken..."

Juliet tilted her head. "You mean the parking lot footage?"

He nodded. "You saw how he handled her. Not rough. Not rushed. He checked her pulse. He carried her like—" He hesitated. "Like someone who cared."

Juliet straightened. "So now you're suggesting the guy who abducted her might have been watching her for years?"

"I don't know." Gabriel's voice dropped to a low, unsettled tone. "But what if he was? What if it's someone who knew her back then? A classmate, maybe. Someone she doesn't even remember. What if he's been circling her life, waiting?"

Juliet was silent for a moment. Then, she exhaled. "It's a theory. But there's no proof tying him—or her—to those deaths. And without that, it's just speculation."

"I get that," Gabriel said quickly. "But we've got nothing else. And this? It's a thread. I'm not saying it's everything we've been looking for, I'm saying maybe someone believed she was important enough to follow."

Juliet was quiet for a moment, eyes scanning the case board in front of her. It was still mostly barren—photos of Angela, a map of the city with a few pins marking last sightings, a blown-up frame of the parking lot footage where the abductor carried her gently into the car. No deaths. No suspects. Just a handful of breadcrumbs and one missing woman.

"You can follow the lead," Juliet said at last, her voice low but even. "Discreetly. And if you do talk to her mother—go easy. It's been hard enough on her without dragging up old ghosts."

Gabriel nodded. "I just want to know if she remembers anything strange. Anyone Angela mentioned back then. Anything that didn't sit right."

She stepped closer to the board, eyes lingering on the empty spaces between the pins, the lines that hadn't been drawn yet. "If what you're saying is right—if someone's been hovering around Angela since college— then he's not impulsive. He's patient. Structured. The kind who waits years for a moment like this."

His brow furrowed. "And you think we've only just now entered the moment?"

"I think," she said slowly, "we've stepped into the middle of a story that's been unfolding for a long time. We just didn't realize Angela was the main character."

He swallowed hard. "Feels like she never did either."

Juliet nodded faintly. "Maybe not. But even if he's been this careful, he must have left traces. Somewhere. People don't just appear out of nowhere— not really."

Gabriel looked down at the open folder in his hands. Class photos. Newspaper clippings. Obituaries. "I'll start pulling alumni. Yearbooks. See if any names connect across those two incidents."

Juliet studied him for a beat, then offered a small nod of approval. "You've got good instincts, Ramos. Just don't get tunnel vision. There might be more to this than meets the eye."

He offered a tired smile. "That supposed to make me feel better?"

She smirked faintly and turned away, but lingered near the board a second longer. Her eyes rested on Angela's face—wide-eyed, frozen in motion. There was still something about it that tugged at her. Not suspicion. Not fear. Just a quiet weight, like knowing the first page of a book and realizing too late it's a tragedy halfway through. She exhaled softly. "Let me know what you find."

"I will."

Juliet turned toward the hall. "And Ramos?"

He looked up.

"If this lead pans out... we won't be dealing with a random kidnapper."

He nodded. "Yeah. We'll be dealing with someone who thinks she belongs to him."

***

The air shimmered. A low hum pulsed through the walls of Marshall's house—barely audible, like the memory of a bell tolling in another world. Somewhere beyond human sight, two forms knelt in the quiet aftermath of a battle not waged in flesh, but in essence. The dim basement light buzzed overhead, stuttering once... then again. Steam rose from Asael's shoulders, tendrils coiling into the air like incense from cursed altars. His skin—if it could be called that—cracked and smoked where Remiel's blade had touched. Beside him, Ravage crouched low, clawed fingers pressed to the floor as faint, hissing lines healed along his ribs. Their forms—fluid and shifting—glimmered slightly out of sync with reality, visible only at the corner of the soul.

Across the room stood Remiel. Silent. Untouched. Wings half-folded, his armor faintly luminous in the dark, casting soft glows along the floor. His face was stern, and the air around him throbbed with a pressure that made the walls creak. A subtle wind had begun to stir the curtains upstairs.

Asael broke the silence with a snarl. "We've made no progress. No *traction*. Every seed we plant, he rips from the soil." He gestured toward Remiel with disdain, but the motion was weak. Empty.

Ravage exhaled, his breath emerging as smoke. "Maybe it's because the great Asael spent too much time whispering into Marshall's head and not enough time watching his flanks."

Asael turned his head sharply. "Don't pretend your presence has improved anything. You're a librarian with delusions of strength."

"And yet," Ravage said, rising now, teeth bared, "*your* failure required my oversight. What does that say about you?"

The room dimmed. The flickering bulb above them popped softly—but didn't go out. A stillness swept over the basement like the hush before a storm. Adapa stepped from the shadows proud and arrogant like a powerful athlete who already declared himself the victor. He didn't walk so much as unfold, emerging as if the air had simply allowed him shape. The walls seemed to lean away from him without moving. Light bent, ever so slightly, at his approach.

"...Master," Asael and Ravage said in unison, the sharpness in their tones drained to ash.

Adapa said nothing. His pale gaze slid past them, resting on Remiel. The angel slowly turned. With one fluid motion, his wings spread open once more—not in violence, but as a warning. His hand hovered near his blade. Though it remained sheathed, its hilt glowed with quiet fire.

"I didn't come to fight. Adapa's voice was soft, kind, but the air responded as if struck—a whisper of wind brushing along the stairwell.

Remiel did not move.

Adapa tilted his head slightly. "Tell me something. Are you truly the guardian appointed to Angela's bloodline?"

A pause. Somewhere upstairs, the wind groaned against the house.

Adapa continued dreamily. "Because I've been wondering... are they all right? Her boy? Her mother?" He smiled, the corners of his mouth too sharp, too knowing. "Sometimes, things slip past us when we're busy with other assignments."

Remiel's eyes narrowed—not with anger, but with a heavy stillness. A realization. He didn't speak, but his wings shifted. "You've done something."

Adapa spread his hands. "I? Oh no. I'm merely a guest here. The harm, if there *is* any, must've happened while you were otherwise occupied."

Remiel took one step back, then burst upward in a flash of argent light. There was no noise, no shockwave—only a faint scent of ozone. He was gone.

Adapa turned his head slowly toward his subordinates. The dim bulb steadied. The air, however, did not. A dreadful hush settled over the room— thicker than silence, tactile. Adapa stood motionless. The faint dripping of water from somewhere within the walls marked time like a heartbeat. Ravage shifted slightly, his breath hitching. Asael clenched his jaw but said nothing. Then the floor beneath them rippled. Darkness seeped like oil from the cement slick, foul, and hungry. Without warning, hundreds of black, sinewed arms erupted from the ground, glistening with ichor. They surged upward with inhuman coordination, wrapping around Asael and Ravage in a grotesque embrace. Clawed hands gripped tightly. Barbed limbs coiled around throats and ankles. The basement light pulsed once.

Asael let out a guttural snarl, already struggling. "No—Adapa—wait—"

Ravage screamed, "We can still fix it! He caught us off guard—!"

They knew this ritual. Every demon in the old orders did. These weren't arms from Adapa—they were lesser ones, swarms of bottom-feeding spirits willingly congealing for one purpose: restraint. No demon escaped once held like this. It was the prelude to pain—and, in the worst cases, to complete absorption. All demons who failed their missions risked being absorbed into a more powerful entity. There was no trial. No last chance. The demonic kingdom did not waste resources—it reallocated them. Individuality, personality, freedom—gone. Subsumed. Demons that had once been trapped in absorption spoke of it only in whispers, when they dared. They described it as a nightmare that never ends. They could only *watch* time pass. Powerless. Forgotten.

Ravage began to writhe.

Asael bared his fangs, jerking against the limbs, panic rising fast. "Adapa—wait—"

But Adapa did not move. He stood perfectly still in the eye of the chaos, eyes closed, hands clasped calmly behind his back, like a professor awaiting silence from unruly students. When he finally spoke, it wasn't a roar. It was a whisper—sharper than steel and twice as cold. "You were two."

The basement creaked. The temperature dropped further.

"You," he repeated, eyes now open and glowing faintly in the dimness, "were two... and he was one."

Asael snarled, venom lacing his words. "He's not *just* one. He's Remiel—"

"SILENCE."

The room vibrated with the force of it. The lights upstairs flickered. A glass clinked faintly in the kitchen cabinet above them. Neither Asael nor

Ravage dared speak again. Adapa's gaze drifted toward the ceiling. He saw through it—not with sight, but with something deeper.

Above them, Marshall moved slowly in the kitchen, stirring a pot. His shoulders were slumped, his eyes empty. The scent of onions and old grief filled the air. The stove clicked and hissed as it came to life.

Adapa's lip curled. "I had to intervene," he said, voice now taut, like a leash stretched too far. "I had to reach where you could not. Because instead of thinking through the problem, you wasted your strength headbutting a glorified hallway monitor."

Neither demon moved. They couldn't. The arms pulsed, tightening slightly—anticipating a command.

Adapa turned toward them again. His voice was calmer now, but all the more dangerous for it. "He is powerful. Yes. But he is not omnipresent. He cannot guard every breath, every thought, every *weakness*. And yet you let yourselves be dazzled by his strength... instead of outwitting it." He leaned in. His shadow grew. "You should have split," he hissed. "One of you could've drawn him away. The other could have shattered the boy's dreams, poisoned the mother's breath. Whispered despair into the seams of their hope until they unraveled."

He took another step forward, the floor cold beneath him. He didn't glow. He didn't brandish flame. But the shadows around his body twisted and writhed like serpents behind glass.

"And yet," he said softly, "I had to sully myself with the work of underlings." He turned his gaze upward again.

Marshall stood still over the pot, staring into it like it contained not soup, but the ashes of everything he'd ever believed in.

Adapa's eyes gleamed. "His heart is softening. That beautiful gash in his heart is beginning to congeal. He is doubting. Reflecting. A man standing in the ruins of his own convictions." Then, with chilling slowness, he turned back to the restrained demons. "You will watch. You will listen. And you will *learn* how to break a man who is already halfway broken."

He stepped back, disappearing partially into the shadows once more. "Because the next time you fail me..." His voice became a rasp of wind through bone. "I will make you a part of me forever."

At once, the black limbs withdrew, sinking into the floor with wet, slithering sounds. Asael and Ravage collapsed, gasping, faces pale and drawn.

Above them, the light no longer flickered. Adapa ascended. He moved without sound, without weight, like a breath passing through the cracks in the floorboards. The staircase did not creak beneath him. The air around him warped faintly, barely perceptible, but deeply wrong.

In the kitchen, Marshall stood with his back to the room, stirring the pot with robotic repetition. The scent of herbs and vegetables simmering in broth lingered in the air, too clean for what was about to happen. Adapa appeared behind him—not so much stepping into place as simply becoming visible. He crouched low and reached into the shadow cast by the base of the oven. His long fingers gently scooped something black and dripping from the floor—like sap harvested from a wound in reality. With slow care, he began rolling it between his palms. It formed into the rough shape of a worm, wriggling subtly in his grasp, a fragile strand of suggestion born from despair.

He cupped his hands around it and raised it to his mouth. "I am better off dead," he whispered into it, his voice delicate and sincere—like a lover's final words before vanishing into the sea.

Then, with reverent care, he moved the worm beside Marshall's ear. It slithered in without resistance. Marshall flinched. Only slightly. Just a twitch of his cheek, a blink that lingered too long. Then he kept stirring. Adapa watched for a moment longer, his head tilted like a biologist observing a specimen. Then he turned and drifted toward the back hallway, where the bedroom door stood ajar. The old woman lay silent in her bed. Breathing. Diminished. Alive.

Adapa stepped into the room like a shadow gaining mass. He loomed at her bedside, a dark monolith framed in the soft glow of a nightlight in the outlet along the wall. He bent low and reached again—this time into the shadow pooled under her frail, unmoving hand. From it he drew a thicker mass, denser, coiling like smoke and silk in his fingers. He kneaded it into a ball the size of a marble and placed it gently into his mouth. Then he leaned down, until his face was inches from hers. Her lips were slightly parted, breath rattling faintly in her throat. Adapa exhaled. A black mist left his lips in a single, focused stream, entering her mouth like a slow-moving plague.

For a moment, nothing happened. Then her chest began to rise and fall more quickly. Her brow dampened with sweat. Her breaths turned shallow, erratic. The nightlight flickered once.

Adapa straightened and vanished. He returned to the basement like a breeze returns to a still forest—impossible to trace, but immediately felt. Asael and Ravage looked up as the temperature dropped again.

Adapa's voice was soft, but absolute. "I've changed my mind about this arrangement. Ecanus, you will return to your old assignment. *James.*"

Ravage flinched but said nothing.

"There's been too much progress," Adapa continued. "Uriel's influence has grown. The man must be pushed deeper into despair. Go remind him what hopelessness feels like."

Ravage bowed his head. "Yes, Master."

Adapa's eyes shifted to Asael. "You will remain. Marshall is your burden."

Asael nodded, shoulders still tense.

"I have given him a whisper," Adapa continued. "A seed of death. It speaks to him now in his own voice. Let him believe that Angela's death is not just necessary—but divine. That it is his *calling*. His redemption." He stepped closer, his tone tightening. "His mother now bears a curse over her lungs. It will devour her from within. Use it. Let it fester into guilt, into fear, into rage within Marshall. Make her illness a reminder that every moment of mercy has a cost."

Asael's eyes darkened with understanding.

Adapa turned halfway, pausing. "The curse I cast on Phoenix is... complex. It will tangle Remiel in enough spiritual red tape to keep him occupied. Bureaucracy is an angel's favorite noose." He raised a finger, pointing it at Asael like a sword. "Finish this."

Then, as silently as he had come, Adapa vanished—leaving behind only the faint, sulfurous scent of something old and unclean.

And far above, Marshall stirred his soup with one hand and rubbed his temple with the other, as if trying to remember something he hadn't yet forgotten.

***

The pediatric room was dim and quiet, painted in soft blues and gentle creams. A monitor beeped steadily, each sound a fragile assurance that Phoenix still lived. The boy lay in the narrow hospital bed, pale and still, an IV taped to his small arm. Beneath the blanket, his chest rose and fell in irregular patterns, his breaths shallow and strained. In the corner, Christine slept slumped in a vinyl chair, a worn jacket draped over her knees. Her face, lined with age and worry, twitched occasionally as if still praying in her dreams.

Beside the bed, nearly invisible in the hush of the physical world, stood Serel. The lesser angel, once bound and humiliated by Adapa, now shimmered faintly—barely more than the glow of a candle in a storm. His wings were dimmed, and faint scorch marks still marred his robes. He watched over Phoenix with a heart full of grief and guilt, hands clasped, whispering quiet pleas into the veil. But his power was weak. Too weak.

The room shifted. The lights buzzed once—then flared. Wind rustled the paper charts on the counter. And Remiel arrived. He did not *enter*. He *descended*. A flare of argent light streaked through the ceiling without sound, condensing into a tall, armored figure in gleaming gold and white. The force of his arrival pressed the room inward, distorting the air like a tremor in the spirit realm. Every molecule of atmosphere held its breath.

Serel dropped to one knee instantly. "Remiel—I—I didn't know he would come. I was watching—I swear to the Highest, I *never left*—but he—he chained me"

Remiel raised a hand, a swift, wordless gesture. Not of anger—of urgency. "I know." His voice was low and thunderous. "Later." His gaze turned to Phoenix.

The boy trembled faintly under the blankets, his skin sheened with sweat. Remiel's eyes burned with divine sight—and there, hovering just above Phoenix's lung, he saw it. A ball of sticky black corruption. Pulsing.

Breathing. Anchored to the boy's spirit like a tumor made of despair and rot. Without hesitation, Remiel reached for it. His gauntleted hand closed around the vile thing, and he began to squeeze—until a voice issued from the ball itself, small and too-calm.

"He sends his rain on the just and the unjust."

Remiel's brow furrowed. The ball twisted in his grasp, a thread of dark ichor connecting it back to the child's chest like a spiritual umbilical cord. As he lifted it higher, the surface split open. A pair of black lips formed on the center.

"This kind can only come out by prayer and fasting," the mouth said. "This kind can only come out by prayer and fasting. This kind can only come out by prayer and fasting."

Over and over. A chant. A riddle. A mocking truth. Remiel's hand trembled with restrained fury. He raised the ball higher—but the black cord pulling back toward Phoenix grew taut. The boy stirred beneath the blankets. His body rejected the separation. Remiel's jaw clenched. He glared at the lips. Then, slowly, he lowered it back to the boy's chest. The ball reabsorbed with a sickening softness, like a leech sinking into flesh. Phoenix shuddered once and stilled again.

Serel stepped forward, shame dripping from every word. "What... what is it? Why can't we—"

Remiel turned from the bed, eyes still glowing faintly. He spoke not with fury now, but with weight. "Prayer is one thing. But fasting..." His voice faded, brows drawing tight in contemplation. "I need to find someone who will *fast* for him."

26

Comfort Each Other and Edify One Another

The room was dark, save for the glow of moonlight through the window. James sat hunched in his recliner, an old leather thing that creaked every time he shifted. The fan in the corner buzzed intermittently, struggling to move the stale air that smelled of liquor, sweat, and cheap takeout. A mostly-empty bottle of bourbon sat on the table beside him. His glass, slick with condensation and fingerprints, hung loosely in his hand, resting on the armrest. He hadn't turned on the lights in hours. Maybe days. The only motion came from the rise and fall of his chest and the slow twitch in his jaw. He stared at nothing. His phone lit up on the table. A message. He leaned forward, squinting through bleary eyes.

[Kendra] *Did you find that bracelet I left at your place?*

James blinked, rubbed his face, and typed slowly.

[James] *I'll look for it.*

A beat passed.

Then her reply snapped through like a whip.

[Kendra] *Just don't expect to find it at the bottom of a liquor bottle.*

He stared at the screen, lips pulling back slightly. The dull throb in his head sharpened. He tapped out a reply.

[James] *Why haven't the kids answered me? I've sent them like 8 messages.*

The dots appeared immediately.

[Kendra] *Why would they want to? You didn't exactly leave a good impression.*

Another beat.

[Kendra] *Are you still doing drugs?*

His grip tightened.

[James] *What does that have to do with anything?*

[Kendra] *Seriously? You're asking that? I don't want them around you if you're still using. Or drinking like you clearly are.*

He could hear her voice now—cold, judgmental, furious and tired all at once.

[James] *So that's it? You told them not to talk to me?*

No response for several seconds.

Then:

[Kendra] *I told them the truth. That you're unpredictable. And that I don't trust you alone with them. What kind of example is that?*

His heart pounded, bourbon bubbling in his gut like acid.

[James] *You don't get to do that. I want to be there for them.*

[Kendra] *You wanted to be there after you lost them. Where was this energy when I was crying myself to sleep wondering if you'd even come home?*

He swallowed hard. The room felt smaller.

[Kendra] *It's too little too late, James. You don't get to screw up for years and expect everyone to just wait around for your redemption arc.*

He slammed the phone down onto the table. The screen cracked against a metal lighter, bouncing once before landing face-up—still glowing. He grabbed the bottle. Poured. Drank. Harder this time.

"I'm still their father..." he muttered, voice barely audible over the hum of the fan.

***

No one answered. But *someone* laughed. High above, pressed against the ceiling like a grotesque spider, Ravage clung to the plaster in complete silence. He had arrived unnoticed, his wiry, muscled frame folded in unnatural angles. His eyes gleamed like two dull embers, watching James drink with a look of delight, lips curled in amusement.

Invisible to mortal eyes, Ravage whispered with a smirk. "Well, *someone's* feeling sorry for himself."

James didn't react—he couldn't hear him.

Ravage shifted slightly, inching sideways along the ceiling with perfect quiet, like a stain crawling across the roof. He peered down at the man beneath him—slumped, sagging, rotting from the inside out. "Kendra's got you pegged." He chuckled, head tilting as he studied James's glass. "You're not just a bad father—you're your *own* father, recycled with a new bottle and a cheaper chair."

He hung upside-down directly over James now, chin touching the air above his head. "Never present. Never strong. Never there when they needed you." He mock-pouted. "And now? They don't need you at all. That's the part that *kills*, huh?"

James took another swig.

Ravage's eyes flicked to the corners of the room. He turned his head, sniffing the air like a scavenger dog. "Huh..." he mused. "No Uriel."

He dropped down silently from the ceiling, landing in the corner like a loose pile of shadow before re-forming into his usual squat, broad-shouldered frame. He paced slowly, hands clasped behind his back, admiring the decay. "Funny how they're never around when you want 'em, isn't it?" He glanced at the door. "No trumpet blasts. No light through the curtains. Not even a flutter of feathers." He gave a low chuckle. "They're real good at showing up when the credits roll. Not so much when it's act two and the hero's puking on himself."

He walked past James, unseen and unfelt, close enough to whisper into his ear. "But *I'm* here, Jimmy boy. I'm always here. Always watching."

James rubbed his face and poured another drink.

Ravage grinned and stepped back into the shadows. "Let's see if we can finally make you honest. About who you really are."

The bourbon was half gone now. James sat slouched deeper in the recliner, eyes glassy and unfocused. His chest rose and fell with slow, ragged breaths. The phone sat silent on the table. Cracked screen. Dead glow.

Across the room, in the shadows just beyond the edge of the lamplight,

Ravage crouched like a gargoyle made of gristle and spite. He watched with wide eyes, grin stretching ear to ear. "That's it..." he whispered, voice tender. "Let's do something *interesting.*"

James's hand drifted to the drawer beside his chair. He opened it slowly and pulled out the old revolver. Heavy. Familiar. Cold.

Ravage straightened up, bouncing on the balls of his clawed feet. "Oh-ho-ho... now we're talkin'. Let's spin the wheel, Jimmy boy."

James popped open the cylinder. Shaking fingers fumbled through the cluttered drawer until he found a single round. He slid it into the chamber, clicked the cylinder back in place, and gave it a spin. The chambers whirred with a metallic rattle, then slowed... then stopped. He raised the gun to his temple.

Ravage leaned in, eyes gleaming, mouth ajar with anticipation. "Come on... come on..."

Just as James pressed the barrel against his skull— Buzz.

The phone vibrated against the table, lighting up with a name:

Brandon – Incoming Call

James flinched. He blinked, staring at the screen like it was a hallucination.

Ravage growled under his breath, eyes narrowing. "Ignore it. *Ignore it.*"

James stared a moment longer... then slowly reached over and hit the silence button. The screen dimmed. He brought the revolver back up. Ravage's grin returned like a beast emerging from the brush. James closed his eyes. Pulled the trigger. Click. No shot. Just a hollow snap of the hammer slamming down on an empty chamber. He exhaled sharply, shoulders shaking. Lowered the gun. Then spun the cylinder again.

Ravage cackled—low and rising, a giddy rasp of mockery and pleasure. He slapped the wall and twirled in place. "Oh, this is *perfect!*" he howled. "Look at you—completely alone, soaked in shame, playing roulette with your own skull!"

He wiped imaginary tears from his eyes. "You couldn't even kill yourself right. And the best part?" He leaned in again, just inches from James's blank, exhausted face. "You *want* to lose."

James leaned forward, elbows on his knees, gun dangling between them.

He rubbed his temple, breathing heavy.

And Ravage, still grinning, whispered, "Let's go another round."

The cylinder spun again. James stared at the gun in his hand. His thumb hovered over the hammer.

Across the room, Ravage leaned forward like a child watching a magic trick. "Round two," he whispered with glee. "Come on, come on, let's see what fate has to say."

James pressed the barrel against his temple again, lips parted, eyes distant—Buzz. The vibration rattled against the wooden table like a knock from the outside world.

Brandon – Incoming Call

Ravage hissed, his grin cracking like dried leather. "Not again..."

James's hand twitched. The phone buzzed once more. Persistent. Insistent. He groaned, closed his eyes, and slowly lowered the revolver. His finger hovered over the decline button. Then he hesitated. With a sluggish breath, he reached for the phone—and answered.

"...Hello?"

Brandon's voice came through the line, warm and familiar, edged with concern. "Hey man. You good? I was just thinkin' about you."

James wiped a hand across his mouth. His voice came out thick, slurred. "Yeah. Yeah, I'm fine. Just... tired."

Brandon didn't respond right away. "I'm really glad you made it to Celebrate Recovery last week. Meant a lot, seeing you there."

"Yeah," James muttered, eyes flicking to the revolver still resting on his thigh. "Great time. Changed my life." He started to pull the phone from his ear, reaching for the end call button.

"Wait—hold up," Brandon said quickly. "You all right, man? You sound kinda... off."

James gave a hollow, bitter chuckle. "Oh, I'm just peachy," he slurred. "Life's a dream, brother. Never been better."

Brandon's voice softened, laced with a quiet sort of humor. "So... life's terrible, and you're at your lowest point?"

James froze. His lips parted, but nothing came out.

Brandon waited. Then added gently, "Talk to me, man. Please."

In the shadows near the recliner, Ravage stood motionless. The revolver remained untouched for now.

James rubbed his eyes with the heel of his hand, the revolver now resting limply on his lap. The silence on the phone stretched. Brandon didn't push.

Then softly, James said, "I miss them, man. My kids." His voice cracked like a dry branch. "I just... I didn't think it would feel like this. I didn't think I'd turn into him. But here I am. Sitting in the dark. Drinking. Ignoring calls. Just like he did." His breath hitched. A sob welled in his throat. "I'm the same damn man I used to swear I'd never be."

Brandon waited. Then said gently, "I know that feeling."

James didn't respond right away. Just breathed. Just cried. "I wanted to be better. I swear I did."

Brandon's voice came through again, steady and calm. "You still can."

In the corner, unseen by mortal eyes, Ravage stood frozen. His hands balled into fists. His grin had withered into a scowl. Then the room shifted. A warm breeze drifted in from nowhere. The air shimmered faintly—just enough to make the shadows twitch. And then— Uriel emerged. He stepped out from the light, as though the very outline of the room had given birth to him. His golden eyes held no judgment—only a radiant calm. He wore a faint, knowing smile, like someone arriving late to a party and content just to observe the embers.

Ravage hissed and stepped back.

Uriel glanced at him without concern. "Human connection," he said, his voice like sunlight slipping through morning fog. "It's a beautiful thing, Ecanus."

The old name hit Ravage like a slap. He flinched.

Uriel didn't press. "It has a way of holding back the darkness," the angel continued, folding his hands before him, "sometimes more powerfully than any angel from Heaven." He looked toward James, who was now hunched forward in the chair, one hand covering his eyes as he spoke into the phone.

"I just want to tell them I'm sorry," James whispered. "I want to hug them. I want to *see* them."

Brandon didn't say much. Just, "Yeah," or "I hear you," when James paused.

But his presence on the line was a tether. And James clung to it.

Uriel looked back to Ravage, his smile still in place—but firmer now, edged with quiet triumph. "You thought him alone. But he has gained something far more dangerous to your kind than just hope." He stepped forward, voice reverent. "He has a community."

Ravage bared his teeth but said nothing.

Uriel didn't need a sword to win this battle. Not tonight. He simply stood by the broken man in the chair—and waited.

27

The Dragon and His Angels

Thousands of years ago, the forest near the village in the Levant whispered with ancient breath—leaves swaying like murmured prayers, branches creaking like old bones. Through the dense trees, a procession of torchlight wound toward the clearing ahead. Their steps were solemn, yet urgent, as if pulled forward by something older than memory. At the head of the line marched the cultists. They wore robes of blood-red, the fabric heavy and smeared with old stains. Their hoods were drawn, their faces marked with coiled patterns of black paint. At the center of the group, Jared, who was separated from his sister stumbled forward, bound by rope. His face was bruised and swollen, his knees bloodied from repeated falls. Every tug of the cords brought a grunt of pain as they dragged him forward like cattle to slaughter.

Among the villagers trailing behind, two men walked with quiet purpose. Cloaked in dusty brown robes, unremarkable to the human eye, they moved unnoticed—but within them burned Holy Fire. Remiel and Uriel, cloaked in flesh. They said nothing as the procession reached the clearing. Rising from the center like the spine of a forgotten god was the temple—a squared stone pyramid layered with tiers of stone steps. Moss clung to the cracks, and vines snaked their way up its sides, but the top platform stood clean, untouched by time or nature. The torches flared brighter as the cultists ascended. The villagers murmured prayers, some in fear, others in awe.

Remiel's gaze rose to the summit. Uriel's lips were tight, his shoulders stiff beneath his human guise. At the top of the pyramid, the summit opened into a wide, flat stone surface. At its center stood a cylindrical altar, smooth and weathered. A serpent—massive, intricate, and coiled—was carved around its base in a perfect ring, mouth open and fangs bared. Its tail wrapped around itself in a loop of eternity. The priests—still robed in red—took their positions without hesitation. The high priest, marked by his robe's black trim and the painted image of a black serpent winding down his back, stepped forward. His face was hidden beneath a bone-white mask carved to resemble a serpent's skull. They bound Jared—his wrists and ankles pulled in each cardinal direction, stretching him over the stone until he trembled.

The high priest lifted his arms. "Come forth, O watchers of the blood...

O serpents of the sky, hear us.

Accept this vessel.

Drink of his breath.

Feast upon his bones.

And show us favor once more..."

The chanting ceased. A long silence fell. Then— Light split the sky. Not one—but twelve. From each corner of the temple grounds, columns of light began to descend. Golden and silver, but cold—like the light reflected off polished bone. They swirled slowly, pulsing like slow, ancient drums, descending until they hovered just above the ground. The villagers gasped. Some fell to their knees.

The high priest shouted, "The gods come! They *see* us!"

But Uriel's face turned grim. Remiel clenched his fists. And the light took shape. Twelve figures, tall and radiant, formed from the beams—wings of gleaming fire, robes of blinding silk, eyes glowing like molten metal. But Remiel knew them. He knew them all. There, on the northern pillar—Asael, his once-brother in arms, now robed in false glory, his expression coiled with disdain. To the east, perched like a vulture, was Ecanus, his smile already forming into something too wide, too eager. At the front, descending like royalty, was Adapa. His gaze swept the crowd—not with mercy, but with hunger. And behind them, others. Twelve in total. Fallen angels in full masquerade.

Uriel's breath was cold mist in the air. "They must have been planning this for a long time."

Remiel's jaw tightened. "And now they want to be worshiped."

The twelve beams of light descended fully now, crystallizing into the forms of radiant beings—wings outstretched, robes aglow, their presence overwhelming. But to Remiel and Uriel, the light was a lie. Their hearts knew the truth of those who stood before them. They had once shared the same sky. The same mission. And now they wore divinity like a stolen robe.

From the front of the gathered angels, Adapa floated forward—arms out, expression beatific. His bare feet hovered just above the stone as he descended upon the altar. The high priest, already trembling, dropped to his knees and touched his forehead to the ground. Jared screamed, thrashing against his bindings, his cries high and desperate—Until Adapa gently touched his forehead. Instantly, his body went still. His eyes fluttered shut. The panic vanished as he dropped into a deep, unnatural sleep. Adapa hovered above him, then slowly turned to face the crowd. He spread his arms. And began to sing. The language was strange, melodic, filled with sibilant consonants and rising vowels. None of the humans understood it, but it struck a chord within their bones—ancient and mesmerizing.

But Remiel and Uriel did understand. It was a hymn. A hymn to the serpent. A song of honor, of rebellion, of glorified treason.

"To the one who slithered through Eden's gates,

To the one who whispered fire into clay.

To the one who bore the burden of exile,

And rose not as villain, but as liberator.

He who defied the One Above,

He who brings knowledge with his breath—

Rise, serpent, rise again..."

As Adapa sang, the other eleven angels joined in. Each voice added a haunting harmony—low, angelic, irresistible. The sound washed over the worshipers like an ocean of ecstasy. Many of the villagers fell to their knees. Others wept. Some reached toward the sky, overcome with awe. The torches dimmed, flickering as if bowing in reverence. And then— The earth trembled. It began as a distant vibration—like a coming stampede. The villagers gasped. The priests froze.

Above the far horizon, something vast and black blotted out the stars. A dragon. Wings stretched wider than the clouds. Scales shimmered like obsidian mirrors. Its eyes glowed like twin furnaces as it flew toward the temple, cutting through the night like a god returning from exile. As the dragon approached the temple, the winds howled. And then—just above the summit—it descended, its form folding inward as it touched the temple's peak. The great beast twisted, turned, and transformed. Where it had hovered now stood a man. Tall. Commanding. Radiant. His blonde hair caught the wind. His blue eyes sparkled like the sea under moonlight. His skin gleamed like carved marble. He wore a simple white robe that shimmered faintly, woven from something not of this world. The very stone beneath his feet pulsed with unnatural life. And as he landed, the twelve angels dropped to their knees in perfect unison. Heads bowed. Wings folded. The crowd below was utterly silent, held in a moment of reverent terror.

Uriel's face was pale now. He breathed, "Lucifer."

Remiel's eyes narrowed, fists curling at his sides. And then—he stepped forward. "This ends tonight," he growled, the illusion of his human guise beginning to flicker at the edges.

But a hand caught his arm. Uriel held Remiel fast, his expression stern beneath the calm.

"Not like this. We can't take them all at once."

Remiel's gaze burned. "We are not just soldiers. We are sentinels. Hosts of light. We don't cower in the face of evil—we confront it."

Uriel didn't flinch. "And we don't throw ourselves into battles we cannot win."

Remiel gestured toward the summit. "There are twelve *fallen angels* bowing before *Lucifer himself* on consecrated earth. Where are the watchers? How have they not seen this?"

Uriel's eyes shifted, scanning the gathered figures, the villagers, the priests, and a growing number of fallen angels materializing around the edge of the temple. Then he answered, voice low. "Because some of them are already here."

Remiel's eyes widened.

Uriel leaned closer, voice like a wire pulled tight. "We get the boy. Now. Before they sacrifice him."

Remiel looked toward the altar. Jared still lay motionless—breathing, alive, but surrounded by wolves.

Uriel continued. "I'll draw their attention. You'll take the boy. Move him to a safe point in the forest. Then go to Heaven. Report this. Bring back the Host."

Remiel opened his mouth to object.

Uriel cut him off. "It's the only way. You know that."

A silence passed between them—thick with dread and brotherhood.

Remiel's jaw tightened. "I know he can't kill you Uriel, but Lucifer... he can..."

Uriel held up a hand. "There's no time."

Remiel's fists clenched at his sides. Then he nodded once.

Uriel gave him a small, reassuring smile. "I'll be fine. He'll recognize me. That's the point." He turned toward the summit. And in that moment, he stood tall—his disguise falling away like dust in the wind. The human skin dissolved. The wings unfurled—vast, radiant, humming with ancient light. He stepped forward onto the temple floor, revealing his full glory.

The fallen angels turned.

And the first voice to speak was Adapa's, his gaze narrowing as the golden radiance of Uriel fell across the stone. "So, the errand boy arrives."

Uriel looked to each of them in turn. "Step away from the child," he commanded, his voice laced with divine authority.

The air vibrated with it, and even the villagers cowered from its resonance.

A hush fell across the summit.

Then a figure stepped forward from the semicircle of fallen. Asael. His wings spread with cruel elegance, his face twisted in mock affection. "You always were the stubborn one." His tone dripped with persuasion. "But it's not too late, brother." He took another step, eyes glinting in the torchlight.

"Bow before Lucifer. Worship him. And I swear there will be a place for you in the new world we are building."

Uriel scoffed, eyes hard. "Is child sacrifice part of that vision?"

Asael's smile faltered, but Adapa stepped in smoothly. "You mistake necessary offerings for cruelty, Uriel. The old ways must end. The new world demands new laws."

Uriel's voice rang like a bell of truth. "You think you'll be gods in this world? No..." He looked around, to each fallen angel, his gaze unflinching. "You'll be servants. Pawns to a harsher master than the one you have rebelled against."

A murmur rippled through the crowd of angels. Uriel raised himself into the air. His wings stretched outward like burning banners. And then—light. Radiant. Blinding. A storm of holiness made visible. The summit bathed in glory as a sphere of divine brilliance surged outward from Uriel's form. The humans collapsed to their knees, crying out, clutching their eyes, crawling along the stone in total blindness. The torches flickered, then extinguished. Shadows fled. The fallen angels squinted, recoiling, wings shielding their eyes. For a moment—just a moment—Uriel stood alone in the air, blazing like the morning star before dawn.

Suddenly, a white-robed blur shot through the radiance like a blade. Lucifer. He launched upward and *snatched Uriel from the air* and hurled him back down to the world below. The two streaked across the sky like colliding stars—and then Uriel hit the stone. The sound cracked the Heavens. He crashed into the temple platform with a thunderous impact, stone shattering like glass beneath him. Dust erupted in a ring.

The force of it sent priests and villagers tumbling backward. Uriel lay in the crater—wings broken, light dimmed, body aching with celestial pain. Before he could rise, Adapa stepped forward and snapped his fingers. Dozens of black, scaly hands erupted from the stone around Uriel, clutching his limbs, his wings, his throat. They pinned him like a captured lion, claws digging into the earth itself to keep him down. Then came the sound of soft footsteps.

Lucifer approached, regal and serene. He knelt beside Uriel like a friend checking on a fallen comrade. His voice was velvet and frost. "What did you expect to accomplish, Uriel?" He tilted his head, blue eyes glowing. "Did you think they would listen to you?" He smiled. "There is no war left to win. Only inheritance."

But Uriel—bleeding, broken, breath shallow—smiled back. Lucifer's smile vanished. He turned his head. The altar was empty. No body. No boy. Only the blood-soaked ropes that had once bound him, now loose and coiled like shed snakeskin.

Lucifer slowly rose to his feet, his calm cracking at the edges. "Find him," he commanded without raising his voice. It echoed through the air like a shattering decree. "He is not alone. Remiel is here."

The fallen angels stirred like hounds loosed from a cage. Without hesitation, six of the original twelve burst into the sky gathering other lesser demons with them, black wings slicing through the darkness, scanning the treetops and shadows. The others spread out across the temple perimeter, vanishing into the night with fury in their movements.

Lucifer turned back to Uriel, who still lay bound in the shattered stone, his smile fading into a grimace of pain. Lucifer's calm returned—but this time, it was cruel. "You're clever." He kneeled again. "Always were." He studied Uriel's face with a strange intimacy. "But you forget—I know the boundaries better than anyone." He raised his hand, fingers glowing with soft white light. "I cannot kill you. Not directly. Not yet."

Uriel gritted his teeth.

"But I know the loopholes," Lucifer whispered. His hand hovered just above Uriel's forehead, his voice dipping into the soft cadence of a memory. "Do you remember when I sang in Heaven?" His tone was wistful now, even reverent. "How the melody would slow the stars? How every being who heard it could dwell in the song for what felt like a thousand years? Time itself bent to the beauty of my voice."

He leaned in closer, a glint of something monstrous behind his perfect eyes. "I can still do that."

Uriel's breath caught in his chest.

Lucifer's voice darkened. "And though I cannot kill you, I can make you suffer… for what will feel like a millennium." He placed his glowing hand gently over Uriel's forehead.

The moment contact was made, Uriel's body arched with pain. His mouth opened in a scream so raw it split the silence across the temple summit. His eyes went wide, then distant—trapped. To the fallen, it lasted only a few seconds.

To Uriel, the torment had only begun. Inside Uriel's mind, time unraveled. The world around him slowed to a crawl. Overhead, birds flapped their wings in impossible slow motion—each beat taking what felt like hours. Dust hung in the air like suspended stars. The clouds didn't move. Even sound became a thick, muffled hum. Uriel tried to move, to speak—but he was frozen, trapped in this warped dimension of suffering.

Lucifer moved freely. He circled Uriel's still form with leisurely grace, untouched by the time dilation. He crouched beside him, examining his helplessness with childlike fascination. Then, with two fingers, he reached out and touched Uriel's foot. It ignited. A small flame at first—blue and pure—licking at the edge of his flesh like a match to paper. Then Lucifer touched the other foot, and it too caught fire. Uriel couldn't scream. The agony crawled up his legs inch by inch, but in this broken partition of time, it was a crawl that would last lifetimes.

Lucifer knelt beside him again, speaking softly—mockingly. "In here, a day will feel like a thousand years. And your body, dear Uriel…will burn like a slow candle."

The fire crept higher by the second. Each flicker stretched into an eternity. And in that prison of flame and stillness, Uriel endured the first eternal minute.

***

The forest was quiet, shrouded in mist and the faint crackle of distant branches. Remiel landed gently in a small clearing, the moonlight spilling down through the canopy like silver threads. Cradled in his arms was Jared—unconscious, limbs slack, and breath shallow. Remiel knelt and laid him down carefully on a bed of moss and leaves. He placed a hand over Jared's chest, and his fingers glowed softly. The bruises faded. The cuts sealed.

Blood vanished into healed skin. With a slow flutter of his eyelids, he stirred awake. He blinked, confused—then startled. When he saw Remiel, he immediately backed away, scrambling on hands and heels until his back hit a tree trunk. His breath came in sharp, terrified gasps.

Remiel stayed still. Then, in Jared's native tongue, his voice soft and clear, he spoke. "I do not serve the serpent." He pointed upward, through the trees, toward the heavens beyond the clouds. "I serve the Most High God."

Jared stared at him, trembling.

Remiel's voice remained calm. "You are safe now. But I must go. A war is beginning." He rose to his feet, wings starting to unfurl behind him, radiant and spectral in the dim light.

But before he could take flight, Jared's small voice stopped him.

"My sister...?"

Remiel paused. He turned.

Jared stood now, unsteady but determined, eyes wide with pleading. "They took her. Before me. To... receive the Serpent's blessing."

Remiel's gaze hardened. He remembered—yes. A girl dragged away by one of the red-robed priests before the march to the temple. She had not been among the villagers at the summit. Remiel turned east, toward the far end of the village. His eyes narrowed, and his angelic sight opened like a lens. The forest and distance vanished. He saw a tower, surrounded by fire pits and banners. On a raised platform, a line of young women in red dresses stood silently, faces painted, adorned in beads and gold. A priest slowly walked the line, stopping before each one, muttering judgments. Attendants fluttered around them like insects—tightening robes, painting lips, fitting veils. And there—her. Leah. Silent. Staring straight ahead.

Remiel exhaled, eyes dimming. He turned back to Jared, voice low and solemn. "She is in the tower. East side of the village."

Jared's face lit with a mixture of fear and desperate hope.

"I cannot go. There was sorrow in his tone. "I must return. But you can. There is still time."

Jared hesitated, trembling.

Remiel placed a hand on his shoulder—strong and warm. "Be brave. You don't need wings to bring down evil. Only courage." Then he stood. Wings opened wide. And in a burst of wind and silver light, Remiel shot skyward, vanishing into the night like a falling star in reverse.

***

Below, Jared looked east... and ran. Eventually he made it to the base of the structure where his sister was being kept and managed to sneak inside. He crept through the outer corridors of the tower, every step measured, every breath held. He expected to be caught at any moment—but no one came. The guards were gone. Distant shouts and trumpet-like echoes rang from the direction of the temple. The village was distracted. The heavens were stirring. And so he slipped through the winding halls of the tower until he reached a doorway veiled by crimson curtains. He pushed through.

The room beyond was softly lit by low fire bowls, their glow casting flickering shadows on the sandstone walls. Incense filled the air—sweet, heavy, and cloying. A dozen young women sat on plush cushions or silk-covered benches, all dressed in red ceremonial dresses, adorned in jewels, gold chains, and thick black eyeliner that turned their gazes into masks. Some were chatting softly. Others adjusted their hair, jewelry, or clothing, as if preparing for something important. There were no guards.

He ducked behind a carved pillar, scanning the room. There. His heart thudded. Leah. She was seated beside another girl, head tilted slightly in conversation. Her eyes were downcast, her face calm—but she looked so different. Unrecognizable beneath the ornate makeup and stiff posture. But he knew her. Even through the transformation. Even now. He waited. Made sure. Still no guard. Then, slowly, he emerged. At first, only Leah's companion noticed him approaching.

But when Leah turned to see who the girl was staring at—her breath caught in her throat. Tears welled instantly. She stood, in disbelief, and ran into his arms. They embraced tightly, her head buried against his shoulder, his arms wrapped around her like he feared she would disappear again. Around them, the murmurs began. The other girls looked up, whispering, unsure whether to be frightened or fascinated.

He pulled away first. "We have to go," he said in a hushed, urgent tone.

"Now. While they're all at the temple." He reached for her wrist and turned, but she stayed rooted to the floor. He glanced back, confused.

"I need to do something first." Leah wiped her eyes and turned back toward the room. She took a deep breath, then stepped forward, raising her voice—not loud, but steady. "Listen to me." She looked at the girls.

They turned, cautiously.

"I don't know what they've promised you—jewels, warmth, comfort—but it's a lie." Her voice quivered but grew stronger with each word. "We're not priestesses. We're not brides. We're offerings. They'll use us until we're not beautiful anymore. Until we're old, or defiant, or broken—and then we'll be cast aside."

Some of the girls looked down. Others blinked, unmoving.

"I won't pretend it's easy outside," Leah continued. "My village was burned. We don't have homes. We don't have soft cushions and incense." She paused. "But we have freedom. And no one makes us wear chains and smile while we die."

A long silence followed. Then, slowly, the girl who had been sitting beside Leah stood up. She walked forward and stood next to her. Another followed. And another. Within moments, half the room had joined her—girls in red, makeup smudging as tears fell, faces suddenly human again. The others remained seated, uncertain, still trapped in the dream they had been sold. But change had begun.

Leah turned to her brother. "Now we can go."

As the group turned toward the exit, hope blooming with each step— a shadow blocked the doorway. A single figure stood waiting. A serpent priest. He was massive—his blood-red robes sleeveless, revealing a torso carved from years of battle. His arms were marked with black tattoos of fangs, coils, and serpent eyes. His chest rose slowly with controlled breath.

Jared froze. The priest stepped forward with deliberate menace, eyes sweeping over the girls, then fixing on Jared. Jared instinctively stepped in front of them and raised an arm in a protective gesture, his body tense. The priest smiled. Then lowered into a stance—feet apart, shoulders squared, fists clenched before him with practiced calm. It wasn't how men fought in Jared's village. This was something else, something he had never seen. Disciplined. Trained. Deadly.

Jared tried to imitate him, lifting his fists, but his footing was unsure—weight distributed unevenly. The priest began to circle, eyes fixed on Jared like a predator sizing up a cornered hare. His feet moved with silent precision, body swaying like a serpent ready to strike. Then he lunged. A quick jab flashed out landing squarely on Jared's cheek. Jared stumbled back, reeling, hand flying to his face. But he didn't fall. He raised his fists again, blinking through the pain. The priest advanced, letting out a harsh hiss, and swung wide with a brutal hook. Jared ducked just in time and drove an uppercut into the priest's chin. The priest staggered.

A gasp rose from the girls. Jared pressed forward, striking again and again, landing shots into the man's gut, ribs, anywhere he could reach. The priest backed up—off balance. It looked like Jared was winning. Until— the priest caught Jared's fist midair, twisting it violently. Jared shouted in pain. Then came a devastating left hook—slamming into Jared's jaw. He crashed to the floor.

The girls screamed. The priest grinned and kicked Jared hard in the ribs, then dropped his full weight onto him. He straddled Jared and began pummeling his face, knuckles drawing blood with every impact. Then—his hands locked around Jared's neck.

Jared gagged, hands clawing at the priest's wrists, his legs kicking uselessly. He couldn't breathe. His vision began to blur. His strength waned. And then— *Crack!* The priest's head jolted violently to the side. His grip loosened. Behind him, Leah stood—both hands wrapped around a heavy stone serpent statue, its tail chipped, its head slick with blood. The priest slumped forward. His massive body collapsed on top of Jared, unconscious. Silence fell.

The girls gasped, covering their mouths. Jared lay beneath the priest, coughing, gasping, trying to pull himself free. Leah dropped the statue. Then dropped to her knees and pulled her brother's arm over her shoulder, trying to lift him.

He looked up at her, dazed and bruised. "I was about to win," he rasped with a bloody grin.

She choked a laugh through her tears. "Come on. We're not done yet."

***

Smoke curled upward from Uriel's body, rising in slow, unbroken strands like incense from a dying temple. His wings were seared, blackened at the tips, his robes charred and clinging to skin that healed only to burn again. The unholy fire licked at him endlessly, a cruel loop of pain that could never end. To the others, it had been minutes. To Uriel—it had been five days. His eyes, once brilliant with light, now stared forward with a distant gloss. His chest rose in shallow, ragged gasps. His mouth twitched as if murmuring prayers he couldn't quite remember.

Lucifer stood over him, calm and unmoved, arms behind his back like a king admiring a ruined painting. "This," he mused, "is what loyalty buys you."

From behind, Adapa approached, wings tucked and face unreadable. "My lord," he said, bowing his head. "The search parties have failed. Remiel is gone. And so is the boy."

Lucifer didn't move at first. The corner of his mouth twitched—either in amusement or fury. Then he spoke, low and cold. "Call them back. All of them."

Adapa bowed again, flawlessly graceful. "As you command." With a gust of wind and black feathers, he soared into the night sky.

Lucifer turned his attention back to Uriel and crouched slowly, resting his elbows on his knees. He stared into the broken angel's blank eyes. "Still in there?" he whispered. "Still clinging to your purpose? Or have you finally learned what it means to suffer without meaning?"

Uriel didn't answer. Lucifer smiled. Then—the air split open. A white spear, enormous and radiant, whistled through the sky like a falling comet. Lucifer's eyes flashed. He leapt back just as the ivory spear plunged into the ground, separating him from Uriel with an explosion of wind and light that sent cracks racing through the stone. Standing on the blunt end of the spear, balanced as easily as if it were the earth itself, was Michael, the Archangel. Bronze curls framed his chiseled face. His eyes burned like fire behind a wall of humor. His armor shone with gilded etchings, and his wings spread wide, glimmering like blades of polished bronze and gold.

He looked down at Lucifer with a wide, easy grin. "Did you forget what happened last time you tried this?"

Lucifer's eyes narrowed. "Things are different now."

Michael jumped down, landing with the grace of a lion and the weight of a falling star. "Mm. Different? Sure. Same snake, new scales." He turned to Uriel, knelt down, and rested a hand lightly on his scorched cheek.

Uriel flinched—his breath shallow, his eyes wide and flickering, twitching like someone trapped in a nightmare.

Michael gently patted his face. "Hey," he said softly, leaning close. "Hang in there, buddy. Cavalry's comin'."

Uriel didn't speak—but a tear slid down his cheek, cutting a clean path through the soot. And behind Michael, light began to gather in the clouds above—an army just beyond the veil.

28

Rejoice in Hope, Be Patient in Tribulation, Be Constant in Prayer

The restaurant sat nestled between a barbershop and a bakery, its windows glowing softly under hand-painted signs that read *La Casa de Luz*. It wasn't flashy. No skyline view. No dress code. But the scent that drifted from its kitchen—smoke, citrus, cumin, and warm corn—spoke for itself. Gabriel parked a few spots down and took a steadying breath before walking in. A bell above the door jingled, and instantly the warmth hit him—both in temperature and atmosphere. Handmade papel picado decorations danced lazily in the air-conditioned breeze, and a framed photo of a younger Gabriel shaking hands with the owner hung behind the counter.

"¡Mira quién es!" a voice boomed from the back. Marco, a broad-chested man in his sixties emerged, apron dusted with masa and a towel flung over one shoulder. "Been too long, mijo."

Gabriel smiled as the man strode toward him. They clasped hands in a firm shake that turned into a quick hug and a back-pat.

"You want it bagged to go like usual?" He stepped back toward the kitchen.

Gabriel shook his head. "Not tonight. I've got a date."

Marco's eyes widened. A grin bloomed across his face, and he gave Gabriel a few light jabs to the shoulder, more affection than impact. "Ay, caray. You bring a lady here and don't tell me? Sit tight—I'll make it nice." He turned

242

with purpose, talking under his breath to himself as he ducked behind the counter.

A moment later, he reappeared with a small glass vase filled with fresh flowers and two candles he pulled from a drawer near the register. He moved to the corner booth near the window—the most private in the house—and began setting the table like a man prepping a stage for something sacred. Gabriel just chuckled to himself, watching the transformation.

Gabriel walked up beside him and gave him a grateful pat on the back. "Marco, you didn't have to do all that."

Marco turned with a shrug and a smile. "Of course I did. Anything for you, *compa*." He walked off toward the kitchen, already calling for his best plates.

Gabriel sat down and pulled out his phone.

Here early. Don't worry, no need to rush. Table's ready.

He set the phone down and glanced around the room. For a moment, his fingers drifted to the utensils—adjusting the knife angle, moving the spoon slightly left, then undoing it all just to reset it again. His thumb tapped restlessly against the napkin. He caught himself and exhaled, then chuckled under his breath. Nervous. He hadn't felt this in a long time.

A few minutes later, the bell above the door chimed. Paula stepped inside, blinking as her eyes adjusted to the dim warmth. She didn't see him right away. Her hand moved down to smooth the fabric of her sundress—light yellow with small white flowers. She shifted awkwardly, adjusting a strap, then took a hesitant step forward as she scanned the room.

Gabriel stood up from the booth. "Hey," he said gently.

She turned—and smiled. "Hi."

He took a step closer and nodded at her dress. "You look..." He paused, searching for a word that wouldn't sound like a line. "Beautiful."

Her smile deepened, a hint of pink blooming in her cheeks. "Thank you. I almost didn't wear this." She gave a small, embarrassed laugh. "Bought it a while back and never found the right excuse."

"Well," he said, gesturing toward the booth, "I'm glad tonight made the cut."

Paula's eyes followed his hand, taking in the table—candles flickering, a modest glass vase with fresh flowers nestled between the settings. It stood out. No other table in the restaurant looked like that. She raised an eyebrow. "This is... definitely not what I expected when you said family-owned spot." She slid into the booth. "Did they set this up for everyone or are we getting the VIP treatment?"

Gabriel chuckled, settling in across from her. "Let's just say the owner likes me."

"Oh?" she teased, picking up her napkin. "And how exactly did you earn this floral centerpiece and mood lighting?"

"Long story," he said, trying to play it cool.

Marco reappeared with a couple of water glasses and a grin that gave him away. "*Ay*, don't let him downplay it. Your date here? He caught the people who stole from me. Didn't just hand it off to some rookie—no. He pieced it together himself. Even got back something I thought I'd never see again." He gestured behind the counter to the far wall.

Mounted in a glass case was a beautiful, amber-toned Spanish guitar—its wood worn smooth from use, the frets still shining. A small photo sat just below it, showing a young man playing that very guitar, head tilted back singing, a mic in front of him.

"My son," Marco said, his voice softening, "used to play every Saturday night—old boleros, rancheras, even some original songs. The customers loved him. We all thought he was gonna make it big someday."

Paula followed his gaze, her expression turning gentle.

"He passed away a few years ago. Aneurysm. No warning. He was twenty-four." Marco's voice caught for just a second before he cleared his throat. "We kept his guitar here ever since. Made the place feel like he was still playing in it." He nodded toward Gabriel again. "When those punks broke in, they took cash, booze, and that guitar. Thought it'd fetch a high price—didn't care what it meant. But this guy?" He clapped Gabriel's shoulder again. "Tracked it down. Got it back in one piece. Didn't just solve a crime—he gave us back a piece of our heart."

He smiled at Paula, but there was a weight behind it. "So when he says he's bringing someone special in here, we light the candles." With that, Marco gave them a knowing wink and turned back to the kitchen.

Paula watched him go, then looked across the table at Gabriel, her expression soft. "You didn't tell me any of that."

Gabriel gave a small shrug, his fingers absently tracing the rim of his glass. "I was just doing my job."

She tilted her head, smiling. "Not every job ends with someone getting their son's guitar back."

He glanced toward the display on the wall, then back at her. "Yeah, well... don't remind Marco. You know after it was all over he tried to name an enchilada after me?"

Paula laughed, and the tension that had built during Marco's story gently unraveled. Their eyes lingered for a quiet second, the candlelight dancing in the space between them.

"You know," Paula said, picking up her water, "our moms would probably be freaking out right now if they knew about this."

Gabriel smirked. "Oh yeah. My mom would be calling every ten minutes asking how it's going. Then she'd start sending me name suggestions."

"For what?"

"Future children. Pets. Whatever's next on her list."

Paula grinned. "She skips ahead, huh?"

"Immediately. And she always says the same thing—'You work too much. Find someone who makes you slow down.'" He met her eyes again, voice dipping just a bit. "She'd like you."

Paula blinked and smiled. "Well, I'm a big fan of moms who know what they're talking about."

Gabriel lifted his glass. "Don't say that. She'll never let me live it down."

Marco returned with two steaming plates balanced effortlessly on his arms. "All right, lovebirds. Enchiladas with *molé negro*—only make it on holidays, funerals, and first dates for people we like." He set the plates down, gave them a wink, and vanished again.

Paula leaned over her plate and inhaled. "Oh my God. I'm not emotionally prepared for how good this smells."

Gabriel chuckled. "You're not even emotionally prepared for the second bite. That's when it gets real."

She laughed and picked up her fork. "All right, detective. Impress me."

He smirked, lifting his own. "Already working on it."

They both took their first bites at the same time.

Paula closed her eyes as the flavors hit—rich, smoky, slightly sweet, with just the right kick of heat. "Oh my God," she said, after a beat. "That's *unfairly* good."

Gabriel laughed, nodding. "Right? This place ruins you for other food."

She took another bite, savoring it, then set her fork down gently. "Okay, now I get it. You weren't just trying to impress me. You were sharing your favorite place."

Gabriel smiled. "Exactly. It's the kind of place that reminds me why I still love this city." He watched her for a moment, then leaned in a little. "So, emergency medicine—what's that really like? I mean, being on the front lines like that."

Paula gave a small, thoughtful shrug. "It's intense. Every day's different. Sometimes it's controlled chaos. Sometimes it's just chaos." She laughed softly. "But honestly? It's rewarding. You get to be there when someone's at their absolute worst, and just... help. Even if it's just stabilizing them, holding their hand, talking them through the panic. You make a difference in real time. That's what keeps me going."

Gabriel nodded, his expression softening. "That's incredible."

She smiled. "Thanks. What about you? Being a detective has to be pretty rough sometimes."

Gabriel looked down for a second, his fingers brushing crumbs from the table. "Yeah. It can be rough." He glanced toward the wall again, where the guitar rested in its glass case. His gaze lingered for a moment. "Sometimes cases end like that," he said, voice quieter. "You put the pieces together. Something broken gets returned. People get a little peace of mind back." Then he turned back to her. "But sometimes they don't. Sometimes you never find out what happened. Sometimes you do—and it's worse than you expected."

She nodded, her eyes softening. "That must be hard."

He exhaled. "Early in my career, that used to eat me alive. I couldn't sleep. I'd stay up going over the same details, convinced I'd missed something. That if I just looked hard enough, I'd find the key." He looked at her, his voice steady but weighted. "I have this drive—I need to know what happened. Not just for the case, but for the people. For the ones left behind."

Paula nodded, her eyes soft. "I can tell."

He gave her a faint smile. "It's not exactly a personality trait that makes you popular."

"I don't know," she said, picking up her glass. "I think wanting the truth is a pretty good start."

He looked at her for a second, something flickering behind his eyes.

Paula's gaze didn't waver. "Still. You're out there trying. That counts for something."

He looked at her for a beat, then gave her a faint smile. "I like that you think so."

She returned the smile, but then her eyes drifted downward, her fingers lightly brushing the base of her glass. "What you said... about needing to know the truth... I get that. I think that's what pulled me into medicine in the first place. Every symptom is a puzzle. You ask the right questions, order the right labs, make sense of the chaos... and sometimes, you get to fix it. You get to save someone." She paused. "But sometimes... you don't."

Gabriel listened, quiet.

"I remember the first time I lost a patient." Her voice was steady, but something distant flickered behind it. "I was still in residency. Sixteen-year-old boy. Car accident. Blunt trauma to the abdomen. He went into emergency surgery and I assisted. It lasted hours... we tried everything." She shook her head gently. "But we couldn't save him. He coded on the table. I knew, in theory, that it was going to happen eventually. That you can't save everyone. But when it actually happened..." She swallowed. "It was like something cracked inside me. I walked out of the OR, took off my gloves, made it to the back parking lot, and just... cried. Hard. I didn't even know I had that much in me. Then I wiped my face, went back inside, and finished my shift."

Gabriel's eyes were locked on hers, gentle. "I'm sorry. That's not something you just forget."

She shook her head. "No. It's not. It's like an old wound that never fully heals. You get better at carrying it, but it's always there."

"That's exactly how it feels with some cases." He looked down at the table, then back up at her. "Have you heard of Angela Ward... the missing mother?"

Paula slowly nodded.

"We've been digging for weeks. Leads dry up. People go quiet. The trail gets colder by the hour. And you think about her little boy, and you wonder if he's going to grow up never knowing what happened to his mom."

Paula looked at him, the same ache mirrored in her expression.

"I keep going back over every interview, every report. Trying to find the piece I missed. Because I know if it were me—if it were my family—I'd want someone who wouldn't give up."

There was a quiet stillness between them—something unspoken but deeply understood.

She reached across the table and gently touched his hand. "She's lucky you're the one looking."

He looked down at her hand, and hesitated for a moment. "We're actually planning to release part of the footage soon. From the parking lot."

Paula's brow furrowed. "Footage?"

"There's a security camera near where the kidnapper parked. The angle's not great, but you can make out enough. Angela fighting back. She didn't go down easy."

A flicker of admiration passed through Paula's expression. "Good for her."

Gabriel nodded. "Yeah. She landed a solid blow to his face—clawed at his eye. Left him stumbling. That's actually one of the details we're including in the press release. If someone sees a guy walking around with a scratched-up eye around the time she went missing, we want them to come forward."

Paula sat back, absorbing the weight of it. "That must've been hard to watch."

"It was. She was terrified... but she didn't freeze. She fought like hell. There's always this moment, watching something like that, where you wonder—if she'd been there just ten seconds earlier... would it have changed anything?"

She held his gaze—steady, compassionate, present. "You're carrying a lot," she said softly.

Gabriel gave a small, tired smile. "I think we both are."

Their hands lingered for a moment longer on the table before Paula gently pulled hers back. The silence between them wasn't awkward—it was charged with something real, something understood.

The kitchen doors swung open and Marco appeared again, balancing a tray with the pride of a man carrying treasure. "I hope you two saved room. Flan and churros with abuelita chocolate—on the house. Because I like you, and because love looks better with dessert."

Paula laughed. "That's dangerously charming."

Gabriel grinned. "Don't encourage him."

Marco placed the plates down with a flourish, then leaned in. "And don't think I didn't notice you two getting all soulful over here. You keep talking like that and I'm bringing out the good tequila."

Before either of them could respond, he was gone again—vanishing into the kitchen like a magician who knew exactly when to exit.

Paula smiled as she looked down at the desserts, but her eyes flicked back to Gabriel after a beat. "Hey... can I ask you something?"

"Of course." He reached for a churro.

"The night Angela went missing—what time was it exactly? Do you remember?"

Gabriel blinked, mid-bite. "She left the bar just before eight. The camera picked her up five minutes later waiting in the lot. And then... the incident starts about fifteen minutes after that."

Paula nodded slowly, her expression neutral, but her fingers tapped lightly against the stem of her glass. "Okay. Just curious."

Gabriel tilted his head. "Why?"

She gave a small, easy shrug. "I don't know. Something about it... just stuck with me. That's all."

He studied her for a moment, but she smiled, took a bite of flan, and changed the subject with practiced ease.

***

Thousands of years ago a divine showdown took place at the village's temple. The night was no longer quiet. The sky had become a canvas of chaos—wings, light, and flame streaking across it in violent strokes. The clash of angelic steel and infernal claws rang like the tolling of apocalyptic bells. Screams—both human and inhuman—rippled through the trees, now lit with unnatural fire. Smoke curled like grasping fingers through the branches. Remiel knelt beside Uriel's crumpled form. Uriel's eyes were vacant—staring, but not seeing. His lips parted slightly, breath shallow. The afterimage of Lucifer's torture still held him in its cruel grip.

Remiel placed a hand on his friend's shoulder, his grip firm but not forceful. "Uriel." His voice cut through the storm like a bell of iron. "Look at me."

No response. Uriel's fingers twitched, but his gaze didn't move.

"Uriel," he repeated, louder this time. "You're not in the fire anymore. You're here—with me."

Still nothing.

So Remiel reached out and pressed their foreheads together, eyes shut, light pulsing between them. His voice dropped to a whisper—not for volume, but for weight. "You are not alone."

For a beat, everything else faded—the crack of battle, the roar of flame, the howling of the damned.

And then— Uriel blinked. His chest hitched as if surfacing from deep water. He gasped, body seizing for an instant. Then his hand shot up, clutching Remiel's tunic. His eyes—wide, glassy, burning—finally locked onto his brother's. "Remiel," he rasped.

"You're safe," Remiel said quickly, slipping an arm under Uriel's shoulders and lifting him up. "You're here. Breathe."

Uriel's lips trembled, and for a moment his strength faltered. Then he saw the sky. And the forest. And the burning trees. And above it all—Michael and Lucifer. They collided like titans. Michael's spear spun in gleaming arcs, singing through the air with divine resonance. Lucifer moved like liquid fire, dodging each thrust with sinuous grace. Then, with a snarl, Lucifer

250

exhaled—and a wave of fire erupted from his mouth, a pillar of unholy flame lashing toward Michael. But, he dove aside just in time. The fire struck the treetops behind him, igniting them instantly. A thunderous crack split the air as one of the ancient pines burst into flame, its trunk splintering, its branches falling like burning arms toward the earth.

Remiel held Uriel tighter, dragging him to his feet. "We have to move."

Uriel staggered but nodded, shaking the last of the mental prison from his mind.

"I'm here," he said again, more firmly this time. "I'm with you."

But before they could step away—

They stopped.

Three figures stood ahead.

Adapa, serene as a corpse-king, robes unmarred by flame.

Ecanus, eyes too wide, grin twitching, licking his lips like he tasted madness in the air.

And Asael—whole again, smoke still clinging to the edges of his form.

They stood at the edge of the blaze, flames licking the sky behind them, casting monstrous shadows across the scorched ground. The three formed a triangle—an unholy trinity of deception, delirium, and destruction—blocking the path forward like wolves before a gate.

Remiel's hand gripped the hilt of his sword. He shifted, stepping slightly in front of Uriel. "You steady?" he asked, eyes never leaving the three.

Uriel exhaled, slow and even. Though still battered, he stood taller now—his light returning like embers catching wind. "I'm ready. Let's finish this."

Remiel gave a tight nod, his voice low. "Adapa and Ecanus are mine." He glanced sideways at Asael—eyes hard as flint. "You take the snake."

Uriel stepped forward, his wings unfurling in a whisper of light and steel. "Gladly."

With that, Remiel drew his sword—radiant and burning like it had been pulled from the heart of a star—and charged. Adapa didn't move. Not until the blade came down like a divine hammer. Then, with a sound like tearing silk, he vanished—dissolving into a pillar of black smoke. The sword passed through nothing. The smoke slithered away, reforming several feet behind

Remiel.

Ecanus, shrieking with delight, launched himself into the air. His body arced high, and then came crashing down—both fists aimed for Remiel's skull like a meteor of flesh. But Remiel spun aside in a burst of light. The hilt of his sword came up with a powerful smash, catching Ecanus in the ribs mid-fall. The impact sent the mad angel flying backward, tumbling through the air before crashing into a burning tree with a grotesque crunch of bone and bark. Remiel didn't watch him land. His focus snapped back to the smoke, which now reformed into Adapa's smiling figure. But the scene shifted. A breathless pause. A stillness before the clash. Uriel and Asael. Facing one another. Their eyes met.

A thousand years of silence passed in a heartbeat.

Asael tilted his head, something tender in the motion. "You know," he said, voice low and smooth, "I had hoped... that you would see it. That you, of all of them, would stand with me."

Uriel's expression didn't shift. "I saw plenty. That's why I stand against you."

Asael's smile faded. A flicker of regret—real or performed—crossed his face. "Why? Why do you still protect them? What is it about these fragile things that makes you willing to burn for them?" He stepped forward, voice rising. "They stumble through their days barely aware of the heavens above, drowning in their own wars, their filth, their noise. And yet—you bleed for them?"

Uriel didn't flinch. "Because they matter."

Asael's composure cracked. The sneer returned—fiercer now, jagged with years of resentment. "This world should have been ours!" he hissed. "We were forged in light, tempered by eternity. And yet we are made to kneel while they—children made of dust—are given rule over the earth? Dominion over creation?" He spat the words like poison. "We watched the stars being born. We sang existence into motion. And now we're reduced to guardians and messengers—while they build kingdoms and call themselves kings."

He paced now, agitated, wings twitching with fury. "I refuse now. I will not be servant to clay."

Uriel's gaze was steady, voice quiet but unwavering. "That's always been your tragedy, Asael. You were too busy envying them to see the truth."

Asael's steps slowed.

Uriel took a step forward now. "This was never about who gets to rule. We are family with them." He gestured toward the burning trees, toward the wounded, toward the chaos beyond. "They may be weak. They may stumble. But they were made with the same breath that gave us life." He paused—let the weight of it settle. "You can't see it because you never looked past your pride. You think servanthood is slavery—but it was always stewardship. And love."

Asael's expression twisted. "Don't speak to me of love."

But Uriel did not yield. "That's all this was ever about. Not power. Not dominion. Love. And you rejected it. You chose exile over family. Jealousy over joy." He drew his blade—gleaming with soft, unyielding light. "And now you call that freedom."

Asael bared his teeth.

The ground beneath them trembled.

Their wings snapped wide.

They moved. Asael's body began to shift as he advanced—bones stretching, cracking, reforming. His legs twisted and fused into a massive, coiled serpent tail, thick as a tree trunk, scaled in obsidian black. It hissed across the scorched earth, muscles rippling with inhuman power. His upper torso remained vaguely angelic, though it had curdled—feathers blackened, arms elongated and ridged with sinew. His fingers ended in jagged, hardened talons, glistening like obsidian blades. His face contorted between man and monster, eyes molten gold, lips split by curved fangs. He slithered toward Uriel with terrifying speed, the ground splitting beneath the weight of his advance.

Uriel stood firm, sword in hand, his eyes blazing with focused light. He raised the blade and swung. The edge carved through the air in a wide arc—but Asael had already slid to the side, tail coiling and propelling him forward like a viper. Another swing—then another—Uriel's movements a storm of precision, his sword singing with holy fire. But Asael was too fast. He twisted and ducked, tail snapping and bending his frame in impossible angles. Every strike met only wind and smoke. Then Asael lunged. His talons came down like axes, both hands slamming toward Uriel with monstrous force. Uriel raised his sword just in time as the claws struck the blade, sparks erupting in a burst of light and shadow. Asael pressed forward, forcing Uriel back with raw power. Then—he gripped the sword. His claws clamped around the blade's edge, black talons shrieking against the divine steel. Uriel gritted his teeth, trying to twist it free.

But Asael leaned in—face inches from his own. From between his fanged lips, a thin, forked tongue flicked out, tasting the air between them. "I was always stronger Uriel, this battle is already decided," he whispered, voice like burning oil.

Then—with a snarl—he *ripped* the sword from Uriel's hands and flung it into the shadows behind him. He roared and swung again, claws whistling toward Uriel's head. Uriel ducked. Another strike. He blocked it with his armored forearm. A third—he turned aside just in time. The talons gouged deep ruts into the stone beneath his feet. But then—Uriel *caught* them. With a shout, he seized both of Asael's wrists in his hands, his arms locked in a powerful grip. Asael hissed and tried to wrench free, but Uriel held fast, wings flaring with radiant light.

"You're nothing like what you were Asael," Uriel growled. He yanked Asael's arms wide and drove his forehead into Asael's face with crushing force.

Asael reeled, staggering backward, black blood streaming from his nose. Uriel didn't hesitate. He lifted his foot and *kicked* Asael square in the chest— sending the half-serpent arching back through the air, crashing into a broken pillar with a thunderous crunch. Uriel stood tall, hand outstretched, fingers open. And then—*Whip!*—his sword flashed through the air like a shooting star, returning to his grasp in a burst of light. It landed in his palm with a solid, satisfying thud.

Uriel's grip tightened. His wings rose. And he stepped forward. "Let's finish this."

Asael stirred amidst the rubble, the stone beneath him cracked and glowing faintly with the residue of Uriel's light. He growled low and began to rise—his serpent tail coiling beneath him like a spring, black claws digging into the ground for leverage. Blood streaked down his face, but the madness in his eyes had only deepened. Uriel stood across from him, sword gleaming in both hands, feet planted like an immovable pillar of Heaven. They stood across from each other—two ancient brothers beneath a burning sky.

All around them, battle raged like a storm. Blinding flashes lit the night—swords clashed, wings tore through flame, beasts and angels collided in a maelstrom of fury and fire. Thunder cracked. Lightning flashed. Trees split and fell. And above it all— Lucifer. His form no longer human. A massive black dragon with tattered wings and eyes like twin eclipses, he launched skyward—tearing through the heavens like a blight upon creation. His roar shattered clouds. Michael followed, ivory spear in hand, chasing him into the stars. Their clash became flashes above—violent, distant, supernatural.

But here—on earth—time slowed. Uriel's gaze returned to Asael. And for a moment, he didn't see the serpent. He saw the angel he used to know. The one who laughed in the halls of Heaven. The one who stood beside him when the stars were still learning to shine. The one who sang so loudly it made galaxies shiver. A tear welled in Uriel's eye. It shimmered.

Asael saw the flicker of grief—and mistook it. With a hiss and a snarl, he lunged forward, fangs bared, claws ready to rend. And then—blinding light. It burst from Uriel like a nova, engulfing the clearing in a radiant shockwave. When the light faded— Asael was on his back, pinned beneath Uriel, the angel's knees planted firmly against his serpent coil.

Uriel's sword was gripped in both hands, the glowing tip hovering just above Asael's chest. Asael panted, chest rising and falling, eyes narrowed. Then he saw the tears still clinging to Uriel's face—and he laughed.

It was hoarse, guttural, a sound torn between mockery and madness. "What's this? Feeling nostalgic?"

Uriel didn't strike. His voice cracked beneath its sorrow. "Why? Why did you have to choose the dark?"

Asael's laughter died down. He stared up—not at Uriel, but at the sky.

"We could've walked together for all eternity," Uriel said softly. "Side by side. We were meant to protect them. To *love* them."

Asael blinked slowly… peacefully. "That's exactly why I left," he said, voice quiet now. "Because I wanted to choose something for myself. No more plans. No more purpose. You call it darkness." He looked at Uriel now, fully. "I call it freedom."

Uriel's grip tightened. He raised the sword high, light streaking from the blade like a divine flare. And then— *A trumpet blast.* It rolled across the sky like a tidal wave of command—deep, celestial, impossible to ignore. Every head turned skyward. The light above parted.

The King was calling. Uriel froze, eyes lifting to the heavens. Around them, the other angels—Remiel, Raphael, warriors known and unknown—turned their wings toward the sky. They ascended like meteors in reverse, pulled home by the voice of God.

Asael smirked from below, lips curling. "Daddy's calling."

Uriel lowered the blade. And in one smooth motion, he stood, sheathed the sword, and without a word—burst into the sky, light trailing behind him like the wake of a comet.

Asael lay on the stone, staring up at the sky. And laughed.

29

But Concerning that Day and Hour No One Knows

Something was off. Marshall had been distant all day. Not in his usual quiet, brooding way—this was something heavier. Angela could see it in the set of his shoulders, the stiffness in his walk. He didn't linger by the TV like he sometimes did. No awkward pauses. No small talk. Just silence and a grim expression stamped across his face like he'd swallowed bad news and didn't know how to digest it. He brought down her food earlier and barely looked at her. A short nod. No words. No checking in. No "How are you holding up?" Nothing. Something was very wrong. She felt it. And though every part of her wanted to believe it had nothing to do with her, she could not afford to assume anything anymore. She stared at the small chalkboard by the bed. Her fingers trembled just a little as she picked up the nub of white and scrawled one word across the surface:

EMERGENCY.

This was it. She needed him out of the house. Even for just a moment. She could not wait any longer—not with that storm cloud in his eyes.

She braced herself and raised her voice just enough to carry up the stairs. "Marshall?"

Nothing.

"Marshall!" She pitched her tone higher this time, laced with forced

257

urgency.

Heavy footsteps thundered overhead. A door creaked. Then a rush of movement down the stairs. The basement door flung open and there he was—panting, disheveled, eyes wide with panic.

"What is it?" His eyes darted around the room like he expected to find blood or a body. "What's wrong?"

She hesitated. She wasn't expecting him to come so fast. This was her moment. She didn't answer right away. Instead, she tilted her head, studying him. "That's what I was going to ask you."

His brows drew together in confusion. Then annoyance. The fear drained from his face, replaced by irritation. He exhaled sharply. "I thought you were hurt," he muttered, rubbing the back of his neck. "Why did you call me like that?"

"I'm sorry," she said gently. "But... Marshall... I've been watching you. Today, yesterday. You've been different. Grim. Distant. Like your mind is somewhere else."

His jaw tightened. She watched the muscles move beneath the skin.

"I'm not trying to push you. I just... I want to understand. I want to know what's going on."

He looked away for a long moment. She was afraid he was going to lie. Or shut down.

"It's my mom. She's sick."

Her chest tightened. "Sick how?"

"Coughing. High fever. It started yesterday, but it's worse today. She's not doing well. I—I gave her some old antibiotics but I don't know if they're working."

There was a rawness in his voice that she had not heard before. He was scared. Really scared.

She nodded slowly. "I'm sorry. That must be terrifying."

He stared down at the floor, as if it might tell him what to do.

She swallowed hard. She could not lose sight of the plan. Not now. "I... I also wanted to tell you something else." She made her voice sound small and hesitant. "I'm about to start my period."

His head snapped up. "You're what?" His eyes darted again in panic. He began to turn around, probably to dig through some forgotten cabinet.

"It's okay, I just— I'm going to need some pads, a specific brand. The ones with the wings. Blue packaging. Ultra Light Long Overnight. Not the regular ones, they don't work for me."

He hesitated, clearly unsure if this qualified as a real emergency. But she could already see him doing the mental math. Mom upstairs. Angela downstairs. This wasn't a fight he wanted right then. She hoped. That one errand might be the crack she needed. One trip. One chance.

He blinked at her. Twice. Then his mouth opened, closed, and opened again—like a goldfish flung out of water. "When... exactly?" he asked, his voice tight.

She had to fight the urge to smirk. "Tonight. I can already feel the cramps starting."

His face twisted in alarm, as if she had just announced a medical emergency. He stared at her like she was about to spontaneously combust. "Oh... uh..." His eyes darted around the room like he was scanning for an instruction manual. "Okay. Okay. What do I... do?"

He was genuinely panicking. He looked like someone had handed him a live grenade and told him it might explode sometime soon.

"I just need that specific kind. Blue package. Ultra Light Long Overnight. Has to have wings. Not the regular kind. Not the short ones. Not maxi."

He just stood there, utterly overwhelmed. Then, without a word, he spun on his heel and bolted upstairs. She heard drawers opening. Then frantic footsteps overhead. For a second, she wondered if he'd actually fled the house right then and there—but then the basement door banged open again, and he came rushing back down the stairs, wild-eyed and breathless.

He had a crumpled piece of printer paper in one hand and a pen clutched in the other like a lifeline. "Say it again," he demanded. "The name."

She kept her voice steady and slow, watching him scribble like he was taking notes in a nuclear physics class. "Ultra Light. Long Overnight. With wings. Blue packaging."

He underlined *with wings* three times, muttering it under his breath. "With wings... wings... blue..."

Then, without so much as a goodbye or second glance, he turned and sprinted back upstairs like the floor was on fire.

He left the door wide *open* in his rush.

Her eyes widened. She listened. Creaking floorboards. The rustle of keys. A pause. Then the faint click of the front door. Gone.

She let out a long, slow breath and turned toward the television. Her fingers moved fast, grabbing the remote from the small table nearby. She hit the power button and dropped the volume low—just enough to hear the announcers talking, enough to track the minutes as they passed. Basketball again. Perfect. A game clock. She counted every second on the timer, each one ticking louder in her head. Fifteen minutes. That was the window. That was the promise. From his last trip to the store, she knew it would take him a little over an hour. And hopefully this trip would take even longer... especially since she had never even heard of "Ultra light long overnight with wings in blue packaging."

The moment the clock hit fifteen, she moved. First, the camera. It had been there since day one—mounted neatly at the top of the television, its glossy black eye always watching. Marshall never tried to hide it. He wanted her to know it was there. A constant reminder that her world was under surveillance. She grabbed her pillow, yanked off the case, and tossed it over the lens in one clean motion. The fabric draped just right, blocking its view. It would be suspicious but she figured that it would be better than seeing her escape, he might think something was wrong with the camera even if that was unlikely - every second mattered.

Next, the light. She looked at the dangling light overhead and unscrewed the bulb. It came free with a faint click. She crouched beside the bed and wrapped it carefully in the blanket, hands pressing firm. The muted crack of shattering glass made her stomach twist. She unwrapped the pieces cautiously. Shards glittered like tiny knives in the blue light of the television. She sifted through them, searching until she found the wire filament inside. She didn't have Tanner the Lockpicking Lifeguard's expertise, just desperation and fingers that wouldn't stop shaking. She gently pulled the filament free and set it aside. Then, from under the mattress, she retrieved the bobby pin. She settled on the floor, ankle turned toward the flickering light of the TV.She bent the bobby pin slightly—just enough to serve as a tension wrench—and slipped it into the lock. Then she inserted the filament carefully above it, feeling for pins the way she'd seen on that episode. Tanner had made it look easy, but he wasn't kneeling on a concrete floor with under an hour before all hell would break loose.

Still, the theory was sound. Apply tension. Feel the pins. Lift gently. One at a time. She drew a deep breath and focused. She gave herself thirty minutes. That was the deal. Thirty minutes to do this clean. No noise. No panic. No fire. If she failed? Plan B. The blanket. A fire. Smoke and chaos. She would find a way to force his hand. Force the door open with her out of the shackle. But not yet. She pressed the filament forward. And she began.

***

Marshall's hands gripped the steering wheel so tight his knuckles blanched white. The tires hummed as he sped down the winding mountain road toward the store, headlights slicing through the dark like searchlights. His mind raced even faster. His mom hadn't opened her eyes all morning. Her skin had felt too hot, her breath too shallow. He'd given her the old antibiotics, sure, but what if they weren't enough? What if he'd waited too long? And now Angela—Angela needing something specific, something he didn't have time to figure out. Pads with wings, blue packaging, long overnight—what the hell did any of that mean? He exhaled sharply through his nose, frustration rising like bile in his throat.

Then he saw it. In the rearview mirror—movement. A figure in the backseat. Marshall's heart skipped. He jerked his eyes upward, blood chilling. There he was. Not like the dreams or whispers or flickers in the corner of his vision. But solid. Human. He looked about five years older than Marshall. Strong jaw, calm eyes, dark hair combed neatly like someone out of an old family photo that never existed. He looked exactly how Marshall had imagined an older brother would've looked. Protective. Confident. Maybe even kind. And yet... something behind his eyes twisted the illusion.

"She's lying," Asael said calmly, like he was reading the weather.

Marshall blinked. "What...?" But when he looked again, the backseat was empty. Just the faint smell of heat and vinyl.

His mouth went dry. He looked down at his phone resting in the cupholder. Was she lying? Would she lie about something like that? Why now? His thumb hovered over the screen, a knot forming in his chest. He opened his phone and started swiping to the camera app, not noticing he was slowly drifting into the other lane. As his thumb hovered over the app he was startled by an angry driver's horn which forced his eyes to snap back up on the road – and his own lane. As the driver passed, an enraged arm with outstretched middle finger flew through the lowered window. Just then, the blast of a siren caught his ears. Red and blue lights flared behind him like angry fireworks.

"Shit," he hissed, jerking the wheel straight. He squeezed the wheel until his knuckles turned white.

The CHP cruiser pulled in tighter, lights flashing. Marshall cursed again and hit the power button on his phone, the screen going black before he ever saw what Angela might've been doing. He tossed it onto the passenger seat like it had betrayed him. His pulse thundered in his ears as he slowed down and pulled over, jaw clenched and breath tight.

The mirror was empty now. No one in the back. But the echo of the voice remained. "She's lying."

The cruiser door swung open and a uniformed officer stepped out, adjusting his belt as he approached the driver's side window. The officer looked like the kind of man who'd seen too many late shifts and not enough sleep. His uniform was pressed, but the fabric strained faintly where his gut met the belt—a quiet war between professionalism and middle age. A strip of gray ran through his close-cropped hair, and his jaw worked as if he were grinding down irritation into habit. The harsh glow of the cruiser's lights carved sharp shadows across his face, deepening the lines around his mouth. He leaned down with the slow, practiced motion of someone who'd done this a thousand times and rarely enjoyed it. His grimace wasn't quite anger— more the weary impatience of a man who'd run out of patience hours ago.

Marshall had already rolled his window down, forcing a neutral expression onto his face and trying to calm the wild thrum of his heart. The red and blue lights reflected across his dashboard, pulsing like a heartbeat.

The officer leaned in, flashlight sweeping across Marshall's hands, his lap, the empty seat beside him. "Evenin'. You know why I pulled you over?"

Marshall gave a small, forced chuckle. "I'm guessing it was the swerve."

"Yup." He stood upright. "You drifted halfway into the next lane. Didn't signal. Seemed a little distracted." The officer's flashlight beam drifted over to the cell phone on the passenger seat. He raised his eyebrows before pulling the light back.

Marshall nodded. "Yeah, sorry about that. It's—uh—kind of a weird night."

The officer raised an eyebrow. "License and registration."

Marshall reached for the glovebox, retrieving the documents with steady hands. No reason to panic. The cop wasn't going to find anything. There was no warrant. No missing person tied to him. Angela was off the grid. He was careful. Still... something inside him gnawed at the edges of his thoughts. That strange look on her face when she told him she needed him to get her pads. The softness of her voice. The timing. Something wasn't right.

But before he could dive back into it, the officer handed his documents back and said, "Weird night how?"

Marshall gave a sheepish grin, holding up the folded piece of paper he had written Angela's request on. "My girlfriend—uh, she's going through... you know, her time of the month. Sent me to get pads."

The cop stared.

"I had no idea what I was doing," Marshall added, trying to sound self-deprecating. "So I tried to write it down." He unfolded the note and read aloud, "Ultra Thin. Long Overnight. With wings. Blue package." He looked at the officer. "Sounds more like a top secret mission than a sanitary product, right?"

The officer didn't laugh, his expression cold. "You swerved going eighty-five in a fifty-five zone."

Marshall's grin faltered. "Right. Yeah. That part's on me."

The officer paused, studying him for a beat longer. "Sit tight. I'll be right back."

As the cop walked toward his cruiser, Marshall leaned back in his seat, the joke dissolving from his face. He stared at the note in his lap, covered in his underlines and scribblings. Something about it unsettled him now. The thought struck him and he sat forward. But the officer was already returning. And just like that, the moment passed.

The officer's boots crunched softly against the shoulder gravel. Marshall sat up straighter, folding the note and tucking it back into his pocket, trying to look appropriately remorseful.

The cop handed him back his license along with a slip of paper. "Citation for speeding and failure to maintain lane. You can contest it or pay it online. Info's on the bottom."

Marshall took the ticket, forcing a tight, polite smile. "Thank you, officer."

The man gave him a slow, assessing look. "Get to the store, but take it slower this time."

"Yes, sir."

The officer lingered half a second longer, then turned and walked back toward his cruiser. The lights dimmed as the patrol car pulled away, merging back onto the road. Marshall sighed and tossed the ticket into the passenger seat. His fingers tapped nervously against the steering wheel as he checked the clock on the dash. He needed to get moving.

Angela's voice drifted through his head again. *"I'm about to start my period."*

Something about the way she said it—it had felt... staged. Off.

Marshall sat in silence for a long beat, the hum of the engine low and steady beneath him. The glow from the dashboard cast faint shadows across his face as he reached for his phone on the passenger seat. He hadn't even opened the app before the cop pulled him over. Now, he thumbed to it—quick, sharp movements—and launched the feed tied to the basement camera. A loading icon spun for a moment. Then the feed snapped on. Black. Not a technical error. Not a disconnect. Just... black. He stared at the screen, thumb tapping the refresh button once. Twice. Still black. His pulse began to thump louder in his ears. He knew what that meant. She covered the camera somehow. His jaw tightened as he locked the phone and tossed it back on the seat, eyes flicking to the road ahead. The store could wait. He flicked the turn signal and swung the car around in a tight, sudden arc, tires crunching over the asphalt as he headed back toward the house—faster now. The pads, the note, the pleading voice—it all twisted in his chest.

She was up to something. And he needed to get back. Now.

***

Paula stood near the reception desk, her clipboard pressed loosely against her chest, eyes unfocused as the low hum of hospital noise swirled around her. Monitors beeped in the distance. A stretcher rolled past. Phones rang. Voices murmured. But her mind was somewhere else. That man. The one with the eye injury. It had been late—near the end of her shift. Something about him had lingered, like the taste of metal in her mouth. It was the same night Angela went missing. She hadn't thought about it until last night, when Gabriel mentioned the injury Angela gave her attacker. Now it wouldn't leave her alone.

"Hello?" a voice cut in sharply. "Earth to Paula?"

Paula blinked and turned.

Tasha stood at the edge of the desk with one hand on her hip and a knowing smirk on her face. "Where'd you go just now?"

Paula shook herself gently, smiling. "Sorry. Just thinking."

Tasha leaned in a little. "Thinking about Detective Tall-and-Handsome, by chance?"

Paula gave a small laugh and looked back down at her clipboard. "Things are going... great."

Tasha raised her eyebrows. "That's it? *'Great?'* Girl, don't you *dare* try to slide out of this. I want details. Like, are we talking 'he's sweet and thoughtful' great or 'I think about him when I'm brushing my teeth' great?"

Paula's lips twitched. "I'm... pleasantly surprised. He's not what I expected. But I'm taking it slow."

"Mmm-hmm," Tasha hummed, crossing her arms. "You say 'slow' but your eyes are doing this glowy thing that screams *fast lane with the windows down.*"

Paula chuckled and glanced back toward the hallway. "I promise I'll spill later. But there's actually something I need to check."

Tasha frowned, surprised at the sudden shift in tone. "You good?"

"Yeah. I'm fine." She was already walking away. "Just something on my mind."

She disappeared down the corridor, her smile fading as she moved. She had notes to check. From that night. And if her gut was right, then something much darker was about to surface.

Paula slipped into an unoccupied exam room, closing the door softly behind her. The overhead lights buzzed faintly, casting the space in sterile white. A computer sat idle in the corner, humming quietly. She pulled up the rolling chair and sat down, fingers already flying across the keyboard as she logged in with her credentials. Her heart beat faster with each screen she navigated. She keyed in the date—Angela's disappearance. The list that populated made her stomach sink. That night had been chaos. Overcrowded ER, a multi-car pile-up, a domestic violence walk-in, an overdose. The files stretched long down the screen.

"Come on," she muttered, scanning names and timestamps.

Then she saw it.

Her own initials in the chart. She opened the note.

Patient unusually evasive. Signs of possible chemical exposure. Injury story inconsistent with observed physical trauma. Recommend follow-up if non-compliance noted.

She froze, reading the words over and over.

It came back in pieces—the man with the eye injury. Flinching at questions. Giving vague answers. She'd suspected pepper spray at the time, everything about the interaction made the hair on the back of her neck stand up. She remembered writing that note with her stomach in knots. How could someone with an injury that dire and at risk of losing their eye refuse surgery? Her fingers hovered over the keyboard as she pulled up his patient file. *Marshall Sewert.* She reviewed the notes, puncture and scleral laceration along the white wall of the eye, the injury clicked like a lock turning. It was him, the kidnapping suspect, she knew it deep down even if it was only circumstantial. The timing, his demeanor, the injury. It all aligned.

Paula leaned back in the chair, her heart pounding in her ears. The pit in her stomach grew sharper. The file sat open before her like a loaded weapon. It could have been exactly what Gabriel needed. The file described a man with a suspicious eye injury coming in shortly after the kidnapping and roughly matching the description on the news. But she also knew what it meant. HIPAA wasn't just a guideline. Sharing this could get her fired. Worse—if the defense ever caught wind of how the information was obtained, it could damage the entire case. Evidence suppression. Chain of custody. Reasonable doubt. This wasn't just a decision about right and wrong. It was about how much wrong could unravel if she chose to do the right thing the wrong way. She stared at the screen, torn between the weight of silence and the cost of speaking.

If it *was* him... if Marshall Sewert was the man who took Angela, then this note—this little scrap of professional suspicion she'd nearly forgotten— could help save a girl's life. If she was still alive. Paula gripped the edge of the desk with one hand, trying to steady herself. Her thoughts were spinning, crashing into one another like waves. The right thing was obvious. She had something real. Something actionable. All Gabriel needed was a spark to follow, and this could be it.

And yet, a voice in her head whispered back: *HIPAA. Confidentiality. Professional ethics.* She felt sick. What kind of person was she, that she was even hesitating? Was she really going to let some red tape stop her from doing what was right?

If that girl is out there somewhere—alive—suffering...

She shut her eyes, her fingers flexing on the desk. She imagined Angela chained, bleeding, praying for someone to see something, say something. Paula could be that person. Right now. But the counter-argument came just as quickly. *What if she's already dead?* What if they'd missed the window? Then anything Paula shared—anything obtained without proper procedure— could become poison. A defense attorney would shred it. The case could collapse under the weight of "unlawfully obtained medical information." The prosecution would be left scrambling to explain how their key lead came from a well-meaning doctor who crossed the line. And what if they lost the case because of her? She chewed the inside of her cheek.

There has to be a legal exception, she thought. Something about "imminent danger." *The HIPAA Exception for Serious Threats.* She pulled up the policy from memory, scanned the language in her mind:

A healthcare provider may disclose protected health information if they believe, in good faith, that the disclosure is necessary to prevent or lessen a serious and imminent threat to the health or safety of a person or the public...

Paula's shoulders sank.

It didn't apply, this was all still circumstantial. Suspicion and intuition. No direct evidence. No confirmed ongoing threat. Just her gut. And a note. And the man's name in a file. If she acted now, she wasn't a whistleblower. She was a liability. And still, the question clawed at her: *What if this silence becomes the reason Angela dies?* She sat there in the quiet room, the monitor flickering gently. Caught in the space between moral clarity and legal chains. Her next move could save a life. Or sink a case. And the clock was still ticking.

A soft buzz broke through her spiraling thoughts. She lifted her head, blinking against the sting in her eyes, and saw her phone light up. Gabriel.

Hey. Just wanted to say last night was great. Also, I don't know about you, but I already crushed the leftovers. No regrets.

A faint smile tugged at the corner of her mouth. She stared at the message for a long moment, her thumb brushing the edge of the screen.

It would be so easy. Just a few words. *The man you're looking for might be Marshall Sewert. Eye injury. Seen the night Angela went missing.* She could send it. Right now. She could give him everything. Her finger hovered above the keyboard. But she didn't move. Because that wasn't how this could go—not without risking everything. Not like this. She exhaled slowly and set the phone down beside her, screen still glowing with the unsent reply. Then... the thought struck her. An anonymous tip!

Her chest rose as she inhaled sharply, the idea snapping into focus like a jigsaw piece sliding into place. No name. No credentials. No trail. Just the truth. And maybe... that would be enough. But as the adrenaline eased, a new thought slipped in—quiet and cruel. *What if it's not fast enough?* She bit her lip, brows pulling together. Anonymous tips go into databases. Get filtered, vetted, rerouted. What if it sat there for hours? What if someone didn't read it right away? What if it got buried under noise? What if Angela didn't have that kind of time? Paula pressed a hand to her mouth, heart pounding again. She had a way to speak. But was it fast enough to matter?

Paula pulled the phone back into her lap, her fingers moving with renewed purpose. She opened her browser and typed *Los Angeles Police Department anonymous tip line.* The first link brought her to the department's official site. There was a form—brief but functional—asking for the nature of the tip, the suspect's name, a location, and any other details. Her thumb hovered for a second. Then she backed out. Not yet. She opened her VPN app and toggled it on, watching as the little icon turned green. Her IP address now bounced somewhere through Nevada. Just in case. She wasn't taking any chances. She returned to the form and started typing.

***

Gabriel sat at the kitchen counter, the empty takeout container pushed off to the side, a lingering scent of carnitas and cilantro still hanging in the air. He tapped the last of a tortilla chip against his plate, chewed absentmindedly, then leaned back in his chair with a quiet sigh. He had just texted Paula— something light, nothing too eager. The date had gone well. Better than expected, honestly. But even with her still hovering at the edge of his thoughts, he couldn't shake the familiar weight pressing on his shoulders. The case wasn't moving. He opened his laptop, screen already glowing with the spreadsheet he'd been staring at for the past hour. It was a list of former student assistants—pulled from a dated but intact archive sent over by the university's HR office after some gentle pressure and a formal request. Specifically, these were assistants tied to Dr. Leonard Marlowe, the tenured statistics professor who had died under strange circumstances two years prior. It was a longshot. Gabriel knew that. The kind of digging that usually turned up nothing but ghosts and old coffee orders. But something kept pulling him back to the idea—some thread of intuition that wouldn't let go.

Tyler, the frat boy who died a year before Marlowe, had taken Marlowe's class. Gabriel had confirmed that last week. Their deaths were a year apart but no known overlap. No hard connection. But it was the *feeling.* Something in both of those deaths smelled like rot covered in good intentions. And if he was going to chase that scent, he had to start somewhere. He scrolled through the names, his eyes scanning the columns: *student ID, major, position title, department hours.* Most were forgettable. Some he vaguely recognized from background checks—now living in different states, now working in unrelated fields. He tapped the down arrow. And paused.

Sewert, Marshall.

Position: Departmental Assistant – Psych & Stats Building.

Years active: Winter 2014 – Spring 2015.

Gabriel's brow furrowed. He didn't recognize the name right away. It didn't match any of the primary suspects or witnesses connected to Angela's case. But something about it stuck. He highlighted the row, stared at the name a moment longer. A student worker. Not rare. Not significant on its own. But if this guy worked in the building... if he had access to Marlowe's office... if he'd ever interacted with Tyler... Gabriel reached for his notebook and scribbled the name in the corner of a mostly empty page. Just in case. At this point, a gut feeling was all he had.

***

This was it. The day Angela would die. The day Marshall would pull the trigger and follow her into silence.

Asael lounged in the backseat of the speeding car, his legs crossed, hands resting easily on his knees. Marshall couldn't see him—not yet. But the demon could feel the frantic energy pulsing off the man like heat from a dying engine. Panic was in full bloom now, sour and delicious. Asael's gaze shifted downward toward the small space beneath the driver's seat, where the sharp corner of a new ammo box peeked out, the label still crisp. He smiled. That had been the final detail. The last variable. He had whispered the urge into Marshall's mind at just the right time—just enough worry, just enough dread. *You'll need protection. You can't leave things unfinished.*

And Marshall, obedient as ever beneath the surface, had listened.

Asael's smile widened, his eyes gleaming. Adapa would be pleased. This wasn't just a clean corruption—it was theatrical. Symbolic. A triumph of despair wrapped in free will. If today played out the way he foresaw, perhaps even the ranks of the deeper thrones would take notice.

With a soft hiss of smoke, Asael dissolved into a swirl of ash and shadow. He streaked across the sky like a stain, a dirty wisp slithering through the trees, until the old cabin came into view. He arrived in the blink of an eye. The basement first. He passed through the walls like fog and entered the dim, flickering space just above the mattress where Angela sat hunched near the door, sweat glistening on her brow. She was still at it. Filament in one hand, bobby pin in the other. Knees pulled tight, her focus absolute. Every few seconds, she paused and shook out her fingers before resuming her careful picking of the ankle shackle's padlock.

Asael floated silently above her, studying the tension in her arms, the strain in her face. Desperation. But not enough. There was no chance she'd make it out before Marshall returned. The clock had run dry. Every pin she lifted was another second wasted. Every breath was one closer to her last. Asael didn't linger. He drifted upward through the rotted floorboards, up to the small back bedroom where the real key piece of the puzzle lay. Marshall's mother. She lay in her bed, still. Quiet. Too quiet. He moved closer, hovering above her like smoke clinging to the ceiling. Her chest didn't rise. Her lips were gray. Her skin, once flushed with fever, had settled into the dull sheen of death.

He knelt beside the bed and took a long, slow breath—though he didn't need to. "Perfect," he whispered.

She hadn't died long ago. Still warm. Still recent. Still fresh enough for Marshall to believe he could've saved her, had he just stayed. He could hear the scream already forming in Marshall's throat. The grief. The guilt. It would snap his mind like brittle wood. Asael rose, eyes scanning the room. No trace of light. No scent of holy flame. No winged interlopers in sight. No angels. Not today. His plan would unfold uninterrupted. And all that remained... was the finale.

30

Blessed Are the Peacemakers

Gabriel was halfway through skimming a report on another cold lead when the alert popped onto his phone—bold red flag, top of the screen.

New Anonymous Tip – Angela Ward Case.

His pulse jumped. He'd removed the filter a week ago. After the media frenzy died down and the tips slowed to a trickle, he'd made sure *any* mention of the Angela Ward case would bypass protocol and go directly to him. Most of them were garbage. This one wasn't.

Marshall Sewert. Treated at L.A. hospital for an eye injury the night Angela Ward disappeared. Puncture Injury and possibly pepper spray. Behavior was evasive. Consider checking ER notes for confirmation.

Gabriel stared at the screen for two seconds—then bolted upright, reaching for his laptop.

Sewert, Marshall.

He'd just written the name down hours before. He pulled up the employment spreadsheet again, scanned down the list of student assistants tied to Dr. Marlowe—the statistics professor who died under odd circumstances.

There it was: *Marshall Sewert. Psych & Stats building. Winter 2014 – Spring 2015.*

Same exact name.

He flipped tabs, fingers moving fast, keying into law enforcement databases. Background check. Public records. Address. An isolated residence off a rural road, north of the city tucked in the San Gabriel mountains. Wooded. No neighbors within sight. Owned under his name. No active landlines. No social media. Sparse work history. Currently receiving SSI and caretaker support benefits. Gabriel sat back, heart thudding harder. It could still be nothing. But... it didn't feel like nothing. He recalled the early interview with the woman from the bar, she thought he said his name was Mark. What if she had caught him off guard, and he almost said his real name, Marshall. He was still scanning the screen when his phone buzzed again. Text from Paula:

If you're still looking into Angela's case... trust your instincts.

Gabriel read it once. Then again. Vague. Careful. But she knew something. He could feel it. She wasn't the kind of person to stir the pot unless there was heat underneath it. He thought back to their date. The way her face shifted when they talked about the case. How quiet she got when he mentioned the footage. And now this? There was something she couldn't say. But she *wanted* him to find it. Gabriel stood, grabbing his coat and keys in one smooth motion. The laptop remained open on the table, Marshall's name glowing on the screen like a warning shot. He didn't need a warrant to knock on someone's door. And if there was even a *chance* Angela was still alive... He had to see for himself.

***

Thirty minutes. That was the deal she made with herself. Angela's hands were cramping, her neck sore from leaning at the same angle too long. The filament had begun to bend from overuse. The bobby pin's tip was dull. And still—the lock wouldn't budge. No click. No shift. No miracle. She exhaled shakily and set the makeshift picks aside. Her pulse was hammering in her ears.

Plan B.

Angela reached for the remote sitting by the mattress and popped the back cover. Two small lithium batteries clattered into her hand. She kept her movements sharp, precise. No hesitation now. She carefully pulled out the cracked bulb from the blanket and began scraping one of the batteries with the broken glass, working off the outer casing. After a few tense minutes, the metallic wrapping split, revealing the tight roll of silvery lithium inside. She swallowed, remembering the demonstration her chemistry professor had given the class showing what happens when lithium touches water.

Angela wrapped the lithium carefully in the edge of the blanket, forming a loose pouch. She crawled over to the open basement door, as far as her chain would allow, and placed it at the foot of the stairs—her only exit. She knew that Marshall would be home soon. She thought the small fire would generate enough smoke to set off an alarm and alert a neighbor. As a last possible resort it might cause him to unshackle her in the commotion giving her a chance to run. She took the bottle of water and poured it directly onto the blanket. Nothing happened. For one breath. Two. Then smoke. A wisp at first, curling up like a question. Then a hiss. The blanket began to darken, small flames licking through the fabric.

Angela stumbled backward, coughing as the smoke grew thicker. She knew this was dangerous—stupid even. She was still trapped in the room. Still tethered. But at this point? *This* was all she had. She dropped to the floor and reached for the lock again, barely able to see in the TV's flickering light. Her eyes stung. Her chest burned. She shoved the filament in one last time. Jammed the bobby pin in with more force than control. She wasn't even picking anymore—just *raking*, scraping the pins with frustration and fury.

"I swear to God—" she hissed through clenched teeth.

Click. A sound so soft it almost didn't register. Her breath caught. She paused. Then turned the bobby pin gently— And the lock *popped* open. Her heart slammed into her ribs. She yanked the shackle off her ankle and scrambled to her feet, kicking the burning blanket away from the stairs. The smoke now rolling across the ceiling. She launched up the stairs two steps at a time, lungs burning, eyes wet. The hatch was just ahead. And for the first time in what felt like forever— She had a shot.

She burst through the basement hatch and into a hallway. The air aboveground was cooler, sharper. Even with the smoke still clinging to her clothes, it felt like breathing for the first time in weeks. She stood frozen for a second, eyes darting across the room. No sign of him. No movement. No voice. *Good.* Her gaze swept over the kitchen, the hallway, the living room beyond. She remembered the first night—her choking on her own vomit while zip-tied and gagged, how he cradled her like a sick dog. She had almost died in that room. But not today.

Today, I make it out. She sprinted to the front door, hands fumbling at the locks. Her fingers moved fast in adrenaline-fueled precision. Then—tires. Gravel crunching. An engine. Close. Too close. Headlights cut through the window like twin blades of light. She froze. The locks. She slammed them back into place with trembling hands, backing away just as the car pulled up fast and hard outside. Her heart thudded in her ears.

No no no no—

She spun on her heel and ran, every nerve screaming for cover. Down the hallway. Doors. Shadows. Nothing useful. She threw a door open and darted inside. The bedroom. She slammed the door shut behind her and turned the lock with a soft *click*, then braced against it, chest heaving. And froze again. Across the room, lying motionless in the bed, was Marshall's mother. Angela stared for a beat, stunned. The woman's skin was pale, her chest still. A wave of cold washed over her.

Is she...?

A pang cut through her—sorrow, fear, something more tangled. She didn't know this woman, but she'd heard the pieces of her life through Marshall, his unraveling. Angela had pictured her as a ghost. But now, seeing her like this—silent, maybe dead—it felt real. Too real. But there wasn't time. Angela's eyes snapped to the window. A small, sliding pane above the bed. It was cracked already. Dirty, but openable. She rushed to it, pushed it wide, and swung her legs through. Her feet hit the dirt hard, knees buckling. Then she ran. No hesitation. No looking back. Straight into the forest. Straight into the dark. Each breath was fire in her lungs, each step fueled by a single, burning word. *Go.*

***

Marshall's car skidded into the gravel drive, headlights bouncing off the trees as he slammed the gear into park and flung open the door. His boots hit the dirt hard. The night air smelled off—acrid. Smoke. His heart seized. He yanked the driver's side door open again and hurriedly grabbed a handful of bullets from the ammo box tucked beneath the seat, dropping some to the floor in his rush and stuffing the rest into his coat pocket with shaking fingers. He didn't have time to load the revolver now. First—Angela. He sprinted to the front door and jammed his key into the lock. But something caught his eye. Smoke. Leaking from beneath the hatch to the basement.

No. No no no—

He quickly unlocked the door and burst inside the house, following the trail of smoke to the basement hatch. He ran, crouched low, and flung the hatch open. A wave of hot, gray smoke poured out. He gagged, pulling his collar over his mouth as he ducked down, peering inside. Flames licked up from a smoldering blanket near the stairs. The mattress was blackened on one side.

The air was thick with the sharp sting of burning plastic and scorched fabric. But Angela was gone. Panic surged through his chest. He bolted upright and ran down the hall, lungs burning.

He arrived at his mother's room, his heart hammering in his chest. He yanked on the doorknob - locked! He smashed his shoulder into it hard, once, twice, and then burst into the room—only to stop cold in the doorway. She was still. Too still.

Marshall staggered toward her. "Mom?"

No breath. No movement. Her mouth slightly open. Her chest silent.

His stomach dropped. "No… no, please—" He knelt beside her, trembling, one hand brushing her cooling forehead. Her skin was waxy, colorless. Gone. He let out a broken sound—half sob, half choke—and leaned his head against her shoulder. "I'm sorry," he whispered, voice cracking. "I should've stayed. I should've been here."

A flash of movement caught his eye—the window. Wide open. Curtains fluttering. His whole body went still. Angela. She had been here. She saw. She ran. And now… now she was gone. He pressed a hand to his chest, as if trying to hold himself together. But the pieces were breaking loose inside. His mother was dead. Angela had escaped. The fire was still building below, and something inside him—something that had barely been holding on— finally snapped.

He whispered, "It doesn't matter anymore."

Tonight was the end. For everything. He stood abruptly, eyes empty, and grabbed the flashlight off the shelf. Without another glance back at the bed, at the house, at the flames, he threw himself through the open window and into the night. And ran after her.

***

The vault of Heaven shimmered with impossible hues—colors no mortal eye could name. In the hallowed chamber where the Archangel Raphael resided, scrolls floated mid-air in rhythmic spirals, their ink glowing softly as they turned. Columns of alabaster light stretched infinitely into the skies, and the sound of distant choirs echoed like wind across still water.

Uriel stood at the threshold, shoulders squared but fists clenched at his sides. His wings slightly askew, bearing singed feathers from an earlier battle with Ravage. He bowed low, but his voice betrayed his haste. "Commander Raphael," Uriel said, breath catching in his throat. "The charge you gave me—James, the man from the ammunition factory—he's improving. He's... holding on."

Raphael, seated upon a plinth sculpted from solid starlight, nodded without looking up. A long scroll hovered before him, unspooling gently as his eyes traced each line. His brow furrowed slightly, but he said nothing.

Uriel pressed on. "He still struggles. Ecanus torments him with memories, with false promises. The ideation hasn't vanished—but now, he turns to others instead of the bottle or the gun. Brandon and the recovery group at the church... they've become his shield. He cries openly. He prays again. He even laughed yesterday—truly laughed. The hold of the darkness has weakened significantly."

Raphael hummed, a subtle sound of acknowledgment, but didn't speak.

Uriel took a step forward, barely restraining his urgency. "With respect, Commander, I believe the worst is behind him. He is not out of danger, but he is walking toward the light. And..." he paused, lowering his head slightly, "...I would ask to be reassigned. Immediately."

Raphael finally looked up, his silver eyes meeting Uriel's with quiet perception. For a moment, neither spoke.

Then Raphael smiled faintly, amusement flickering in the corners of his mouth. "You're worried about her."

Uriel didn't deny it. "Yes. I believe she's in immediate peril. I believe Asael is ready to make his move."

Raphael returned his gaze to the scroll, flipping it closed with a flick of his hand. A seal burned itself into the parchment with divine fire. "You have done well with James, Uriel. As you say, the worst is behind him for now. You are now reassigned to Angela." He lifted his hand, letting the scroll drift into the ether. "Effective immediately." When he looked up, Uriel was already gone.

A streak of blazing gold and crimson tore through the upper sky, vanishing past the horizon of Heaven in a heartbeat. Raphael leaned back, watching the fading trail with the weariness of one who has seen much and expected all of it.

He chuckled to himself, shaking his head. "Always in such a hurry." He turned to the next scroll as it floated toward him, murmuring softly, "Go, guardian. Let love burn brighter than fear."

***

The tires screeched as Gabriel's unmarked sedan veered off the main road and onto the cracked shoulder. A plume of dust kicked up behind him as he sped up the winding path toward the cabin. His jaw clenched when the first orange flicker danced across his windshield. When the trees broke, the full sight hit him. The house was ablaze. Flames poured through shattered windows, curling like serpents into the night sky. Smoke bled into the treetops, thick and fast. Gabriel slammed the brakes, the car skidding on the dirt driveway before lurching to a stop.

He threw open the door and stepped out, already reaching for his radio. "Dispatch, this is Detective Ramos—I need fire response at one eight four Woodline Drive now! Structure's fully involved. I also need backup and paramedics in case of injuries. Possible hostages involved."

The radio crackled its confirmation, but Gabriel was already moving. As he circled the front of the car, his eyes swept the perimeter—no sign of movement at the cabin, just the roar of fire devouring timber and memory.

Then, a flicker. A beam of light—small, erratic—bobbing deep in the tree line.

Gabriel's eyes narrowed. He clicked his radio again. "Possible suspect moving northbound through the woods. I'm in pursuit. Send additional units to triangulate on foot—I'm heading in." He unholstered his weapon and broke into a sprint, his boots crunching over leaves and old pine needles as he plunged into the dark.

The flashlight beam ahead danced like a distant ghost, weaving between trees, too fast for a stroll—too shaky for control. Then—A gunshot cracked through the trees.

Gabriel ducked instinctively, pivoting toward the sound. His own weapon came up, steady in both hands. "Damn it," he muttered, adjusting his grip as he moved faster, his breath steady despite the pounding in his chest.

The beam of light jerked violently—then disappeared. Gabriel slowed, senses sharpened, ears straining for any shift in movement. The woods held their breath, as if waiting for the next act of violence to unfold.

***

Branches clawed at Angela's arms as she ran, her breath hitching in ragged gasps. The night air was cold against her sweat-slicked skin, and every step felt more desperate than the last. She didn't know where she was going— only that she had to keep moving, deeper into the woods, away from him. Her bare feet slapped against dirt and rock, stung by thorns and broken twigs. She stumbled, caught herself, and kept going. The darkness was suffocating. Trees loomed like shadows of giants, and the forest floor twisted unevenly beneath her. Then, her foot caught on a root. She cried out as her body pitched forward, tumbling down a slope masked by brush and leaves. Her body crashed against the ground with a painful thud. A sharp, stabbing pain bloomed in her ankle. She clutched it, biting her lip to stop the scream. It probably wasn't broken—but at least sprained, badly. She tried to put weight on it and collapsed again.

Up above, the beam of Marshall's flashlight slashed through the trees like a hunter's gaze.

"Angela!" he shouted, his voice cracked and breathless. "Please—don't run! I'm not going to hurt you!"

She dragged herself upright, gritting her teeth. Her ankle screamed with every step, but she moved—hobbling, limping, using nearby trees as crutches. The light was getting closer. She couldn't outrun him. Her heart pounded. She turned sharply and ducked into a patch of denser brush, moving off the path and slipping behind a wide, moss-covered tree. She crouched low, hugging herself to stay still, to vanish into the dark. The beam of the flashlight appeared again, far too bright—brighter than it should've been. It flooded the forest like a spotlight, casting harsh white across every surface as it swept left and right. Then it stopped.

Angela froze, barely breathing. She heard him above her, somewhere near the top of the incline where she had fallen. She could imagine him now, scanning the area, calculating.

Leaves crunched.

"There's no way you made it far with no shoes in the dark. You're hiding." He stepped forward, slowly now. Calculated. "I don't want to do this," he called out, voice trembling. "God, I didn't want any of this..."

Angela's breath caught in her throat.

"I tried," Marshall said, louder now. "I tried to make something right. All I ever wanted was to protect someone. You don't understand what it's like... growing up in a world where no one protects you." His voice wavered.

The flashlight paused again—illuminating the exact spot where she had fallen just minutes earlier.

His eyes tracked the crushed underbrush. The direction her prints had gone. "You fell. You're hurt."

Angela's hand flew to her mouth to stifle a whimper.

"I couldn't save my mother. I couldn't stop my father from nearly killing her that night. I didn't do anything. I failed her. You know that pain, don't you? Even now, in her final moments, I wasn't there for her... again." He took a few more steps forward, slowly turning, his flashlight dancing across nearby trees. "All I wanted was to get it right this time," he whispered. "Just once."

Angela stayed perfectly still, her lungs burning. Every inch of her wanted to bolt—but she knew if she moved now, he'd hear. He was too close. Too alert. Too... broken. The light swept within inches of her. And then—it passed. Marshall kept walking.

Angela allowed herself one shaky breath.

The flashlight beam moved past her tree... and then—Darkness. Angela blinked, but the black was complete. The unnatural spotlight had vanished without a sound, leaving her surrounded by thick silence and shadows. Her heart thudded against her ribcage. Why did he turn it off? She strained her ears, listening for anything—footsteps, branches, breath—but the forest was dead quiet, like it too was holding its breath. Nothing moved. Even the insects had gone still. Was he gone? No. She knew Marshall well enough now. He wasn't done. He was waiting. Angela's skin crawled. Every second that passed without sound felt like a needle to the nerves.

She stayed frozen for what felt like minutes, her mind racing. Then—slowly, painfully—she began to crawl away. Inch by inch. Her injured ankle dragged behind her like a dead limb. She kept her body low, trying not to rustle the leaves, biting down on every wince, every urge to sob. One arm forward. Then the next. Push. Slide. Breathe. Silence. Finally, when the trees seemed farther apart and the air a little more open, she rose to her feet, clutching a low-hanging branch for support. She took one step. Then another.

Snap.

A dry branch gave way beneath her weight. Before she could even gasp, the forest lit up again in a burst of white. The flashlight flared on—directly pointed at her. She froze in place, blinking wildly against the blinding beam.

"Angela!" Marshall's voice roared from the darkness.

A gunshot cracked the air. Angela flinched violently, hands flying over her ears.

"Don't move!" he shouted. "Don't take another step!"

Tears sprang to her eyes as she slowly raised her arms above her head. Her voice was barely a whisper. "Okay... okay."

The light didn't waver. She turned toward it, step by step, until her face was fully exposed in its glare. Marshall stood somewhere behind the light—she still couldn't see him clearly, but she felt him. The weight of his pain. The fury of his disappointment. And the terrifying quiet of a man who believed this was the only way the story could end. Angela's chest heaved as she met the beam head-on. She was done running.

The light dimmed. Marshall angled the flashlight down from her face, casting it low against the forest floor. The harsh white faded into a soft wash of shadows. Angela blinked rapidly, her hands still raised, heart pounding in her throat. Marshall stood a few yards away, the flashlight now trembling in his grip. His eyes—haunted, one purple and the other red-rimmed—were locked on her face.

***

Marshall looked at Angela and in that moment he saw something in her. A flicker. A memory. He saw his mother. Not the fragile, broken version he'd spoon-fed medicine to for years. But the young version. Before the brain trauma. The way she used to look at him, wide-eyed and worried, right before his father's belt would come down. The way she cried afterward, mouthing apologies she couldn't say out loud. That same fear. That same softness. In Angela's face. His throat tightened. The flashlight dropped slightly, and he ran one trembling hand across his mouth, still holding the revolver.

He shook his head slowly. "What am I doing? Is this… protecting you? Is that what this is?"

Angela didn't respond. She didn't move.

***

Angela watched him look up again at her, eyes glassy.

"I told myself I was saving you from the world. From what it does to people. From what it did to me. But… I don't even know anymore." He turned away from her briefly, hand clutching the side of his skull. "It's like my brain—it's full of noise. Of him. Of everything I should've done different."

The revolver caught the edge of his temple as he pressed his palm there. He didn't seem to notice. "I failed my mom," he said quietly. "I let her stay with a monster. I was a kid, but I knew. I knew, and I didn't stop it. And when I finally did, it was too late."

He looked at Angela again, and the pain in his eyes was bottomless. "I thought maybe... if I could do this right—if I could keep you safe—maybe I'd matter. Just once. Maybe I'd be something more than what he made me." Tears slipped down his face, and he didn't wipe them away. His voice cracked. "I'm sorry. I'm so... sorry." He dropped to his knees, the forest swallowing his shadow.

Angela's arms slowly lowered. She took in the broken figure before her— this man who had once held her captive, who had terrorized her, who had also, somehow, brought her soup when she couldn't sit up. Who wept now not for her, but for every moment he lost to pain and silence and fear.

She closed her eyes. *God... please. I don't know what to say. I just want to go home. I want to be safe. But if there's a word left in me that can reach him... show me. Let it be enough.*

She opened her eyes and stepped forward once. Carefully. "Marshall," she said softly, voice trembling but steady. "There is good in you. I saw it. Even on the worst nights."

He shook his head violently, like he was trying to dislodge the memory from his skull. "How can you say that after everything I've done? I killed people. I can't wash away the stains of that." His voice cracked. "I kidnapped you. I took you away from your son. I robbed you of your humanity because I thought I was protecting you." He stood up, but he did not look directly at her. His hand clenched around the revolver, not raising it, not lowering it. Just holding it like something he didn't know how to let go of. "You're not some goddamn bird that I can keep locked away in a cage. You're a real person."

Angela's eyes shimmered, but she held her ground. She saw the tears in his—hot, confused, childlike. "I know that. But I think you forgot it."

Marshall's jaw trembled. He took a step back, then another. "I didn't know what else to do. I just—every day I woke up and I could feel it slipping. The world. My mind. The lines between what was real and what wasn't. I'd see her—my mom—and then I'd see *him*, and then I'd hear things that weren't even mine. And the only thing that made sense was keeping you close. Because if I could keep you safe, maybe I'd finally get it right." He looked up slowly, uncertain.

"You are not your father," Angela said. "But you are so scared of becoming him that you're turning yourself into someone else you were never meant to be."

He clutched his chest, as though her words physically struck him.

"I know you want to protect people," she continued. "So protect me now—by choosing something different. Something harder. Let this end here. Please."

His lip quivered.

***

A familiar chill spilled into the air, so subtle it could've been mistaken for a breeze. But Marshall felt it—like the temperature dropped, like the shadows themselves were holding their breath. His spine stiffened.

From the corner of the woods a figure emerged visible only to Marshall—not in monstrous form, but as a man. Calm. Serpentine.

His eyes gleamed with a mockery of sorrow. "She left your mother, you know," he said, his voice smooth as oil. "Didn't even call for help when she saw the flames. She ran. You think that was noble? She gave up on her. Just like everyone gave up on you."

Marshall flinched. He didn't look at the man, but his hands clenched at his sides. He recognized Asael's cruel tone.

Asael continued, and circled him slowly, casual, cruel. "You saw it in her. The hesitation. She's not different. She's just a few wounds away from becoming like the rest of them. This world—it infects people. And when it finishes its work, it'll hollow her out, too. You'll see. Give it time."

"Shut up," Marshall whispered.

He kept circling, gaze now turned toward Angela. "What happens when the next person comes along and breaks her? When she feels the same betrayal you've felt every day of your life?"

"Shut. Up." Marshall turned, yelling now, eyes flashing with fury. "I said I'm done listening to you!"

He faded like smoke in the wind, his presence evaporating—but the chill remained. Marshall's shoulders heaved as he caught his breath. He turned back to Angela, who hadn't moved, who watched him now with wide, aching eyes.

***

His voice was hoarse. "Even though it's selfish... the house felt warm when you were there. You made me feel like I was a person again. Even after what I did to you. Even after the worst of it—you sat across from me, and I didn't feel like a monster. I felt... human."

She took a breath, lips parting to speak.

"I know you pray," he said quietly. "I could hear it... on the camera. Down there in the basement. The whispering. The way you talked to the ceiling like someone was listening." He looked up at the stars, his eyes glinting with unshed tears. "Do you think your God could forgive someone like me? For all of this?"

Angela opened her mouth. "Marshall—"

His eyes were still turned skyward. "I'm sorry," he whispered. "I need to tell you something." He looked back at her, and now his face was steady. Quiet. Honest. "When I left the house, I was in a rush. I only had time to grab two rounds from the box. Two." He held up the revolver now, slowly. "I shot one into the air earlier." His voice cracked. "The other one... I never intended to use on you."

Angela's breath caught. Marshall closed his eyes. And lifted the barrel to his temple.

31

He Will Wipe Away Every Tear

The forest held its breath. Marshall's finger hovered on the trigger, the revolver pressed against his temple, his eyes closed. One heartbeat. Two. Then— A *blazing streak of fire* tore across the night sky. A roar, like the sky itself had cracked open, echoed across the woods as Uriel descended like a meteor. His wings, wreathed in gold flame, sliced through the air. His sword blazed with divine light, trailing heat and power. He *slammed* into the earth like a thunderbolt, and the ground shuddered. Dirt and leaves scattered in a blast of wind.

Uriel's sword was already drawn, its edge pointing at Asael hiding in the shadows. "Not tonight," he growled, voice shaking the trees.

Asael grinned, face flickering between human and serpent. "Too late," he rasped. His glowing eyes shifted past Uriel—toward Marshall, still standing with the gun to his head.

Uriel's eyes widened. "No—"

Angela's voice broke through the chaos, trembling but clear as a bell. "Marshall, please!"

He didn't move.

"You don't have to do this." She stepped forward, her voice desperate and filled with something purer than fear—compassion. "You *can* make a different choice."

His grip on the gun trembled. His eyes darted to her, confused and swimming with pain.

"I know what you're thinking. That this is justice. That this is how you atone. But you've been carrying a weight that was never yours to carry." She limped closer, wincing with every step. "It wasn't your fault, what happened to your mom. You were just a boy. A scared, wounded boy. You couldn't save her then... and it's not fair that you've been paying for it ever since."

Marshall's jaw clenched. A tear slid down his cheek.

Angela reached out—slow, deliberate—and placed a hand over his trembling arm. "I see you," she whispered. "The part of you that loved her. The part that tried to protect me, in your own broken way. There is still something good in you, Marshall. Something *human.* No more violence." Very gently, she guided his arm downward, her own shaking.

The revolver lowered inch by inch, until it hung at his side. He let out a ragged breath—half relief, half collapse.

Behind them, Uriel kept his sword steadily pointed at Asael, eyes not leaving the demon for a second. "You've already lost," he said coldly. "You gambled on his pain and came up empty."

Asael's expression warped into something feral. "You think this is over?" he hissed. With a sudden snarl, he lashed out—a reptilian claw cutting through the air and shattering Uriel's guard, driving him backward.

Before Uriel could recover, Asael's massive tail whipped around with bone-cracking force, slamming into him and hurling him through the trees. Immediately, Asael's form *fractured* into smoke and shadow—and *launched* toward Marshall like a spear of black fire.

***

Marshall arched backward violently, a guttural noise tearing from his throat as smoke poured from his eyes and mouth. His body jerked once— twice—and then went completely still. Silence. Then— He stood upright. Slowly. Too slowly. When he opened his eyes again, something was wrong. They gleamed—not like a reflection, but like burning coals flickering behind glass. He turned his head and looked down at Angela. His mouth curled into a crooked, *wrong* smile.

"Angela," he purred, voice low and unrecognizable—Marshall's tone overlaid with something else, something darker. "You really *are* beautiful when you're afraid."

Angela stumbled backward, confusion washing over her as her eyes met his. And then the visions hit. Like lightning behind her eyes. She *saw* him— Marshall, but *not* Marshall—grabbing her by the throat and slamming her into a tree. She saw herself thrown to the ground, saw the flash of a blade in his hand, *felt* the steel cut her skin. She gasped. Another vision: His bare hands around her neck, squeezing, her lips turning blue— And then, like a final shard driven into her mind, she saw a *face.* Not Marshall's.

Its skin was black and scaled like a snake, with no whites in the eyes—just molten red. A snarl of pleasure stretched its inhuman lips, and horns like ivory curved back over its head.

Angela's breath caught. She looked up at him, wide-eyed. "You're real," she whispered.

The thing wearing Marshall laughed—a sick, broken sound that distorted his voice just slightly, like a chorus of two beings speaking through one mouth. "Of course I am. I've been real since Tyler knocked you up at that party. Since the moment you prayed and no one answered. And now..." He leaned close, "...now, I'm going to splatter your brain all over this lovely little forest."

His hand snapped up, gripping her throat with crushing force. His other arm raised the revolver, pressing it firmly to the side of her head.

Angela gasped, grabbing his wrist, her feet scrabbling against the forest floor. The gun didn't fire. It *shook.*

His smile faltered. His brow twitched. "Pull it," he growled to himself. "Pull the damn trigger."

The tremor in his hand grew worse. His eyes fluttered for a moment, conflicted.

"Don't start this now, Marshall. You *know* what happens if we don't finish this. You've *seen* what comes next. Just let me do this. Let me end it!"

His grip faltered—just a moment, just enough. Angela *twisted,* gasping as she slipped from his grasp and tumbled backward, hitting the ground hard and scrambling away.

"No!" he barked.

Marshall turned, raising the revolver again—not at her this time, but at his own head. His voice dropped low. "It's fine. I'll settle for plan B." Marshall's hand lifted the gun slowly, steadily.

The muzzle touched his temple.

Angela's eyes widened in horror. "Marshall—no!"

But Marshall's expression didn't change. And the demon's eyes burned with triumphant fury.

Angela lay sprawled in the dirt, heart pounding, lungs gasping for breath as Marshall—no, the demon—raised the revolver to his temple. And then— A presence. It swept in beside her like a warm wind through winter, strong and still and pulsing with light. She turned, confused, and *froze*. There, standing beside her, was a man—not quite a man. His form burned faintly, as though the stars themselves had carved his outline. His armor shimmered like forged lightning. Wings, vast and powerful, folded behind him, radiant with fire and dawn light. His sword hung at his side, glowing faintly with restrained power. Angela's breath caught. She *saw* him. For the first time. And somehow—somehow—she *knew*.

"Uriel..." she whispered, her voice shaking.

The angel didn't take his eyes off Marshall, who now stood trembling under the weight of the demon's control, gun to his own head.

Uriel's voice was calm, deep, and filled with something ancient. "Pray, Angela," he said gently. "Now."

Angela stared at him, wide-eyed. "You're real. You've been here this whole time."

He nodded, only faintly.

Tears sprang to her eyes. "Then *do something!*" she shouted. "Please! *Help him!*"

Uriel's expression darkened—his eyes, filled with sorrow and fire, flicked down to meet hers. "I can't. Not without harming him."

Angela looked between him and Marshall, her voice cracking. "But he's going to die!"

Uriel's voice was lower now, full of weight. "This is a battle of the soul now. Not of flesh. I can strike Asael, the demon, but I cannot save the man from himself."

Angela covered her mouth, a sob tearing free.

"He has to choose," Uriel said. "He has to want to be free."

Angela knelt in the dirt, her palms pressed together, trembling. Her voice was barely more than a breath. "God... please. I don't know how this ends. I don't know if I'm strong enough. But he is still in there. Please... reach him. Don't let it end this way."

The forest grew colder.

Marshall's body jerked slightly—his eyes blazing with that unnatural glow. His lips twisted into an inhuman smile, too wide for a human face. His voice came out layered, warped: Marshall's pain behind it, the demon's venom lacing every word. "Do you really think your pathetic prayer can help him?"

Angela looked up, tears streaking her cheeks.

The voice sneered. "Your prayers won't save him. When I'm done with this husk, I'll find you again. I'll never stop hunting you. One day, when you're weakest, when your hope is gone—*I'll finish what he couldn't.*"

Angela closed her eyes and kept praying.

His smile widened, that sick grin stretching unnaturally as he pressed the revolver harder to Marshall's temple. "Let's make this holy," he whispered.

Click.

The hammer pulled back.

Pop.

A soft, empty sound echoed through the trees—nothing more than a hollow cough of air.

No bullet.

Angela's eyes flew open. Marshall didn't fall. There was no spray of blood. No collapse. Just silence. The gun hung loosely in his hand. A *squib.* Time held its breath.

He roared—*not in pain*, but in rage. "You cheated!" he screamed, the forest reverberating with his fury. "*You broke the rules, Uriel! This was ordained! That round was supposed to be live!*"

Uriel stepped forward now, sword glowing brighter, the calm in his voice cutting deeper than a shout ever could. "I did nothing Asael."

His chest heaved. "*Liar!* This was divine interference!"

Uriel shook his head once, slowly. "That round wasn't mine. It came from another soul you discarded. A man your kind once whispered near death. A broken factory worker you tormented for years. You thought he was weak. Useless." The angel's eyes narrowed, and he gestured slightly toward the gun. "But he found healing. He found people who reminded him what hope looks like. And one night, he left behind a single squib round in a box of live ammunition. Not because he had a vision. Not because he was told to. But because he *hoped* that maybe, somehow, it might save someone one day."

Uriel's voice dropped like thunder. "You weren't defeated by a miracle. You were defeated by *human mercy.*"

Asael snarled, twisting violently inside Marshall's skin, fighting the truth that now clung to every fiber of the moment. Angela staggered back, eyes fixed on Marshall—no, *them.* His body began to *tear.* Not in flesh, but in essence. A sickening *ripple* moved through the air as Asael's torso began to wrench itself from Marshall's, the two forms splitting along an invisible seam. Their legs remained rooted together—entwined like cursed roots— and their shared arm still gripped the revolver, a grotesque tether of will and bone.

Marshall's face twisted in agony as he fought, every muscle resisting, sweat dripping down his brow. "No," he growled, straining against the force inside him. "You don't get to take everything. *Not this time!*"

Asael's upper body hovered grotesquely beside his, grinning through gritted, demonic teeth. His corrupted skin pulsed with shadow. "You were *nothing* before me. Just a boy sobbing in the dark. You think you've got strength now? That gun was mercy, Marshall. Let me finish this for you."

Marshall screamed, wrenching his body to the side, trying to throw off Asael's grip. The revolver shook violently in their shared hand, shifting wildly. Then—

A *crack* of twigs. Heavy boots slamming into the forest floor.

Gabriel burst through the trees, gun raised, eyes immediately locking on the threat. "DROP IT!" he shouted, voice hard and commanding. "Now!"

Marshall gasped, "Wait—!"

But Asael turned. His red eyes flicked toward Gabriel, and he *smiled*—something cold and calculating flashing behind the smirk. "Perfect," he whispered to himself. With one final surge of strength, he jerked the shared arm upward, angling the revolver toward Gabriel—just enough. The split-second shift was all Gabriel needed. He fired.

Crack.

Marshall's body jerked violently as the bullet tore into his chest. The forest went silent. Asael slowly stepped away—no longer tethered, no longer bound. He rose to his full height, now standing separate and whole, a dark specter breathing in the mortal air. Marshall collapsed to the forest floor in a heap, blood blooming beneath him, eyes fluttering.

Angela screamed. "*No!*"

Gabriel rushed forward, realizing too late the trap he'd been forced to spring.

Asael tilted his head, watching the pain ripple across their faces. "How poetic. I didn't even have to pull the trigger this time." He stood over Marshall's fading body like a victor atop a battlefield.

But something deep in the trees began to stir. As Asael took a slow, mocking step toward Marshall's body, the Heavens *ripped open*. A searing bolt of light screamed down from the sky like a divine blade hurled by wrath itself. It struck Asael with the force of judgment, *crushing* him into the forest floor in a thunderclap of wind and brilliance. Remiel landed atop him like a meteor, one large armored hand locked around the demon's throat, driving him down with wings of blinding fire. Asael shrieked in fury, limbs thrashing, smoke pouring from his body as Remiel's power seared into him.

Angela didn't watch. She was already running—hobbling—toward Marshall. Uriel moved beside her, keeping pace, his sword vanishing into light as he stood beside Angela.

Gabriel approached behind them, unaware of the angels and battle that had taken place. His gun was still drawn, expression taut with confusion and adrenaline. "Get away from him!" he barked. "Angela, he's dangerous—he could still—"

But she ignored him. She dropped to her knees beside Marshall.

Gabriel watched, baffled. He backed off, pressing his radio. "Dispatch, this is Detective Ramos. Suspect has been neutralized—gunshot wound to the chest. I need medics now. Repeat, I need medics. Hostage has been found. Alive."

Angela's world had narrowed to Marshall's face. Blood bubbled at his lips. His breaths were shallow, shuddering.

He opened his eyes, barely able to focus. And saw her. "I'm sorry," he whispered.

Angela's voice cracked. "I know."

His gaze drifted upward—and widened. Behind her, bathed in divine glow, stood Uriel. His form radiant and solemn, his expression grave but tender.

Marshall's lips trembled. "Jesus..." he whispered.

Angela blinked, confused. Uriel said nothing.

Marshall's eyes welled with tears. "Please... forgive me."

Angela held his face gently as he took one final breath. His eyes closed. The forest was silent again.

Then, in Angela's vision—*only hers*—a gentle light rose from Marshall's chest, like a flickering flame. Uriel bowed his head slightly, as if in reverence. Behind them, Remiel still pinned Asael to the earth, his expression carved in steel. But in that one fragile moment, it was not the angels or the demons that Angela watched. It was the face of a dying man. And the peace he never thought he could find.

***

Marshall opened his eyes to a silence deeper than death. No pain. No weight. No body. Just light. He stood—not in the forest, but on a vast grassy plain, windswept with warmth and stillness that pressed into his bones like sunlight after a bitter winter. The sky above stretched forever, pale gold and endless. There were no shadows. No echoes. Just a breathless peace that felt almost... wrong.

His brows furrowed. "Where... am I?"

He turned slowly, trying to orient himself, but the landscape offered no landmarks. Just open space and that strange, humming quiet. But then—he saw something. Or someone. A figure, far in the distance. So far, he couldn't make out her features, but there was something about the way she stood— soft, open, waiting—that tugged at something deep inside him. A memory without a name. He took a step forward. Then another. The wind shifted gently, carrying the scent of lilacs and something else—something he hadn't known in years. Home. As he walked, the figure began to move too, walking quickly, then running. And that's when he saw her clearly. His breath caught. It was her. His mother. But not the way he last remembered her—frail and half-lost, slumped in her aged floral chair, eyes dulled by damage and years of sorrow. No, this was the version of her from old, scattered memories. Her hair flowed with shine and life. Her skin glowed with youth. Her eyes— God, her eyes—they were whole. Vibrant. Filled with light and joy. She was smiling. She was crying. And she was running toward him. Marshall froze. His feet rooted to the grass as she closed the distance and flung her arms around him, laughing through tears.

"Oh, my sweet boy!" she sobbed, holding him tight, her voice rich and unbroken. "My beautiful boy..."

He didn't move. Couldn't. Her embrace was foreign. Not unwelcome, but unknown. The kind of touch he used to dream about, long after it had disappeared from his life. She pulled back just enough to kiss his cheek, her hands cradling his face like it was treasure.

He stared at her, disoriented. "Mom?" he whispered.

She nodded, tears running down her cheeks as she smiled with a love so pure it hurt to look at. "Yes, baby. It's me."

Marshall's lip trembled. And for the first time in his life, he was seen not with pity, not with fear, not with judgment— But with delight. They stood locked in each other's arms, weeping—two broken souls being made whole in a place beyond time. Marshall's chest heaved as he tried to speak, but the words tangled in his throat.

His mother ran her fingers through his hair, rocking him gently like he was a child again. "I saw you, Marshall," she whispered, voice thick with tears. "Every day. Every hour you spent taking care of me. I know I couldn't speak... I know I couldn't move—but I saw you. I felt your hands. Your voice.

I wanted so badly to tell you then how much I loved you."

Marshall blinked through the blur. "You... you knew?"

She nodded, more tears spilling down her cheeks. "I heard you reading to me. I saw you feeding me, washing my hair, turning the pages of my old books like I still mattered. You never gave up on me."

He looked away, his face twisting with guilt. "I didn't do enough."

"Marshall," she said softly, cupping his cheek again. "You did more than enough."

His shoulders hunched, as if the weight of his past was trying to crush him even now. "I should have protected you. I should've stood up to him. I should've—" His voice cracked. "I should've saved you."

But she shook her head, grief washing over her. "I'm so sorry. I never meant to put that weight on you. I was your mother. I was supposed to protect you, not the other way around."

He opened his mouth to speak, but she placed her hand over his heart.

"I need you to know something," she said. "When I looked at you, especially in those early years... sometimes I saw your father—the way you'd clench your jaw, the way your eyes would flicker when you were angry. And it hurt, not because you were like him, but because I was scared. Scared that one day I'd look at you and not see my boy anymore. Scared I'd see him instead."

Marshall's lips parted in silent shock.

"But over time... I saw who you really were. I watched you grow into this quiet, gentle boy who never stopped trying to be good. And there were days— so many days—I let him hurt me, because I thought... maybe if he hit me instead of you, you'd be spared. Maybe if I took enough, you'd be okay."

She broke then. The sobs that came out of her were raw—full of the kind of regret that outlives death. "I'm so sorry," she cried, her whole body trembling against his. "I'm so, so sorry that I didn't tell you. I should've told you every single day. I should've wrapped you in my arms and said it a million times—that you were good. That you were loved. That I was proud of you."

Marshall held her tighter, tears falling silently.

"When I was dying, you looked at me, and I couldn't say a word. But inside, all I could think was—*My sweet boy. Please be safe. Please don't carry my pain any longer. Please know I love you. If I could live again, I would give you everything I never did. I would protect you.*" She kissed his forehead, trembling, whispering, "I love you. I love you. I love you."

And for the first time in his life, Marshall believed it.

They sat in the grass now, side by side. Marshall leaned his head on his mother's shoulder like he had always longed to but never dared. They talked—about nothing and everything. About the time he spilled flour all over the kitchen when he was seven. About the poem she once recited to him when he was sick. About the long nights he sat beside her bedside, not knowing if she knew he was there. She remembered it all. And every word healed a part of him that had been broken for as long as he could remember.

Not far off, two figures stood on a gentle hill. Uriel and Remiel. Silent. Watching. The radiance of their forms shimmered faintly in the sunlit breeze, cloaked in quiet awe.

Uriel's expression was serene, his arms folded across his chest. Remiel stood slightly behind him, smiling—a rare, warm smile that softened the edge of his celestial presence.

"Look at them," Uriel said softly, his voice like the rustle of tall grass. "Two lives the world would have thrown away. A mother and son the world deemed too shattered to mend."

"And yet," Remiel murmured, "here they are. Whole."

Uriel nodded. "There is no scar Heaven cannot unwrite."

They began walking forward—slowly, reverently—toward the mother and son still seated in the grass. Laughter echoed gently across the field. Marshall had just remembered a story from when he was five, about hiding under the table with his favorite blanket during a thunderstorm. She'd found him and crawled under too, and they'd waited the storm out together. He laughed, and she laughed with him, hand on his back. Then she looked up—past him. Her smile widened.

Marshall followed her gaze. Two shining figures approached, radiant and calm, robes moving like water over the grass.

His mother stood and reached for his hand. "Come on," she said gently. "There are some friends I want you to meet."

He rose with her, unsure, letting her guide him.

As they drew closer, she gave a small bow of her head to the angels. "Uriel. Remiel."

The angels returned the gesture with a grace that rippled through the air itself.

Marshall looked between them, awe-struck. "You... you know them?"

"I do," she said, smiling toward Remiel. "They've walked with me here."

Marshall swallowed, his voice suddenly small. "Why am I here? I didn't earn this. I don't deserve any of it."

Remiel's eyes softened. "Heaven is not for those who deserve it, Marshall. It's for those who accept it."

Marshall looked down, overwhelmed. There was a pause. Something shifted. His mother and the angels exchanged a look—gentle, solemn. As if sharing a truth that hadn't yet been spoken.

She turned to Marshall again, took both of his hands in hers. And her voice broke. "You can't stay."

Marshall froze. "What...?"

Tears welled in her eyes again, but now they were peaceful. Resigned. "Not yet, baby. Not yet."

Marshall's lips parted, his hands still clutching hers. "But... I don't understand."

She reached up and gently brushed his hair back, just like she used to when he was a boy—when the world felt too loud and cruel and he just needed to be held. "You're needed down there. Not forever. Just for a while."

His brow creased. "Needed? For what? I've done terrible things. I broke people. I—"His voice faltered. "I don't think I'm the kind of person God can use."

She smiled, eyes shimmering. "And that's exactly why He will."

Marshall blinked.

"There are people, my sweet boy, who are buried in their own darkness. Who don't believe they're worth saving. Who think their story ends with the worst thing they've ever done." She squeezed his hands. "You're going to show them that it doesn't."

He stared at her, a lump rising in his throat.

"You've walked through fire, Marshall. You know what it's like to feel unlovable. Unseen. But you also know what it is to be rescued." She touched her chest. "Let them see that in you. Let them see that even the most broken hearts can still beat with purpose."

Marshall swallowed hard. "But I'm scared."

She nodded, her smile tinged with grief and pride. "I know. I know."

He looked into her eyes, suddenly desperate to stay, to cling to this moment.

Her thumb stroked his knuckles. "But you're not alone anymore. Not ever again. And one day, when your work is finished, I'll be right here... waiting to tell you everything I didn't get to say."

A breeze swept gently through the grass. The warmth around him began to shift. The sky brightened. Everything began to glow.

She leaned forward and kissed his forehead. "Go shine your light in the dark," she whispered. "And remind them that even the lost can be found."

And then— The light engulfed him. And he began to fall— not down, but back.

BANG.

Marshall's body jolted violently on the table, the jolt forcing a ripple through the team gathered around him.

"Clear," Paula said firmly, lowering the defibrillator paddles. Her tone was measured, steady—but inside, her chest was tight, breath held.

Monitors beeped. No rhythm yet.

She glanced at the surgeon beside her still working quickly to clamp a torn vessel, blood slicking their gloves.

"His pressure's dropping. We're losing him," someone said.

"Again." Paula pressed the paddles back to his chest.

BANG.

The second shock arched him off the table. And then— A beep. A flicker. The monitor stuttered... and then resolved into a rhythm. Weak, but present.

Paula exhaled, long and quiet.

"He's back," one of the nurses murmured. She didn't smile—didn't celebrate. She just reached for a suction tube and stepped back in to help with the bleeding.

"Let's stabilize him. We're not out of the woods yet," Paula said.

Marshall's eyelids fluttered, just for a moment. His body was pale and soaked, motionless apart from the slow rise and fall of his chest. But his pulse was there. And for now, that was enough.

32

Then Shall Your Light Break Forth Like the Dawn

The graveyard was silent. No wind. No owls. Just rows of broken stone and crooked headstones leaning into the darkness like forgotten sentinels. At the far end, near an unmarked grave veiled in moonlight, knelt Adapa. He wore a crisp white suit, clean and pristine despite the dirt beneath his knee. His silver hair shimmered faintly in the dim light, and his pale hands were folded reverently on his leg. He stared at the grave with a hollow stillness, as though he were waiting for something—or someone—to rise from it.

Behind him, chains rattled. Asael—in his true, coiled, serpent-demon form—writhed and spat, dragged forward by two towering figures in obsidian-black armor. The knights' armor was jagged and ancient, pitted with battle scars. Their faces, mostly obscured by tangled black hair, were sagging and sunken, their dark red skin glistening with oil and time. Eyes like cinders glowed faintly beneath their brows, expressionless. They held Asael firm, one at each arm. His scales scraped the dirt as he tried to twist away, screaming.

"Adapa, please," he hissed, thrashing. "It wasn't my fault! I had them—I was so close—I *was* winning! I just need a little more time."

Adapa didn't turn. He simply looked at the grave, his voice as cold as the earth. "You had your time."

"I gave you millennia of devotion!" Asael cried. "One mistake—one—and you cast me aside?! I was loyal!"

Adapa finally turned, his glowing eyes unreadable. "You were *loyal*, Asael. That is not the same as effective."

Asael strained harder, desperation leaking into his voice. "Please. I can do better. I'll do whatever you want—just give me one more chance."

Adapa stood.

The wind stirred.

"You'll shortly join the others who failed before you," he said quietly. "But not yet. We are still missing a piece."

As if summoned by the words, a low howl of air tore through the graveyard. A third knight descended from the black sky in a spiral of smoke and flame, dragging another demon by the throat.

Ravage. He kicked and clawed, wild-eyed and laughing bitterly despite the chains that bound him. His skin flickered between forms—sometimes a mass of jagged teeth and limbs, sometimes the lean shape of a snarling man. "You're wasting your knights on me?" he barked, voice echoing with layered malice. "What's the matter, Adapa? Afraid of getting little old me by yourself?"

The knight said nothing, only slammed him down beside Asael with brutal efficiency.

Adapa slowly approached them both. "I thought I'd offer you a lesson. A final courtesy."

Asael snarled. "We don't want your lessons!"

Adapa smiled faintly, as if that had been the answer he expected. "You will listen anyway." He looked back at the grave behind him, the wind gently stirring his white suit.

"So many lie here in the dirt. Unmarked. Unclaimed. Forgotten. Criminals, most of them—at least that's what the world calls them. But I know better. They were the byproduct of tragedy, worn down by the slow grind of the machine *we* built."

He paused, the faintest smirk curling at the corner of his mouth. "It's easy to blame them, but they were simply shaped by what we gave them—

violence, neglect, silence. And despite the wreckage they left behind... we don't actually want a world full of them. That kind of chaos? It draws too much attention. Too much prayer."

He turned back to Asael and Ravage. "You understand, don't you? We need *order*. A society we can manipulate. Just enough pain to make people question a good God. Just enough pleasure to make them forget the suffering of their neighbor. It is a delicate rhythm. A hymn of distraction."

He took a step closer, his voice growing quieter and colder. "Angela disrupted that rhythm." His glowing eyes locked with Asael's. "I saw it. Her death would have cracked generations open—left them wondering where God had gone. Doubting. Hurting. Searching."

He turned to Ravage. "But her survival? Her life? That will echo longer. Deeper. She will turn hearts back to faith in ways none of you anticipated. Your failure was not small. It was seismic." He folded his hands behind his back. "I won't pretend you weren't brilliant. Each of you brought terror and genius in your own way. But your usefulness has ended." He looked up to the sky briefly—then down again, the glow of his eyes intensifying. "Now, you will better serve the kingdom of darkness grafted *inside* of me."

Adapa stood in silence, gazing down at Asael and Ravage as the wind stilled again, like even the night was waiting. Then, without a word, his body began to *change*. Slowly, deliberately, he started to rise—his frame stretching, expanding, ascending. His immaculate white suit split at the seams, and dissolved into shadow as his skin darkened and thickened into hard, glistening *scales*—layer upon layer of jet black, glinting like wet stone under moonlight. His arms grew longer, more sinewed. Claws the length of swords burst from his fingers. Massive, obsidian *wings* unfurled from his back with a sickening crackle, blotting out the stars above. His neck extended, coiling like a serpent's, and his face elongated into a monstrous draconic visage—a maw wide and jagged, eyes glowing like eclipsed suns. By the time he had finished growing, he towered at least three stories high, casting a long and dreadful shadow over the graveyard.

The knights remained motionless, unmoved. But Asael and Ravage—They were *silent*.

The fight, the struggle, the snarling rebellion—all of it had drained from them. They now stared up at him, frozen in place. No courage. No pride. Only terror. Adapa leaned in, lowering his monstrous head until his breath washed over them, sulfurous and searing. Then he *opened* his mouth slowly, a low, guttural growl resonating in his throat like the stirring of the pit itself. Rows upon rows of razor-sharp teeth gleamed with fresh venom. Thick strands of saliva stretched between his fangs like webs. And then—his tongue *spilled out.* It slithered toward the dirt, long, slick, and glistening. But it was not smooth. Dozens—*hundreds*—of *faces* pulsed just beneath the surface of his tongue. Twisted, sunken, contorted in agony. Demonic features, once proud, now vacant and dazed. Their mouths opened and closed soundlessly. Some wept. Some smiled, hollow and mindless. Each one trapped. Each one fueling him.

Asael let out a tiny, broken whimper. Ravage could only shake his head slowly, as though trying to reject what he saw—his mouth opening to scream, but no sound emerging. Adapa let the moment linger, savoring it.

The faces writhed subtly beneath the translucent film of his scaled tongue, like dying embers struggling to move inside cooled ash. Their conscious-nesses hadn't fully vanished—they were still *aware*, still *suffering*—and they powered him now. Small, eternal batteries. He exhaled, and the wind that followed smelled like scorched bone and old nightmares. And still, he said nothing. His judgment had already been spoken.

They stared upward into the abyss of Adapa's open jaws—into the shim-mering web of fangs, the heavy breath curling in the air like smoke, the long, slithering tongue writhing with the trapped faces of their fallen kin. The tongue retracted slowly. The jaws began to rise higher. Higher. Then— With a guttural growl that shook the headstones from their foundations, Adapa *dropped.* His massive head came crashing down in a single, devastating motion—jaws snapping shut around the two demons like a great black guillotine.

CRUNCH.

The ground quaked as his teeth collided, and for a moment, everything vanished inside him. No screams. No struggle. Just the wet, echoing sound of bone and flame and soul being *crushed* into submission. He lifted his head again slowly, jaw dripping with thick, black saliva. There was no trace of Asael. No sign of Ravage. Only silence. Adapa stood still for a long moment, exhaling steam through his nostrils like a furnace cooling after a long burn. Then, his form began to shrink, the scales receding, the wings folding in, until he once again stood as a man in a white suit before the now-ruined grave.

He looked down at the cracked earth beneath him, brushing a speck of dust from his lapel. "Balance restored."

Then he turned and vanished into the night.

***

The morning sun poured golden light across the quiet neighborhood streets, dancing through the windows of Angela's car as she pulled into the drop-off lane at Phoenix's school. She shifted into park. "All right, buddy."

Phoenix—seven years old and growing faster than his clothes could keep up—unbuckled himself with practiced ease. His backpack was too big for him, as always, bouncing a little as he slid out of the seat.

Angela leaned toward him, her hand resting briefly on the steering wheel—where a simple gold engagement ring caught the light. "Have a good day, okay? Be kind. Pay attention."

"I know, Mom," he groaned with a smile.

She smirked. "I love you."

He rolled his eyes, but then leaned in and gave her a quick kiss on the cheek. "I love you too."

She watched him as he ran off toward the building, waving once before disappearing into the flow of students. Angela exhaled slowly, letting the warmth of the moment settle in her chest.

Her phone buzzed in the cup holder.

Mom Calling...

She answered with one hand as she pulled back onto the road. "Hey, Mom."

"Hey, sweet girl," her mom's voice came through, warm and familiar. "You doing all right?"

"Yeah, just dropped Phoenix off. He was in a good mood."

"That's great. Oh—listen, I ran to the store this morning, out of milk again."

Angela chuckled. "I told you to start writing things down."

"I *do* write them down. I just forget where I wrote it. Anyway—while I was there, I ran into Diane."

Angela blinked. "Diane?"

"You probably don't remember her. I haven't seen her in *years*. We used to be in that old book club together. She asked how we were doing."

She laughed. "What did you say?"

Her mom gave a dry chuckle. "I laughed. Because *how* do you answer that? After everything that happened?"

Angela smiled softly, eyes still on the road.

"I told her about your nonprofit. She couldn't believe it. It was the most Diane thing in the world to start crying right in the middle of the dairy aisle."

Angela chuckled. "Wow."

"And when I told her you work with young mothers—helping them finish school and get housing and support—she just kept shaking her head. Said she always knew you had a calling."

"Really?"

"Uh huh."

There was a pause.

"You seem distracted," she said gently.

Angela didn't answer at first.

Her mom's voice softened. "...Are you going to see him today?"

Angela's fingers flexed on the steering wheel. Her eyes flicked to the mirror, where Phoenix's empty seatbelt swung gently. "Maybe. I haven't decided yet."

The line was quiet for a moment—gentle understanding hanging in the silence.

Angela let the silence hang for another moment, eyes drifting out the windshield as traffic thickened ahead. "Well," she said gently, "I'm almost at the office."

Her mother sighed on the other end, warm and knowing. "All right. Just... don't forget to breathe today."

Angela smiled. "I'll try. Love you, Mom."

"Love you too."

She set the phone back in the cup holder, taking a moment to adjust the ring on her finger. The gold glinted in the sunlight as she pulled into the lot of a modest business park tucked between an elementary school and a coffee roastery. The building was unremarkable—simple concrete and glass—but as she stepped out and crossed the parking lot, her pace quickened with purpose. She opened one of the framed glass doors and made her way inside. She climbed the stairs two at a time, the click of her flats echoing softly in the stairwell. Down the hall, she moved with familiarity until she reached a pair of frosted glass double doors. Etched into the surface in clean, welcoming font it read:

Second Chapter

She pushed them open. Inside was a cozy but professional space—soft greens and muted earth tones, with natural light pouring through the windows. A handful of offices branched off from the main hub, and in the center, a large meeting table was already occupied.

May, the secretary, a young woman with tight curls and wide eyes, looked up from her desk and smiled. "Morning, Angela. You're just in time—the meeting barely started."

Angela nodded, smoothing a hand over her blouse. "Thanks, May."

As she entered the conference room, heads turned her way. A few respectful nods from her team. Familiar faces—administrators, program leads, case workers. They made room at the head of the table as she approached. On the mounted screen at the far end of the room, a Zoom call was in progress. The faces of several university representatives blinked into view, each in their own little square.

"...We've looked over your proposal," one was saying, "and honestly, what you're doing is something we should have implemented years ago."

Angela took her seat and smiled as the screen brightened.

The banner across the bottom read: *Discussion: Second Chapter – Proposed*

Campus Charter for Mothers' Support Network. The meeting was beginning. And Angela was exactly where she was meant to be.

***

The moment Gabriel and Mackenzie stepped out of the unmarked cruiser, the suspect took one look at them—and *ran.* Gabriel had been on his trail for months tracking down the person running credit card scanners at gas stations until he finally found him.

Gabriel sighed. "Here we go."

The guy was overweight, huffing before he even cleared the sidewalk. He tried to vault over the low chain-link fence at the back of the gas station but *caught his belly* halfway over and toppled onto the other side with a grunt.

"Stop! Police!" Mackenzie called out, trying not to laugh.

The suspect scrambled to his feet, arms flailing, and took three more steps before *tripping* on a soft spot in the grass and going face-first. Gabriel didn't waste time. He leapt over the fence, closed the distance, and *slammed down* onto the guy's back with a practiced tackle. Dirt flew.

The suspect wheezed, helpless. "I didn't do nothing! I know my rights, you need probable cause!" he shouted, face half in the grass.

Gabriel pulled his arm behind his back and snapped the cuffs into place.

As Gabriel rolled him over, a cascade of *blank credit cards* spilled from his hoodie pocket onto the ground like fallen leaves.

Mackenzie caught up, panting. "So... just a random guy carrying twenty blank cards?"

"I'm a collector," the guy wheezed.

Gabriel shook his head, already hauling him up by the cuffs. "Of course you are. You have the right to remain silent..."

They loaded him into the back seat. Gabriel shut the door and was about to start the paperwork when his phone buzzed in his jacket pocket. He glanced at the screen. Paused. "...Really? Right now?" he muttered, eyes wide.

Mackenzie looked over. "What?"

Gabriel was already sliding into the driver's seat. "We need to make a pitstop." He threw on the lights.

The sirens screamed to life, and the cruiser lurched forward, cutting through city streets with surgical precision. Gabriel's grip on the wheel was solid, his pulse racing with something *other* than adrenaline this time.

Mackenzie sat in the passenger seat, giving him a sidelong glance. "Wait, is this *it*?"

Gabriel didn't answer. His eyes were fixed ahead. He turned the last corner and pulled directly in front of the hospital entrance, tires screeching slightly as he braked hard. For a second, no one moved.

Gabriel turned to Mackenzie with a grin. "Today I'm gonna meet my daughter."

Mackenzie smiled, and let out a breath. "You *got this*, man."

From the back seat, the scammer blinked at the hospital sign. "Congratulations, detective!"

Gabriel let out a nervous, half-laugh and pointed a finger through the metal grate. "Shut up." He jumped out, slammed the door, and turned to Mackenzie. "Handle the booking. I'll be back."

Mackenzie grinned. "Go."

Gabriel sprinted through the sliding glass doors, weaving through hospital corridors like he'd been here a dozen times before. Nurses pointed. An orderly stepped out of his way.

Someone shouted "Room two one two!"

He didn't stop to thank them. He burst into the delivery room, heart thundering.

Paula was already in the bed, her face glowing with pain and sweat, her hair a little wild—but her smile broke through the moment she saw him. "You're late," she said through a contraction.

Gabriel crossed the room in two strides, grabbed her hand, and kissed her forehead. "I'm here," he whispered. "I'm not missing this."

***

The prison yard was quiet, the early afternoon sun casting long shadows through the reinforced windows. Inside the chapel, Marshall sat alone, elbows resting on the table, thumbing the worn edges of a small, blue-covered Bible. Its corners were bent, the pages creased and underlined with a mixture of reverence and hesitation.

A guard stepped into the room, clipboard in hand. "Sewert."

Marshall looked up.

The guard nodded toward the hallway. "You've got a visitor."

Marshall blinked, startled. Visitors were rare—almost nonexistent. He closed the Bible carefully, setting it down like something sacred, and stood. His hair had grown longer—unkempt but clean—and a modest beard framed his face, softening the harsh lines that had once been etched there by madness and grief. The fire in his eyes had long since cooled, replaced by something steadier. Something quieter. He followed the guard down the corridor, his boots scuffing the linoleum with every step. The visitor area was half full—other inmates murmuring through scratchy phones, some laughing, some not. Marshall's eyes scanned the room—and then froze. On the other side of the glass sat Angela.

He stopped for a second, as if unsure whether to keep walking. Then he did. He sat down slowly, picked up the phone, and raised it to his ear. Angela mirrored him. They stared at each other through the glass, a dozen emotions flickering between them—recognition, memory, uncertainty. Then they both opened their mouths to speak—at the same time. They paused, half-smiling.

"You first," Marshall said gently.

Angela looked down, shyly touching the gold ring on her finger.

He noticed. His brows lifted. "You're married."

She smiled, still fidgeting with the ring. "Engaged."

Marshall nodded slowly, warmth in his expression. "Congratulations."

"Thank you. I met him at work." She shifted in her seat, then looked up again. "After everything happened, I thought a lot about how much of a struggle it was for me trying to go to school and raise Phoenix. I wanted to make a difference. It's funny, the company I worked so hard to get a job for replaced me and I was out of work. I figured I might as well take it as an opportunity to do something that I really wanted. I started a nonprofit. We help young mothers—finish school, find housing, build something stable. Something better."

Marshall's lips parted in genuine surprise. Then he smiled—a real, deep smile. "I'm so happy for you. That's... amazing."

They sat in silence again, not uncomfortable this time. Just full.

Angela broke it. "How have *you* been?"

Marshall's shoulders lifted slightly. "It's been good. Better than I thought it could be."

She looked at him curiously, a hint of softness behind her guarded expression.

He nodded slowly, eyes lowering. "I've been sharing my story. There's a recovery group in here—guys who've seen and done terrible things. Some still in denial. Some broken past repair. But a few... a few are ready. I get to help lead those meetings." His voice was calm, but firm. Grounded. "Not because I've got it all figured out. But because I've been to the edge. I know what it looks like when the darkness tells you you're beyond saving."

He paused, eyes drifting down to the scuffed counter between them. "And... I never got a chance to tell you this before, but... I saw them that night. The angels. I know you did too."

Angela's breath caught.

His voice dropped to a reverent hush. "When I was dying... I saw my mother."

Angela's eyes widened.

"I hadn't seen her like that in years—free, whole, *smiling.* She looked younger, peaceful. We talked. We laughed. We cried. I didn't even realize how much of me was still aching for her until I saw her again." He glanced up at her now, his eyes shining with something deep and quiet. "She told me I'd come back. That I still had work to do. That there were people drowning in the same darkness I barely survived—and that I was meant to help them find their way out."

He let out a breath, not quite a sigh, and managed a small smile. "And, well... here I am."

Angela sat back, still holding the phone to her ear, her fingers gently wrapped around the cord. Her eyes searched his face—older now, calmer—but still familiar. "I believe you."

Marshall blinked. He looked surprised.

"I do. Back then, I didn't know what to make of it. The visions, the light—it all felt... bigger than us. But I think some part of me always knew it wasn't just trauma or hallucination. Something *broke through.* Something real." She hesitated, her voice catching. "I used to pray for peace, for healing, for answers. And sometimes I still do. But mostly now I pray that the pain I lived through can help someone else too. That it can mean something."

Marshall nodded slowly, every word seeming to land like a balm.

Angela smiled faintly, her fingers still idly twisting her ring. "It's strange. There was a time I didn't think I'd ever look at you again without fear. But... I don't feel afraid now."

His eyes dropped for a second.

"I see the man in front of me. Not the man who took me. Not the broken child who needed someone to save. I see someone who *chose* to change. And I'm proud of you for that."

Marshall swallowed hard, emotion flickering just beneath the surface. He didn't speak—just gave a small nod, jaw clenched to hold back the tears welling in his eyes.

Angela leaned a little closer to the glass. "And I don't know if you need to hear this, but... I forgive you."

The words hit him like a tidal wave, washing away years of the aching guilt he had held so tightly it had become part of his bones. For a moment, he couldn't breathe. His heart squeezed hard in his chest before loosening in a way that felt impossible, like something inside him finally exhaled. A trembling breath escaped him. Tears flooded his eyes before he could stop them, hot and sudden. He squeezed his eyes shut, shoulders shaking with the force of it. When he opened them again, his vision shimmered. His hand rose on its own, weightless now, and he pressed his palm to the glass.

Angela hesitated—then lifted her own hand to meet his, palm to palm, the thick pane between them the only thing that kept them from touching. The silence between them wasn't heavy this time. It was sacred. Angela's hand rested against the glass, mirroring his. Marshall kept his there, his eyes closed now—not in shame, but in peace. For a long moment, they simply stayed like that. No more words. No more wounds. Just the stillness of two souls who had passed through fire and come out changed—each on their own path, each bearing scars, but no longer defined by them.

Outside, the sun dipped lower, casting warm amber light through the high, barred windows. The prison buzzed faintly in the background, life going on. But here, in this quiet corner of the world, there was only stillness.

And the beginning of something new.

www.ingramcontent.com/pod-product-compliance
Lightning Source LLC
Chambersburg PA
CBHW071534110726
47908CB00007B/1877